A Promis

A Promise on the Horizon

Ann Pearson

GRANVILLE ISLAND
PUBLISHING

Copyright © 2019 Ann Pearson

All rights reserved. No part of this publication may be reproduced, stored in a retrieval system or transmitted, in any form or by any means, without prior permission of the publisher or, in the case of photocopying or other reprographic copying, a license from Access Copyright, the Canadian Copyright Licensing Agency, www.accesscopyright.ca, 1-800-893-5777, info@accesscopyright.ca. Due to the dynamic nature of the internet, website addresses and contents may have changed since publication.

ISBN: 978-1-989467-02-2
ebook ISBN: 978-1-989467-03-9

Book editor: Cheryl Cohen
Book designer: Omar Gallegos
Proofreader: Rebecca Coates

Cover image: Vue du village de Simplon.
Artist: Gabriel Lory fils.
1811 © The Trustees of the British Museum.
All rights reserved.

Granville Island Publishing Ltd.
212 – 1656 Duranleau St. Granville Island
Vancouver, BC, Canada V6H 3S4

604-688-0320 / 1-877-688-0320
info@granvilleislandpublishing.com
www.granvilleislandpublishing.com

Printed in Canada on recycled paper

For Allan

Contents

PROLOGUE
1811: The Year of the Emperor's Comet ... ix

ONE
Encounters on the Journey ... 1

TWO
A Halt en Route to Rome ... 49

THREE
The Dream of Italy ... 106

FOUR
Autumn Fog ... 225

EPILOGUE
1812 and After ... 303

TO THE READER ... 307

Prologue

1811: The Year of the Emperor's Comet

Dim at first, the new comet was to prove one of the largest and brightest ever seen and its discovery within days of a blessed event in March was hailed as an omen. The Emperor Napoleon's own birth had coincided with the apparition of just such a cosmic phenomenon and now the birth of his son had been marked by another. It was surely auspicious. The arrival of this long-awaited heir had set the seal on the emperor's reign, guaranteeing the permanence of an empire that now incorporated most of the smaller states of Europe. The old order was being swept away and after a succession of ruinous defeats Prussia, Austria and Russia had little choice but to accept it. Spain and Portugal still resisted with English help, but England itself would have to seek peace now that the closure of all European ports to its ships was crippling the trade on which its prosperity depended.

1811: The Year of the Emperor's Comet

By September, the comet was visible to the naked eye just above the horizon. Reports of its exceptional size and brilliance drew crowds of observers to the open places of Paris, but in the countryside peasants who spotted it as they returned from the fields at dusk feared some great calamity must be at hand. For if to some it heralded the birth of a new dynasty, there were others who whispered that it might portend the emperor's downfall. His power seemed unshakeable, but there were signs that he had overreached himself. The ban on trade with England had caused a general European slump. Grass was growing on empty quaysides; men and machines stood idle. Russia was openly defying the embargo, but the emperor would not tolerate infringements when he was on the verge of breaking the English. Conflict was obviously inevitable.

In that balmy autumn, though, who wanted to think of war? The vintage was one of the best in living memory — thanks, many believed, to the comet, though vintners knew the exceptional weather was responsible. But celestial events may influence earthly affairs through their impact on the superstitious. It's said that the comet confirmed the emperor's sense of destiny, though the astronomers' calculation of its three-thousand-year-long orbit might have made a humbler man reflect on the transience of empires. For who could contemplate that immense sweep of time without a pang at the brevity of human existence? Even the most rational, watching the comet voyage through the autumn sky, might be moved to seize the chance of happiness before their own brief journey ended.

One

Encounters on the Journey

A traveller should always be provided with paper, pen and ink. All that one sees and hears worthy of record should, insofar as is possible, be written down on the spot, ideally with one's reflections added. Every evening before bed one should transpose the day's rough notes into the journal proper.

— Hans Ottokar Reichard, *Guide for Travellers in Europe* (1793)

You will meet every species of humanity on the road — pilgrims and truants, pleasure lovers and philosophers, the upright citizen and the downright rogue. Be wary of them all but most especially of the writer, eternally scribbling in a dog-eared notebook. Do not seek to be interesting or you may meet yourself some day portrayed in a most unflattering manner in the pages of a 'Tour'.

— Anonymous, *Memoirs of a Literary Peregrination* (1820)

Politics [says the author] will mortally offend half my readers and bore the other half who have seen a far livelier and more pertinent version in the morning paper.

If your characters don't talk politics, replies the editor, they aren't men of 1830, and your book is no longer a mirror as you claim . . .

— Stendhal, *The Red and the Black* (1830)

Tonnerre, Friday 30 August 1811

Was it only yesterday he'd left Paris? It feels as though he's been travelling for days. Last night, with a full moon and a good straight road across the plain, the diligence didn't stop except to change horses, and the passengers had to sleep in their seats. But tonight they're staying at an inn and he has time to record the day's impressions before they fade. The room doesn't offer the luxury of a table, so he's set his notebook and candle on the chest of drawers.

First, a quick sketch of his fellow-travellers. There were five of them starting out. A little cotton-seller (less bashful than she appeared, judging by what he overheard in the dark last night). A fat, vulgar, prosperous woman with a well-brought-up small boy. And two Italians who'll be with him all the way to Milan — a charming man in his late thirties (whom he'd mistaken for a Milanese bourgeois, but more of that later) and Scotti, a young naval officer on his way home to Genoa having just made his escape after four years as a prisoner of war in England. *If he weren't completely witless he'd have strange things to tell, but he's like a bottle that's floated seas and rivers with a filter in its neck to keep out anything interesting.*

For his own part, he's determined not to miss a thing. Why else endure all the discomfort and fatigue of travel if not to return with a deeper understanding of human nature and a pack of clever anecdotes to entertain one's friends?

To keep himself awake this afternoon after the nearly sleepless night, he spent two or three stages in the open cabriolet under the driver's seat — less comfortable than the interior but a superb view. *I found a book there — the conversations of someone or other, by Maria Wollstonecraft-Godwin. I skimmed a few pages in which Maria immediately brings into play the darkest despair and ends with madness. It's odd that a book like this should have reached the masses in our countryside.*

Pausing to trim his quill, he wonders about the reader. A woman most likely. They adore these dark English novels. Perhaps the one he glimpsed on the stairs tonight — a slim figure in grey, her face hidden by a travel veil. She didn't join them at supper.

His pen scratches on in the tiny pool of candlelight. Dull, flat countryside until Joigny. Dinner in Saint-Florentin where the serving girls were shy as savages. Spanish prisoners of war, very young. He gave them a few coins. Stony soil beyond, but beautiful vineyards on the slopes. Character sketches, conversations — he could keep going for several pages more, but he's starting to flag and the diligence will set off again at three, about the hour he normally falls asleep. Poor little Angel, he thinks, stowing his notebook — for the next two months she'll be eating her supper alone and going to bed without him. There were actually tears in her eyes when she kissed him goodbye. It made him a little ashamed of being so eager to leave. But he'd be an idiot not to seize this chance of returning to Italy.

He snuffs the candle and stretches out on the bed. How much has changed since he last saw Milan ten years ago. Was it there or in Paris he'd begun keeping a journal? He should have looked for that old notebook before leaving. It would be amusing to see his first impressions of Italy. Juvenile, no doubt, but frank and unaffected since he'd vowed from the start not to worry about style or spelling.

Unwelcome as a flea in the bedclothes, a memory springs from the dark — the scowling face of Count Daru checking his first letter and pointing out a spelling mistake in front of the whole office. One of many small humiliations that still make him squirm, though no one on his cousin's staff escapes them. He turns on his side, easing his shoulder into a hollow in the lumpy mattress, but there's no evading the anxiety that the thought of his cousin induces. He's taking a risk, setting off now instead of waiting till his colleague returns from leave. But everything's up to date in the office, and while Daru is with the emperor in Holland, there won't be anything needing attention.

Besides, it's owed to him, really, this trip. He'd been led to expect it, with all the talk last spring of sending him to Italy. Crozet had taken a leave of absence to go with him, their bags were packed. And then Count Daru sent someone else instead. Why raise his hopes only to disappoint them? But now, with the chief himself away for two months, there's nothing to stop him taking a private trip. And when he asked — careful not to specify why or for how long — if he could absent himself for a while, Daru was quite agreeable. A family visit, he'd have said if pressed, which was true enough since he'll pass through Grenoble on his return. It's time he went, with his good old grandfather nearing eighty and in failing health. And talking to his father in person may achieve more than letters.

All that aside, he needs a change of scene. There's no other way to escape the madness that's possessed him — for what else is it but madness to fall in love with a virtuous wife, and this one above all. It's three months now since the evening in the garden when he plucked up courage to tell her, and her reply that only friendship was possible between them should have ended it. But he can't stop hoping each time he sees her, finding encouragement when perhaps she's merely being kind or maintaining appearances so as not to betray him to her husband. For that reason alone, it's wise to absent himself now. And maybe if she misses him she'll have a change of heart. He'd hoped for some hint of sadness when he said goodbye. They were alone briefly, but she'd busied herself around the room — hiding her feelings, perhaps? 'I'll try to return more reasonable,' was all he'd dared to say, though he longed to tell her he adored her. At least he'd given her his letter, but will she read it?

He turns onto his back, staring into the darkness. Here he is, leagues from Paris, still engaged in the same futile speculation that's filled too many pages of his journal this summer. Taking a mistress was supposed to cure him. It did for a while, the first few weeks — watching Angéline onstage knowing that many men would envy him. She's ardent, pretty, sweet-natured, and sings his favourite arias. But she's empty-headed and after seven months of sleeping with her every night he's bored. It's reached the point where he can only get an erection by thinking of the other woman.

But would it be any different with *her*? Could he hope for more than a year of happiness when he's bored so quickly? She's just an ordinary wife and mother. But that's part of her charm. He likes watching her with the children, or entertaining them himself for the reward of a smile that includes him in the inner circle of her affection. Even in her pregnancies, she's desirable. There's a ripeness to her looks, a warmth and directness in her manner that attracts him more than any young girl, no matter how lovely.

Soon, though, he'll be back among the loveliest women in the world. It thrilled him just to utter their names again tonight, all those beautiful *Milanesas* who'd bewitched the officers of the French army a decade ago, though he'd nearly made a gaffe telling the older Italian he knew Mme Ghirardi. 'I met her when I lived in the French envoy's residence —'

'She's dead, poor girl,' his companion interrupted.

He should have heeded the emotion in the other man's voice, but he'd rattled on unthinkingly: 'That's tragic! Such a pretty woman. The finest eyes I've ever seen! Wasn't she the sister of Giuseppi Lechi?'

'My brother,' his companion broke in quickly, with a melancholy smile, just as he was about to mention General Lechi's arrest for corruption. What an embarrassment that would have been!

But what luck to be travelling with one of Count Lechi's sons! They were famous for having led the insurrection in Brescia — five of them marching arm in arm beneath a Revolutionary Italian tricolour sewn by their beautiful sister. Ten years ago, he could only admire them from a respectful distance, and now here he is, chatting easily with this one. Of course, that's mainly due to Lechi himself: a man of the nobility who travels by diligence instead of his own carriage is a rare being. Not a trace of self-importance, but gracious to everyone, even the coarse travelling salesman at supper tonight. And it's genuine, unlike French graciousness in which the satisfaction of acting admirably is always too evident. A manner on which to model his own, if he weren't too easily irritated to be capable of it. And that Italian naturalness — what Frenchman of Lechi's rank would stroll into the kitchen and lift the saucepan lids to see what was on offer? Or suggest a dip in the river before supper?

He'd hesitated at first, afraid of looking foolish since he can barely swim. Luckily the water wasn't deep, and after two sweaty days in the diligence with no hope of a bath in these village inns, it felt wonderful. In the glow of well-being afterwards, listening to Lechi praise the joys of country life, he was ready to adopt it as his own philosophy.

But rustic bliss is all very well for the rich. A man like himself can't afford it. Of course, if he'd been content to remain a provincial mediocrity he could be spending his Sundays roaming the hills or reading under the limes. But Paris is the only place for a man with ambition, soulless though it is with its filthy streets and flat horizon. It was the greatest disillusion of his young life, those first miserable months in Daru's office, and the sad, pollarded lime trees in the courtyard where the clerks went to piss seemed to warn what the city would do to him. Naturally, he'd seized the opportunity to escape as soon as one came his way. What boy with spirit wouldn't have?

It's galling nonetheless to think that if he'd stuck to the path laid out for him then, he could be meeting Lechi as an equal now. But he's made up for his youthful escapades, and even if his present appointment is nothing to boast of, his admission to the Council of State has set his foot on the ladder. Obviously, there's heavy competition. Three hundred new auditors were admitted last year, each one seeking promotion, but he has one great advantage: the Daru brothers are rising in the world, with the count now Secretary of State and Martial the Intendant of Crown Property in Rome, and he has every hope of rising with them. In a few years, if all goes well, he'll be Baron Henri de Beyle, prefect of a department, instead of a nobody whose name wasn't even spelt correctly on the list of candidates.

But Lechi's talk of happiness has unsettled him. Perhaps it's a mistake to aim for a prefecture when he'd be happier in some lesser post. Secretary to an ambassador, for instance, in a capital with a good opera house. But two months away from Paris will give him a fresh perspective, a chance to take stock of himself at twenty-eight. And he'll call on Mme Pietragrua in Milan, and little Livia B. in Ancona, who perhaps hasn't entirely forgotten him since she returned to her native land. It's just as well after all that Crozet can't come with him. He'll be freer travelling alone.

Remembering his last sight of Livia at the carriage window in her widow's veil, he's reminded of the woman in grey. What does her veil hide — grief or some reason to avoid public scrutiny? How dull the world must look through that grey gauze.

Tonnerre, Friday 30 August

For the first time in my life I am completely alone. Though I had anticipated the discomforts of the road I had not foreseen this anguish on finding myself at nightfall in a place where I do not know a single soul. But I cannot turn back now.

Don't exaggerate, she tells herself. You can always return to Nogent — and stagnate for the rest of your life. The first step is the hardest.

It isn't easy to be thrown among strangers in a public conveyance, but she must travel as cheaply as possible. The fare includes meals and lodging, though today she'd brought her own provisions, not ready to face the common table. Fortunately, the long-distance diligence has wider seats, so one isn't crammed elbow to elbow with one's neighbours as in a regular coach. Even so, she'd found it disagreeable.

Most of the passengers were sleeping when I joined them early this morning, but I was seated opposite a young Italian in a shabby uniform whose persistent stare unnerved me. At the next halt, I noticed that the cabriolet was unoccupied. It is exposed to the sun and the dust thrown up by the horses' hooves, but the wide view is worth the discomfort, and my veil offered sufficient protection, as well as shielding me from the curiosity of strangers. Every inn has its clutch of idlers who have nothing better to do than gawp at new arrivals.

I enjoyed the view in solitude until after the midday halt when I found that a young man had taken my place, although I had left my book to indicate that I was returning. Not wishing to be alone with him, I took my seat in the interior again. I should have retrieved my book before we came in for supper, but the young man stood there joking with the driver and I was too timid to approach them.

But enough of these complaints. Today's journey has brought her through pleasant country and she has a mass of pencilled notes to transcribe. Nine years in the flat northern chalkland with its thin pasture and meagre crops had dulled her senses, but here among these ripening orchards and vineyards they are stirring almost painfully back to life. There were moments in the late afternoon when something quite mundane — the pitch of a roof, the play of sunlight on a limestone wall — seemed charged with meaning, like the hieroglyphs of a dead language, or those obscure signs that guide the flocks of migratory birds to the very spot where their forebears have nested since time immemorial. When the diligence paused at a crossroad, the arrow on the milestone pointing to a familiar name merely confirmed what instinct had already told her. They were not far from it now, that country between the two rivers, where colchicums would be unfurling their lilac petals in the meadows and wild clematis silvering the hedges. It couldn't be more than a few leagues to the west and for an instant she'd been tempted to pause on her journey south. But the gates would not swing open to admit her now, and what point would there be in peering through the bars?

For a long moment the page swims out of focus, then she pulls herself together and continues. She writes slowly, leaving space at the bottom of each page for afterthoughts or omissions. The set of leather-bound notebooks is one of her few indulgences, and she would hate to mar their pristine pages with an ill-chosen word or clumsy phrase.

A burst of laughter in the corridor — the loud, over-emphatic voices of men who have enjoyed a convivial evening. Floorboards creak in the next room. Something falls with a thud, then another. A muffled sound or two more, then silence.

It's time she tried to sleep herself, though she's apprehensive of bedbugs. She's covered the bed with deerskin, recommended by her travellers' guide as a barrier, and set her own linen sleeping sack on top. The drawstring at the neck reminds her of a shroud. But it's good to be lying still, her head on her own small pillow, after a day of constant motion. She's left the shutters ajar and a current of cooler air flows into the stuffy room, bathing her face agreeably though it brings an ammoniacal whiff of the stables in the yard below.

If she can sleep now she might manage four hours before the chambermaid knocks. But her mind is still too active. She should have rescued her book from the cabriolet. It would have distracted her, held at bay the panic that keeps rising. A foolish panic — she has adequate funds (unreal as that still seems), she has letters of introduction, she's equipped with every necessity — but for the second time in her life she's cut adrift from everything familiar, heading into the unknown.

Nineteen years now, almost to the day. Her mind swerves like a horse sensing danger; the past is always waiting in ambush, and in the darkness of the unfamiliar room it rises up with all the vividness of a child's perceptions. The hurried departure in a shabby vehicle instead of the family coach, her parents strange in borrowed clothes, with tricolour cockades in their hats, her own petticoat weighted with mysterious packages that Jeannette had stitched inside. No questions, no complaints, Jeannette had warned, and she'd dutifully held her tongue through the night, terrified at every halt by the brutish faces peering in, the harsh voices demanding their papers. Was it one night or two? She remembers trying to sleep with her head on Jeannette's lap, waking to painful sunlight and a strange new smell, as piercing as the shrill cries of birds that seemed part of it, then gripping Jeannette's hand in terror as they were rowed out to the ship and hauled up the side in a roped chair. A long, dark and nauseous interval for which memory furnishes only a metal basin; then shore again, the ground still moving beneath their unsteady feet. A babble of foreign voices, another coach ride through country where the most ordinary things had become strange — little houses with straw roofs like nightcaps pulled down over their ears, larger ones of brick as red as the coachman's face. Then a snarl of carts and coaches heading into a seemingly endless tangle of streets, and a new terror — how would they ever find their way in this labyrinth where even her father seemed lost?

But she'd learnt to brave the streets, to note waymarks to guide the return, to be alert for pickpockets and other wandering hands, to hold her head high while avoiding the eyes of men. She'd learnt too what a coin might buy and how to inspect every stall in the market before spending it. And how to move and dress differently, to become inconspicuous, to hold her tongue among strangers but to greet the humble neighbours politely and win acceptance, or at least toleration.

She's faced the unknown before. But never alone — always with Jeannette by her side. Jeannette would have lessened the discomforts and embarrassment of travelling in a public vehicle. It would have been an extra expense, though, and the constant presence that was reassuring once would be intrusive now. Besides, it would be selfish to ask anything more of Jeannette. After years of loyally sharing the tribulations of exile she deserves a peaceful old age among her own.

A clatter of hooves in the yard below, a late arrival. Voices, then silence again. A dog barks in the distance, answered by others in a spreading chorus of agitation that slowly subsides. Turning over cautiously, so as not to roll off the deerskin, she breathes in her pillow's comforting scent of soap and lavender, and feels sleep at last overtake her.

Saint-Seine-l'Abbaye, Saturday 31 August

I believe I saw a comet today, he writes. They'd set off at three in the morning beneath a beautiful starry sky, and not long afterwards he'd spotted it just above the horizon. He draws a rough sketch from memory. The comet vanished once dawn broke, the light first blue, then copper, till the sky flamed red with the rising sun and the countryside stirred back to life.

A grand spectacle worth the discomfort of the cabriolet, but after breakfast he'd returned to his seat inside. The woman in grey immediately took his place. She hid there all day, didn't eat with them, slipped in and out of the inns like a nervous cat.

At the afternoon halt in Montbard, they'd visited the garden of the great naturalist Buffon, which he takes some pains to describe. The Gothic tower had caught his imagination — 138 steps spiralling to the top and walls five feet thick, with window seats in the embrasure where one could sit and dream. Six gardeners had once swept the leaves from the plane-tree walks for the master's passage. The remaining gardener showed them round — a thin, vigorous old man who'd seen Jean-Jacques Rousseau himself kneel in homage before the little pavilion where the thirty-six volumes of the *Natural History* were composed in long solitary days with nothing but bread and water before dinner.

There was a lesson for himself in such discipline, no doubt, but only a man with an independent income could have produced a work of that length, he thinks, labelling his sketch map of the garden. The revenue from the Montbard estates brought in around forty thousand francs, the gardener said. What he could do with even a quarter of that! When his father dies, he'll inherit property that should generate an annual income of ten thousand francs. If he had half that settled on him now — on paper at least, which is all that matters — it would give him the standing required for a high administrative position and he could apply for the title of baron. But his bastard of a father evades his requests, or sends a small advance on the inheritance from his mother, as if that would help (though it's certainly come in useful for this trip). Perhaps if he talks to the old man in person on the way back, he'll have more success. A good father would surely do everything in his power to assist his son's career, but his own seems more interested in the flock of merino sheep he's breeding. It's hard to fathom this mania for agriculture in a man who was legal counsellor to the Grenoble parlement until the Revolution, a post that entitled the family to letters of nobility had his father not been too stingy to pay the necessary fee. What the old bastard can't see with his provincial mentality is that to succeed in life you must make the right impression. Arrive in a carriage and you're smiled upon; on foot, in mud-spattered boots and a shabby coat, you're ignored. If it means going into debt, so be it. Debts are a necessary means to an end: once he has his prefecture he'll pay them off. And if he's a little precipitate in signing official letters as De Beyle, it's only a matter of time before he gets the title that will justify it.

He'd have brooded all afternoon across the dry stony plateau where there was nothing to be seen but an occasional clump of trees. Fortunately, Scotti had entertained them by singing. An unexpected talent — the man sings well, in the best Italian style. There's nothing like music to banish gloomy thoughts.

A good supper tonight and shapely maids. He has a weakness for the girls at inns. They're glad to earn a little extra and if you tip generously, you can get one up to your room. The girl tonight was clearly willing — 'Is that all you'll be wanting, sir?' she asked in a knowing way when she cleared the table — but the officious landlady hurried her back to the kitchen.

Still, pleasure aside, it's better to have spent the time on his journal. If he's assiduous it will give him the basis of a book on Italy. Not that there isn't a surfeit of 'Tours' already. His will be different, though: it won't be a hackneyed catalogue of sights seen and inconveniences endured, but a study of the Italian character and society at this moment of transformation. His conversations with Lechi have made him all the keener to see Milan again now that it's the capital of the emperor's Kingdom of Italy. It will be fascinating to observe the effects of political change on the pleasure-loving Milanese. And Rome without the pope, Naples free of the Bourbons! Truly this is a turning point in history worth witnessing.

Saint-Seine-l'Abbaye, Saturday 31 August

I descended well in advance this morning only to find that the young man had again taken my place in the cabriolet. There is something irritating about him — that air of self-satisfaction on his plump face, and the silly trinkets on his watch chain. Fortunately, after breakfast he rejoined his companions and I returned to the cabriolet, relieved to find my book still there.

Today's journey saddened me. I had not expected so many reminders of the cataclysm along our route. But even the smallest places were swept by violence, as sudden and destructive as the hailstorms that devastate the vineyards. Here in this peaceful wooded valley where we are spending the night, scarcely a stone now remains of the great abbey to which the village owes its existence. In Montbard, the monument raised to the memory of the great naturalist Count Buffon was torn down by those who saw in it only a symbol of aristocratic pride. I heard the story at the inn, where we stopped for dinner. I had asked to be served in a private room although it costs more, and the landlady waited on me herself. She and her husband had been in service at the château, she told me.

The curtsy and some lingering obsequiousness had already betrayed that fact, though the woman imposed her presence with all the freedom of the new ways.

'Everything's changed, Mademoiselle, since the old Count's death. He died just before it started, God be thanked. The young count's widow still lives in the château. They left her that, poor lady, and the gardens. But the lands were confiscated after the young count's arrest.'

She'd guessed what was coming and felt an urgent desire to block her ears, to prevent her mind from envisaging the hideous scene. But there was no escape.

The woman has probably been telling the story for years. To have witnessed the downfall of the great is her one claim to interest, and the inn with its daily arrivals offers a perpetually renewed audience. The story haunted me for the rest of the day, though I tried to banish it by immersing myself in my book.

Not the best book for the purpose — gloomy, as though it foreshadowed its author's fate. Poor Mrs Godwin. Dead before she could finish it, and that poor child left motherless. Such a happy little creature, babbling in her mixture of French and English. Without that child and her French nursemaid, the meeting with Mrs Godwin would not have happened. A life may turn on such chance encounters.

It was the fifth year of their London exile, the year she lost any lingering childish illusions that the world was ruled by a benevolent God. It stands out from all the others like an envelope bordered in black in a pile of correspondence. She has a sad tale of her own to tell if she finds her mother's old friend tomorrow.

They'd moved that summer to the city's northern edge in hopes her mother could breathe more easily away from the smoky centre. Two rooms, clean and vermin-free, in a newly built cluster of streets, not too distant from the comfortable homes of the pupils her father had found to tutor. Other émigrés nearby, a French chapel, and fields beyond to ease their longing for the countryside of home. On their very first stroll through the hay meadows, Jeannette heard the French nursemaid calling her little charge and introduced herself. Soon the four of them were meeting most afternoons.

Once or twice Mrs Godwin had joined them, walking slowly with the heaviness of late pregnancy but happy to converse in her fluent though accented French. They'd met other Englishwomen (the ladies who commissioned the embroidery with which she and her mother contributed to their scanty resources), but this was the first with whom she had really talked. Learning that their most deeply felt hardship was a lack of books, Mrs Godwin had lent them a few, including a copy of her travels in Sweden and Norway. She was writing a novel, she'd told them, and hoped to have it completed before the new baby arrived.

And here that novel lies on the table in front of her, one of the first books she's bought, now that she can permit herself the luxury. She'd been astonished to find it listed in a Parisian bookseller's catalogue. Mrs Godwin — or Wollstonecraft, as she was known — was more famous than they'd realised. She'd saved it for this journey, but it's too sombre a tale at a moment when she needs encouragement. Tomorrow, in Dole, when she recovers her baggage from the luggage rack, she'll take out Mrs Godwin's book of travels.

She stares at the author's portrait in the frontispiece. But it doesn't restore that half-remembered presence. Nor do the words on the page; the author's voice is lost in translation. Is it even a translation? 'Imitated from the English', it says, which does not promise fidelity.

A bang on the door makes her jump: the chambermaid, come for her supper tray. She intended to ask for hot water, but the girl flounces off impatiently. They're all the same now. The idea of service has vanished. Next time she must have a coin in hand, the only way to get their attention. She was longing for a full sponge-down after the sultry day, but she'll have to manage with the single ewer of water on the washstand.

At least the air is cooling. She goes to the window and peers out cautiously at the village street. The young man in the shabby uniform is pacing up and down, smoking. His two companions must be sitting on the bench directly below because she can hear their voices — the one bluff, assertive, with a sarcastic edge; the other softer, Italian-accented. Catching the name Buffon, she strains to hear more. They'd visited Buffon's garden, apparently. If she were less reserved, she might have gone with them, but a woman travelling alone cannot permit herself that easy engagement with strangers that a man enjoys.

They're setting off now for an evening stroll. She watches their backs recede down the street. The villagers are sitting in their doorways, resting from the day's labour. Swallows dart and glide in the golden evening light. The air smells of woodsmoke and animal dung.

Buffon was one of her father's favourites. How often in his final years she'd read to him from a volume of the *Natural History*. To enjoy a plenitude of books again (albeit his nephew's, not his own, which were in God knows whose hands now) had been his one solace on their return to France. And for her, when his failing eyesight required a reader, it was an extended education, introducing her to thinkers whom she might not have had the discipline to read by herself.

But in their book-starved exile, any book was precious. The night they fled, her father had put Ovid's poems from exile in one pocket and Voltaire's *Letters on the English* in the other. For a time it was all they had, apart from an English dictionary. Through the generosity of his pupils' parents he'd slowly acquired the tiny collection of Latin classics required by his tutoring, and it was with those volumes that her own education progressed. So a new and original work like Mrs Godwin's *Letters from Sweden and Norway* had been a greater luxury than the occasional cherries or fresh green peas Jeannette brought home in triumph from a street seller. It was an entrancing book, even her father thought so, though had he known as much about its author as she did (thanks to the nursemaid's gossip), he might have viewed it less positively. But that was immaterial after Mrs Godwin's death, poor woman. Whatever her sins, she did not deserve so cruel a fate. The baby would survive, the nursemaid said. But what consolation was a wailing infant sister to the little orphan? It broke their hearts to see her.

And then they were in mourning too, after a winter so cold that the Thames had frozen, then weeks of fog that worsened her mother's cough till every breath was a struggle. It was the darkest moment of their exile, that chill February day they buried her, in the distant corner of the churchyard reserved for the Catholic dead. Sometimes, when they visited the grave, they'd see Mr Godwin and the two little girls at Mrs Godwin's tomb. No monument for her mother. Their resources could not stretch to it, but grass and wild flowers, gentler than a heavy stone, had slowly clothed the naked mound.

Now, poor exile, she rests unvisited in that foreign soil. Father too lies alone, not laid to rest with his ancestors in Vernet, but interred in the public cemetery of a town with which he had no connection. And she herself may end her days in some unknown place among indifferent strangers. But with time the painful sense that she belongs nowhere may come to seem a kind of freedom. And perhaps she will find fellow spirits, others whose world has been turned upside down and who, like herself, are seeking a new life.

The sky is turning rose and gold above the rooftops. Rooks in ones and twos, then a gathering flock, wing slowly over the village to their roost. Two boys drag a handcart piled with logs under the archway opposite and an old man hobbles out to shut the double doors behind them. The village is closing in on itself for the night. It's the time of day when she feels her friendless state most painfully.

Here come her three fellow-passengers, still deep in conversation. She draws back from the window quickly, though she would like to know what they are talking about. They seem respectable, cultivated even, with their interest in Buffon. She might join them for supper tomorrow. It will be her last day with the diligence, so if the acquaintance proves undesirable it will not be prolonged.

On the Road, Sunday 1 September

Ten to four in the morning, their first halt of the day, and there's time to write while the horses are changed and the driver makes some necessary adjustment. The others are too benumbed with sleep to leave their seats, but he's awake, his mind active, and the servant has found him pen and ink, along with some bread to silence the growl in his stomach.

He's been pondering what makes a good travel book. It's an enterprise in which every amateur imagines he can succeed, as he discovered when he made the mistake of reading some accounts of Italy. Intolerable for the most part, the only ones worth a second look were those by Duclos and the Englishman Arthur Young because both manage to be themselves.

That's what he aims at in writing: to be his own unvarnished self, the naked animal with all his defects. Self-knowledge is the first step towards happiness, the Greeks said. There's no point in keeping a journal unless you're honest.

He butters another slice of the coarse country bread and bites into it hungrily. Naturally you have to practise some concealment in case it falls into the wrong hands. Anyone contemptible enough to peek inside would think him a veritable Lovelace with all his references to women — Countess Palfy, Mme Z., Lady A. But they're disguises for the one he loves, whose real name — Alexandrine, so formal and dignified — he can't imagine uttering. Sometimes he changes her name several times on the same page to confuse an indiscreet reader, or makes some passing reference to the real woman that seems to distinguish her from the object of his passion. Occasionally (enclosed in parentheses where fantasies belong) he allows himself to enact with her alias what he hasn't dared in reality, as though he were a character in a novel, bolder and more enterprising with women than his diffident self, who's never ventured more than a cousinly kiss on her cheek.

Not that he hasn't taken some risks. Like the Turkish letter. He thought himself clever at the time, disguising a love letter as a printed page from a book and pasting it inside the cover of a novel he lent her. She claimed she hadn't seen it, though she said that she didn't like the novel because it put things too crudely. Perhaps that was her way of letting him know that his little fiction of a jealous sultan, a favourite slave and a despairing lover had offended her. But isn't there some truth in it? What is a wife, beneath the veneer of civilisation, but a slave — six pregnancies in nine years of marriage, and she's only twenty-eight, there could be half a dozen more, though perhaps her husband will exercise some restraint now she's given him a second son. It's fatigued her. She no longer dances all night at a ball but simply walks through the steps. Of course, she's learnt to manage the man as a sensible woman does. I want a peaceful life, she says. But is she happy?

'We're leaving, Monsieur!' the driver shouts. He stuffs his journal in his coat pocket and heads back to the cabriolet.

Later that night he makes a stab at describing the day. The heat is suffocating in his room though he's in his shirtsleeves with door and window open for a cross-draught.

They passed through three large towns today — Dijon, Auxonne and Dole. He gives them each a few sentences, but once you've seen two or three of them these provincial towns are all the same. Dole at least has a picturesque setting with a fine view from its promenade. He draws a sketch to show where the new Napoleon Canal joins the river.

Yawning uncontrollably, he closes his notebook. If he weren't so sleepy, he'd record the supper conversation. They'd all been stimulated by the presence of the woman in grey. It was the first time he'd seen her without her veil. Features too sharp for beauty. Blue eyes, pale complexion that flushed painfully when she spoke. Too shy to utter a word unless obliged to, but then she'd surprised them. Obviously he'd piqued her; perhaps he had been rather forceful. But if you stand on ceremony, conversation goes nowhere.

Padding barefoot across the room to close his door, he catches a glimmer of candlelight across the passage. Her door's ajar. Curious, he positions himself behind his own, straining to see into the shadows opposite.

Dole, Sunday 1 September

Though I descended early, the young man was already in the cabriolet. Having no desire to watch the sunrise with him, I took my seat in the interior till after breakfast when, as though by unspoken agreement, he ceded possession to me.

The heat was intolerable today. I understand now why we leave before dawn: the driver wishes to cover as many leagues as possible in the cool of early morning. The beauty of the awakening countryside compensates for the lack of sleep, but by afternoon I am drowsy. The post horn woke me as we crossed the Saône, and I remembered dear Mademoiselle Robert's lesson on the rivers of France, and wondered where she is now.

We dined in Dijon, which still bears the scars inflicted by the vandals — churches smoke-blackened, statues mutilated, the palace of the Dukes of Burgundy in ruins, every symbol of the past profaned.

She stops to fan herself. The accumulated heat of the day is stifling in the tiny room, though she's opened the windows wide to let in fresh air, leaving the door ajar for the chambermaid, who's promised to bring more water.

Tonight I had supper with my fellow-passengers. I had expected to find at least one other woman at table and almost fled when I saw the gentlemen seated by themselves.

But the diligence driver had spotted her in the doorway and rose to his feet.

'Mademoiselle is honouring us with her company tonight.' He pulled out a chair for her and told the servant to set an extra place. 'Don't be afraid, Mademoiselle — the conversation is entirely proper. These gentlemen are talking about happiness.' His ironic smile told her not to take them too seriously.

'The question we are debating, Mademoiselle,' said the older Italian courteously, 'is whether happiness is a state of well-being derived from inner tranquillity, or the most intense joy of which we are capable and therefore necessarily intermittent.'

'You philosophers ask too many questions!' the driver protested. 'Happiness isn't a mystery. All it needs is a sunny morning, a meal in pleasant company at the end of the day — and good health, of course. To yours, Mademoiselle, Messieurs!' He raised his glass.

'You opt for well-being then, Monsieur, like me,' said the Italian. 'But we must admit that there are also more intense forms of happiness, no? What would bring you the greatest happiness?' Ignoring the driver's broad wink, he turned to the young man in the faded uniform, who said in his broken French: 'To see my home again after all these years, to embrace my mother!'

'May your reunion be joyful!' said the older man kindly. 'And you, my friend?' he asked the young Frenchman.

'To read love in the eyes of the woman I adore.'

'And Mademoiselle?'

She'd hesitated, embarrassed. 'To see with my own eyes places that I know only from the writing of travellers.'

'But it's folly to base your hope of happiness on travellers' tales!' exclaimed the young Frenchman. 'Half of them are pedants, and the others — Chateaubriand and his like — are too keen to make fine phrases. They're the most dangerous because their inflated descriptions can only lead to disappointment — or false emotion if you try to feel the sensations they promise.'

'How can emotion be false?' the older man objected.

'When we convince ourselves that we are feeling what we ought to feel,' said the Frenchman. 'Or when we misinterpret our feeling. For example, the traveller who expresses rapture in front of a sublime view or a work of art may be taking as much pleasure in his own sensitive soul — it's all vanity, in other words.' He looked at them smugly.

'Buffon says that what we call love is largely vanity.' She felt a blush flooding upwards from the base of her neck but she wanted to return his attack. 'Vanity of conquest, vanity of possessing that which others desire, vanity of being desired.'

'How cynical you are, you French!' the older man exclaimed. 'We Italians are simple souls when it comes to happiness, are we not?' he asked his young compatriot, who was devouring his soup as if there were no greater joy than a full stomach. 'We don't doubt the truth of our feelings. How can you be happy with such an attitude?'

'I'm not saying that all emotions are false,' the Frenchman protested. 'Only that some may be. There are pure emotions — the enjoyment of music, for instance. I owe some of the happiest moments in my life to Mozart.'

'But what makes you sure that no vanity enters into it?' the Italian asked, giving her a conspiratorial glance. 'The satisfaction of possessing superior musical tastes, for instance?'

'We're all prone to the vanity of feeling superior to others,' the Frenchman riposted, clearly stung. 'But those of us who try to cultivate lucidity aren't deceived by such petty satisfactions.'

'But does the lucid man — or the lucid woman — feel pleasure with the same intensity?' The older man's smile invited her to speak but left her tongue-tied. His charm was as intimidating as the young Frenchman's stare.

The conversation moved too fast for me, a duel of wits in which I was merely a spectator, though I was pleased to have scored my own hit. No doubt they thought me a bluestocking exhibiting my knowledge of Buffon, an old maid ignorant of life outside books. But I felt incapable of defining happiness. What do I know of it? Have I even felt it since childhood ended? I have experienced neither the conjugal affection nor the maternity in which woman's happiness is said to lie. And I refuse the name of happiness to the satisfaction of doing one's duty, which religion tells us is the only reliable joy we may experience in this world.

Had I not feared to be thought sentimental, I might have said it was to stand beneath a tree after rain, listening to a song thrush. But that is a fleeting joy. For the moment happiness is a promise on the horizon towards which I travel, a name on the map, as it were, that perhaps I shall never reach though I believe it exists.

Naturally an exile would imagine happiness as a place, she thinks bitterly. With what anxious joy they'd learned of the amnesty permitting their return to France. Jeannette's happiness was unalloyed (though she'd wept when she said goodbye to them), for she could return to her native village, where no doubt she's astonishing the inhabitants still with her tales of the English. There was no such homecoming for herself and her father. Any illusions they'd had of recovering their confiscated property were immediately dispelled. Their home was in the hands of a grain dealer who'd amassed a fortune and bought the house and park to dignify his wealth. It had made her father so angry that she feared for his mind.

Nothing was left. Not a shred of their personal possessions. They were destitute. And her father no longer capable of the teaching that, with her embroidery and Jeannette's resourcefulness, had kept them alive in London. They couldn't have survived if her cousin and his wife hadn't taken them in, Armand kind enough in his dutiful way, but Marie-Cécile's welcome forced.

Five years she'd lived with them in Nogent, five long years of making herself unobtrusive, trying to ease her father's decline. And then he was gone. Despite her grief, she'd had a guilty sense of a burden lifted, but what did life hold for her now she was free? She was twenty-six and she'd had no suitors. Marriage was unthinkable while her father was alive and she his only comfort in this longed-for but now alien land. And who would want her anyway — a returned exile, liable to harbour royalist sympathies, and unblessed with the beauty that might distract a man from her lack of dowry? She seemed doomed to live out her life at her cousin's, just another of the penniless spinsters whom families grudgingly harbour.

How can they talk so easily of happiness, these gentlemen, as though it were simply something to be grasped — they who move through the world of their own volition, ignorant of the prisons in which dependence confines so many women, for whom happiness can only lie in calm acceptance of their lot.

Her writing loses its habitual smoothness as her pen races across the page, letting all the bitterness of the last nine years overflow. Her only escape from dependence was servitude in another family. She'd thought of seeking a post as a governess, for which she possessed more than sufficient education — not to mention expertise in the ladylike arts of embroidery and self-effacement. Then the *curé* mentioned that an elderly parishioner, the childless widow of a magistrate, was seeking a lady companion. It was not without misgiving that she accepted. But Marie-Cécile's covert hostility was making her life intolerable, and even the two little boys had begun to treat her superciliously (like the servants, who had their own subtle ways of indicating her status). It would at least be a change of scene. And Mme d'Aumont, though demanding, wasn't unkind. They'd grown attached to each other in the three years they spent together. But it was sad at times, nonetheless, to be living the life of an elderly woman, the precious years of her youth passing untouched.

It's a luxury to be able to define happiness, I should have told those gentlemen philosophers. Only the privileged can debate its meaning . . .

Her pen stops in mid-sentence, for she's one of the privileged now. It is sad to owe one's freedom to another's death. Her grief when the heart attack felled poor Mme d'Aumont was genuine, though mingled with self-pity since it made her homeless again. She was steeling herself to seek another position when, unbelievably, the lawyer informed her that she was the sole legatee. It was no dream: she'd become an independent woman.

That was happiness. To wake every morning with the knowledge that I was my own mistress. I should have told them that.

But it wasn't enough by itself. Ownership of the gloomy old house and a small annual income hadn't transformed her existence. Of course, other possibilities soon declared themselves. An inheritance made any woman alluring. Beyond the indignity of being courted as a woman of property, though, she felt an instinctive resistance. She hadn't gained independence only to surrender it to a husband.

And then one day in the dull seclusion of the year-long mourning with which she'd honoured her benefactress, it came to her that she was no longer tied to Nogent. She had no need of a large house; she could let it to tenants. With that regular income and Mme d'Aumont's small capital to draw on, she could live anywhere she chose.

At first the thought was too frightening. I would still be there without Mrs Godwin's example. What lucky impulse inspired me, seeking escape in a book on that bleak January day, to take out her Letters from Sweden? *I had leafed through it before in search of a favourite passage, but this time the words that met my eyes struck me with the force of a revelation, almost as opening the Bible at random might have done for a pious soul. Mrs Godwin had proved that a woman could travel alone, that she wasn't condemned to know the world only through the accounts of men. I too, if I found the courage, could wander those distant shores, enjoy the eerie brilliance of a northern midsummer night.*

A sea voyage was out of the question, though, while war with England continued, and besides, she knew none of the Scandinavian languages. She'd returned the book to the shelf, dispirited.

But there alongside was Mme de Staël's *Corinne*, with its captivating descriptions of Italy, as though fate (and not her own two hands) had placed the books together on the shelf to point the way. What was there (except fear, and a woman's ingrained self-limitation) to prevent her from going to Italy? She had studied the language, the whole peninsula was now under French governance, and the newly opened road through the Alps had simplified the journey. As for the cost, her years of exile had accustomed her to frugality, and with all the riches of art and antiquity to explore, what more would she need than clean lodgings and the simplest of meals?

I am fully aware that Mme de Staël's book has all the exaggeration of a novel. That arrogant young man had no need to warn me against travellers' tales. But I shall be following in my father's footsteps, taking the road to Rome he took in his youth. I shall sit in the Coliseum as he did, reading the Roman historians, and see for myself the splendours of Renaissance art and architecture. And perhaps, if I find congenial society, I shall settle there. But even a solitary existence in Rome will surely be preferable to the monotony of Nogent.

In the distance a drum sounds the order for lights out at the barracks. It must be late. Clearly the chambermaid forgot her promise.

As she goes to shut the door, she catches a furtive movement in the doorway across the corridor: someone was standing there. A familiar stocky silhouette. Has he been spying on her? If so, it's entirely her own fault, for leaving her door ajar. She bolts it, ashamed of her thoughtlessness. What must he think of her?

But who is he anyway, this insolent fellow, that she should care what he thinks? Educated certainly, but expensive tailoring can't disguise that plebeian appearance. And those ridiculous trinkets on his watch chain! Tomorrow he can have the cabriolet to himself since she's spending another night in Dole. Thank heavens, she will never see that smug face again.

Champagnole, Monday 2 September, mid-afternoon

Before going to bed, I kept a watch for some time on the room of a woman I'd sat opposite at supper. Her door was ajar and I had some hope of catching a glimpse of thigh or bosom.

'No sign of the lady from the cabriolet,' Lechi remarks, as though he can read upside down. 'A pity. It's not often you meet a woman who can cite Buffon. I was looking forward to a second bout between the two of you.'

'Yes, I'd like to have avenged my honour.' He rests his forearms on his notebook protectively, waiting for Lechi to finish drinking the substance that passes for coffee outside Paris and leave him in privacy. Not that he has anything salacious to report — she had her back turned, so absorbed in writing that she hadn't sensed his gaze, and he'd seen nothing more than a patch of bare nape between her dress and the plait of fair hair that encircled her head. But it had made him curious. Such intense concentration suggested an inner life. She was clearly well educated. Travelling alone, reading an English novel, drab as a mouse — a governess perhaps, on her way to take up a position, though the touch of haughtiness in her manner suggested she hadn't been born to subservience. Of course, a woman travelling alone had to hold herself aloof, or she'd be the object of advances from every man she met. There was something about her, though — a hunger for experience in her definition of happiness — that suggested she'd be open to the right approach. Lechi had been very gallant; was it for him she'd left her door ajar?

It certainly wasn't for himself. In any case, she was too thin, no bosom to speak of, and a woman who thought love a delusion of vanity was probably cold. Nonetheless, he'd admired her graceful attitude as she wrote, her slender back perfectly upright, her blonde head aureoled by the candle. It was a rare glimpse into a secret feminine existence.

'Coming for a walk?' Lechi interrupts his thoughts.

'I'll catch up with you in a minute,' he says. Lechi joins Scotti, who's smoking outside. He picks up his pen again.

A woman who in my bed would have no effect on me gives me delightful sensations when seen unawares. She's natural, I'm not preoccupied with my role and can give myself to sensation. He pauses to underline the final six words.

He's never completely natural with women, even in bed. He's too self-conscious, that's his problem, and it interferes with all his pleasures. Like yesterday in Dole — superb full moon lighting the city and instead of enjoying it he was wondering what impression his face and his watch chain were making on the women, and trying to walk with disdainful indifference past some insolent young dragoons. But he's still young; surely these anxieties will eventually pass.

Today at last they reached the kind of densely wooded hill country he loves, though he'd been too absorbed in conversation with Lechi to give it full attention. This section of Imperial Highway 6 is brand new. It shortens the route from Paris to Italy by forty leagues, thanks to the emperor.

'*There's* a man who's always in a hurry,' Lechi said. He'd met the emperor in person, it turned out, when his family had offered hospitality on Napoleon's triumphal progress through Lombardy.

'I saw him at Versailles with the empress the other day,' he'd been able to tell Lechi, adding casually, 'I'm often at one of the palaces in the course of my functions.' He'd been carefully vague as to their exact nature — inspector of imperial furnishings would sound menial to a man of Lechi's rank — but he is, after all, attached to the imperial household thanks to his association with Count Daru, and the conversation had taken a turn that made him feel obliged to reveal it.

Lechi was highly critical of the emperor, yet it was clear he admired him. Without a doubt he was the greatest man of the times, they agreed.

'A force of nature, like Vesuvius,' Lechi said. 'Though whether he'll transform Europe or leave it covered in ashes remains to be seen. We welcomed him in '97, young Jacobins that we were, aspiring to our own revolution. He promised Italy freedom, and we took him at his word. But we wanted an independent republic, not a monarchy with a French ruler.' Perhaps the new Kingdom of Italy was still the best hope for the future, as his brothers believed. But personally he'd declined the offer of a place in government, having no wish to underwrite the emperor's dictates.

'Surely, it's just a matter of time,' he'd protested, troubled by Lechi's disillusion. The emperor was setting in place the institutions of modern government that eventually Italians would be capable of sustaining by themselves.

'Shall we live to see that day?' Lechi asked. 'It's too soon to know what these great changes have wrought. We've lived through a volcanic eruption that wiped out the old society, but we can't yet judge the solidity of all this fine new construction rising among the ruins. It may come tumbling round our ears. The one certainty is that things will never revert to what they were before. A new spirit has arisen.'

Lechi had quoted Virgil, and he tries to remember the line now — *Novus saeclorum nascitur ordo*. A new order is being born of the ages. But at what cost? Unlike his conservative family, he's always rejoiced in the Revolution for the excellent institutions it created (still slightly clouded by the eruption, admittedly), but recently he's begun to worry that it's exiled joy from Europe for a century to come. Lechi had assured him that happiness is still to be found in Italy.

Hearing that has strengthened his desire for a post there, though perhaps — he writes now, in a mix of Italian, French and English to confuse a snooper — it wouldn't serve his literary ambitions to live so far from the objects of his satire. He must observe them daily to complete his play, the portrait of Parisian society he's been working on for seven years. Living in Italy, he'd lose touch with his material, though of course the contrast of other national types helps you see your own more clearly. Lechi, for example, has made him conscious of the artificiality of French manners.

Nothing could be further from Lechi's amiability than Z.'s, he writes. *The one natural, playful, whimsical as a girl, the other pedantic, pretentious, heavy, boring.*

Z., also known in his journal as Count Palfy, or Probus the honest administrator — his formidable cousin, Pierre Daru, pompously affable when he isn't red with fury, shouting at his subordinates, making everyone cringe. Why, even now, seventy leagues from Paris, can't he escape the man? He's worked hard the last few years to overcome his reputation as an irresponsible young hothead; there are moments when he feels Daru has finally developed some respect for him. The letter recommending him for a post said he was capable of writing reports with clarity, precision and intelligence. The most generous praise he'd ever had from his cousin; it made him happy for a whole day.

But with a man like that you're always an underling. It's Daru's need to have everything under his control that makes him so difficult. All the more so now he's Secretary of State as well as Intendant of the

Imperial Household. That he can fill both roles (with a master even more obsessed with detail than himself) testifies to his extraordinary capacity for work. But those with driven natures can't understand that others want to live differently. Can Daru even imagine why a young man might want time off for a little trip to Italy? You're forced to prevaricate with a man like that.

The post horn is sounding the departure. Stupid to let thoughts of Paris cloud the day.

Dole, Monday 2 September

I rose late this morning, making up for lost sleep, though even in my dreams I seemed to hear the jingle of harness bells. But my hope of finding Mme de Sancerre was disappointed. I knew that there was little chance that she still resided at her former address, since I had received no response to my letter, but I could not have passed through Dole without trying.

She'd found the house without difficulty, and her knock brought a maid, then the master. Cold eyes observed her suspiciously over a pince-nez. 'There's no one of that name here, Mademoiselle.' He closed the door before she could question him further.

As she turned away, a voice called from an open window across the narrow street. 'Mademoiselle! Whom do you seek?' A wrinkled face in a widow's cap peered out of the shadows.

'I was hoping to find Madame de Sancerre or some member of her family. I believe that they lived here?'

'But that's a long time ago, Mademoiselle! They emigrated, or so we heard. One day they were there, the next the house was empty. Then the bailiffs came with the confiscation order and not long afterwards that gentleman moved in.'

'And they have never returned? Do you know where they went, Madame?'

'We heard nothing more of them, Mademoiselle. But you could ask at the mayor's office.'

To satisfy myself I made enquiries, without success. Against all reasonable expectation, I had hoped for this reunion, longing to confide to a sympathetic ear all the sorrows of which I have spoken to no one since our return to France. But Monsieur de Sancerre must have been one of the loyal officers who left the army when the republic was declared.

Unlike her cousin, who'd continued to serve even after the king's execution and through all the changes that followed — defending France, he claimed, whatever the government of the day. He was a great admirer of the emperor (the usurper, as her father privately called him). Fortunately for them, whatever his political views, Armand had retained a sense of family duty.

She hadn't recognised the battle-scarred man with the empty sleeve and the decoration in his lapel who'd met them in Calais on their return from England. As a child she'd hardly known this cousin ten years older than herself, who'd paid her scant attention on the few occasions they'd met. She'd understood, even as a little girl, that he would inherit Vernet since her father had no surviving son. Did he bear her father any resentment for its loss? He'd insinuated once that her father had brought his misfortunes upon himself, but she was too loyal to ask what he meant. In any case, Armand has little reason to complain. He's prospered since his wound put him out of active service. Marie-Cécile had a substantial dowry (and graceful manners that banish all hint of its mercantile source). He's acquired property, a share in his father-in-law's business, and a field of action for his talents. He cannot feel the loss of Vernet as she does.

If she closes her eyes she can resurrect it, as though she were walking with Mademoiselle Robert along the sanded path to the wild part of the garden, where a stream wound under the trees to a lily-covered pond. Or down the long avenue of limes in June when they hummed with bees drawn by the honey-scented blossom. The sunlight through the heart-shaped leaves had a greeny glow. Beyond lay the gates and the world outside the borders of the park . . . She recoils as though she's seen a viper on the path, then retreats to the safety of the box-edged parterres below the terrace and runs under the stone arch into the walled potager, where she would brush her hands against rosemary and mint and sample the first strawberries of which she's never tasted the like since. All lost, like her books, and the herbarium she was making with Mademoiselle Robert, and the little porcelain shepherdess with her lamb.

'Look back and all you get is a crick in the neck.' Jeannette's homely saying shakes her out of her trance. It's foolish to let the bitterness of dispossession blight the present. She's young still and healthy, she has resources. She must keep her eyes resolutely fixed on the horizon.

I spent the afternoon exploring Dole, admiring some fine old buildings of past centuries, most of which have been put to less noble uses since the

Revolution. It is still a garrison town, the promenades invaded by loud young officers, but the view from the belvedere of the forested hills beyond raised my spirits in anticipation of tomorrow's journey.

The moon rose early tonight, full and brilliant. I caught sight of it at the end of the street like a great eye peering over the rooftops at earthly doings. It seemed closer than usual, no doubt an optical illusion.

A distant drum roll signalling lights out at the barracks reminds her that she has an early start tomorrow. She packs her writing case and goes to the window for a breath of air. The moon is above the rooftops now, but less brilliant; there's a shadow along the lower rim, though the sky is cloudless. Something uncanny is happening. The shadow is creeping slowly upwards across the luminous surface in too regular an arc for mist. Already, the bottom quarter is obscured, the light above it dim. Can this be an eclipse? She leans out of the window seeking other observers, but there's no one on the street. If she'd left with the diligence this morning, she might be watching it with her companions from last night. But the experience would be dissipated in conversation. The sublime is best experienced in solitude.

She watches until half the moon is darkened before she closes the shutters. If she hadn't reserved a place in the early mail coach, she would have waited to see the moon re-emerge from Earth's shadow. But even to have seen this much has compensated for the day's disappointment. It seems a harbinger of all the new experiences that await her. Two days from now she will see the Alps. And in a month, if all goes well, she will watch the moon rise over the Coliseum. Already she feels emboldened and she's only been three days on the road.

Geneva, at the Golden Crown, Tuesday 3 September

It's eight in the evening and the words are pouring onto the page. Last night, after finishing his diary, he'd joined Scotti at the window and noticed that the moon had lost a quarter, though it had been full earlier. But it wasn't till the maid told them this morning that only a tiny sliver remained that they realised they'd seen the first stage of an eclipse. He might have seen it all if he hadn't been obsessed with the gauche behaviour and laboured jokes of a group of commercial travellers, whose greatest achievement apparently was to have drunk eight bottles of wine with a beef salad. The bourgeois at his most

Encounters on the Journey

ridiculous. The evening had had its compensations, however. He'd screwed front and rear a serving girl who was passable, and listened to a clarinet and violin which weren't but which had nonetheless given him pleasure.

But was his pleasure in the girl and the music any different from that of the commercial travellers? And yet he has a mistress like Angéline and the opera every night, which should fill his heart but don't. It must be a powerful antidote to boredom to have one's heart entirely occupied. These reflections clouded an otherwise memorable day.

At five in the morning the diligence halted and they'd woken chilled to the bone, startled by the thunder of machinery. He and Lechi got out to investigate. A stream, tumbling down the hillside, powered the giant wheel of a hobnail factory where eight to ten women, mostly young, were already at work. Two blows from a heavy mechanical hammer produced a nail. It had made a strong impression on him — the quick fingers placing the metal, the twenty hammers shaking the floor with their force. And all for two sous a thousand, so at a rate of ten to twelve thousand a day the women earned about one franc. What kind of man made his money from such an enterprise?

Another slightly bitter political discussion with Lechi had depressed him until the view of Mont Blanc and Lac Léman sprang upon them mid-morning. A magnificent spectacle that he should have sketched on the spot before fatigue wiped out his impressions.

They reached Geneva at four and were dropped inconveniently at the diligence offices instead of the inn. The city was silent and gloomy as a prison, the main square deserted, grass growing through the paving stones. Everyone they dealt with was surly and grasping. Probably the effect of centuries of republican government. Manners are more graceful in a monarchy.

He continues writing for another page or two — Genevan girls, Rousseau's education, Scotti's ignorance — but it's badly phrased because he's tired. Tomorrow he'll send this notebook back to Paris to keep it safe from prying eyes. Not that he's been as indiscreet as he might have been — about his conversations with Lechi, for instance, who'd challenged his complaints about the Genevan character over supper.

'But they have good reason to be surly! The city had been an independent state for two hundred years. You can't expect them to accept annexation cheerfully.' Lechi had lowered his voice, though the group of French officers playing cards nearby was making too much noise to overhear. 'As a department of France, they're subject to French taxes and conscription, and their manufacturers have been ruined by the ban on exports to England — do you expect them to welcome you kindly?'

Now, thinking it over in bed, he wonders if Lechi was right. Of course, Genevans might have grievances, but national character lies deeper than temporary circumstance, as he'd told Lechi: 'Think of Geneva's harsh religion — good God, theatres were prohibited here!'

Were Genevans as morose eleven years ago, when he first visited the city? Would he even have noticed then? He was too turned in on himself by the misery of his first winter in Paris to pay attention to others. It had nearly killed him, sixteen-year-old innocent that he was with his dreams of life in the capital — the comedies he'd write, the actresses he'd court — only to find himself alone in a rented room like a prison cell with a dirty window framing a patch of grey sky. He might have died there of the fever he'd caught (or the quack's vile black medicine which made his hair fall out) if he hadn't been taken in by the Daru family, who had him nursed back to health (and a restored head of hair, thank heavens). But in that industrious household there wasn't a chance he'd be allowed to sit in his room all day awaiting the Comic Muse, and since he couldn't face taking the École polytechnique entrance exam — the very reason why his father had sent him to Paris — or the humiliation of returning to Grenoble, he'd had to accept a lowly position in his cousin's office at the Ministry of War. An inauspicious start to the new century (or, as it was being called then, year VIII of the Revolution). But suddenly the whole office was on the move, and he had instructions to follow. It was spring, orchards and meadows in bloom, and like the countryside he was coming back to life, far too absorbed with his own sensations to pay attention to the good citizens of Geneva. His main concern (once he'd satisfied his wish to see the birthplace of Rousseau) had been to hide his own incompetence from the campaign-hardened soldiers of the reserve army in whose company he was to travel.

Besides, things had been simpler then. France was still a republic, and the French army was fulfilling the Revolutionary promise to help all nations that wished to regain their freedom. Italians needed their help to throw off Austrian tyranny, and Genevans, as good republicans, were backing their cause. Now, eleven years later, nothing seems so clear. And it's souring his conversations with Lechi. He'll avoid politics tomorrow.

With the toenails of his right foot he scratches a flea bite on his left ankle, souvenir of last night's inn. He hopes it's the only one. He'd used a condom with the maidservant, but it's still risky. He hasn't had the pox since that episode in Vienna, but the doctor warned him last year — a few more doses of the clap and he'd need a catheter to piss. It had shaken him: he's forsworn the girls on the street since he took up with Angéline. For the first time since leaving Paris, he misses her. The thought of her, humming a line from an aria as she pulls off her stockings, stirs him. He pictures her lifting her petticoat over her head, exposing the curly black bush of her sex, her opulent singer's chest. Turning and twisting her in his mind's eye to the most provocative arrangement of her supple limbs, he brings himself to a release that guarantees sleep.

Saint-Laurent, Tuesday 3 September

The diligence passes only three times a week, so I left Dole this morning with the mail coach. It is faster than the diligence, but unfortunately one must share the cabriolet with the driver, so I travelled inside with two lawyers who discussed their cases interminably. After my late night I feared making a spectacle of myself by falling asleep, but the interest of the changing landscape kept me awake.

The highlight of the day was our ascent into the Jura — the first mountains that I have ever seen. In the steepest part of the climb, we got out and walked to lighten the horses' load, pausing at the top to enjoy the view of sunlit fields and vineyards below. From then on, the land was rocky and uncultivated. Towards evening, the road followed a torrent through a ravine above which the dark spires of fir trees stood out in silhouette against the silver disc of the rising moon, a sight as romantic as the Norwegian landscapes that Mrs Godwin's book describes.

I felt exultant to be fulfilling my dream. Yes, this was happiness, whatever that young man said, though it could not be prolonged once we reached this isolated village. The sordid inn is little better than a tavern with its loud music and blowsy servants, exploiting every opportunity to make money from those condemned to its resources for the night.

Closing her journal, she goes to the window, inhaling the resinous scent of the firewood stacked beneath. The glow of a lantern is all that distracts from the beauty of the night sky. Standing there, bathed by the incoming tide of air, as she's stood so often before on one of those blossom-scented spring or summer nights when she couldn't sleep, she contemplates the high, pale moon. Down below, the music plays on interminably. Whether by request or because of a limited repertoire, the players keep returning to the same piece, a crude but haunting little tune that seems to promise some climax it never achieves. She listens, affected in spite of herself, till the mountain air sends her shivering to bed.

Voices, male and female, so close they seem to be in her room, wake her just as she's fallen asleep, but it's only her neighbours on the other side of the thin partition wall, preparing for bed. A brief exchange, the man loud, the woman hushing him, then a succession of grunts as he makes himself comfortable in a bed that creaks with every move. Only when the movement becomes frenetic does it dawn on her what's happening. Hot with embarrassment, she pulls her pillow against her ears. The room is the dirtiest she's slept in, and she hasn't even left France yet. But if it's the price to be paid for a day like today, she must overcome her disgust.

Saint-Maurice, Wednesday 4 September

A picturesque spot with a castle guarding the ancient fortified bridge across the Rhône, yet strangely he has no recollection of the place, though he must have come through eleven years ago. Memory is like an old campaign map, torn at the folds and so spattered with rain and mud that entire sections of the route are obliterated. But whatever else he's forgotten, he vividly recalls his departure from Geneva, and he tells the story over a good supper of trout and a nice little wine poured by the landlord (who claims to have served the emperor on the famous march):

'My cousin had gone ahead with the advance guard, but he'd left me a horse and instructions to follow him with the reserves. The only problem was that I'd never learnt to ride! And the animal had been stabled for a month, so it was frisky. My portmanteau was strapped to its back — it weighed a ton because I'd brought thirty books! — and I mounted. The minute we were through the city gate the horse took off at a gallop. Just as I was about to be tossed in the lake, someone grabbed the bridle. A captain who'd been asked to keep an eye on me had sent his batman to my rescue. Between them they taught me the rudiments of horsemanship. Swordplay too — I was no more competent with a sabre than a horse.'

He was soft as a girl, thanks to his father's over-protectiveness, with a boy's bravado, practising the moves under the captain's eye at every halt, though heaven knows what would have happened if he'd faced an Austrian charge. But the satisfaction of passing those tests of manhood had been nothing compared to the exaltation of riding through the setting of Rousseau's *Héloïse*. That evening in Rolle, hearing the great bell of the village church ring out, reverberating through the stillness like ripples from a pebble thrown in water, his whole being had expanded with it in waves of joy. He'd never experienced such emotion. It wasn't the trivial happiness of childhood (of which he'd known all too little after his mother's death), but something approaching ecstasy. Moments like that shouldn't be spoken. He doesn't confide it to Lechi, nor had he to the cynical captain.

'A good fellow in his way. He stopped me going over a precipice in the Saint Bernard pass.'

'That was one of the emperor's most brilliant exploits!' Lechi exclaimed. 'Slipping through the Saint Bernard to take the Austrians by surprise in the south when they were expecting him from the north! Of course, it might have been disastrous. There's snow in the passes even in May. Weather can wreck a general's plans.'

'There was plenty of snow, I can tell you!' he said, happy to hear the admiration in Lechi's voice, which wiped out the sourness of yesterday's discussion. 'I hope I'll never experience such cold again! But the emperor — or rather, the First Consul as he was then — knew what he was doing.'

Or did he? After all, they hadn't been able to haul their cannon through the snow, had they? But his own impressions, following with the rearguard, may be unreliable. And even the things you're sure you remember can't be trusted.

'A brandy with your coffee, gentlemen?' asks the landlord. There's a man who doesn't doubt his memories, though the general he waited on may well have been some lesser figure sufficiently self-important to be taken for the leader. But which of us doesn't like to boast that we witnessed history in the making?

It's disconcerting to retrace the footsteps of that younger self who'd envy his new assurance, when what he's actually feeling is a sense of loss. Back then, he felt things with an intensity he rarely experiences now. Does age inevitably dull sensibility? Or is it Paris? The deadening routine of work, the cultivation of tedious people who might advance his career, the shallowness of it all. Perhaps this journey will prove that his soul can still soar as it did that evening above the lake. If anything can restore that lost emotion, it's Italy.

Geneva, Wednesday 4 September

This morning, not wishing to get my first sight of the Alps through the small window in the mail-coach door, I asked the driver, who seemed a respectable man, if I might sit beside him. I am glad to have found the courage, for nothing in my experience hitherto can compare with that instant when I saw across the horizon the line of snow-covered peaks crowned by Mont Blanc. Below us stretched Lac Léman, of a celestial blue and vaster than I had imagined. No words can do justice to the sight.

But, sublime though it was, there were many more ordinary spots on our route where I longed to halt. I could gladly have spent all day botanising in a rocky pasture among the firs. This mode of travel is too fast, its impressions quickly effaced. Ideally one should make the journey on foot, with a donkey to carry the baggage, like the wayfarers we overtook. But a woman could never do it alone. Even Mrs Godwin, who writes as though she travelled unaccompanied, must have had a local servant to deal with boatmen and innkeepers since she did not know the language. I have reread the first few chapters on Sweden with great interest during the halts today.

Looking back over what she's just written, it occurs to her that she too might publish her travels. Of course, she's not capable of treating the economic and political topics that give Mrs Godwin's book its weight, but the experiences of a woman travelling alone might interest the public. She'd use a pen name, for discretion's sake and not to embarrass her cousin.

The young man in the diligence was always scribbling during the halts. Perhaps he too was writing an account of his journey. She would not like to find herself in its pages. But she could take her revenge by putting him in her own — with his top hat and side whiskers and the trinkets on his watch chain.

She starts to reread her journal from the beginning, trying to see it with an outsider's eye. Of course, she would have to eliminate everything too revealing, all those pages where memories have jostled aside the present. If she were to write with publication in mind, she would be more circumspect. But the mere possibility of a reader would change what she wrote — and how much might then be suppressed, how many details judged unworthy of inclusion. No, she must write for herself alone, without readers in mind.

And yet there's always a reader. Not just her future self, for whom she's trying to retain the myriad impressions of the day, but the readers in her head — Mademoiselle Robert, for whose approval her first compositions were shaped, and her father, whose acerbic judgement preserves her from the feminine weakness for exclamations and superlatives. And now that unpleasant young man, whose scorn for the hyperbole of travellers inhibited her as she recorded her first sight of the Alps. But it's one thing to recognise their influence, and quite another to escape it.

She takes up her quill to continue, wishing it could lift her pedestrian prose into flight like the wing from which it originated.

I went out before supper and saw the house where Rousseau was born. To wander through these streets familiar to his youth, to contemplate the lake and mountains that formed his sensibility, was one of those experiences for which I am ready to endure any discomfort. The landscape in which our earliest days are passed shapes us as deeply as the influence of our parents. One may know something of a man's soul, I believe, by visiting the places dear to his childhood.

This inn is the best so far, especially in comparison to last night's wretched lodging. (There is, to be honest, an unpleasant odour at the end of the corridor, but once my door is closed I no longer perceive it.) I have decided to stay two nights, and reserved a place on Friday's diligence.

Brigue, Thursday 5 September

He pulls off his boots and scratches his flea bites with the satisfaction of long-delayed relief, brooding over a discussion with Lechi that began on their walk before supper. They'd paused on the bridge across the Rhône, trying to spot where the new road penetrated the mountains that closed the end of the valley. 'Someone prospered here,' Lechi had said, nodding at the huge château that dominated the little town.

'Some great lord who controlled the pass,' he'd speculated in return. 'A toll on every mule train, and you'd soon amass a fortune. It was high time the Revolution abolished seigneurial rights.'

'It's under the control of a greater lord now,' Lechi said drily. 'Who still exacts payment.'

'But not for his personal enrichment!' he protested. 'The Simplon road cost eighteen million francs. A huge investment. The annexation of the Valais was necessary to guarantee its security. And the local inhabitants benefit from the trade and travellers it brings.'

He undresses and snuffs the candle, sinking into a deep feather bed that's as welcoming as a woman's body, though he's in no mood to appreciate its embrace. The discussion with Lechi was amicable, but it's made him uncomfortably aware of the change in his own views. Seven years ago, watching the pope and the emperor enter Notre Dame for the coronation, he'd called it (in the privacy of his journal) an alliance of charlatans — religion consecrating tyranny for the alleged good of mankind. But the advantage of imperial power, he's come to realise, is that it's simply the most efficient way to bring about change. Left to themselves, all the small backward states that France has annexed would take a century to make their own way towards reform, with the inevitable strife of revolution and civil war. It's in their best interest, surely, to have an effective modern government, even if it has to be imposed on them by a superior power. Would Italy, with its multiplicity of tiny states, ever change left to itself, he'd asked Lechi.

'You northeners were enlightened. But the south, with that Bourbon imbecile on the throne of Naples and Sicily! And the papal states — ruled by an ultra-conservative church that had made them the poorest and most backward in Europe. As departments of France, they'll benefit from investment in agriculture and manufacturing —'

'And France from guaranteed cheap supplies,' Lechi interjected slyly.

'But look what else they gain: the Inquisition abolished, the Ghetto opened —'

'You think that's pleased them?'

'Trial by jury, a modern law code,' he persisted.

'The best laws in the world couldn't win their hearts after the pope's arrest,' Lechi interrupted. 'And on top of that to name the emperor's infant son king of Rome! I'm no defender of the papacy, but that was a fatal error.'

Did the pope not have enough to do as head of the Church without being a secular ruler too — and a bad one at that, he'd asked. But he'd had to concede that the arrest had simply created a martyr. He'd wanted to prove (to himself as much as Lechi) that he's still capable of critical judgement even if his own future is bound to the empire. And Lechi himself admits that the emperor is developing the countries under his rule to a degree they'd never known before. It's remarkable how much has been achieved in just ten years — all these new roads and canals, the educational reforms, the encouragement of science and manufacture. It's a great time for ambitious young men, so many careers now open to the talented that were once the exclusive preserve of the well-born. A capable young man can rise rapidly in this new world.

It was here, on the very road they travelled this morning, as he'd told Lechi, that he'd first grasped that fact, eleven years ago. He remembered it vividly — shivering in a cold dawn, watching a chaos of men, mules, cannon and munition waggons turn into an orderly column under the command of a young general on horseback. 'That's Marmont,' someone had told him. 'Only twenty-six, and already a general!' It was enough to inspire any seventeen-year-old.

'So you joined the army?' Lechi's smile was pitying.

'My cousin got me a commission in the dragoons. I was attached to the staff of General Michaud.' For a few months anyway, until (being a mere sub-lieutenant) he was ordered back to his regiment. If he'd become Michaud's aide-de-camp it would have been different, but he was stuck in a dull garrison town among coarse ignorant companions, and his military ambitions waned.

'Then I caught some kind of recurrent fever.'

'Very opportune!' Lechi laughed, not unsympathetically.

'Yes, I was lucky.' He'd gone home to convalesce and his father, desperate to rescue his only son from the perils of a military career, had offered him an allowance if he resigned his commission. It was just enough to live in Paris and pursue his dream of becoming the new Molière. He was serious about it, spending his nights at the theatre, taking lessons in declamation, writing his first play, but above all reading voraciously, immersing himself in ideas and literature.

But then along came Mélanie and threw him off course. Not that he regrets Mélanie. He's been thinking of her since the dip the other night — how she'd waded into the river at La Pomme in her chemise, refusing to be denied the pleasure of a bathe just because she was a woman. But he'd made himself a fool over her, taking a job in business so he could follow her to Marseilles when she joined a theatre company there. It had upset his father (a son in commerce, living with an actress!), and led him into deception . . .

His flea bites are itching intolerably. The heat in these feather beds inflames them. He throws off the quilt and scratches fiercely.

The affair hadn't lasted, anyway. Mélanie moved on with another company. Marseilles was a dead end. And he'd had enough of living on a pittance. Four years had gone by and he was nowhere. There'd been nothing for it but to humble himself, beg his cousin for a second chance. The time was right, war with Prussia imminent and Daru by then chief commissary of the army. Even if birth no longer matters, you still need connections — would Martial have got such a plum position in Rome if he weren't Daru's younger brother? As for himself, he'd never have got the post in Brunswick without a little influence. Adjunct war commissary wasn't much, but it was a foot on the ladder, and he's worked like a mule since.

Of course, if he'd stuck to the beaten track, he might now be a decorated hero, or an intendant in one of the annexed territories, like Martial or Alexandre Petiet in Florence. But there's no point regretting the lost years. They formed his mind and he wouldn't be who he is now without them. And there are still positions to be had — in Spain, for instance, once it's been pacified. A year or two there would give him a whole new perspective on human nature.

Geneva, Thursday 5 September

I slept well in this impeccable room that confirms the Swiss reputation for cleanliness, which is perhaps less a result of Protestant virtue than of the abundance of fresh water, for when I crossed the bridge over the Rhône after breakfast I saw the washerwomen beating their linen in the swift-flowing current, which must render it pure as the glacier from which the river takes its origin.

Satisfying a desire to walk in the country which these past few days on the road had aroused, I followed a path beyond the city gates where every few steps there was something to delight me — even a few wild strawberries, which recalled Mrs Godwin's disembarkation on the Swedish coast. My only disappointment was that this morning the mountains were hidden by cloud.

The path led her down through vineyards to the lake, where a man and boy mending nets on the shore looked up curiously at her approach. On impulse, she asked if it were possible to go out in a boat.

'Where to?' the man asked.

'Just to see the view from the water,' she said timidly.

'The lad can take you for half an hour.'

He named a sum to which she agreed. The boy got up and dragged a skiff to the water's edge. With lifted skirts, she stepped in nervously, but the motion of the little boat was steady as the boy dipped his oars and pulled away from shore. She raised her parasol and asked his name.

'Thomas,' he mumbled.

'And how old are you, Thomas?'

'Twelve.' He seemed abashed by the question, his eyes avoiding hers.

'Do you go to school?'

'In winter. When there's no work.' She could have guessed from his sunburnt limbs. His shirt and breeches were worn but carefully patched.

'Do you live in Geneva?'

'No.'

Discouraged, she gave up. Freed of the duty to show a benevolent interest in her fellow man, she could give her full attention to the view. On one side lay the city, clustered round its cathedral like a congregation beneath a pulpit. On the other, below the wooded hills, pleasantly situated country houses stood out among the fields and vineyards that sloped down to the lake-shore. How avidly she'd read Rousseau's description of this landscape, and now here she was herself, through her own will and resolution, afloat on Lac Léman under a blue September sky.

But there was still something lacking, she recognised, sitting erect under her parasol, her dress smoothed decorously over her ankles. The problem lay in her dependence on others to take her where she wished to go, her female helplessness in the face of the physical world. This boy, scarcely more than a child, could already assume the freedom of a man in the ease with which he moved the boat, secure in his strength. But Mrs Godwin had learned to row in Norway. What pleasure to be propelled by your own effort, or simply to drift like Rousseau, lying on his back in his little boat, watching the clouds float by in the summer sky. She had not yet achieved such independence. But here she was nonetheless, imitating however modestly the writers she admired, whose lives — whatever their misfortunes — seemed more intensely lived, richer in experience than the ordinary. She slipped off a glove and trailed one hand over the side, enjoying the ripple of water against her wrist.

On shore again, having paid the agreed sum with an extra coin for the boy, she walked back to town. But her shoes had got wet as she disembarked and by the time she reached the inn, her damp stocking had rubbed a blister on one heel.

Nine in the evening. I did not walk far beyond the city gate this afternoon, but the clouds that obscured Mont Blanc had vanished and its full grandeur was visible again. I understand now why the ancients deified mountains, for the great peak that dominates the others seems an image of the Creator — perfect, majestic, self-sufficing, and infinitely remote from human suffering. It amazes me to know that man has now set foot on the summit, that boots have left their imprint on the eternal snows. But I marvel still more that one of the climbers was a young woman. Mademoiselle Paradis must be an exceptional individual.

After dinner I joined the strollers on the shore. Watching the summits turn rose in the sunset, I felt the lack of a companion with whom to share the moment. As I made my way back, my solitary state oppressed me. At dawn I shall be on the road again and the thought of the difficulties ahead alarms me. How shall I set about finding cheap but respectable lodgings? And will it be safe to walk alone in a southern city?

Back at the inn, the comfort of hot water brought a sudden temptation. Nothing obliges me to continue — I could settle in this clean, well-ordered town, by this beautiful lake. There must be individuals of my own kind here whose acquaintance I might seek. Mme de Staël lives nearby. But that name renewed my courage. Italy is my goal. It would be cowardly to give up now. Tomorrow I shall take my seat in the diligence again, ready to cross the Alps.

Domodossola, Friday 6 September

'Now there's an achievement you can't deny!' he exclaims, as they sit down to supper. 'What a feat of engineering!'

He's exhilarated tonight, not so much from the dramatic switchback climb to the Simplon pass as from the descent into his beloved Italy — the first campanile rising above the chestnut woods, the first exchanges in the lilting rise and fall of an Italian dialect, and that haunting snatch of song he'd caught as the diligence halted outside a courtyard where peasant women seated in a circle were stripping hemp.

'It was Italian engineers, you know, who found some of the most ingenious solutions,' Lechi remarks. 'The Gondo tunnel, for instance.'

'I grant your engineers their share of the glory, but isn't that a sign of the collaboration the emperor is encouraging between our two nations?'

'May it prove so! The road is one of the wonders of the modern world, even if we owe it to the difficulty of hauling cannon through the Alps. Was the Saint Bernard crossing truly as hard as they say?'

'The path was slippery as the devil and nothing but a low stone wall to keep you from going over the edge. In places it was blocked by horses that had dropped dead from exhaustion — mine reared at the sight. I had to dismount and lead it. Fifteen to twenty of them had gone over the precipice, just lying there on a frozen lake below.'

He's caught their interest. Scotti has put down his soup spoon. It's tempting to exaggerate. He thinks of the portrait of the emperor that he's seen in Saint-Cloud — astride a white horse, one arm raised to point out the upward path, horse and rider almost airborne in the fierce wind that's billowing the rider's cloak. On a boulder, newly inscribed, the name of Bonaparte above those of Hannibal and Charlemagne. An artist's flattery! Everyone in the army knew the First Consul had ridden a mule. Reality had been anything but heroic.

'Everyone was grumbling, especially the foot soldiers with their heavy packs. They swore at us when the captain ordered them to make way. They'd gladly have stolen our horses. It was every man for himself, none of the comradeship I'd imagined. Our reward for all this when we reached the hospice was half a glass of freezing red wine!'

'I thought the monks had brandy,' says Scotti, his glum face registering one more of life's disappointments.

'For the generals perhaps, not for forty thousand men! Luckily, we weren't relying on the monks. Our rations had been sent ahead by the supply corps — that was my cousin Daru's role. We'd have died of hunger otherwise.'

'Yes, up there the army couldn't live off the local population. No cows or chickens to be commandeered in the Alpine snows!' Lechi contributes drily.

'The descent was just as dangerous. And then we had to get past the Austrian cannon at the fort in Bard.'

His baptism of fire, though he was too late for the real excitement. By the time he descended from the pass, Marengo was fought and won, the Austrians in retreat. He'd visited the battlefield the following year — a paltry memorial, and the bones of men and horses still lying around awaiting the scavengers who grind them up for fertiliser.

'The difficulties have been exaggerated,' he says abruptly. 'It was uncomfortable, nothing more.'

'Still, it's to your travails that we owe the ease of our journey today.' Lechi raises his glass. 'I drink to a future of good roads, even if they're built for armies!'

Saint-Maurice, Friday 6 September

A beautiful sunrise as we left Geneva. Outside a village a group of men were cutting back the vegetation that encroached on the road. As we passed, one of them glanced up into the cabriolet and our eyes met for an instant. The hostility in his gaze brought back ugly memories. The Revolution may have abolished the corvée, but it is still the peasant who maintains the roads, and his resentment towards those who ride in carriages has not diminished. The incident would have troubled me all day had I not had companions to distract me.

She'd thought herself safe from intrusion. The other passengers — two elderly ladies, a well-dressed couple, and a gentleman whose stiff demeanour proclaimed the pastor — seemed unlikely to dispute her possession of the cabriolet. But as she returned from the breakfast halt, the couple asked if they might join her. The husband, a tall lean man with an open friendly manner, put his hand on her elbow to steady her as she climbed in, while his plump little wife gathered up her skirts to follow.

He stepped in beside them and they introduced themselves. They were Lyonnais, Payot by name. She asked how far they were going.

'To Baveno. We're making a tour of the Italian lakes. And yourself, Mademoiselle?'

'To Milan.'

'Then we shall cross the Alps together,' he said cheerfully. Her heart sank.

'My husband often makes the journey on business,' Mme Payot confided. 'But this time he's persuaded me to accompany him. We have just married off our youngest daughter, so there's nothing to keep me at home.' She herself seemed as happy as a girl on her wedding journey.

'I'm eager to see the new road through the Simplon,' Payot said. 'We shall return by the other new road through the Mont-Cenis pass, which permits the convenience of a circular trip. Now you'll see the advantage of the cabriolet,' he told his wife, as the diligence rolled out of the inn yard. 'A little dusty, but an incomparable view.'

The loss of my solitude was mitigated by the pleasure of sharing impressions. Mme Payot takes a lively interest in everything. Her husband is astute, more cultivated than one might expect from a man of his class. He is a silk manufacturer in Lyon and travels frequently to Italy, where he obtains all his raw silk. But the trade has declined, he told me, since the ban on commerce with England. Many silk weavers are unemployed. He predicts unrest if nothing is done to assist them.

She'd heard Armand express similar concern over the cotton weavers in the north, and felt a secret satisfaction that the emperor's schemes of ruining England were having unanticipated consequences. Whether the English were justified in their pursuit of the war she was not prepared to say, but she could not forget that England had given her family refuge.

All such matters were soon forgotten in the beauty of the countryside, though. Whatever was happening elsewhere, here at least the people were thriving, their houses wreathed in vines, their fields and orchards fertile.

We are spending the night in this village huddled in the shelter of an immense grey cliff above the Rhône. Caesar, it's said, may have taken this route on his way to conquer Gaul, followed in later centuries by Lombards and Saracens. The French army (as the innkeeper did not fail to remind us) passed through eleven years ago to invade Italy.

Before supper I walked down to the river and stood on the bridge above the fast-flowing current, meditating on the inexorable movement of history which carries us all along in its turbulent path.

'It's dangerous to look at the water too long, Mademoiselle. They say it induces melancholy.'

She was startled, not having heard Payot approach. 'It's magnetising, the force of these alpine rivers, for someone accustomed to the slow rivers of the north.'

'That's where you're from?' His eyes, deep-set and piercing, studied her with a friendly curiosity that provoked contradictory impulses of self-revelation and concealment.

'I was born in the centre, just south of Auxerre, but I have lived for some time now in Nogent-sur-Seine.' She suppressed the years of exile.

'And you are going to Milan — do you have family there?'

'No. But I have letters of introduction.'

'I am glad to hear it. Milan is a civilised town, but a lady travelling alone needs friends.'

He was too discreet to ask any further questions, but I sensed that he was trying to place me. No doubt I betray my origins in my speech and manner. 'We are who we are,' as my father said about the Revolution's abolition of rank. 'No law can change what is innate.'

But I must change — she underlines the words fiercely — *so that I can feel at ease in whatever society I find myself. Today, in response to the frank and natural manner of my companions, I introduced myself simply as Honorine Vernet. It is a first step towards a new life.*

Was she deluding herself, she wonders, brushing her hair and replaiting it before bed. There was nothing bold about that unpremeditated omission of the giveaway 'de', just instinctive self-concealment. And if invisibility is her goal, why not go further and use her first baptismal name, Marie, which she shares with half the female population? Her other names place her too clearly among her caste: Félicité (which strangely her parents had never used, afraid perhaps to tempt fate by proclaiming the happiness her birth had brought them), and Honorine, a name she's never much liked, after a godmother she'd barely known. Marie-Félicité-Honorine de Vernet. Marie Vernet. They sound like different women.

She stops in the middle of a plait, three strands of hair hanging loose, and stares at her dim reflection in the mirror above the washstand. Alone in this strange room, a hundred leagues from everything that's defined her till now, she feels she could discard her identity as easily as the dress she's just taken off. Of course, it's not true: her passport, her cousin's letters of introduction, the documents for Italian banks, all bear her full name. She cannot escape it even if she wishes. But she's glimpsed the void and it makes her shiver. The sense of herself that she clings to may be arbitrary, a product of heredity and upbringing and social conformity, but who, what is she without it? Could she stand alone without the props that sustain her?

Tonight as she slides into her sleeping sack it seems less shroud than cocoon, the protective covering of a creature in metamorphosis. For no matter which name she uses, the journey itself is changing her. The woman who arrives in Rome will not be identical to the one who set out. And this, at least, is her own free choice; she has stepped off the beaten track. Perhaps, even at thirty, one may enter upon a new form of being.

Baveno, Saturday 7 September

All the same elements of beauty as Geneva, he thinks, looking across Lake Maggiore to the wooded hills and snow peaks beyond. Minus the Protestant gloom. This is a people who know what happiness is — the boatmen singing as they row in to shore, the barefoot girl pattering past with a basket of grapes on her head. Even the stiff old men sunning themselves on a bench are happy here.

'The advantage of the Simplon route is that it brings one down to an earthly paradise,' Lechi remarks.

'Nothing on the descent from the Saint Bernard can equal this,' he agrees.

But he'd discovered a paradise of another kind. They'd entered a small town, already ransacked by the troops who'd preceded them, where they found a billet with an old priest, which they'd had to defend against their own soldiers — men with dirty, haggard faces, bent on removing the door to make a roof for their bivouac. And it was there, in that ordinary little town, that he heard his first opera. They were doing Cimarosa's *Secret Marriage*. Not the greatest performance — the prima donna was missing a front tooth — but what a revelation! He couldn't imagine a greater joy than to hear such music every night.

Few men can boast as dramatic a passage into adult life, he reflects, as they set off again. Not just the ordeal of the crossing, and his first experience of being under cannon fire, but that momentous arrival in a strange new world with its first intimation of the pleasures of manhood — music, women, love (though the latter was only a dream as yet).

As they leave the lake and strike out on the new road to Milan, he's glad to be riding up on the roof with the baggage. You roast in the sun, but the view is priceless. Scotti has joined him but Lechi prefers the interior, so conversation will be limited; he can stay with his memories.

Once again, he marvels at the countryside — maize on either side of the road so high and dense you can't see more than a hundred paces, wheat fields bordered with vines strung like garlands between fence poles. Nowhere in his travels has he seen such fertile land.

It's Scotti with his sailor's eyes who makes out the spire of the Duomo in the afternoon haze at the end of the long white road. Soon they can see the city walls and for a few seconds he's once again a boy riding behind the captain, feigning an indifference he's far from feeling.

How joyfully the Milanese had welcomed them after the Austrian withdrawal. Balls, fireworks, illuminations, the cafés open to all hours, the opera house and theatres crammed. An atmosphere of euphoria, licence even — all those pretty women responding to the presence of hundreds of men fresh from the victory at Marengo and eager to reap its fruits. He'd watched from the sidelines, dumb with longing, while his older comrades won the hearts of Milanese beauties. If only someone had taken him in hand, pushed him into the arms of a woman — not just any woman, but one with the sensitivity to discern the passionate soul behind his unpromising exterior. His whole life might have been different.

The diligence comes to a halt in front of the Customs building. He consults his watch; he has to find an inn, change and dine before the '*corso*', the early evening promenade on the ramparts. But with luck he'll catch a first glimpse of the woman who above all others embodied the seductive charm of Italy. Will she remember the tongue-tied boy who dreamt of returning one day to conquer her?

Brigue, Saturday 7 September

We left Saint-Maurice just before dawn. I feared we would miss the famous waterfall, but lit by the sun's first rays it was a ravishing sight. Monsieur Payot persuaded the driver to halt a moment so that we could admire it. Madame Payot and I regretted its vulgar name. 'Pissevache! The Swiss know nothing beyond their cows!' she exclaimed. It reminded her of a lace veil and I thought an angel's wing. Monsieur Payot said the naming of waterfalls should clearly be left to ladies.

Their good-natured banter enlivened the hours on the road, though there were moments as they penetrated deeper into the mountains when she would rather have been alone. She tried to fix it all in her mind to record later — the terraced vineyards rising to the very base of towering cliffs, the farmhouses perched high among pastures almost lost in the clouds, the ancient fortifications guarding the road, scarcely distinguishable from the rocky outcropping to which they clung. When the diligence rolled into Brigue, where they were spending the night, the gilded onion domes of the château gave the little town the air of some exotic outpost on an oriental caravan route.

She couldn't resist going out again after supper, though Mme Payot had retired to bed. Payot, his greatcoat over his shoulders, followed to smoke his cigar, and they strolled up the lantern-lit street under the high wall of the château, glancing into its courtyard where waggons loaded with bales were sheltering for the night. At the top they passed under the great stone arch of the town gate through which the diligence would head at dawn.

'It's like a door into the unknown.' Her voice echoed under the vault. It was darker on the other side. The moon hadn't risen above the mountains, and the line where their solid mass gave way to the black void of sky was marked only by a scattering of stars.

'You are courageous to undertake such a journey alone,' he said. 'But Italy isn't France, you know. Don't be too trusting.'

'I am not without experience of the world.'

'And not all good experience, one guesses?' His voice was sympathetic.

'Good and bad — one learns from both.' She fought a desire to confide. It was chilly up here in the mountains; she gathered her shawl tighter.

'Are you cold?' He shrugged off his coat and wrapped it round her before she could protest. The scent of eau de cologne and tobacco enveloped her in its warmth.

'It's late — we should go in,' she said. His kindness threatened her equilibrium. In two days she'd be on her own again. She didn't want to think about it.

SUNDAY, VILLAGE OF SIMPLON *I must briefly describe our ascent to the pass before we set off again. We left at sunrise with extra horses. As the road climbed, the mixed forest of the lower slopes gave way to larch woods, above which sheer cliffs, their rugged surface broken only by the white line of a waterfall, rose to snow-covered peaks. Intimations of the titanic violence that produced these jagged forms fill the soul with terrified awe. In mine they confirmed the belief that creation is not benign. Yet it is a stupendous spectacle. I told my companions that I should like to travel on foot, to have time for contemplation instead of being rushed ever onwards.*

'You would need stouter shoes,' Payot observed. 'But ladies never consent to sacrifice elegance to practicality.'

'Would you have us do so?' His wife glanced complacently at her own delicately shod foot.

'No, my dear. But Mademoiselle, I wager, would don hobnailed boots to reach a waterfall.'

'Why not?' she said, feeling defiant. 'Mademoiselle Paradis did not ascend Mont Blanc in dancing shoes. But I am afraid you would laugh at me.'

'Never!' he assured her, smiling. 'Boots I accept, though I hope I do not live to see a woman in breeches. My grandchildren's prosperity depends on women's love of finery.'

'Good silk stockings will never go out of style,' Mme Payot said cheerfully.

The Simplon pass was not the narrow defile she'd pictured, but a high open valley surrounded by snow-covered peaks. As they reached the summit, a troop of soldiers on horseback clattered past, a reminder that the great natural barrier of the Alps had now been opened to trade and travel, but also to invading armies. In recognition of the fact, a massive barracks was under construction opposite the ancient travellers' hostel still kept by the monks. The diligence did not stop there but headed down to the tiny village of Simplon, a primitive place that hadn't yet grasped its new importance.

Two gentlemen travelling in their own carriage joined them at the inn, where the wonders of the road provided the main topic. The diligence driver praised its safety. He was still new to the route (the service had only been running a year) and as proud as if he'd designed it himself.

'But it was built with conscripted labour,' the Genevan pastor complained. 'And at great cost to life — three hundred men died in the construction of the Gondo gallery.'

'And that's not counting the maimed and disabled,' said a woman who'd joined the diligence in Brigue. 'They've built a hospital in Domodossola just to take care of them.' She was visiting her daughter there, who'd married one of the Italian engineers.

'They were pushed too hard,' the pastor said. 'Tunnelling six metres a week through solid rock!'

'The conquest of nature has its inevitable casualties, Monsieur,' said one of the carriage travellers, a stout prosperous-looking individual. 'It is, alas, the price we pay for progress.' He cut himself another wedge of cheese and called for more bread. While the servant hurried to the kitchen, he told them of his first trip to Italy. 'There was no road wide enough for a vehicle. So carriages had to be taken apart, the pieces loaded on mules and reassembled at the other end. Passengers rode mules, or hired porters to carry them. But now I travel in the comfort of my own carriage!' He took a slice of bread from the basket the servant proffered. 'This road will bring prosperity to the region.'

'To all of us, Monsieur,' Payot said. 'The new road facilitates the exchange of Italy's raw materials for France's manufactured goods. It will benefit both countries.'

'But is there not a danger,' the other carriage traveller asked, 'that when these natural barriers between nations are abolished, the individual character of each people is lost?'

'If that's so,' the stout gentleman said, 'it will only be regretted by artists like yourself who admire the primitive. I welcome change if it means that the civilised northern nations will have an improving influence on the backward south. I'm sick of picturesque squalor.'

The stout gentleman spoke for the majority who were on the side of progress. But for my part, it troubles me that these lonely heights, formerly traversed only by muleteers and shepherds, will now be invaded by a horde of travellers whose presence may well destroy the sublimity they seek. I marvelled at the road nonetheless — the tunnels through the mountainside, the galleries that protect it from avalanches, the refuges for snowbound travellers. The ingenuity that its construction demanded is as impressive as the mountains themselves. For the first time I grasped the immense power of this empire and its will to transform the world, though it irks me that the road will glorify the name of an upstart.

We are being called for departure — I must stop. The most dramatic part of the road still awaits us. Tonight we shall sleep in Italy!

Two

A Halt en Route to Rome

In this country where people think only of love, there is not a single novel because love advances so rapidly and publicly that it does not lend itself to any kind of development, and to give a true picture of people's behaviour you would have to start and finish on the same page.

— Madame de Staël, *Corinne, or Italy* (1807)

To whoever finds this notebook: you are requested, Sir, in the name of honour and on account of the boredom it would induce, not to read it, but to send it to Monsieur Fournex, hôtel de Hambourg, no 18, Paris.

— Stendhal, *Journal* (1811)

Milan, Sunday 8 September

He's been on the verge of tears from the moment he arrived yesterday and hurried (with Scotti in tow) to the *corso*. Too late; night was falling, everyone had left. *But there I was at last back at that Eastern Gate which, no wordplay intended, saw the dawn of my life.*

It was there on the Corso della Porta Orientale that his eyes had first opened to a world of pleasure beyond the limited imaginings of Grenoble, there he'd discovered the dolce vita of Italy and the beauty of its women, the most feminine in the world. But all his memories centre on one: Angela Pietragrua — he writes the name then scratches it out, leaving only the initial — whose love he couldn't aspire to because she was Louis's mistress, but who'd filled a million daydreams in which he returned as a colonel (or anything more elevated than Daru's most junior clerk) and took her in his arms.

'Why didn't you tell me?' she asked him today. As though . . . But he mustn't get ahead of himself. Begin from the beginning.

He'd feared the city wouldn't live up to his memories, or that he'd grown too cold to respond. But his feelings are still as powerful as if it were yesterday. He must have been poor company for Scotti, who'd dogged him all evening till the Genoa mail coach left.

Should he write what affected him most? Why not — after all, he's only writing for himself. It was the smell of manure peculiar to the city that, more than anything else, convinced him he wasn't dreaming. The city was no mirage, but a solid reality in which everything he saw brought tears to his eyes because it reminded him of his love. He was afraid he'd make a fool of himself when he saw her. If he possessed the magic ring that confers invisibility, he could enter her salon unseen and shed happy tears.

Not possessing that useful ring, he resorted to another means to diminish his sensibility. (Easy enough, though Italian inns don't have chambermaids. The valet who lit his lamp asked if he wanted a girl and five minutes later one tapped at his door.) He'd slept like a log afterwards and today in Mme P.'s salon he had the appearance at least of a rational man.

But before he records their meeting, he wants to portray himself as he was eleven years ago. Seventeen years old. No experience of the world, but a head filled with novels. Rousseau's *Héloïse*, of course, but also *Dangerous Liaisons*. Their protagonists had shaped his idea of what a man could be: Saint-Preux, tender, romantic, worshipping a woman he can never possess, and the rake Valmont, who takes every woman that comes his way.

Back then, he'd longed to pass for a rake, but in reality he was as innocent as Mozart's Cherubino — though utterly lacking Cherubino's grace, with his one jacket bursting at the seams and his unkempt hair. To think he spent those precious years from seventeen to twenty-two, the most ardent in a man's existence, without a woman! If some kind-hearted soul had taken pity on him, he'd be confident with women now. But perhaps those years of silent longing had given him his poetic sensibility, which might never have developed if he'd been bolder instead of waiting for a stroke of fate (like a carriage accident in a novel) to throw him into the arms of a beautiful woman.

It's ten years since he said goodbye to her, showing off his brand new uniform and the helmet with the horsetail plume that her little boy had played with. He'd told her, in hopes she'd take pity on him, that he'd soon be a corpse on the battlefield. Charming way to court a woman!

He paces the room, caught up in the emotions of the past, until he's calm enough to continue recording the present.

At one o'clock today, his heart in his mouth, he knocked on her door. He had to wait before she could receive him, which gave him time to rehearse his compliments. And then she was there. A moment's shock — he recalled a slender girl with flowing hair, not this regal woman coiffed and gowned in the latest fashion. Her father was with her, looking prosperous. Eleven years of French troops in the city must have doubled his business.

'Monsieur de Beyle?' She addressed him in French, his card in her hand. So she didn't remember him.

'It's ten years since we last met, Madame. Louis Joinville introduced us.'

'Why yes, of course, I remember you!' She turned to her father: '*È il chinese.*' His old nickname. She hadn't forgotten!

'Ten years . . .' she said with a melancholy inflection. 'And what brings you back?'

'I've long dreamt of returning. I've seen Berlin and Vienna since, but there's no city like Milan.'

'What makes you say that?' She sat down on the sofa, one arm gracefully extended along the back (a posture that showed to full advantage the curve of a magnificent bosom).

'The enjoyment of life is raised to an art here. You're two centuries in advance of Paris. And no other city has such beautiful women, of whom you, Madame —'

'No compliments, please, I beg you!'

'I've never forgotten you,' he said, rescuing what he could of his prepared tribute 'But I hope you have no recollection of the young fool I was then.'

'I remember a lively boy.'

So his dumb adoration hadn't made him ridiculous. He could joke about it now.

'Why didn't you tell me?' she asked.

He transcribes as much of the conversation as he can recall. They were both a little awkward. Naturally; after a ten-year gap, it's as though they're new acquaintances. The arrival of other callers gave him time to observe her. She's still superb. Ten years ago she had the lithe, sensuous grace of youth, but her beauty is majestic now, there's wit and intelligence in her face. Still that pensive downward gaze, like a Leonardo angel, the same enigmatic smile. He watched her with the man who may be her current lover — graceful manners, military bearing, pleasant face. Count Lodovico Rezzonico Widmann — colonel in the viceroy's guard of honour, income of fifty thousand francs, her father told him.

When he took his leave, she invited him to her box at La Scala. 'There's so much I want to tell you,' she said. 'I've done a lot of foolish things since we last met.' All this in front of the others, with no concern for appearances. The possibility of a brief affair with her begins to seem real.

He puts away his writing things and selects a ruffled shirt and silk waistcoat for the evening. Tying his cravat in front of the mirror, he tries to see himself as she saw him this afternoon. There's no denying he's ugly — he's been told so since he was a boy. Nature unkindly disguised his poetic sensibility in the physique of a butcher. Good tailoring (and Léger is the best in Paris) can slim his heavy torso, and sideburns diminish his round cheeks, but nothing can ennoble his cleft chin or his short fleshy nose. Only his eyes redeem him. If eyes are the mirror of the soul, perhaps a sensitive woman can see what lies behind his unpromising exterior.

PAST MIDNIGHT He must briefly record the evening. A full house at La Scala for *The Disappointed Suitors*, the new opera that's just opened. He met Lechi, who took him up to Mme Lamberti's box. Another Milanese beauty, with the distinguished manners of a woman who's moved in the highest circles. (He suspects she's Lechi's mistress.) But to his disappointment Mme P. wasn't in her box. She must have meant tomorrow.

Domodossola, Sunday 8 September

Only a day's journey separates this little town from Brigue, but the evening 'passeggiata' and the strolling musicians under the arcades of the 'piazza' testify that we have entered another world. The local women in their red skirts and kerchiefs are as different from their counterparts on the other side of the Alps as the style of their houses. On our arrival, barefoot urchins ran alongside the diligence offering fruit for sale, and two little singers entertained us most charmingly before supper. But just as one is on the point of succumbing to the charm of Italy some irritation or inconvenience breaks the spell, for it is, alas, a very primitive country. The general backwardness is immediately apparent in the dilapidation of the buildings. Though the walls are often decorated with frescos, the windows are unglazed, covered only with oiled paper. It must be cold in winter. Dung heaps offend both eye and nose. The shock is all the greater when one descends from the pure alpine air and the grandeur of the peaks.

Moreover, I find that the Italian phrases I have practised these past months are of little use here where Piedmontese is spoken. Tomorrow it will be Milanese! How can one communicate with a people whose language changes every few leagues?

This is the last evening I shall spend with my amiable companions. Three days of shared experience have given us the ease of old acquaintance and I shall miss their company. Mme Payot urged me to stay in Baveno a few days and visit the islands on Lake Maggiore. But I resisted temptation. Their kindness touched me, but it would only make it harder to face the road on my own again.

Needing distraction from feelings that threaten to overcome her, she opens the shutters and steps out on the balcony. Her first night on Italian soil. As if on cue, a man in the shadows below begins to pluck an instrument. A singer joins him, addressing his song to her. Embarrassed at provoking their attention, she draws back quickly inside the room, but the melody continues. When it ends, she hears the clink of coins tossed from another balcony and the musicians begin another song. The words are probably trite, but the sentimental melody pursues her through her preparations for bed. She isn't sleepy yet, her body restless with unused energy, and even in the chaste confinement of the sleeping sack a familiar urge overcomes her. The pleasure it brings is intense but guilty, though it's not the act itself (hardly more significant than relieving an itch) that shames her but the imaginings that accompany it. She should not have allowed herself to entertain such thoughts, but now that they're released they fill her with a longing no less blameworthy for being mere fantasy. A hazard of travel she had not foreseen.

Milan, Auberge Royale, Contrada delle Tre Alberghe, Monday 9 September

Midnight. He's just returned from the opera, but he must briefly record the day's events. He moved to a better inn, engaged a valet, and purchased an elegant cane that gives him something to do with his hands instead of holding them behind his back à la Papa. He's already practised a dozen moves that make him look like a man of the world, successful with women.

This afternoon from two to five at Mme Pietragrua's. (He hasn't yet called on Mme Lamberti, not wanting to seem too eager.) Dinner at Veillard's, the French restaurant near La Scala (where there's no risk of macaroni on the bill of fare). A pretty girl there who may be a working girl — he'll try to find out tomorrow. The *corso* next, then the Lentasio theatre. Filthy place, but they were doing one of the operas that initiated him to music ten years ago. A sorbet afterwards in a café by the Duomo.

He'd hired a carriage to impress Mme P., though it's not a necessity here as in Paris. Parisians think their city so advanced, but it's primitive compared to Milan. Drains should be under the street as they are here. Of course that's probably due to the Austrians, like the double line of flat paving stones in the cobbles that gives smooth passage to carriage wheels. Italians aren't concerned with practicalities. But their country is the fatherland of the arts. You find proof of their artistic nature wherever you go. Like today in San Fedele — he was admiring the magnificent interior and suddenly the notes of a sonata rang out from the organ followed by a gay and brilliant rondeau, played by a young man in the company of two women. Where else but Italy could that happen?

What a delightful year he could spend here, as secretary to an ambassador, or in some other position that didn't entail much work. How could one not be happy surrounded by such happy people, with all the pleasures of women and the arts, and a circle of men like Lechi.

He's felt such a sense of homecoming all day that it makes him wonder if he isn't partly Italian on his mother's side. The Gagnons may well have Italian blood in their ancestry, as great-aunt Elisabeth used to claim, if only that of some ruffian Gagnoni forced to take refuge in France. It would explain his instant response to Milan eleven years ago. He's so happy to be back that he couldn't resist informing his sister Pauline, though he warned her to burn his letter and not reveal his whereabouts to anyone, even Grandpapa, but write to him in Rome where he'll be twelve days from now.

Madame Pietragrua was more reserved today, but she made him sit in the place of honour beside her on the sofa and told him, as she'd promised, how her affair with Joinville ended. A long tale of jealousies, misunderstandings, reconciliations. But in the end Joinville had left for Paris in a fury. Scorning gossip, she'd followed him to justify her conduct before breaking with him definitively. So Italian! No Frenchwoman would expose herself like that.

It's significant that she's already advanced him to such intimacy. And if a man like Joinville (good-natured and intelligent, but with the manners of a peasant and no compensating wit) could inspire such passion, there's surely hope for himself.

Antonio came in at the end of the afternoon — the little boy who'd played with his helmet all those years ago, now a handsome youth of fifteen. Back then, he'd envied the child his unquestioned right to the attention of an adorable and adoring mother, and now, observing Antonio's natural grace and self-assurance, he saw with a pang all that his own mother's death had deprived him of. What a different character he'd have now if he'd grown up with his mother's love instead of Aunt Séraphie's scolding.

Antonio greeted him politely enough but with the distracted air of an adolescent for whom nothing holds any interest outside his own existence. It was an awkward moment and he was glad when the boy left.

'I can't pretend to be young any more with a son on the verge of manhood,' she sighed, and gallantly he offered reassurance. She seemed, surprisingly, to need it. A pardonable vanity in a woman, as was the way she'd talked about Count Méjean, the viceroy's chief adviser, who'd been courting her. She was clearly flattered by Méjean's attentions, while feigning indifference. Was she trying to make him jealous? Or did it simply prove that she'd admitted him into her confidence? Either way, he felt encouraged.

Summing up the afternoon, he writes, *It seems possible that I might possess Mme P. To have her here, Mme B. in Ancona, Naples and Rome on top of that, what more could I desire! As I have no time to waste, I'll try to ascertain tomorrow if, without further commitment on either side, she would like to enjoy a few happy moments with me.*

Milan, Monday 9 September, evening

This morning when we halted in Baveno on the shore of Lake Maggiore, I said farewell to my companions.

Tears spring to her eyes. Once again, she's alone, and it feels all the harder in these hot, crowded, stinking streets after the beauty of the countryside. Last night, with Payot smoothing any difficulties at the inn, everything seemed easy, but today, when the diligence deposited her at the Customs building, she was on her own. She'd chosen the most honest-looking driver from the several clamouring for her attention and asked to be taken to a good inn, only to realise belatedly that she'd paid him twice what he asked. The thought that she must face the same ordeal in every town on her way to Rome overwhelms her. But she must not give way to fear.

After two weeks on the road, it would perhaps be wise to halt for a while and rest. The journey south will be less daunting once I have accustomed myself to Italian ways. There are no chambermaids here — a manservant brought my hot water this morning, which made me uncomfortable. In any case this inn, though tolerably clean and comfortable, is too expensive for a prolonged stay. I must look for cheaper lodgings. Tomorrow I shall make use of one of the letters of introduction with which Armand has furnished me.

She had shocked him, and Marie-Cécile even more, when she'd announced her plans. To travel so far and alone! It was almost unseemly and certainly dangerous. But once Armand had seen that she wasn't to be deterred, he'd given her letters to French officials in every major town on her route. The mere sight of them reassures her now. In readiness for the morning, she's taken out the one addressed to a Monsieur Larocque in the offices of the supply corps.

Despite the necessity that I felt of continuing on my way this morning, it was with frustrated longing that I admired the serene beauty of Lake Maggiore as the diligence followed its shore. How I should have loved to embark on its tranquil waters for the islands! Partings are melancholy, but friendships of the road must necessarily be of brief duration. It is better thus, for the vicissitudes of the journey introduce one to individuals — she pauses on the brink of utterance but propriety dictates the conclusion *— with whom one would not normally associate.*

How many inadmissible thoughts have been thus rerouted. A trace remains, of course. The most innocuous statement can stir a memory on rereading, and certain phrases are ciphers that she alone can decode. Still, she's far from Nogent now, among indifferent strangers; there's no reason why she shouldn't confide anything she wishes to these pages.

She dips her pen, charged with the impulse of the words she hasn't written, but the ink dries as she hesitates. Propriety subjects her to a control as strict as the rules of syntax. And syntax itself is a constraint. Her sentences must be well constructed, their elements harmoniously combined, an imperative all the more powerful because learnt so young. Beyond the neatness of hand inculcated by Mademoiselle Robert, she had been exposed to the magisterial paragraphs of writers she studied with her father, which still govern the shape of every sentence taking form in her head. But the well-formed phrase leaves no room for the rush of competing thoughts and conflicting emotions, just as decorum prohibits the relief of an outburst, a confession.

Perhaps she'll find greater freedom in Italian. But first she must master it. The last few hours have shown the limits of the knowledge she's acquired from her grammar book. It's not enough to formulate a request correctly if you cannot understand the reply. If she settles in Milan for a month she must look for a tutor. Everything will be easier once she acquires greater competence in the language.

Before closing her notebook, she pencils in the margin, *Monsieur Payot asked this morning if I had enjoyed my serenade. I had the impression, perhaps false, that it was he who had paid the musicians.*

A Halt en Route to Rome

Milan, Tuesday 10 September

First thing in the morning he spoke to an honest-looking *vetturino* who'd take him to Rome in a vehicle guaranteed to be clean (which probably means passable) in nine and a half days for six and a half louis. Another man gave the same price. It's cheap enough, but nine days will eat up his leave. Hiring his own vehicle, with fresh horses at every halt, would halve the time, but it's beyond his means, unless he finds companions to share the cost. With that thought in mind, he'd called on the French consul (a personage of an obesity that must seriously impede thought) who put him on the track of a government official headed for Rome. With luck the man won't be leaving yet; he'd like to delay his own departure another week or two.

But now it's time to change for his call on Mme P. Splashing himself with eau de cologne, he pulls on a clean shirt, humming the third suitor's aria which has been running through his head since he heard it at the opera the other night. 'I am but eight and twenty and I've just arrived from Cosmopoli.' If he finds her alone, he'll make his move.

Midnight He flings his new cane on the floor in a fury. He's made a fool of himself. He's provoked the contempt of Mme Pietragrua, who made it clear that she isn't interested in his love, and he's probably offended Widmann. His poetic memories of Milan will be ruined forever.

At five o'clock he was in a state of perfect happiness and now he feels savage enough to rip something to shreds. His notebook offers an outlet but he can't bear to put his foolishness into words. It's no use going to bed — he'll simply lie there brooding. He picks up a book and plunges into it until his eyelids droop.

Milan, Contrada Passerella, Tuesday 10 September

Thanks to Armand's acquaintance, I have moved into clean and comfortable lodgings and begun to explore the city. I could not have accomplished so much in one day without the assistance of this Monsieur Larocque, whose consideration had no bounds. If all the officials to whom I have letters of introduction are as helpful, I need no longer fear arriving in an unknown city.

Anxious to be settled, she'd decided to present her letter in person and set off on foot to avoid the expense of a carriage. A foolish economy, she soon realised, struggling to follow directions. She'd almost despaired by the time she found the place and handed Armand's letter to a clerk. A moment later, she was ushered into an office where a man of middling age greeted her with a look of astonishment. He'd clearly just pulled on his shabby uniform coat at the announcement of a visitor. No doubt a solitary woman traveller was a rarity. He seemed flustered by her arrival and she apologised for disturbing him.

'Not at all, Mademoiselle, I assure you. But I regret that you have had the trouble of coming here. Had I known that you were in Milan, I would have called at your inn. Colonel de Vernet tells me that you are on your way to Rome. I trust you left him in good health?'

Responding to his enquiries, she tried to recall what Armand had said about him. They'd served in the same regiment, she thought, and his bronzed, weather-beaten features suggested a man more at home in the saddle than behind a desk.

'So you are making a halt in Milan?' he said. 'If I can offer any assistance during your stay, please believe me entirely at your service.'

With a flush of embarrassment, she asked his advice about inexpensive lodgings.

'I cannot recommend any of the cheaper inns,' he said. 'Even the best would expose you to disagreeable encounters. You would be more comfortable in a *pensione*.' A colleague and his wife had boarded with a respectable widow when they first arrived and found the place satisfactory. If she wished, he could send someone to see if the accommodation was available. Would she like to wait? And a glass of lemonade perhaps after her long walk?

She accepted gratefully. On the messenger's return with confirmation of a vacancy, Larocque called a carriage and took her to view it. The widow occupied an apartment above a watchmaker's shop on a quiet side street close to the centre. For a surprisingly modest sum she could have full board and a spacious room with a balcony. One could live in Italy for half the cost of France, she saw with relief. From there her kind helper had taken her to a bank to present her letter of credit, and back to the inn to collect her baggage before depositing her at her new lodgings. He seemed embarrassed by her thanks, saying that it was the least he could do, it was an honour to assist any member of her family. He must owe his advancement to Armand, she supposed, and this was a way to repay it.

While she was unpacking, the shy little maid, Perpetua, brought up a small parcel with his compliments. It contained a guide to the city in French. Decidedly, the man was very thoughtful. After lunch, which she ate in solitary state, she unfolded the map inside the cover (on which Larocque had marked her street). It showed a city tightly contained within a double circle of canals and ramparts. A few broad thoroughfares radiated from the centre to the half-dozen city gates on the perimeter. One could easily lose one's way in the web of smaller streets between, but if she kept to the nearest thoroughfare, the Corsia dei Servi, she could follow it across the inner canal then take the Corso della Porta Orientale as far as the public gardens by the ramparts.

She waited till mid-afternoon when the heat had lessened, then took her parasol and set out, joining the crowd of strollers. The Milanese seemed to live on the street; from cafés and balconies, people with time on their hands greeted acquaintance and surveyed the passers-by. As a woman alone, she must run the gauntlet of male appraisal. She felt like retreating, but quickened her pace and continued. Only the most fashionable women had adopted the French bonnet, she saw; the rest wore a graceful veil, attached to the crown of the head, thrown back or lowered over the face. On her way home, she stopped at a milliner's to purchase one. It would make her less conspicuously foreign.

After dinner she exchanged a few words on practical matters with the landlady, Signora Colombo, who was both obliging and accustomed to dealing with foreigners. Her laundry could be sent out to a trustworthy laundress and if she wished to take a bath the maid would accompany her to the Alamanni bathhouse, a respectable establishment.

Settled now in her cool high-ceilinged room, with her books arranged, she sets out her writing things on the table in front of the open window.

My impression of the city has improved. The elegant town houses along the Corso Orientale and the proximity of the vice-regal residence suggest that it is a quarter where one may safely walk unaccompanied, as also in the public gardens which are frequented by the respectable. The shade of its tree-lined paths was most welcome in the heat, but agreeable a promenade though it is, I could not help regretting that in my haste to reach Italy I did not stay longer in the Alps. I feel relieved, though, to be fixed in one place for a month. Tomorrow I shall look for a tutor.

Milan, Wednesday 11 September

Summary of September 10: Yesterday at five I was so satisfied that I feared a storm might descend on me from Paris. My mind was troubled by a vague fear that a pleasure so absorbing might have made me neglect some duty.

But he'd left everything in order at the office, he's worrying needlessly. His pleasure was short-lived in any case. He's been in a rage with himself and everyone else all day.

To punish himself for his gauche behaviour last night, he isn't calling on Mme P. today. A wise move, anyway, given her complaints about tedious admirers. Let her feel uncertain about his feelings! The empty hours will give him time to catch up with his diary and analyse yesterday's mistakes.

The afternoon had begun well. He'd arrived early, hoping for an hour alone with her. But Widmann turned up a few minutes later with a permit for the Brera gallery and politely invited him to join them. Returning the courtesy, he put his carriage at their disposal.

While Mme P. was getting ready, a Signor Migliorini arrived — aide-de-camp on the viceroy's staff, cheerful, good-natured but completely witless. The only thing to be gained from such fools is their goodwill and it was amusing to win this fellow's. By the end of the afternoon they were on such friendly terms that Migliorini confided a secret recipe for a long-lasting erection. You take a tarantula, burn it to a cinder, mix with olive oil into a paste, rub it into the big toe of your right foot and you're hard for as long as you want. When you've had enough, you simply wash it off with warm water. Migliorini claimed to know at least thirty women to whom he could demonstrate the potion's effect, if prudence were not the best policy.

Earlier, Migliorini had shown them the portrait of his mistress, and his affair was joked about in a free and natural manner that would make hair stand on end in Paris. The fellow confided that he gets a couple of fucks a day, while his general (Lechi's younger brother) manages up to five or six.

But he's written too much. Widmann is the important one. A lively character, fond of music, not given to serious reflection. In their youth these types are wholly occupied with love affairs. Afterwards, they're left with the very small number of thoughts that have occurred to them in the intervals between pleasures. Hence the lack of ideas in a man who's clearly not unintelligent. Birth and money have given him the manners of high society insofar as Italian naturalness permits.

A concise but telling character sketch, he thinks. Material like this will fill out his 'Tour of Italy' very nicely. This is exactly the kind of analysis of Italian character and attitudes that he'd promised Crozet.

Widmann's manners would have intimidated him ten years ago, he writes, but now he's acquired some knowledge of the world, he can respond in kind. Let his friends sneer if they want: success justifies it.

When Mme P. was ready, she invited him to give her his arm. But he deferred to Widmann, who insisted on deferring to him. Finally, as the newcomer, he'd accepted the honour of offering his arm to this divine woman.

For divinity she truly appeared — her hair in a Grecian knot beneath a gauzy veil, her muslin dress embracing every curve of her magnificent body, she seemed a statue of Venus come to life accompanied by three worshippers. It reminded him of Mme de Staël's observation that in Italy every fashionable married woman has three *cavalieri* to escort her: the favourite, the one who aspires to be favourite, and the one who stands no chance. Mme P.'s behaviour at the gallery made him feel he'd moved to first place, but after last night he's no longer sure.

She'd certainly been encouraging. Her hand, when he helped her out of the carriage, rested in his several seconds longer than necessary, and he'd judged the pressure of her arm against his sufficient to respond in kind as they entered the Brera.

The picture gallery occupied a new wing, created by the annexation of an adjoining church. 'To the indignation of the devout,' she told him.

'What's the loss of one church in a city which has so many?' he replied. 'Museums are the new places of pilgrimage.'

A couple of other visitors had turned to stare at him. He was feeling heady, sure of himself. 'As capital of the Kingdom of Italy, Milan must have a museum to equal those of Florence and Rome. The emperor wishes to give all Italians the means to become acquainted with the great artistic works of their past.'

'Those that His Majesty hasn't carried off to his museum in Paris,' she retorted.

'It appears that he's left you more than enough,' he said, examining the crowded walls around them as the cicerone led them into the first room.

'And a plaster cast of himself so we don't forget our benefactor.' She pointed down the vista of archways between the rooms to a nude colossus at the far end: 'The face is a good likeness, they say. No doubt there are ladies in Milan who can vouch for the resemblance of the rest,' she added, *sotto voce*.

'I'm surprised it's on display here,' he said. 'The original is hidden behind a screen at the Louvre. His Majesty informed Monsieur Canova that while the Romans portrayed their emperors in a state of godlike nudity it didn't befit a modern statesman. And you know what Canova replied? Even God couldn't produce a masterpiece if He had to portray His Majesty in breeches and boots.'

The cicerone was getting impatient. To mollify the man, he remarked that the collection was impressive even for someone familiar with the Louvre.

'Is that where you exercise your functions?' she asked. So she'd remembered the title on his visiting card. But he didn't want her to think him a flunkey inspecting the silver.

'I supervise the inventory of the emperor's museum, which gives me access to the collections.' She looked impressed, Widmann too. Only now he'd have to sound knowledgeable about painting and there wasn't a single name he recognised in the cicerone's lecture.

They paused in front of a canvas in which a white-bearded man raised his hands in a gesture of dismissal to a woman clutching a small boy. The child was rubbing tears from his eyes with his fist. The mother too was red-eyed. '*Abraham Repudiates Hagar and Ishmael*,' said the cicerone. 'By Guercino.'

She examined it, clearly moved. 'Only a man who understood the feminine heart could have captured that expression. It's Hagar's feelings he makes us see.'

'But you have to admit that Abraham is disadvantaged as far as feelings go — who knows what's going on behind that beard?'

He'd made her laugh more than once with his repartee and by the time they parted for dinner, he was in a state of perfect happiness, sharing his excellent bottle of burgundy with his table companion at Veillard's.

And then it all collapsed. At six o'clock he realised he was falling in love and self-doubt flooded back. Even the opera couldn't hold his attention now that he could think only of how to make a graceful appearance in her box. When he finally went up, having waited till the entr'acte so as not to appear too eager, she was surrounded by men, all unknown to him apart from Widmann, who left abruptly. 'I don't know what's wrong with Widmann tonight,' she said. 'He seems upset.'

One by one her visitors took their leave, but paralysed by shyness once he was alone with her, he could think of nothing to say except to ask who they were. The familiarity of their behaviour had shocked him and he made the mistake of showing it. She said she'd be considered a prude if she took offence, but she seemed troubled that it had given him a bad impression.

Widmann returned, followed by Migliorini (who hadn't changed out of the riding coat he'd worn all day, the kind of negligence you couldn't get away with in Paris). Widmann seemed put out to find him still there. Jealous perhaps, and too natural to conceal it as a Frenchman would have done. He should have left with Migliorini after the three suitors' trio, but he stayed till halfway through the second act. When he reached the pit, he glanced back up at her box and saw her in intense conversation with Widmann. A call in Mme Lamberti's box couldn't distract him. For the rest of the night he was in the blackest rage with himself and the world. But as usual his hypersensitive pride has made him exaggerate his errors and imagine slights where none were meant. Mme P. had in fact shown him many small signs of favour. Her eyes had held his several times, and when his hand touched hers in passing a snuff box, she returned the pressure unmistakably. Really, he had every reason to be satisfied.

I ask that it be borne in mind that all this is a rapid two-month passage through Italy by a man who is a little crazy, as shown above, he writes for his future self.

A year's experience would refine my judgements. All I can do now is note the resonance of each thing as it strikes my soul.

But what, finally, is he to make of her? That's the important question.

Character of Mme P. An imposingly beautiful woman, Mme P. has the seriousness of one who reflects. But her eyes no longer have the romantic look I recall.

She seemed disillusioned, hardened even. 'Love affairs here are like marriage,' she said. 'Pleasurable for the first four months, then a matter of yawning together for a year or two out of deference to public opinion. Monotony kills pleasure.'

'That's true when pleasure is the only goal of life,' he'd argued. Ruled for centuries by outsiders, the Milanese had become soft, but the new Kingdom of Italy would give them higher aims. 'They're participating in its government, they're defending it in the Italian legions, they'll become what they were in the days of the Sforza.'

She was unconvinced. 'They have a certain cunning when it comes to pursuing their interests, but nothing more. And they lack the essential talent that enlivens society — they have no wit.'

'You're a little unfair,' he said (though it gave him hope for himself: wit was where he could outshine them). 'Monsieur Lechi, with whom I travelled from Paris, is a master of the witty phrase.'

'Ah, so you know Lechi?' She seemed impressed. 'There are exceptions, I grant, but for the most part if a Milanese happens to say something clever it lacks the light touch and that spoils it.'

She'd analysed Milanese society with great discernment, beating him at his own game. It's clear she finds the French superior in every way. Isn't there some hope then that a completely unexpected affair with him might tempt her? It would at least break the boredom of which she complains.

He's written twenty pages! It's much easier to write in the afternoon than at the end of the day when he's exhausted. His black mood has evaporated and he's made some progress in self-understanding. Tomorrow he'll plan the next move in his campaign.

Milan, Wednesday 11 September

This morning I sought Signora Colombo's advice on finding a tutor. Unable to advise me herself, she fetched an amiable neighbour who addressed me in fluent French. Though Milanese, Mme Garreau is the widow of a French officer and lives with her son in her parents' home. We spoke Italian for a while and she made a proposal that I accepted. What I need, she pointed out, is the opportunity to accustom my ear to Italian and to practise what I know. An hour's conversation every morning would be more useful than formal lessons. She refuses payment, saying it will be a pleasure to converse with me. It makes me a little uneasy as I fear being trapped in an arrangement that could prove burdensome, but it is only for a month and she is truly charming.

Unlike herself, always guarded in what she revealed, Mme Garreau had immediately poured out her life history. It was the effect of speaking French again, she said. 'I have scarcely spoken it since my poor husband's death, five years ago.'

'But you are so young! You cannot have been married long?' The pretty heart-shaped face beneath the widow's black veil seemed too smooth to have known any sorrow, apart from the vertical line between the eyebrows.

'We had only two years together. I married at twenty. My husband was billeted next door to us when the French arrived. We welcomed them with open arms — everyone was so happy the Austrians had gone.'

'But did your parents not object to their daughter marrying a foreigner?' An indiscreet question, but the young woman's frankness permitted it.

'My mother refused her consent. It forced us to wait a year. But then Pierre's regiment was sent north. We married so that I could accompany him.'

'That must have been difficult for a young bride, so far from home.'

'Ah Mademoiselle, when you're in love, you'll do anything to be together. We always had decent lodgings. And the towns where we were quartered were pleasant. We led a gay life even after my son was born. Poor little mite, he was still a babe when he lost his father. My husband died at Jena.'

She remembered the name and Armand's elation as he read the despatches. 'Two victories in a single day! The Prussians wiped out!' She'd pretended to more interest than she felt; a returned exile couldn't afford to seem unpatriotic, and no doubt it was good that the Prussians no longer threatened peace. But now she was hearing another side of the story — the farewells, the days of anxious waiting, then the messenger bearing a letter.

'I refused to believe it.' Mme Garreau's wide brown eyes welled up at the recollection. 'I was sure they'd made an error. It was weeks before I resigned myself to make the journey home.'

'It must have been a comfort to return to your family.'

'At first, yes. But it's like being a child again. I can't do anything without my mother's permission. In fact, I should go now or she'll complain! But tomorrow morning, if you'd like, I'll come after breakfast.'

It was good to have the prospect of Italian conversation every morning, though belatedly she wondered if it would be of the purest Italian. Still, Mme Garreau's command of French suggested she had enough education to speak more than Milanese.

But now the rest of the day stretched before her. She decided to visit the Duomo. As she set off (less self-conscious now, in her Milanese veil) towards the dazzling white pinnacles and spire that towered above the end of the street, a man came out of a café ahead who seemed familiar. He put his hand to his hat as though to salute her, but he was merely adjusting it against the sun. It was the annoying young man from the diligence. She was half tempted to raise her veil and acknowledge him. It might be interesting to exchange impressions. But before she could decide, he turned and walked away.

The coincidence of their being on this same street at the same moment gave her an odd sensation, as though it were fated to happen. But of course it was entirely fortuitous, like all the random encounters of the journey; other lives with which her own had briefly intersected had left in each a trace as minute as the plucked thread in a shawl snagged by a branch, itself marked by the tiny scar of a broken twig. Abruptly, the sensation of Payot's coat on her shoulders came back to her; she shook herself free of the temptation to linger there.

Approaching the Duomo from behind, through a stonemasons' work yard, she was surprised to hear the tap of hammers high above, though she knew from the guidebook that the building was still unfinished. The work underway was in the purest Gothic, as if she'd been transported four centuries back to the time of the original builders. Much of the marble was newly quarried and it shone like snow in the morning sun, unlike the weathered exterior of other churches, greyed by the passage of time like venerable old men. Indeed, this cathedral had an almost feminine aspect, its stone tracery as delicate as lace or the finest whitework embroidery. Each of the hundreds of slender pinnacles crowning the buttresses and roof was graced by a statue, as though a multitude of angels and saints had descended from on high. It was truly a celestial sight.

She circled it slowly, averting her eyes from a workman shamelessly relieving himself in the angle of a buttress, and entered. The dim interior was a relief from the glare of sunlight on marble outside; she wandered the shadowy aisles, admiring the rainbow colours cast on pillars and arches by the stained-glass windows. High above, in the shaft of sunlight from a clerestory window, a myriad dust motes hung like the numberless souls of the departed. On an impulse more tender than pious, she paused before a statue of the Virgin and lit candles in memory of her parents and Mme d'Aumont, without whose generosity she would not be here.

When she returned for the midday meal, she found a note from Larocque, hoping she was satisfied with her accommodation and asking if she would like a tour of the city one afternoon. She hesitated before accepting. But it was a courtesy on his part; it would be ungracious to refuse.

In the anonymity of a foreign town one may use one's own judgement in such matters. As Count Berchtold observes, 'The traveller's existence is free of all the bonds that numerous considerations and political and private views do not cease to impose when one vegetates in one's native land.'

Two days in this city and already I am making new acquaintance and venturing through the streets alone with more courage than I thought to possess. I feel that I have entered upon a new way of life.

MILAN, THURSDAY 12 SEPTEMBER

I've resolved to make my little declaration to Mme P. and find out if I'm to stay in Milan or leave. Nothing keeps me here any longer but her.

He weighs his chances of success like a general pondering battle. It's barely four days since he arrived: a declaration of love will seem premature. But four days suffice, he'll say, for a man who's dreamt of her for ten years. Besides, he's already used up two weeks of his leave. He can't lay siege indefinitely. It's time to attack.

Can he trust the many signs of interest, though, or is she using him to make Widmann jealous? What if she laughs, treats him as another tiresome suitor? That would be unbearable. But the greatest risk is that she'll put him to the test of a prolonged courtship. Does he want her enough to give up Rome? Yet how can he leave without trying? He'd regret it for the rest of his life.

He'll call on her at one and make his move. Meanwhile, catching up with his journal will settle his nerves.

An instructive morning, professionally: he visited the state rooms at the vice-regal palace, unimpressive for anyone who's seen the Tuileries: the mirrors small, the clocks inferior, too many old-fashioned tapestries. What it needs is some handsome furniture from Paris. The portraits of the emperor are grandiose, but Appiani has made him a visionary — the only way painters can imagine genius. They don't understand that the mark of genius is superior reasoning and cold judgement.

Later that night, he records his meeting with Mme P.

He'd set off in a state of tender excitement, checked with the concierge that she was in, climbed the stairs to her apartment with a beating heart, only to hear her maid (a pert little creature) announce with a knowing smile that Madame was not at home. Thwarted, he went to the Brera, to stare distractedly at the paintings, trying to achieve a state of cheerful indifference. At half past three, he made his way back to the Contrada dei Meravigli. The street of marvels. Apt name for the dwelling of this Circe, half goddess, half witch, who has so many men under her spell. Miraculously, he found her alone.

'We thought you'd left for Rome.' Her tone was cool.

'I didn't come yesterday because I'm in love with you. I wanted to avoid the pain of unrequited love.' Nervous, he was sticking to his rehearsed speech.

'You're joking,' she said. (Were those her words? He can't recall clearly now.)

'I'm entirely serious, I assure you.' He continued his advance resolutely, though his heart was beating like a drum. His voice sounded strange. It reminded him of his acting lessons: the harder you worked at finding the intonation that spelt true emotion, the more artificial it became. He sounded too rational for a man trying to convey deep emotion.

'I was piqued that you didn't come yesterday,' she said in a little burst of frankness that seemed genuine. 'When four o'clock passed and you weren't there I fell into a dark mood. I went out today to punish you.'

'But I was punishing myself by not calling! I knew I'd stayed too long in your box, but I longed to talk to you without all the others around.'

'I too. I feel I can talk freely with you. Come here!' She patted the place beside her, and he sat down, light-headed. 'You remind me of a time when I was still passionate, when I wasn't jaded. It gives me pleasure to talk about the past with you. You remember a thousand small things that mean nothing to most of my acquaintance.'

'It's a past that's precious to me too.' He took her hand in his. She didn't resist.

'I'm touched that you hadn't forgotten me. It's rare to find such constancy in a man.' There were actually tears in her eyes.

'You are a woman that a man cannot forget.' He lifted her hand to his lips. Meeting no resistance, he reached out and drew her to him, venturing a kiss that she evaded.

'Receive but never take!' She gave him a playful tap with her fan.

A good maxim for a character like mine in which the determination necessary to carry things out deadens feeling.

Letting her take the lead allowed his feelings to flow again and before long they were in each other's arms. If they'd been alone all afternoon he'd have reached the goal.

Everything happened so fast he still can't believe it. 'It's like a novel!' she said of his boyish passion, his return after so many years. Does she truly feel what she says? But he'll make her fall in love with him even if she isn't as yet. He managed a grand gesture, showing her the inscription on the glass of his watch that Angéline had had engraved for him, then breaking the glass in two.

He suppresses a guilty pang at the thought of his little Angel, helping him select the ornaments for the chain while the watchmaker engraved the words she'd chosen. He'll take back some Italian trinket for her and concoct a story about the broken glass.

The names are conveniently similar should he ever forget himself, but the variation captures the difference between them: 'Angéline' — light, quick, vivacious, like the roles she sings. 'Angelina', or 'Angiolina', as the Milanese say, with that little pouting *-gio* like a kiss — a fuller, richer, more voluptuous sound.

He stares at the fragments of glass. It wasn't so easy to abolish time. It was their enemy, both in the immediate moment, when other callers could arrive at any moment, and in the longer term with his leave slipping by.

'Go, go!' she kept saying. 'Tomorrow, I won't have the courage to send you away.'

'My journey through Italy will be empty if I've left my heart in Milan.'

'But you'll have the certainty of being loved.'

Voices in the hall. They leapt apart. She fanned herself vigorously: 'I hope no one sees we're blushing!'

A moment later a Signor Scagliotti entered, followed shortly after by Signor Turcotti, the *cavaliere servente*. It was the first time he'd met this important personage, who'd been conveniently absent till now. A strange institution, remarked on by every observer of Italy. A wife can't run around town unescorted, but a husband has better things to do with his time, so the *cavaliere servente* stands in for him. It's said that the *servente* is often a lover, tolerated by a husband whose own affections lie elsewhere. Thus family honour is preserved and the tedium of monogamy relieved. That was the cynical view. The reality might be different.

Avoiding her eyes, he discussed philosophy with Scagliotti (an earnest pedant), and the arts with the *servente*, a man in his forties, clearly intelligent, his face marked by a combination of shrewdness and world-weariness. When other visitors arrived and Turcotti's back was turned, he managed to ask in a whisper if Turcotti was her lover. She shook her head emphatically. No threat as a rival then, but as the guardian of marital honour a man to be reckoned with. Yet he obviously hadn't impeded her long affair with Joinville. But perhaps he was new on the scene, brought in by her husband to prevent further indiscretions. She certainly behaved with greater circumspection in Turcotti's presence.

This evening at the opera, she was surrounded again; impossible to say or do anything beyond the briefest touch of their arms. He was a little bored, though he's beginning to follow conversations in Milanese, even the ribald humour. Anther visitor — Count d'Azas, a Piedmontese — laughed with the others but remarked that in Turin people were starting to tire of indelicate talk.

He has to admit that he's not feeling the happiness he anticipated. It would have been different if he'd found her at home when he first called, in the full flood of his emotions. The delay had banished his tender mood. Perhaps just as well, he thought, recalling the 'battle' of May 31 when he'd declared his love for Mme Palfy, and emotion had made him tongue-tied. This time he'd been eloquent, though he'd had to exercise too great a control over himself to feel much.

Nonetheless, it's a victory to be proud of. A mere four days in Milan and he's in reach of his goal.

Milan, Thursday 12 September

Today I had my first lesson with Mme Garreau. She brought her son, Pierino, a charming little fellow with his mother's brown eyes and long lashes, who teased Signora Colombo's cat while we conversed. Mme Garreau does not try to explain my errors but simply gives my clumsy phrases a correct or more natural form. I seek the explanation in my grammar book and dictionary later.

They began where everything begins — la famiglia. *Mme Garreau has two sisters and two brothers, a dozen nieces and nephews. Her father is a leather manufacturer with workshops in town and tanneries on the outer canal. Her elder brother runs the tanneries, the younger assists her father.*

'And you, Signorina?'

'I'm the only one.' She struggled with a verb, repeated the correct form after her instructress. '*Avrei avuto*' — I would have had — '*una sorella.*' A gentle, lilting word, as soft as the face on the miniature her mother carried. 'The eldest. She died at six. And three brothers. All dead in infancy.' She managed the last verb unaided: 'We would have been a family of five like you.'

Past conditional. The grammatical mode of my life, she thought later, practising it: I should have been, might have had. If there had been no economic crisis, if the king had not faltered, if the moderates had not fatally misjudged — all her father's hypotheticals, obsessively pondered.

'Your poor mother! To lose four children! You must have been very precious to your parents.'

Precious. And overprotected. Alone in schoolroom and garden, only adults for company. Carriage rides with her mother. A daily visit to her father's library for instruction in Latin and history. And then, overnight, out of that hothouse into the poverty of exile, where, despite the coarse food, the damp, the coal smoke, she'd flourished, more resilient than her parents. Learnt to help Jeannette with the daily chores, to mend their increasingly shabby clothes, to contribute to their survival by selling her embroidery.

It wasn't easy to be an only child was all she said. 'My parents worried too much about my health. And after my mother's death my father became very dependent on me.'

'Is he still alive?'

'No, he died four years ago.'

'You're an orphan, poor thing! What brings you to Italy?'

'I have always wanted to see Rome.'

'You're going to Rome?' She might as well have said China by the look on her companion's face. 'But it's too dangerous for a woman to travel alone! There are bandits on the roads, men who have no respect for women.'

It was a disheartening reaction. To restore her courage she threw on her veil after mother and child went home, and set off for a walk.

Having carefully planned my route on the map, I made my way to the inner canal and followed it round as far as the Corso Romana. I had intended to turn back there, but a spirit of adventure possessed me and I continued along a street of handsome residences towards the Porta Romana through which the road to Rome departs. Standing in its shade, I watched carts and carriages head south. In a few weeks I shall be among them!

It was time to return for the midday meal, but I had glimpsed a part of the city's history — an early Christian basilica, the Spanish ramparts of the sixteenth century, the Great Hospital, and the column commemorating the end of the plague. And I had set eyes on the road to Rome! To do all this and to do it alone restored my confidence. No one accosted me except an old beggar to whom I gave alms.

Carefully retracing my steps, I was reminded of my first exploration of London with Jeannette. After the tranquillity of Vernet, the excitement of London's swarming streets tempted us daily beyond the bounds that my father had set. That I am here now, exploring an Italian city alone, is perhaps due as much to Jeannette's adventurous nature as to Mrs Godwin's book.

I spent the afternoon on Italian. Reflecting on my exercise in the hypothetical mode, I find that I must also put it in the interrogative. If my life had not been set on a different path by the Revolution, would I have found happiness with the husband chosen for me? Would I have loved and been beloved? Would I have survived childbed? Would the children I bore have lived? When I consider the lottery of women's lives, I see no certainty that mine would have been happy had the Revolution not occurred. But the question scarcely matters, for sitting here at my window in the mellow evening light, with the sound of Italian voices rising from the street below, I feel for the first time in years content to be where I am.

Milan, Friday 13 September

Love, he heads the page in English, and notes an odd coincidence. He'd worn the same pair of trousers in the 'battle' of May 31 at Palfy as in the 'battle' of Milan yesterday.

But while Mme Palfy's response had been full of feeling (even though she'd dashed his hopes), Mme Pietragrua's struck him as disappointingly reasonable. Still, he writes, Italians being more passionate by nature clearly need to exercise more reason in anything that concerns their happiness, which makes them appear colder, more level-headed. And Angela has certainly committed her share of follies, so she's learnt to conduct herself with the utmost circumspection. Unfortunately for him.

Even in the midst of tender kisses, reason had prevailed.

'You must leave. If you stay any longer you'll make me commit a folly!'

'How can I leave when I've only just found you again?'

'How can I give myself to a man who'll go back to Paris and forget me?'

'I'd give up Paris for the joy of seeing you every day! I'd resign my post if I could find a position here.'

'If you were here, I'd close my door to all my friends and tell them they could see me at the theatre if they wanted!'

'My love!' He raised her hands to his lips and kissed them tenderly.

'But we must be reasonable,' she persisted.

'I can't be reasonable when I'm with you!' But perhaps if she were assured of his departure she might surrender. 'You're right,' he said, moving away from her in a show of resolution. 'We can't go on like this. It breaks my heart but I must leave.'

He went in search of his potential travelling companion, who was fortunately not to be found, then walked to the Porta Orientale pondering his next move. If she surrendered, he'd give up his journey — a month in Milan as her lover would be worth the sacrifice of Rome and Naples.

But immediately a cloud seemed to pass over the sun, dulling his beloved landmarks. How often could he hope to see her alone? A stolen hour here and there whenever she could evade Turcotti's watchful eye. What would he do with himself in all the empty hours without her?

A chill recognition struck him. If she didn't love him, it would have destroyed his pleasure in Italy. But she *did* love him and he was bored at the thought of a month in Milan. Is it really love he's feeling, or merely the thrill of being singled out by a woman that every man desires?

What is love anyway? He'd imagined himself in love with his cousin Adèle, and later with Mélanie. Even with Mme Palfy the feeling comes and goes. Perhaps it's something he's yet to experience. But if he doesn't find it with a woman like Angela, will he ever? Truly, there's something exceptional about her that's kept her memory vivid the last ten years. The heroine of every novel he's read has borne her features; he's measured all other women against her, and though she's no longer the romantic girl he worshipped, she's still magnificent.

No, he can't leave without doing his utmost to possess her. He owes it to that yearning boy of ten years ago. If he doesn't lie in her arms as he'd dreamt of doing then, he'll regret it for the rest of his life.

Milan, Friday 13 September

This morning Mme Garreau proposed walking to the public gardens during our lesson, so we set off with the child. On our way, we ran into her brother on horseback with an acquaintance, a captain in one of the Italian regiments. They dismounted and accompanied us a little way. It is obvious that the captain admires my tutor, and I suspect that our encounter was not accidental. The brother, Signor Giovanni Rossi, has a gentlemanly appearance, and one would not take him for the son of a leather manufacturer (apart from his resplendent riding boots).

'The signorina speaks Italian very well,' he said. They were walking together, while his sister followed with the captain, who had a slight limp.

'No, I make many errors. But I hope to improve with your sister's help. She is very generous to spare me her time.'

'But it's no sacrifice to spend time with so charming a lady. My sister is honoured to have made your acquaintance, and I too.'

She was unaccustomed to the company of fashionable young men and his gallantry made her awkward. That afternoon, when Larocque came to fetch her, she was grateful that, though infallibly courteous, he avoided the artificial compliments that falsified relations between the sexes. He seemed different out of uniform, younger than his greying hair and the deep furrows on either side of his mouth suggested. It wasn't easy to place him — he was clearly educated, but his speech retained a hint of rustic origins, and though he'd acquired a certain polish, she guessed him to be of humble birth, which probably explained his diffident manner.

They circled the city along the top of the old ramparts, which had been turned into a pleasant drive lined with chestnut trees. On one side they looked down upon the gardens of wealthy residences; on the other, out to the surrounding countryside. Across the entire northern horizon, the Alps seemed to float like the foam-capped crest of a wave above the heat haze veiling their lower slopes.

On the north-west, beyond the castle, the ramparts had been levelled for a parade ground. Nearby stood a huge new arena which, like the Roman Colosseum, could be flooded for mock naval battles — 'for those who like that kind of spectacle,' Larocque said dismissively. It was part of the emperor's plan for the whole area. Milan had once been the second city of the Roman Empire, and now as capital of the new Kingdom of Italy, it was to have a forum with public buildings as grand as ancient Rome — once the money had been found to pay for it.

Some irony in his tone emboldened her to ask him if the Milanese were content with their new ruler.

'I believe the welcome they gave us eleven years ago was genuine — the Austrians had made themselves hated. In any case, the Milanese are used to it; they've had one foreign ruler or another since the sixteenth century. Most acknowledge what the emperor has done for the city — it's thanks to him that the facade of the Duomo is finally being completed. The Milanese have argued over its design for three centuries. But he set a thousand masons to work and it's almost done. There's no doubt that Milan has prospered since I arrived eleven years ago.'

'So you made the famous crossing of the Alps?'

'Yes. And like your cousin I fought at Marengo, which ended my career as a soldier.'

'You were wounded?'

'A trifle compared to your cousin's loss of his arm. Just a bullet in the shoulder. But unfortunately when it healed I no longer had full control of my right hand. I couldn't grip a musket firmly or load it fast enough.' Brushing off her commiseration, he said, 'It's what soldiers call a lucky wound — not crippling, but sufficient to escape the army. Without it, I'd be in Spain now, fighting the English.'

'But you didn't return to civilian life?'

'I could see no way to do so. Before the wars I was a law clerk.' He gave her a strangely apologetic look. 'But since my injury I can no longer write the even hand that legal documents require. In my present employment with the supply corps it doesn't matter. I have a clerk to write for me. What's important is that I know the local language and character well enough to prevent our suppliers from cheating us. But it's not an occupation I'd have chosen.'

'Supplies are surely crucial to military success,' she said politely.

'Indeed they are — but they're too often inadequate, however carefully planned at headquarters. Soldiers blame us, and with some justification — certain commissaries are out to fill their own pockets. And in wartime we're detested by the local population from whom we must requisition the foodstuffs and animals we lack. But enough of that. If you look over there you can see the Apennines . . .'

He told the driver to halt so she could trace the misty summits along the horizon. From then on, as though embarrassed by revealing so much about himself, he confined himself to the points of interest along their route.

Their tour ended in a café opposite the Duomo. It was the first time she'd entered one. Even had such a thing existed in Nogent, a respectable woman would not be seen there. But here in Milan, she saw, a lady might enjoy coffee or a sorbet without damning herself. The coffee with whipped cream that Larocque ordered was excellent, though she was intimidated by the fashionable clientele.

They sat outside on the piazza, dominated by the great cathedral which glistened in the late afternoon sun like a confectioner's extravaganza in spun sugar. Two fiddlers and a tambourine player competed with the cries of fruit and flower vendors. On the shady side, a puppet show had drawn a crowd.

'I have never seen people as carefree,' she remarked, watching the merry crowd in front of the puppets. 'They have an ability to enjoy themselves that most of us lose after childhood. One cannot help envying them, even if their pleasure seems a little shallow.'

He sometimes found it irritating, he admitted, though the Milanese joie de vivre had intoxicated him when he first arrived, after the hardships and privations of military life. He stared into space under a momentary spell, then came back to himself and asked if she was interested in art.

Monsieur Larocque has offered to take me to the Brera gallery tomorrow. I am pleased to have made his acquaintance, for whatever his origins he is intelligent and cultivated. It is another of these chance encounters that have brought me into contact with individuals whom I would never have known had my life not deviated from its expected course. Normally I would hesitate to enter into relations with an individual who is not of my own milieu, but (as with Mme Garreau and her brother) the acquaintance is unlikely to prove burdensome in the space of a single month. It is one of the advantages of travel that one can permit oneself to be less reserved than at home.

Milan, Saturday 14 September

He's written nothing today, being in no mood to describe another frustrating tête-à-tête. Twenty-five minutes! Were they never to be alone for longer? If only he could have two hours with her, enough time to be natural, to be himself. He'd risked a small liberty, only to meet with resistance.

'Not even a little kiss down here?'

'If I permit that, where do we stop? The further we go the more painful it will be to part.'

The doorbell rang: callers already! Hastily, they composed themselves. Widmann came in, followed (as though they'd all conspired to thwart him) by Turcotti, Count d'Azas, and a Captain Del Fante whom he hadn't met before, aide-de-camp on the viceroy's staff. Was he imagining it, or did Widmann and Turcotti greet him coolly? But how could they not be jealous? Within a week of his reintroducing himself to Angela, he's become the favourite.

To give credence to his promise to leave Milan, he told Count d'Azas in her hearing that he hoped to travel to Rome with the former imperial prosecutor in Turin. 'You know him perhaps?'

'Saint-Romain? By reputation only. He's a gambler, I've heard. One can never trust their promises.'

So that explains the man's elusiveness, which at least has bought him time. Even in a society as free as this, a woman may feel the need to delay her surrender till a decent interval has elapsed. And she's given him a rendezvous at the Alamanni baths in the morning, which seems to promise some development.

Milan, Saturday 14 September

Today I visited the Brera gallery with Monsieur Larocque. We talked for a long time in a café afterwards. Between the gallery and that conversation I am so full of new impressions that I scarcely know where to begin. My experience of art (other than vague memories of my father's prints of Rome) has hitherto been limited to the volumes of engravings in Armand's library. After those sober black and white plates, the gallery literally dazzled me. Surrounded by such extravagance of scarlet and gold, such a gamut of greens, such heavenly blues, I felt like a blind person whose sight had been restored.

It wasn't the day on which the public was admitted, but Larocque had obtained the necessary authorisation. They had the gallery to themselves, apart from the students who'd set up their easels to copy particular works. The atmosphere of hushed concentration and the predominantly sacred subjects on the walls gave her the feeling she'd entered a church.

A cicerone greeted them at the entrance, but Larocque politely declined his services.

'A guide will overwhelm you with facts,' he said. 'The first time it's best to wander freely, discover what interests you. You can benefit from his expertise later.'

'But I should like to get some idea of the history of Italian painting . . .' She heard her father's voice: 'method, discipline, don't be a butterfly'.

'Then let's begin with the earliest works. They're in the room at the end. Under the emperor's patronage,' he added drily, as they made their way towards a naked colossus framed in the pillared archways of the intervening rooms. She was embarrassed. Nudity in classical sculpture was acceptable, but one didn't expect to see a living individual represented in that state, least of all the emperor. She averted her eyes, which wasn't difficult given that some thirty pictures, hung three deep, competed for her attention.

Her eyes settled on a nearby black-and-white-robed saint with a cleaver in his tonsured skull (no doubt the instrument of his martyrdom). He was flanked by a bishop and an abbot whose sombre faces suggested concern with human wickedness. But behind them, through an open archway, lay meadows on the banks of a lake, with a little white town on its farther shore. A road wound up to a fortress against a backdrop of blue mountains.

'These are remarkable character studies,' she said, examining the three austere faces. 'But what really pleases me is the landscape. It's a whole world in miniature.'

'You're right,' he agreed, examining it. 'I've never really looked at it before. I must admit that I have an aversion to priests, particularly a Grand Inquisitor like this one.'

'He spoils the view,' she said daringly. The eyes of the small angel at the martyr's feet bored into her, detecting heresy.

'Since you like landscape, may I show you another?' He took her over to a Virgin and Child. Behind them lay an autumnal scene — stubble fields, haystacks, a farm on the outskirts of a walled town. 'It's a more commonplace view — familiar to the artist, perhaps.'

'Yes. One feels he didn't invent it.' She looked back at the other picture. 'That landscape is charming but imaginary; this shows the world as it is. I admire its truth.'

'I'm glad you like it. It's a favourite of mine. May I show you something else by the same artist? Very different, but it too possesses truth.'

He took her into an adjoining room, to a Virgin and Saint John with the dead Christ. Only a glimpse of landscape here — all attention was focused on the faces of mother and son. And what faces they were — the son's exhausted by an extremity of suffering, the mother's drawn and shadowed by her vigil beside the cross, raised to the son's as though to detect some lingering breath, with a look that seemed the very essence of grief.

She contemplated it in silence for a long time before she spoke. 'What must the artist have seen, to capture such sorrow as that?'

'It haunts me,' he said. 'I've thought each time I see it that if all the mothers of the dead were present on our battlefields, the generals would not sleep at night.'

His tone surprised her. She would have expected a soldier to be inured to death. But perhaps he'd joined the army against his will. Later, when they were sitting in a nearby café, she asked if he'd been conscripted, struck as she uttered the word that it was the first time she'd used the ugly new term spawned by the Revolution.

'No, I volunteered. I was caught up in the enthusiasm of the times, convinced we must defend our liberty against those who would restore the old regime. The first battles only increased my ardour. When I followed General Bonaparte here, it was to help Italians gain their liberty. When he became First Consul, I was confident that he would correct the excesses of the Revolution and that the republic we had fought for would flourish under his rule. But now . . .' He glanced around and lowered his voice. 'The wars continue, with no end in sight. Conscription has been doubled. With the huge casualties in Spain, the army will soon be full of raw recruits. It sickens me to be part of it still. But what can I do? I must work, I can't live on an officer's half-pension.' He spread his hands helplessly.

'Do you have no family in France who might assist you?'

'I wouldn't accept their assistance even if it were to be offered,' he said curtly, and she feared she'd trespassed. 'In any case, I have ties here that make it difficult to leave. I have a daughter — she's only eight, too young to be parted from the grandparents with whom she's lived all her life. My wife died giving birth to her.'

'How sad!' She was taken aback, almost embarrassed, as though she'd opened a door to an empty room and found it occupied. 'Do you see your daughter often?'

'Every Sunday, and during the week when work permits. She lives in the country.'

'What is her name?'

'Lucia — for her mother, whom fortunately she resembles more than her father.' His smile smoothed out the furrows round his mouth.

'A pretty name. She must bring you some consolation.' The moment she'd said it she regretted the conventional sentiment.

'There is no consolation for such a death,' he said, in a tone that made her feel inept. 'At the beginning I could scarcely bear to look at the child. I left her with her grandparents. What else could I do? I forced myself to visit out of duty. And then one day this little creature stretched out her arms to be picked up . . .' She saw that his eyes were moist and her own filled in sympathy. 'I cannot imagine life without her now.' He pushed away his coffee cup. 'Would you like to drive back along the ramparts?'

I regret that my sympathy was so ill expressed. I have known no one intimately, and I am unaccustomed to such openness, which would shock me, like the rapid progress of my intimacy with Mme Garreau, did I not feel a sincere interest in these two individuals whose kindness has eased my arrival here.

I had the feeling at moments that Monsieur Larocque felt obliged to justify himself to me. It was almost a confession. I hope that he will not regret his frankness. There is still a certain malaise between us, no doubt owing to the difference in social position which even in this changed world cannot be forgotten. Given his acquaintance with Armand, he must know who I am — who I was, I should say. Despite his support of the Revolution, he treats me with a deference that seems to acknowledge my former rank.

I mentioned my desire to see Leonardo's Last Supper *and he offered to take me there next week, though he claims it is scarcely worth the effort since it has badly deteriorated over the centuries and what one sees now is a third repainting by an unskilled hand. But I look forward nonetheless to seeing it with him.*

Milan, Sunday 15 September

I've just left her apartment filled with admiration — and close to passion. She will make me shed tears on leaving Milan.

This afternoon not only Widmann and Turcotti were there, but the whole family: her parents, her sister Peppina, and her handsome stupid husband. But for a full three quarters of an hour, while the others talked among themselves, she'd spoken to him alone, telling him about the grave illness that had brought her close to death. To think that while he was entertaining the sweet hope of seeing her again, she might have been lost to him forever!

He's never felt anything like this with Mme Palfy. But there's something sublime in Angela that exalted him from the start, and this afternoon, with her hair in a mass of rippling waves on her shoulders, she seemed again the girl he'd fallen in love with in 1800.

'You haven't aged at all since we first met,' he told her. 'But I find you more pensive.'

'I'd lived unthinking till my illness. But to come so close to dying opens one's eyes.' Her voice was serious, without the playful tone she maintained in company. 'Faced with death, the promises of religion seemed to me nothing but pious deceptions.'

He nodded, silent. He wanted to tell her what he'd felt at seven when his mother died and the priest said, 'This comes to us from God' — how he'd hated God from that moment on. But he didn't trust himself to speak. He'd never opened his heart to anyone about that, not even his sister Pauline.

'It made me doubt everything,' she went on. 'I read Dupuis on the origins of religion. You know the book? And my favourite, Helvétius. Who can read them without acknowledging that most religion is mere superstition? But my doubts troubled me. I confided in Turcotti' — she glanced across the room at the *servente,* who (though engaged in conversation) was observing them covertly. 'He helped me resolve them.'

He wanted to say something cutting and dismissive. Turcotti, he was sure, would offer the rationalisations that allow doubters to cling to faith. But she was talking about the experience of being close to death, her eyes intense.

'I felt that I'd passed through some profound transformation, that my life couldn't continue in the same way. Yet here I am, leading the same aimless existence when I long for something greater.'

He felt he'd glimpsed a grandeur of soul that answered something in his own. How sweet it would be to shed tears with her.

Still, as an anatomist of the human heart, he owes it to himself to assess his feelings honestly. Reading back over the last few tumultuous days — is it really no more than a week since he arrived? — and noting his fluctuations of feeling, he concludes that he doesn't love her enough to stay in Milan if he can't be with her constantly, but that he could be happy if they were together all the time, if only that were possible! To leave without possessing her, knowing that others have meant more to her, would be misery.

What was it about those others, he wonders, that gave them the victory that eludes him? There have been four 'comets' in her life, so far as he knows: her husband (with whom she no longer has conjugal relations, or so she'd told him this morning at their rendezvous in the bathhouse courtyard, speaking enigmatically because her maid was with her), the painter Gros, then Louis Joinville, and another French commissary. (And myself, he writes in English.) But for the last two years she's led the life of a nun. Will she abandon her new-found prudence for him?

Perhaps the reality of his departure will soften her heart. This morning he'd finally met with the elusive Saint-Romain; if this gambler is to be trusted, they'll leave the day after tomorrow. Which means, as he told her, tomorrow may be their last day together.

After dinner, the whole of Milan was at the Porta Orientale to watch Mme Blanchard's balloon ascent. But he'd already seen her in Paris and all he could think of, scanning every carriage frantically, was Angela. At eight he went to her parents' where her sister had promised to sing for him to Widmann's accompaniment, but Mme Borroni's piano needed tuning, so they all walked over to Angela's apartment. He'd offered Angela his arm, though with Widmann and Peppina close behind, he couldn't take advantage of the darkness, but the pressure of her arm against his made him ask if she'd give him reason to hope.

'You know my answer,' she said.

In response, he slashed his cane against the wheel of a carriage with such force that it snapped in two.

The music, when they reached her salon, wasn't to his taste, though Peppina's voice was as smooth and strong as the coffee with whipped cream at the Caffè Nuovo. He'd assumed a melancholy air in hopes of softening Angela's heart, but she'd scolded him for his taciturnity so he joked with her sister and talked with Turcotti and Widmann. If he weren't in love with Angela, he'd see as much of them as possible; they're distinguished men — yet another proof of her superiority.

Now it was Angela's turn to be melancholy while he was making the others laugh. It hurt her, she told him, to see him so light-hearted while she was sad, thinking of his departure. Then abruptly she said: 'Come at half past twelve tomorrow.'

The earlier hour seems to promise the fulfilment of his hopes. But how long would it last before they were interrupted? He's had enough of these brief encounters, this daily suspense and disappointment. If he's to sacrifice his tour of Italy, he wants to be alone with her in some romantic spot like lovers in a novel. Otherwise he'll leave. But the thought that he might never see her again is unbearable. Once he's back in Paris, he'll scrimp and save, and ingratiate himself with everyone who could help him obtain another leave of absence. Or better still, a post in Italy. A woman like Angela deserves better than a man who'll leave her after a few weeks. She's right to refuse him.

Yet wouldn't a single passionate encounter between lovers with their history be richer in sensation than many might experience in a lifetime? How can he make her see this?

Milan, Sunday 15 September

This morning I attended Mass at the parish church, where I met Mme Garreau — Maddalena, as I am to call her now in the informal Milanese way. She was with her mother, who invited me to visit them in the afternoon. The whole family was gathered when I arrived. Signor Rossi, the father, is not at all the coarse artisan I had expected but an affable businessman with some knowledge of the world. As for Signora Rossi, I fear that she distrusts me.

It was not surprising. A citizen of France could hardly fail to rouse antipathy in a devout Italian whose most sacred traditions had been violated by the French. And a woman travelling alone must be doubly suspect. She was made welcome, but she guessed that Signora Rossi wished to scrutinise her daughter's new acquaintance. The signora was not one of those women whom motherhood had rendered plump and comfortable; maternity seemed to have sucked her dry, unless what kept her thin was the fierce energy with which she continued to exert her governance. Her daughters reacted according to their individual dispositions. Signora Teresa, the eldest (already mother of five herself), simply shrugged her shoulders, unlike Maddalena, who seemed constantly on the verge of exploding. The youngest, Signora Caterina, little more than twenty but already nursing an infant, wore an air of sullen endurance. Their sister-in-law, Pulcheria, whose advanced pregnancy exempted her from criticism, sat placidly indifferent.

The sisters were friendly. The conversation, though, was more Milanese than Italian and hard to follow, interrupted as it was by the babble of half a dozen small children. She stayed as long as courtesy required, then made her escape.

After dinner, Maddalena and Pierino came to invite her to watch a balloon ascent by the famous Mme Blanchard. Young Signor Rossi accompanied them and they joined his friend, Captain Trezzano, in the large crowd outside the city gates. The balloon was already in place. Its gondola seemed scarcely large enough for a child.

'Does she really ascend in that?' she asked, her stomach contracting.

'She's light as a sparrow, look at her,' said Rossi as Mme Blanchard appeared, a tiny figure in white with a huge ostrich plume on her bonnet. She stepped into the gondola, her attendants released the ropes, and the balloon lifted off to cheers that redoubled as the aeronaut unfurled a red, white and green banner. 'The flag of Italy,' Trezzano told the child. With the imperial French eagle spread across it, she noted silently.

Once the balloon was over the treetops, the aeronaut lit fireworks, launching them on tiny parachutes. It seemed more dangerous than the brief explosion of colour was worth. If a spark were to ignite the balloon, its passenger would plunge to her death, like Icarus. But as the breeze wafted the balloon south across the city, she imagined the exhilaration of floating above the rooftops, higher than the gilded Virgin on the Duomo spire, looking down on the labyrinthine streets and canals below, on hidden courtyards and walled gardens, grasping the whole in one sweeping glance like a windhover — a perspective unknown to the citizens, mere ants in the swarming colony. The very thought gave her vertigo and yet it inspired her.

I should not wish to emulate Mme Blanchard, but like the alpinist Mlle Paradis she shows what women can accomplish when they free themselves of the prejudice that they are too frail to attempt the same feats as men. At present such women appear exceptions to the general rule, but they encourage me in the hope that women will one day overcome the many barriers to their exploration of the world.

Observing Captain Trezzano with Maddalena, I saw that his feeling for her goes beyond admiration, and I suspect that it is mutual. On the way back, he invited us to have a sorbet at the café on the corner. Maddalena accepted, though the child should have been in bed. He was overexcited and noisy. Eventually he fell asleep and his uncle carried him home. I was exhausted myself by the effort of listening. I appear to make progress, then suddenly I am lost and speech seems mere cacophony. How much time will it take before I can follow an entire conversation?

Milan, Monday 16 September

Only my heart is Italian, he writes with regret. If he'd mingled with good society ten years ago, he'd have acquired Italian manners — that blend of charm and naturalness that's so attractive — but also their common sense and sagacity. He's always despised common sense (a quality overvalued in Grenoble), but he suspects that if he'd come to know Italians better he'd have held it in high esteem instead of judging it synonymous with a lack of passion.

Angela's good sense is maddening, however. This morning he arrived at half past twelve with high expectations, only to hear that her sister would be arriving shortly. Were they never to be alone together, he asked, frustrated.

'It would only lead us into folly,' she said in her most maddeningly sensible tone. If only she were as reckless as ten years ago. He's come back into her life too late.

There's no word from Saint-Romain, though they'd agreed to leave tomorrow. If he'd left with the *vetturino* a week ago, he'd be halfway to Rome by now. Unless he leaves soon he won't have time for Florence and Naples, not if he's to be back in the office by November for Count Daru's return from Holland. Must he choose between Angela and Italy?

Trying to view the situation with the cold rationality of a besieging general, he considers his options. There are three possibilities as he sees it:

1. Angela will never surrender, so there's no point lingering in Milan.
2. She's testing him: if he proves his love by giving up Italy, she'll surrender.
3. There's no hope *at present*, so he's wasting his time. But with a month to regret her coldness she might have a change of heart when he comes through Milan on his way home.

In the first or third case, he should leave at once — then at least he'll have Italy. In the second case, he should stay, on the almost certainty of possessing her. But if she doesn't surrender he'll have sacrificed Italy for nothing. Besides, even if he fails the test by leaving, there's always the possibility that she'll relent when she sees him again. On balance, therefore, the best decision is to leave now. He leaves another message for Saint-Romain and waits.

Milan, Monday 16 September

Maddalena embarrassed me yesterday by asking about Monsieur Larocque, for she had seen us return on Saturday. Conscious that my comings and goings are observed, I was relieved that there was no one on the Rossi balcony this afternoon when we set off. I thought to have escaped such anxieties on leaving Nogent, but now that I have acquaintance here I cannot escape the burden of preserving my reputation, which weighs so heavily on all women.

As they headed towards Santa Maria delle Grazie on the outskirts of the city, she asked after Larocque's daughter and he described his Sunday. They'd gone to see a foal that Lucia had named *Belle Étoile*, for the star on its forehead and its birth in the year of the comet. His face softened when he talked about his little girl, the harshness of his features dissipated.

'So she speaks French?'

'Yes. I want her to know her father's language as well as her mother tongue. We read together too, otherwise she'd remain in the grossest ignorance. Her grandmother sees no reason to educate a girl. It's enough if she can write a letter and keep her household accounts. I thought of placing her in one of the new schools for girls, but she would be locked up all week. I cannot impose that on her at such a tender age. So I'm her tutor. It's impossible to do much in the time we spend together, but I can at least encourage her desire to learn.'

'A father may play an important role in a girl's development,' she said. 'It's thanks to mine that I learned Latin. And whatever I know of history and philosophy I owe to him. Of course, it was in part because he had no surviving sons. But he believed in educating girls.'

'Your father was an enlightened man . . . exceptional in many ways . . .' He cleared his throat nervously as though about to say more, but they'd reached their destination.

Like many of the city's former monasteries, the buildings had been adapted to a secular purpose, commercial or military. The monks for whom Leonardo had painted his masterpiece had been replaced by a cavalry squadron, and a musty odour pricked her nostrils as they followed the custodian into the famous refectory.

'Is it true,' she asked Larocque, 'that the army used it for stabling?'

He had the grace to look embarrassed. 'When they first arrived, yes, though it was against the express wishes of General Bonaparte, as he then was. But the monks themselves, you know, hadn't respected the painting. It was they who pierced that doorway in the middle — cutting off the Saviour's legs — to facilitate the passage of hot dishes from the kitchen. You must bear in mind that the original was nearly invisible within a century. The paint flaked off very rapidly. And the place is on low ground, with rising damp. Mould has damaged certain sections.'

It was indeed sadly disfigured, and she would have gained only a general idea of the composition were it not for the custodian, who identified each disciple by the gestures that individualised them.

'It's rather theatrical, do you not find?' she murmured to Larocque.

'Necessarily,' he said. 'Seen from below, the gestures must be large to convey their meaning. It's like communicating by semaphore instead of face to face. But we northerners are less given to gestures, so naturally we find them exaggerated.'

We prefer to read faces, she thought, looking at his, where despite his surprising openness with her she sensed reserves that she couldn't penetrate. Something she'd said earlier had made him uncomfortable, she sensed.

'Would you like to drive back outside the walls?' he asked when they returned to the fiacre.

'With pleasure. What I saw of the countryside on my journey made me long to see more.'

'In that case, we could go farther. It's safe for the moment — the hay is drying. Once it's lifted, they'll start spreading pig manure again, which doesn't make for a pleasant excursion.'

'Is that what causes the odour in the city? It seems worse some days than others.'

'It depends which way the wind is blowing. One gets used to it.'

It was the price to be paid for the region's extraordinary fertility, he explained, as they headed out through the city gate. The meadows round the city produced seven crops of hay a year thanks to a system of irrigation and manuring devised centuries ago.

They turned up a lane, past a brick farmhouse. In the field on the other side a line of crouching women were weeding a crop. 'Turnips,' he said, 'and over there, onions. This is Milan's kitchen garden. It's excellent land. I sometimes think of renting a little farm from my father-in-law. It's not the life for which I was educated, I know . . .' Again, he seemed oddly apologetic.

'I can see why it tempts you.' She looked back across the fields at the city walls above which rose a multitude of cupolas and bell towers, all dwarfed by the massive Duomo and its glistening spires. 'To have the pleasures of country life so close to the stimulation of a city seems to me the ideal existence. Is your father-in-law a landowner?'

'A cattle merchant originally — one of our suppliers. He's prospered since we arrived. When the monastic lands came up for sale, he saw an opportunity and now he's breeding horses, of which the army has an inexhaustible need. He's one of those men with little education but a practical intelligence that can turn to anything profitable.'

A type the Revolution had favoured, she thought silently. Like the grain trader who'd acquired Vernet.

They passed through a village — a few solid old houses backing onto a river. Beyond, where a cart track led along the river bank to a watermill, he asked the driver to stop.

'You can see the essential element of this landscape here. It's worth a look,' Larocque said.

Beside the road a stream of clear water bubbled up and ran between pollarded willows into the fields. 'It's a natural spring. The country is full of them. That's why it's so green even in the summer heat. For centuries they've been carefully channelled. Otherwise, the land would be an unproductive marsh.'

She looked around her. The view might have been monotonous without the trees that masked the flatness. Poplars, willows, or mulberries lined the fields and irrigation channels, marking boundaries. Everything had its use: willow stems for weaving baskets, mulberry leaves for feeding silkworms. Nothing was planted for pleasure, yet the sight of nature made productive by human labour and ingenuity was pleasing in itself.

They walked up the track as far as the mill. Dragonflies skimmed the surface of the millpond, flashes of azure more brilliant than the patch of sky reflected there. The current was barely enough to turn the mill wheel. 'If the water weren't so low, it would be pleasant to walk along the river,' she said.

'The rivers are almost dry by September — the water is drawn off upstream for irrigation. But there are pretty walks along the canals, if you're not put off by a little dung on the towpath.'

'I have walking shoes,' she said with a smile.

'Then perhaps we may give it a try.'

There was still a certain unease between them, she felt, as they regained the carriage. No doubt some discomfort was inevitable between a man and a woman alone together. There was the driver, of course, an odd kind of chaperone with his battered hat and his pipe. But it was an intimacy she had never experienced before and it made her a little awkward. She hoped her manner with Larocque was not too stiff.

TUESDAY *This morning I went to the Alamanni bathhouse with Maddalena and afterwards we called upon Signora Teresa, her eldest sister, who lives nearby. Her husband is in the manufacture of silk, which according to the guidebook is Milan's most important trade.*

They were drinking lemonade on Teresa's balcony when young Signor Rossi dropped in. He'd just delivered a consignment of shoes for the soldiers housed in the castle. 'Three hundred of the cheapest quality as ordered, and a pair of expensive made-to-measure boots to thank the commissary for his custom.'

For an unpleasant moment she feared he was speaking of Larocque, but he was describing his father's approach to business. A man like his father couldn't grasp the fact that there were men with a sense of honour who'd be offended if you offered a bribe. 'Father thinks everyone has a price,' he said contemptuously, tossing his wavy black hair off his forehead in a habitual move that reminded her of a spirited horse.

'Was it your brother's choice, or family expectation that he enter the business?' she asked Maddalena as they walked back.

'It seemed natural at the time. But now he wishes he'd entered the army when his number came up.'

'He was conscripted?'

'Yes, but my mother could not bear to let him go. He's always been her favourite. So father paid a young bootmaker to go in his place. The army likes men with a useful trade. Every battalion needs cobblers. Father made a generous offer — there was no pressure on the young man. But now Giovanni regrets it. He thinks the army would have given him a chance to distinguish himself. Here, he's just the son of the padrone.' She quickened her pace to catch up with the child who was running ahead. 'But he'd be sent to Spain. Trezzano was wounded there. You must have noticed his limp? And for what reason? Not to defend us from the Austrians but to fight another of the emperor's wars. Wait for me, Pierino!' she shouted at the child, who'd nearly run into the path of a loaded waggon.

A labourer set down his barrow, grabbed the boy round the waist and laughingly delivered him to his mother, who held him firmly by the hand from then on despite his protests. 'He needs a man to keep him in check,' she said in French. 'Giovanni doesn't help — he indulges him as he himself was indulged. A boy needs a father's authority.'

Was Maddalena seeing Trezzano in that role, she wondered. The captain would certainly bring a needed firmness into Pierino's life, but she felt sympathy for the boy. It would be hard for him to have a rival for his mother's attention.

We strolled with the evening crowd after dinner. As usual, the Captain joined us. I observed that he is trying to win Pierino's acceptance, but the child seems torn between the desire to respond to his overtures and a hostility that he cannot quite overcome. Poor little fellow!

Conversation turned to the comet. Viewing conditions are apparently ideal at present, with a clear sky and only a crescent moon to rival it in brightness. We shall walk outside the city walls tomorrow evening to see it.

Milan, Wednesday 18 September

He's too depressed to write, brooding over the decision he's finally taken. Yesterday he'd felt he was making progress. They'd driven out to her country house to taste the first grapes. She was adorable in a straw hat and rustic dress, and the sweetness of an hour and a half together had plunged him into a tender melancholy that he recognised as love. But this morning's brief tête-à-tête advanced him no further, and she's forbidden him to see her again till evening. He wandered the streets all afternoon and drank too much coffee. Still no word from Saint-Romain.

At seven he went to the rendezvous at her parents' shop, but Peppina was there with her husband and the inescapable Turcotti.

'I thought he was going to Venice,' he muttered.

'He says he won't leave till you do.'

To placate Turcotti, he mentioned his difficulties with Saint-Romain. Peppina's husband suggested the mail coach and offered to take him to the post office to book. Before he knew it he had a reservation for Saturday night. Was there a conspiracy to get rid of him? He's acted as impulsively as a child and now he regrets it. And he paid 120 francs for his seat instead of bargaining it down to a hundred.

To add to his distress, when he returned to the Borroni shop Angela had left. He prowled up and down the street, then found her on the Duomo piazza with Turcotti and the bore, Scagliotti, who was talking about the comet. He told them he'd booked his seat. If she was upset, she hid it well, but there was a hint of reproach in her voice: 'So Milan can't compete with Rome?'

She *had* been testing him. But what could he say with the others there?

'The attractions of Milan are infinite. I shall leave with the deepest regret.'

'Let's go to the parade ground and see the comet,' she said impulsively.

She took his arm and the four of them set off. Near the castle they crossed paths with another group and one of the women caught his eye with a half smile of acknowledgement. He couldn't place her at first, but something in her eyes as they met his brought back the recollection of a verbal skirmish across a supper table. It was the woman in grey from the diligence, on the arm of a handsome young Italian. A disagreeable sensation hovered at the threshold of memory like a black speck on his field of vision, but it was soon dispelled by the spectacle of the comet.

'It appears so suddenly,' Angela murmured. 'And then it's gone again . . . But what an effect it produces!'

'We must not fall into the errors of our ancestors,' Scagliotti cautioned. 'These phenomena have no impact other than scientific.'

He sprang to her defence: 'But poetic souls may associate them with significant events in their own life. To find an association is not to claim causation. Poets have always looked to the heavens — Shakespeare's Juliet imagines her lover scattered in starry fragments across the sky.'

'An example of the grotesquerie that makes him unreadable,' Turcotti said curtly.

'Only by those who follow the dictates of academies,' he replied with all the scorn he could muster. 'Personally, I believe him the greatest poet who ever lived. I've learnt English expressly to read him in the original.'

Angela's pressure on his arm warned him not to pick a quarrel. To mollify Turcotti, he spoke of Italy's great dramatist Alfieri, whose tomb he hoped to visit in Florence. On the way back, Angela's love for him seemed so evident that when they reached her door he judged it wiser not to go in with the others.

Three days left. There's still time. But where and how can he be alone with her long enough? If only they could meet on the road south, spend a stolen night or two together in some little town where nobody knew them.

The thought reminds him of the woman from the diligence. Had she seen him watching her that night at the inn? He squirms at the idea. It's one thing to look — no warm-blooded male could resist an open door — but humiliating to be caught in the act. It's galling to think that this woman, insignificant though she is, might carry that image of him in her head, as though he were pinned to a board like a particularly repulsive specimen in a natural history museum. Still, tonight she'd seen him with Angela on his arm: a man who's clearly successful with women.

Abruptly it comes back, the memory that's been nagging him since they crossed paths. They'd talked of happiness that night and he'd been foolish enough to reveal his longing for love. And then she'd cited Buffon's statement that love was merely vanity, as though he were an inexperienced youth needing to be stripped of his illusions. Of course, there's an element of vanity in his love for Angela — no man is immune to the satisfaction of conquering a woman that all men desire. But that counts for nothing beside his longing to know her intimately, to meet her soul to soul. The woman from the diligence was just envious, belittling something she's never likely to experience. It surprised him to see her with a man, and a handsome rascal of the Migliorini type, moreover. Perhaps a man like that, who could have any woman he wants, enjoys the challenge of a cold one.

MILAN, WEDNESDAY 18 SEPTEMBER

It is little more than a week since I arrived in Milan, not even a month since I set out, but I have seen more in that short time than in the last nine years. A lunar eclipse, the Alps, and now a comet!

At sunset we made our way to the parade ground outside the city walls where a small crowd was gathering. One group had a telescope. But Captain Trezzano assured us that it was unnecessary and that we would spot the comet easily. It is now at its closest to Earth.

'How long will it remain visible?' she'd asked him.

'Another month. It's travelling in a north-easterly direction — the Russians will see it this winter.'

'And where will it go then?'

'Beyond the reach of our telescopes.' But its orbit had been calculated; it would return in three thousand years.

Three thousand years! What an unimaginably immense distance that time implied! Would the world still exist in three thousand years? For an instant she was a child again in her father's library discovering that the sky was not the solid dome she'd imagined, enclosing the world as securely as the ceiling above her bed, but boundless space. One grew accustomed to the idea, but an event such as this brought back that first terror, made the universe strange again.

The last streaks of sunset faded and the sky paled. As darkness fell and the first stars appeared, the atmosphere in the crowd grew expectant. Soon, not far above the horizon, they spotted what appeared to be a larger star but with a luminous tail that identified it as the comet. Even the child could see it, though it did not hold his interest long.

'Mamma thinks it a sign of God's wrath,' Maddalena whispered. 'He will smite the emperor and the Holy Father will return to Rome.'

'Mamma sees doom in every unusual event,' her brother said impatiently. 'Perhaps on the contrary the comet is the forerunner of a new age, like the star that led the Magi to Bethlehem.'

Trezzano was sceptical. 'There have been thousands of comets over the centuries. This one is only notable because of its size. If it does prove a harbinger of change, it will not be through some power of its own but because its appearance inspires men to act.'

A rational way to view it, she thought, though not necessarily reassuring. For what acts might the comet inspire in those who saw confirmation of their own hopes in its apparition at this moment in time? In the accounts of the Roman historians a comet almost always presaged the death of an emperor or some disaster befalling the state. Whatever one might think of the usurper, the present stability was preferable to another revolution.

Pierino was starting to whine; it was time to go home. In the darkness she stumbled on the rough ground and Rossi offered her his arm. As they re-entered the city, they crossed paths with a group heading outwards. Among them, she recognised the young man from the diligence, with a tall and strikingly beautiful woman on his arm. He must have sensed her gaze because as they came abreast under the street lantern, he turned his head and their eyes met. Catching the belated flash of recognition in his, she was glad he could see that she too had friends in Milan.

It seemed an age since that supper-table conversation when he'd mocked her faith in books. What other knowledge of the world was available to women, barred from so many domains that men might freely enter? But she'd overcome one barrier, she was seeing the world for herself now. She felt a surge of pleasure at being in Milan, the same happy sensation of disbelief with which she woke now every morning. Walking back through the crowded streets, past the Duomo glittering with its own celestial radiance, she was no longer the timid creature who'd hesitated to join the men at the supper table that night in Dole.

I am becoming less reserved, though this is due more to the kindness I have met with here than to any resolution on my own part. I have never truly had friends. My childhood was passed in the narrow circle of my parents and teachers. Though exile enlarged my experience of the world, it did not bring me into intimate contact with others, and even in my cousin's house my isolation did not cease. Dear Mme d'Aumont was perhaps my first friend, despite the difference in our ages. But Maddalena, being of a frank and open nature herself, has penetrated my reserve, and though we are of a different character I enjoy her company and that of her brother and his friend. There is, I believe, something characteristically Italian about this rapid intimacy, though it is also a consequence of the loneliness that besets a traveller. But I was lonely before and I did not seek to escape it. No, something has changed me, and for the better, I believe. With Monsieur Larocque too, I am discovering the possibility of friendship. The barriers that would once have made it unthinkable are gone and I see no reason to regret it.

Milan, Thursday 19 September

I won't say anything for the moment about my journey, he writes to his sister.

There'd be too much to tell. But in a word, I'm happy. If you have the patience of an angel and the eyes of a lynx you'll be able to read the why and the how of it in a badly written little journal I scribble every evening when I'm not too tired.

He rarely uses his own name on letters to Pauline, but he can't be 'William Crocodile' or 'Baron Tenderbum' tonight; he needs an alias to fit his mood. Running through the events of the day for something with historic associations, he comes up with 'Romorantin', where in the early years of the sixteenth century an ageing Leonardo had sketched the designs for a palace for the king of France. He'd been reminded of those sketches (now among the treasures of the emperor's museum in Paris) on today's excursion with Angela, who's become quite reckless now that his departure is fixed. They'd hired a carriage near the castle (Angela seemingly unconcerned that anyone might see them) and driven out of the city to the Villa Simonetta, a grand Renaissance country house where generations of the nobility had savoured rural delights amid long-vanished gardens.

Two whole hours together without interruption, alone except for the guide. But happy though he was to have her to himself, Angela's new imprudence worried him, and he'd had a bad moment when they reached a room at the top with an open window and the guide pulled out a pistol. It was only to demonstrate the famous echo, which rebounded some twenty or thirty times between the three wings of the building as though a band of assassins were hidden in the loggia, but the shock had made him feel the risk in his pursuit of her. One false step in this country of high emotions could have more serious consequences than in Paris.

But how lovely she'd looked, the Leonardesque character of her beauty emphasised by the setting. He imagined her in Renaissance dress, reigning over a little court of followers in these gracious frescoed salons, her wit and beauty celebrated by poets and artists. His Lady Simonetta.

I think that this is really love, he writes in his diary. *And she appears to love me too.*

Milan, Thursday 19 September

My walk along the canal with Monsieur Larocque this afternoon brought the most unexpected revelation. It has left me in turmoil. I wish that I could remember and record every moment of the conversation, but the surprise was so great that I could not assimilate it all.

She'd looked forward to the excursion as she tied the ribbons of her straw hat. Since the day was hot she wore a light cotton dress, protecting her shoulders from the sun with a blue-and-white-striped fichu that had always seemed to promise rustic pleasures, though she'd only worn it to Sunday Mass in Nogent.

On the busy high road every passing vehicle sent up clouds of dust, and they soon left it for a lane heading towards a distant line of poplars that marked the canal's course through the fields. When they reached the bridge, Larocque told the driver to await them at the hostelry near the next lock and they set off on foot along the towpath. He'd cut a willow switch to keep insects at bay. It was utterly tranquil in the afternoon heat, a barge vanishing in the distance but not a soul on the path, no sound but the breeze rustling through the poplars, whose slender spires were mirrored in the water.

'This reminds me of a place I loved in childhood,' she said. 'A bend in the river not far from home. My mother always asked the coachman to halt there so we could admire the reflections. I longed to cross to the other bank. There was a meadow behind the trees that I imagined full of autumn crocuses.'

'You'd have found nothing but thistles, I'm afraid.' He paused. 'You mean the spot where the road runs beside the river, just before the bridge?'

'You know it?' She stopped in her tracks, astonished.

'I walked that road many times as a boy.'

'So we're from the same part of the country?' But of course! How could she not have recognised what she'd been hearing all along — that hint of Jeannette's accent, familiar and reassuring, that she'd responded to without recognising its cause.

'Did your cousin not tell you?' He seemed taken aback.

She tried to remember. 'All he said was that you had served in the same regiment. But our conversation was interrupted, I recall.'

'I assumed since he had sent you to me that you must know who I am.' He was suddenly stiff. 'But I should have informed you myself. You might not have wished to make my acquaintance had you known.'

'I am sure that nothing could cause me to regret it.' She might have been making conversation in Marie-Cécile's salon for all her voice betrayed, but she felt light-headed. Something she hadn't allowed herself to think about in years was rising to the surface. 'Just boys, bad boys,' Jeannette had said.

A shout from behind made her jump — a boatman leading a pair of horses pulling a barge. They stood aside to let the horses pass in a small commotion of dust and jingling harness. The barge slid by almost soundlessly, briefly shattering the reflection of the poplars that slowly recomposed as the wake subsided.

'So you are from Vernet too?' she asked nervously.

'Yes — we lived in the last house as you left the village. My father managed the woodlands on your father's estate, as my grandfather had before him — and my eldest brother might have in his turn.'

'Then we may have seen each other as children.' She spoke as though it were the most natural thing in the world, trying to disguise her shock, remembering the road, the peasants removing their hats as the carriage passed.

'At least once, if I'm not mistaken.' He smiled at the recollection. 'But you were too small to remember. I was waiting to be admitted to your father's library — you watched me from the top of the stairs, a solemn little girl with your nurse.'

She could picture the staircase, though no memory of the incident emerged. 'Why were you going to see him?' Her voice sounded strangely distant as though she were hearing herself from the outside.

'You didn't know? It's to your father that I owe my education. Each time we've met I have wanted to tell you how much I revered him, how grateful I am to him, but I could not find the right moment —'

'Tell me how you came to meet him.' She was trembling from the shock.

'The *curé* introduced me. He ran a school in the village, as you may know. I was a studious child and the good old man saw in me a future priest. He'd started to teach me Latin. He told your father about me and your father offered to pay for my education if my Latin was equal to his test. I was so frightened I could scarcely say my name when I entered his library. He handed me a book, asked me to read aloud and translate. It was the opening of Caesar's *Gallic Wars*.'

'I too have been interrogated on that text. *Gallia divisa est in partes tres* . . .' For a moment it seemed to bridge the gulf between their worlds till she saw the irony of the words. Caesar had thought only of a geographical division, but the France of her childhood had seemed immutably divided into three social castes, and was her discomfiture at Larocque's revelation not a sign that those social distinctions that the Revolution had sought to abolish were not erased in her own mind?

'It won me an education. It's a privilege for which I'm deeply grateful, but I must admit that it wasn't easy. It was hard to leave my family, to lose my freedom to roam. And I soon realised that what I'd learned with the *curé* meant nothing. The other pupils were more advanced. My first lesson was to adapt to their ways in order to escape mockery.' He waved away a cloud of gnats with the willow branch. 'For weeks I scarcely opened my mouth. Eventually I found a few comrades — boys like myself, helped by a wealthy relative or a benevolent patron like your father.'

'He never spoke of this.' She searched her mind for some recollection. 'But it does not surprise me. He valued intelligence above all things. And, as you know, he had no sons to educate.' She tried to imagine her father's feelings on seeing in the robust young peasant the son who might have been in his place, and a possibility flashed through her mind, dispelled so quickly that she barely had time to feel ashamed of conceiving it.

'I'm not the only one he assisted — he was a generous man. My father had the deepest respect for him.' The warmth in his voice brought tears to her eyes. 'He was not among those who believed that the people should be kept in the ignorance to which Providence had destined them. I met him each time I returned for the holidays. Once he saw that I merited his interest he seemed less severe. On the last occasion, after my final year, he gave me a little collection of Latin literature — Virgil, Horace, Livy. I have the volumes still.'

'When exactly was that?' She was anxious to fix events in time.

'In '87, before I entered the seminary. I'm ashamed to say that when I left it, after a year, I did not tell him in person as I should have. I simply wrote to the *curé* and asked him to inform your father that finding in myself no vocation for the priesthood, I was seeking employment in a lawyer's office. I was cowardly — I couldn't face their reproaches.'

'But my father would not have wished you to remain there without a calling! He was not a believer. He conformed outwardly to please my mother. With his recommendation you could have found a position as tutor, or secretary to a man like himself.'

'I wished to be independent,' he said gruffly. 'Though it might have been more agreeable than being a lawyer's clerk. Copying documents was as boring as the seminary. But it offered some possibility of advancement and saved me from returning to the village. Had I done so, I might now be a timber merchant like my brothers, who are richer than my father could have dreamt.'

There was something apologetic in the statement that she chose not to explore, and she sidestepped it as she would a muddy patch on the path to reach the safer ground of a part of his history she already knew. 'But you volunteered for the army. In what year?'

'In the spring of '92 when France was threatened with invasion.'

So he'd already left Vernet. He could have played no part in events that September.

'I met your cousin two years later,' he said. 'The volunteer battalion in which I'd enlisted was attached to a former royal regiment — he was one of its few remaining officers. I was a junior officer myself by then. In that army of untrained volunteers any man with an education was quickly promoted. But it took me a while to find the courage to introduce myself and ask for news of your father. I'd heard of your emigration in letters from home. All your cousin could tell me was that you were in London. I couldn't imagine your father away from his library.'

'He was lost without it. It was the worst privation he suffered. We were almost destitute after a year in England, and by then, as you know, the sanctions against those who had fled made it dangerous to return. He had to find employment as a tutor.' She'd never talked to anyone about those years, but it poured out of her now, as she recalled her father setting off on foot in his shabby coat to the homes of his pupils, overcoming his pride when he had no other recourse during her mother's illness but to appeal to the Relief Committee. 'When we returned to France everything had gone, everything! His library . . .' She paused to recover herself. 'What had he done to deserve that? He had not clung to privilege, he supported reform.'

Larocque listened gravely. He seemed at a loss for words. It was perhaps just as well that they'd reached the lock. Over glasses of lemonade at the hostelry with other people around them, she was glad to fall back into ordinary conversation and he'd questioned her no further.

When they drew up again in the Contrada della Passerella, her fear of spectators on the Rossi balcony as he helped her out made her stiff. He too had reverted to formality and she realised as Perpetua closed the door behind her that he'd made no suggestion of another excursion, as though he needed assurance that his revelation hadn't changed her attitude towards him.

Once again, I regretted the social awkwardness that so often prevents me expressing my feelings. I shall write to Monsieur Larocque tomorrow, when I have had time to reflect on his story. He too must surely be pondering the strange turn of fate that has brought us together after so many years.

Milan, Friday 20 September

He's happy this morning in a moody Italian kind of way quite unlike the easy cheerfulness of a sanguine type. It's pouring with rain and he's finally caught up with his journal. He was three days behind and already confused about what happened when. But sometimes it's best to write later: it cuts the self-pity when things are going badly, and as for the happy moments, description spoils them so it's wiser not to try.

His imminent departure reminded him that he hadn't written to his friend Crozet since he arrived, though it was almost cruel to describe the pleasures of Milan to a man who's stuck in a village where the people are as dull as the landscape, trying to console himself with a peasant mistress while he supervises the construction of a lock. He'd been careful not to boast, though he couldn't resist dropping hints if only to excuse his silence.

My observation post in Milan has been Mme Pietragrua's circle, composed mainly of distinguished individuals, and Mme Lamberti's opera box.

He'd tried to convey the atmosphere in those groups, so utterly unlike anything in Paris — the unselfconscious gaiety, the readiness to laugh at everything, the jokes they play on each other. Milanese humour is spontaneous, but they lack real wit; they're incapable of the sallies, the bons mots, the well-turned rejoinders so characteristic of the French. And they're shockingly ignorant. What they do possess, along with that remarkable naturalness and lack of vanity, is a certain shrewdness. They're all good observers of character.

But only in Milan could a fellow like Migliorini with his negligent appearance and indecent stories pass in good society. In Paris he'd be judged immediately for the careless way he ties his cravat. And as for his general, nowhere in France would you find a man of that rank using such uninhibited language to a woman of high society like Mme Lamberti. But with what love the general spoke of music. Mme Lamberti said he was one of the best musicians in Milan.

All things considered, Italians seem happier than Frenchmen. You see it in their smile, a smile not so much of the lips as of the eyes.

When he's finished the letter, he copies the best sentences into his journal. In his obsession with Angela he's written too little about Milanese society since he arrived and this will compensate. By the time he's done the rain has stopped. Out on the balcony, the air has a cleansed freshness that makes him buoyant. Down below, a caged bird welcomes the returning sun with sweet trills that fill him with optimism.

Midnight This time tomorrow he'll be on the road again.

He has a headache from the strain of trying to spot Angela in the darkened theatre where she'd given him a rendezvous. He'd gone early, eagerly watching for her arrival until it became clear she wasn't coming. Making his way through the crowd, his eyes swollen with unshed tears, he'd realised that he was truly smitten. What else could it be but love when it took you over like this, this longing that no other woman could satisfy, the dizziness in her presence, the emptiness away from her. If this isn't love, what is?

Tomorrow morning he has a rendezvous at quarter to ten to say goodbye. His last hope.

Milan, Friday 20 September

Rain and indisposition kept me indoors today, which accorded with my desire to be alone after yesterday's discovery. After several false starts I succeeded in writing to Monsieur Larocque, and Perpetua delivered the letter this afternoon. Regretting the awkwardness of our parting and anxious to assure him that his revelation has not altered our friendship, I said that I hoped to continue our conversation soon, and proposed that we return to the Brera if he is not too occupied. I told him how much the story of his education had moved me, and I thanked him for restoring my father to me, for his account of their meetings brought back memories of the father of my childhood, effaced in recent years by the sad state to which age and misfortune had reduced him.

But they were not the only memories his story had revived. She'd woken in the night from troubled dreams to the dull pain that signalled the start of her monthly bleeding, and had lain awake till dawn. Like raiders infiltrating a city under cover of darkness, memories she'd long kept at bay had penetrated her defences.

It was the sound that came back to her — the heavy thud of something hitting the carriage as she and her mother returned from a drive. An overhanging tree branch, perhaps. But then another and another, a barrage on either side, and a shouted warning from the groom that had made her mother pull her to the floor just before the window glass shattered. The coachman must have set the horses to a gallop, and her mother started the 'Ave Maria', its repeated invocation — 'Holy Mary, pray for us now and at the hour of our death' — so often recited without thought, now urgent, until the blare of the coach horn then the clang of the park gates closing behind them announced they were back in safety. The lamps in the open doorway glowed with more than their usual welcome as the groom helped them out, and Jeannette was there immediately to calm her fears. 'Just boys,' she'd said. 'Bad boys up to mischief.' But her mother had gone straight to her father in his sanctum, and the following night they'd set off after dark on the road to the coast.

It was the first intimation that the violence in Paris could reach even their peaceful backwater. News took several days to travel — they hadn't learnt of the September massacres till later — but the firing of a neighbouring château followed by the stoning of their carriage had convinced her parents to seek refuge across the Channel.

The question that has troubled her since (a question she'd never dared ask her father) is whether the incident was merely a local manifestation of the general violence (like the spread of a virulent plague that struck at random all those in its path, deserving and undeserving alike), or whether the peasants on their estates had cause for anger. Her father, she believed with all her heart and Larocque's story confirmed it, was a principled and benevolent man. He could surely not have permitted the injustices that reigned elsewhere to exist within his own domain. He would have done his best to alleviate the sufferings of the poor in those years of failed harvests. Her mother too, less advanced in her views but sincere in her piety, would have felt a Christian duty to assist the unfortunate. It was impossible, she felt, that her parents had in any way deserved what befell them. Yet there was an uncertainty in her mind that Larocque, knowing that world from the other side, could perhaps put to rest if she found the courage to ask him.

Milan, Saturday 21 September

He's whiling away his final hours in the café by the post office till the courier leaves. The *Moniteur*, just arrived with the Paris courier, lies on the table in front of him but its week-old news can wait till he's posted his own bulletin.

The 21st of September, at half past eleven, I achieved the victory so long desired.

So that his future self won't laugh at the naïve satisfaction of twenty-eight, he writes another line: *Nothing is lacking to my happiness, but that of it not being a victory (which can only make a fool happy).*

True pleasure, he's learnt, only comes with intimacy, which takes time. And only after that comes perfect happiness — if one loves a woman of intelligence and character.

The victory wasn't easily won. At quarter to ten this morning he slipped into the church at the end of her street, but didn't find the promised signal. He tried again at five past the hour, then at twenty past. This time it was there. Outside her apartment he took a moment to compose himself. He mustn't advance too fast. She had a dozen reasons not to surrender, against which he had but a simple plea: for eleven years, he'd dreamt of making love to her — could she really be cruel enough to send him away disappointed?

After a serious moral struggle, in which I feigned an unhappiness close to despair, she was mine.

It wasn't the grand emotional climax he'd imagined. The cool head needed to overcome her resistance precluded passion. But it was a victory even so, and afterwards he wandered the streets in a strangely detached elation, seeing everything from a changed perspective. She'd murmured his name in Italian when he entered her. Like a baptism into a new life. What he'd give to stay here forever!

Glancing at the newspaper, his eye is caught by a familiar name. Count Daru has been replaced as Intendant of the Household by the Duke of Cadore. It's been expected since Daru became Secretary of State. Even a man with his prodigious energy couldn't hold both positions. The decree was signed on the ninth. So for the last two weeks Daru has had no jurisdiction over him! He can banish his guilt about leaving before his colleague's return.

But the timing is unfortunate. Cadore will expect to meet his staff — including Second Inspector Beyle, who's on leave, duration unspecified, whereabouts unknown. That won't look good. But he can't give up his journey now.

Stuffing his journal in his portmanteau, he heads out towards the Bologna mail coach.

Milan, Saturday 21 September

This morning I received a note from Monsieur Larocque in reply to my letter. It was in his own hand, not dictated to his clerk, and I saw for the first time the effect of his wound, which is scarcely apparent otherwise. He apologised again for not having introduced himself properly at our first meeting and he deeply regretted the shock it must have caused me to learn who he was. He too, he said, was moved by our conversation and would like to continue it. I replied at once to suggest Monday if he was free.

But why was he so apologetic, she wondered, rereading his note. There'd been no deception on his part. It was natural for him to assume that Armand had informed her who he was. And though he might feel guilty that he hadn't pursued the vocation for which he'd been educated, there was nothing to forgive in a young man's realisation that he wasn't made for the priesthood. His education wasn't wasted. It had lifted him beyond the village, though perhaps an education that differentiated him from his family had been a source of pain? There'd been a strange look on his face when he spoke about his brothers — embarrassment perhaps? She tried to recall what he'd said about them. Rich beyond his father's dreams. But still in Vernet, which puzzled her because even if they'd continued to work on the estate under its new owner, it would scarcely have made them rich. But they were timber merchants, he'd said. With a shock it came to her that they must have acquired some of her father's confiscated land. That was the real cause of his discomfort.

She jumped up from the table in a state of agitation that demanded outlet. For a moment she thought of confiding in Maddalena, but it was impossible to tell Larocque's story without revealing more of her past than she wished. She could write to Armand, find out what he knew about the sale of the land. She took a sheet of writing paper, wrote the date, then pushed it away. No, she could not expose her friendship with Larocque to her cousin's all-too-predictable judgement.

She called Perpetua to bring her a tisane. Sipping it slowly, her hands cupped around its warmth, she felt calmer. Admittedly, had she known of Larocque's origins she would not have wished to meet him, or any member of a family who had profited from the losses of her own. But the more she thought about it, the more reason she saw to be grateful for her ignorance. It had allowed them to become acquainted without prejudice from the past. Of course, she could never say this to him. She could assure him, though, that he had no need to apologise, and that she was delighted to share memories of Vernet. But she must not exaggerate that connection, she told herself, for almost certainly Larocque could not feel the same nostalgia for the place as herself.

I have spent the day in solitude, thinking about the past, but this evening another subject preoccupies me. Maddalena came to see me after dinner with an invitation to accompany the family to the grape harvest on her grandparents' farm at the end of the month and afterwards to make a week's excursion to Lake Maggiore with her and her brother. I could see no way of refusing her kindness, though the idea of spending several days with the Rossi family makes me anxious. But it is perhaps my only opportunity to revisit that beautiful region of which I caught such a brief and tantalising glimpse on my way here, so I must be grateful.

Three

The Dream of Italy

There is nothing to be compared to the new life which the sight of a new country affords to a thoughtful person.

— Goethe, *Italian Journey* (1816)

The more considerable the extent of the journal the more careful the writer should be not to risk losing it. A prudent traveller will always arrange to make two copies, one of which should be kept in a safe place. A cipher or coded alphabet will be of great utility.

— Hans Ottokar Reichard, *Guide for Travellers in Europe* (1793)

I shall say nothing about Pavia, of which you will find accounts by all the travellers who go in for description (see, for example, the Journey of Monsieur Millin, member of so many academies). Be grateful to me for not giving you twenty pages on the natural history collection.

— Stendhal, *Rome, Naples and Florence* (1826)

Milan, Monday 23 September

To the Brera again with Monsieur Larocque. We were both ill at ease, he no doubt still uncertain of my reaction to his story, and I anxious to show that nothing had changed. I was relieved to reach the gallery. My recollection of the pictures we saw has been slightly blurred by our subsequent conversation, but I found an enchanting landscape by Previtali, a painter whom I had never heard of before.

A kindly, white-haired cicerone greeted Larocque like an old acquaintance but did not press his services upon them. As before, they bypassed the showy canvasses of later centuries — leaving them to the copyists at their easels and a party of earnest Germans — and returned to the pensive saints and virgins of the quattrocento.

She wanted another look at the landscape behind the martyr. But today, preoccupied with the question she intended to ask Larocque, she saw beyond its naïve charm. The village, the château, the church portico framing the view were a microcosm of the old order, in which the human figures — the three churchmen, the mounted nobleman with his bodyguard, the peasant watching his flock — had their divinely appointed roles. Clergy, nobility, people: the three estates of the realm. But in the centre, inescapable, the violence always threatening the social order: the axe in the martyr's head.

Not ready to share her new perception of the scene with Larocque, she looked around for a safer subject and found a depiction of Christ in a meadow. The snow-white robe of the sacred figure had caught her eye, but it was the green that drew her across the room. Here too was an entire world in miniature. Beyond the verdant meadow and its sheltering grove of trees lay a fertile plain with a little walled town, and a river flowing down from distant blue mountains. The artist's delight in nature was manifest — every plant in the meadow accurately drawn.

'I feel I could walk into it,' she said. 'It seems so real.'

'But idealised, don't you think? No thistles to spoil the meadow.'

Thinking of his brothers, she resisted the temptation to point out the ragged stump of a felled tree among the innocent daisies. 'Do you think the artist has painted an actual view?'

'Possibly. Previtali was from Bergamo, I believe, and this bears some resemblance to the Adda valley. It's beautiful country, not far from Lake Como. You should try to see the lakes before you leave for Rome.'

She told him about Maddalena's invitation. He seemed surprised that they were already on such intimate terms and it renewed her anxiety at being drawn into social commitments, which was increased by an encounter as they left the gallery. They were heading towards the café when someone called his name from an approaching carriage. An elegant woman, in whose features a certain willed vivacity stood in for beauty, leant out, her eyes darting avidly between them.

Introductions could not be avoided, but Larocque's mention of her cousin's name seemed to satisfy the curiosity of the lady, whose husband had also served with Armand. After a brief conversation, Mme Picard expressed the hope that Mademoiselle de Vernet would honour them with her company in their box at La Scala, and took her leave with a wave of an impeccably gloved hand.

'Do not feel obliged to accept unless you wish,' Larocque said awkwardly. 'I will explain that you are going away.'

It would be a pleasure to attend the opera, she assured him, though the encounter had made her uneasy about how others might judge their acquaintance. If anyone were to see them sitting at the back of the café, might they not seem to be in hiding? It made her stiff again, uttering banalities until the waiter had set their coffee before them. But then she gathered her courage and raised the question that had troubled her since their last meeting.

'I have been thinking about the past since our conversation — in particular about an incident that led to our departure. One evening, when my mother and I were returning from a drive . . .' She had to pause before she could utter the words. 'Our carriage was stoned.' She saw from his embarrassment that he knew. 'I was too young to understand anything at the time. But I have wondered since if it was only the general violence of those days, or if perhaps' — her throat was tight, but she forced the words out — 'if some injustice on my father's part had provoked it?'

'Your father was the most just, the most generous of men. No one who knew him could doubt it.'

Sensing his discomfort, she persisted. 'But those who did not know him?'

'Those who knew him only through his bailiff — a callous individual. He managed the estate with a harshness that created resentment. His sole aim was to increase your father's revenues — and probably his own.'

'It's what I feared.' She had to master her emotion before she could meet his eyes again.

'I should not have told you,' he said awkwardly. 'Forgive me for causing you pain.'

'I had already guessed something of the sort. My father told me nothing, but I sensed that he held himself responsible for what happened. I thank you for telling me the truth.'

She was sincere, but nonetheless his words had broken the connection between them that she'd imagined over the past few days. Their memories of Vernet, which had seemed to link them beyond all differences of birth, could not be the same. It was fortunate that they had the paintings to fall back on as they finished their coffee.

What Monsieur Larocque has told me confirms what Armand once hinted, that my father himself brought about our losses by his negligence and his over-hasty decision to seek refuge abroad. We might have ridden out the storm like most of the provincial nobility. The conversation saddened me. But I comfort myself with the knowledge that whatever responsibility my father bore for our family's misfortunes (and the hardships of the people), his assistance to Larocque proves his fundamental goodness of heart.

Tonight, however, I am agitated as much by the trivial anxieties of the present as by thoughts of the past. I could not refuse Mme Picard's invitation any more than Maddalena's, though both make me nervous. But since I can go neither to the opera nor to Lake Maggiore alone, I must be grateful to them.

Bologna, the Albergo Reale, Tuesday 24 September

The dénouement of September 21st restored me to a sense of my task and I made use of a half-hour of liberty to write. This postscript is an apology for the coldness of that account . . .

What will that victory bulletin, scribbled in a café, tell him twenty years from now, when the memory has faded? It was all analysis, no feeling. At least it was honest; he hadn't pretended to perfect bliss. Besides, even if the encounter had been everything his heart desired, he'd have spoilt it by writing about it. Happiness can't be described.

But now it's time to start a proper record of his travels. Two weeks of logging his siege of Angela's heart and examining the fluctuations of his own have distracted him from his account of Italian life and manners.

A paragraph on the journey first: Pizzighettone — the river running high. Bozzolo — talk of bandits. Supper in Mantua, where he wrote to Angela and was viciously attacked by mosquitoes. Virgil's country. A line from the Georgics (that bane of his childhood) came back to him: *Ulmisque adjungere vites* — attach the vines to the elms. They're doing it still!

He nearly died of hunger. The fare included meals, but the courier, a lean, sober, silent type, was cutting costs. He was stiff as a board by the time they reached Bologna, though it hadn't kept him from the opera. A shabby place after La Scala, but the prima donna had a perfect sweetness that French singers could learn from. Italians haven't succumbed to the fashion for embellishment that's perverted little Angel's taste. When he gets back he'll have her sing some of the music he's heard here.

This morning he'd hired a guide who took him to the Neptune Fountain, two churches and a gallery. He lists the pictures that struck him, but it's a challenge to walk through room after room of canvasses that blur in the memory as one succeeds another. It's made him feel his ignorance. Of course, his artistic sensibility puts him above the crowd, but a book on painting, something on the order of La Harpe's introduction to poetry, would enhance his appreciation. At present he can only judge a work by its feeling, imagination, naturalness. For everything else — light, colour, composition — he relies on the cicerone. But he won't be deceived by reverence for a name.

Whenever a work by one of the great masters is highly praised, I always ask myself: 'If I found it on a street corner, would it catch my attention?'

The city impressed him, though the filth behind the grand facades is shocking. Dust, dirt, cobwebs everywhere. Italians are barbarians in matters of domestic order. But everything's much cheaper than in France.

Not a single striking woman. 'We're just country folk here,' his guide said. 'Besides, pretty women don't go out on foot in the morning.'

The humour of Italian men is not of a style that appeals to women, he writes later. *So any Frenchman with wit and graceful manners is assured of success, all the more so if he's ennobled himself with elegant attire.*

This afternoon he'd had a little encounter in a gallery that transformed the day. He'd noticed her immediately — a shapely figure, black-veiled in the local fashion, and alone, studying a picture that gave him a pretext to approach her. Nothing special about her, except for those wonderful Italian eyes in which he could read the impression he made, but their conversation took quite a personal turn — until her husband and her father arrived. It made him feel that happiness could be found even in a provincial town like Bologna.

But what a backward place it was! The famous Tanari collection was hung in private apartments so filthy they sickened him — disgusting beds backed up against the frames of magnificent paintings. He'd seen an exquisite Guido Reni Madonna — if she raised her eyes to yours, you'd fall madly in love.

There had been an even more beautiful Venus, his guide whispered. But when the Marquess Tanari died, his wife's confessor told her that the anger of God had struck the household because of the immoral art on the walls. So poor Venus was thrown on the fire. She was naked, and so beautiful it would give any man sinful thoughts, said the guide. If the story was true and this priest-ridden country still burnt works of art, there was every justification for taking the best to Paris. Moreover, they'd be properly displayed in the emperor's museum.

The Marescalchi collection had an enviable room full of choice works by Guido Reni, Guercino, and the Carracci. Nothing second-rate. It was there he'd met his Italian with the sensitive soul and expressive eyes.

They reminded him of Livia's. It's three years since the night in Brunswick when he escorted the carriage that was taking her home to Italy after her husband's death. The letter she'd sent him afterwards had made him blush like an inexperienced boy. He should have kept it. A man like himself, not blessed with the looks that make women lose their heads, won't get many letters like that. He must definitely stop in Ancona on his way back.

But he only has thirty-six days of freedom left! And his time in Rome will be taken up by social obligations. He can't avoid Martial and Chancenie, since he gave them as his forwarding address. Then there's cousin Adèle in Florence, now her husband is intendant there. He's never liked Alexandre Petiet, but he's curious to see what marriage has made of Adèle.

Four days each in Rome and Naples, two in Florence and Ancona. Probably ten days for the journey between, since travel here is so damnably slow. Another ten for the return to Paris via Grenoble — but what does that leave for Milan?

As he stares at the itinerary he's outlined, a solution strikes him. He takes a sheet of letter paper and inscribes it in his most careful hand *To Monseigneur the Duke of Cadore*. No, a letter from Italy will raise questions. Better get Faure to request it on his behalf. He crumples the page, starts another to Faure. He needs a month's extension of his leave. For personal and family business.

Of course, he won't get an answer immediately, given how long mail takes. But surely his new chief won't refuse. He's only asking for another month after all, and a second inspector's duties aren't onerous; he'd have had time on his hands this year if he hadn't been doing the Holland correspondence for Count Daru. His colleague can surely handle anything that comes up.

He tries to run his mind over likely business, but Paris feels remote, his life there, even his love for Mme Palfy, erased by Milan like a scene change at the opera. Everything seems unreal, though — the last three weeks no less than the past year — as though he's an actor who's played his role in whatever performance he's called to, and now, costume and greasepaint removed, is left with nothing but scraps of half-forgotten dialogue on a darkened stage. A strange sensation fills him, as if he were sleepwalking and had woken to find himself on the edge of a void.

It's just the disorientation of travel, he tells himself. All he needs is a good night's rest. Stretching out between the sheets with almost voluptuous relief, he calls up the look on Angela's face as he entered her, which gives him a little thrill of amazement each time it comes back to him. To spend time with her on his way back would be worth any sacrifice, even the postponement of his prefecture.

Milan, Tuesday 24 September

Last night I lay awake worrying about Mme Picard's invitation to La Scala. I should like to have preserved the anonymity of my first days in Milan, but it would have been discourteous to refuse an invitation from an acquaintance of Monsieur Larocque.

'What will you wear?' Maddalena asked when she heard.

She had only one suitable dress — an ivory silk that Marie-Cécile had passed on to her after her second pregnancy. But everything of Marie-Cécile's was of the highest quality, and with her own merino shawl she could survive scrutiny, provided nobody looked at her feet. Her evening shoes were also Marie-Cécile's cast-offs, and she'd hoped they would do a little longer, but the left one had a tear where her toenail had worn through the satin. Recalling Mme Picard's immaculate appearance, she decided she must replace them.

'We'll go to Pontarelli's,' Maddalena said. 'They'll give us a special price.' She held the shawl to the light, admiring the border of acanthus leaves. 'You embroidered all this yourself? It must have taken months!'

'I had time on my hands.' Long grey afternoons in which the dark carnelian red against the ivory wool had offered a rare sensuous pleasure, though she'd imagined no other occasion to wear it than Marie-Cécile's dinners.

'You should arrange your hair differently for the evening, Marie. Sit down and let me show you.' Within seconds the hairpins that held her plaits in their tight coil were removed. A shiver of pleasure ran through her as Maddalena's quick fingers loosened her hair. No one had touched it since Jeannette. 'Such a pretty colour!' Maddalena was saying. 'It's rare to keep it after childhood. And so fine! You shouldn't hide it in plaits. There! Look in the mirror — doesn't that become you?'

Her hair was now coiled into a loose knot on the crown of her head with a single braid concealing the hairpins. She had to agree that it was flattering.

'So you'll try it?'

'Not tomorrow when I must meet all those strangers. I should feel self-conscious with a different style. I have worn it like this since I was fifteen.'

'But leave it for today, won't you? It suits you so well.'

They set off for Pontarelli's, which turned out to be the most elegant establishment on the Corsia dei Servi. Did Maddalena imagine she was wealthy, she wondered uneasily. But she opted for quality despite the cost, persuading herself it was an economy in the long run.

There was a milliner next door where they stopped to look at winter hats. After trying on a number of the latest Parisian models, Maddalena succumbed to a dark green winter bonnet with green-and-blue-checked ribbons and carried it off in a state of guilty exhilaration.

Evidently Maddalena has decided to abandon her widow's black veil, but she has left her purchase with me until our journey to the lake, for fear her mother will scold her. It is no doubt a folly on the pension of an officer's widow, but after my own extravagance I cannot blame her. The 'special' price was far more than I had intended paying, but I was too embarrassed to refuse. My foolish pride has led me into an unnecessary expense, for who is going to look at my feet in a crowded theatre? I can only hope that I shall have occasion to wear the shoes often enough to justify my folly.

Signor Giovanni's compliments on my new coiffure tonight made me uncomfortable. It is only a change of style, but I had the sensation of being untrue to myself.

On the road, Wednesday 25 September

He set off for Florence mid-morning by the cheapest form of transport — an open vehicle, which exposed him to the full blaze of noon. At first the view hardly warranted the discomfort. The Apennines, mere hills separated by winding gorges, lacked grandeur. But by early evening he was high enough to look back at the whole plain of Lombardy with its villages and farms bathed in the glow of sunset.

As the road wound upwards, the driver pointed to a chapel on the summit: 'The Madonna of the Ants. If the signor had come this way two weeks ago he'd have seen them.'

'Ants?' He couldn't believe he'd heard correctly.

'Yes, Signor, ants with wings. They come every year for the Madonna's feast — thousands of them, a black cloud that darkens the sky. It's well known — all the winged ants in the world come to die at the Madonna's chapel. People put out cloths blessed by the priest to catch them. They grind them to a powder: it's an excellent remedy against all kinds of ills.'

Another example of Italian credulity. Only in Italy would you find a Madonna of ants!

For the next few miles the road ran through chestnut woods. The bold silhouette of their branches against the twilight sky and the great rocks along the edge resembled opera scenery. All it lacked was a romantic figure wrapped in a cape — a fugitive risking his life to see the woman he adored, or a young man descending from a solitary mountain lookout to confront his destiny.

Reality, however, was brutish peasants, like the trio on mule-back they passed — a woman in grubby petticoats mounted astride like a man, her male companions scowling. Not the cheerful rustics of an opera buffa. They made him uneasy. He questioned the driver about bandits, though it was hard to understand the Bolognese accent. But the fellow's exaggeration was comic. This was the way to travel — alone and needing diversion, he had to talk to whoever he found himself with, which was more useful for his study of the Italian character than the most observant companion. Not for the first time, he felt grateful that Crozet couldn't obtain another leave.

Two Frenchmen in a good carriage with an intelligent servant would bring the sociability of Paris and the pleasures of the salon to the middle of the Apennines, but they would not appreciate the Apennines as I do, travelling alone in an open vehicle, he wrote at the supper halt, by the flickering light of a fire where pigeons were roasting on a spit.

They set off again in the moonlight, and then, on an empty stretch of road far from shelter, the rain began. Isolated drops at first, raising an odour of dust and dry leaves. But before long the moon had vanished and a regular downpour assaulted him, finding every gap in the ineffectual cover the driver offered. Each time he dozed off, he was woken by a violent jolt as they hit another pothole. Clinging to the front of the vehicle so as not to be thrown out, he prayed for refuge. But no lantern gleamed in the pitch-black night. So much for the romance of an open vehicle.

Milan, Wednesday 25 September

I received a message from Monsieur Larocque asking if I would like to visit the gardens of the Marquess Cusani's villa in Desio. We drove out into the country north of Milan. The villa possesses every luxury deemed necessary to a rustic retreat, including an orangery and a glasshouse for exotic species. But the greatest luxury to my mind is the pure country air that one breathes there.

The head gardener conducted them down a long grass walk bordered by young trees, many recently introduced from North America. Larocque, she was impressed to see, could identify most and discuss their characteristics with the man. At the far end a sunken path wound among overhanging trees to an English garden. More fanciful than the one her parents had created, it had a Gothic tower and a grotto, and a lake with a little island graced by a temple of Venus. A boat moored among the water lilies would have taken them there, but they preferred to admire it from a seat beneath a spreading tree.

'This is a cedar of Lebanon, is it not? There was one at Vernet, I recall.'

'I hope it does not awaken sad memories.'

'No, it gives me great pleasure to see such a beautiful garden.' But she felt an urge to be frank with him. 'I must admit that I can never think of Vernet without sadness. I feel like Eve expelled from Paradise. But it was a paradise from which others were excluded. We possessed it only through the accident of birth.'

She wanted him to know that exile had opened her eyes. The fruit from the tree of knowledge was bitter, but once you'd tasted it you saw the world as it was.

His reply, though perhaps intended to console, had the reverse effect. 'Those who took your place do not deserve it, from what I hear. When the privileges of rank are merely replaced by those of wealth, society is no further advanced. My father, if he were still alive, would deplore what's happened to the woods he managed.'

'You are very knowledgeable about trees yourself,' she said, directing the conversation into a safer channel.

'It's in my blood, coming from a family of foresters. As a child, I often accompanied my father on his inspections. It wasn't work for him — he loved the woods and knew them intimately.'

It was the first time he'd spoken about his father and she was touched by the affection in his voice. 'Did he have a hand in planting the trees in the park at Vernet?'

'He did, and it gave him much pleasure to advise your father on some of the new species. He once said that could he live his life again he'd work his passage to the Americas to see the virgin forest for himself. But he was contented with his lot. Whether by temperament or through his occupation he possessed the secret of happiness.'

She was reminded of the supper-table conversation at the inn in Dole and told him about it. 'Each of us gave a very different response to the question as to what would make us happy.'

'Would it be indiscreet to ask your answer?'

'I said that it would be to see with my own eyes the places I knew only from books. But I could not speak freely in the company of strangers.'

'We're all afraid to reveal our deepest aspirations. Afraid of tempting fate, perhaps.'

'What would you have said? Those gentlemen would not have let you remain silent, I think.'

'The greatest satisfaction I can imagine,' he said hesitantly, and she wondered if he would speak honestly, 'would be to own a piece of land like this and shape it to my ideal. The creation of something beautiful must be a great source of happiness. But since I'm not the Marquis Cusani I'd content myself with a small farm where I could plant a tree or two.'

'It's a life more conducive to happiness than most, if we believe the Roman poets.'

'You've found me out!' He gave her one of his self-mocking smiles. 'Yes, I see myself under a vine arbour in the noonday heat, reading Horace's odes. In reality I'd be cleaning out the cow shed. But at least I'd be independent of the outside world.'

'Independence is precious,' she said, though for a moment she thought of challenging him. Was not the ownership of land the origin of social inequality in the eyes of certain thinkers? But she resisted. In his youth, he must have known in those around him the hunger for land that promised freedom from servitude. Some, like his brothers, had now acquired land (or so she assumed) but how many of the peasants had truly benefited from the Revolution? The impression she'd formed from her journey across France was that their poverty was only a little relieved by the abolition of seigneurial privilege. She ought to question him about the present condition of the inhabitants of Vernet, but she was reluctant to cloud the pleasure of the afternoon.

'Would you like to walk a little farther?' he asked. 'We haven't seen everything yet.'

The gardener, sensing he wasn't needed, had departed. There were no other visitors. For the moment the garden was theirs. They followed a path to the top of a little rise where a north-facing belvedere offered a view of the Alps.

We looked out across the wooded plain towards Mount Resegone. Its sawtooth crest bears witness to the violence of the natural forces that shaped it, a reminder of nature's harsher aspect which brought out by contrast the gentle beauty of the garden and the countryside surrounding it. We talked of the opposition between the human desire to shape and perfect nature and our nostalgia for a nature as yet untouched by human hand such as Monsieur de Chateaubriand has described in the Americas.

Each of our meetings has had its awkward moments, and today was no exception, but our mutual sympathy and our common tastes permit us to surmount them. I believe that my father, astonished as he would be by the fortuitousness of our encounter, would not disapprove of the friendship that has resulted, for Monsieur Larocque could not be more respectful, nor more eager to repay through his kindness to myself the debt of gratitude that he owes my father. Before I leave for Rome I must find some way to thank him, perhaps something pretty for his daughter — a scarf or a sash that I could embroider with some simple flowers that would please a little girl.

Florence, Thursday 26 September

An exceptional day, filled with experiences he should have described immediately. But he'll write first thing in the morning. Snug in bed, he tries to fix the details in memory.

He'd reached Florence at five in the morning, soaked to the skin, shaken to pieces, and beside himself with fatigue. He took a room at Schneider's, the best inn. No seat available with the Rome courier before the twenty-eighth, but at least his two nights here will be spent in comfort. The Petiets would probably have offered him hospitality but then he'd have been stuck with them. As it was, the mere thought of Adèle diminished his pleasure in the city.

The stormy weather wasn't ideal for visiting churches which are dark even on the sunniest day. But nothing could keep him from Alfieri's tomb, so he'd hired a carriage and guide to visit Santa Croce. The rough barn-like exterior shocked him. It needed facing with marble like the Duomo in Milan. But inside, the first thing that met your eyes was Michelangelo's tomb! As if that wasn't enough, beyond Michelangelo lay the remains of Machiavelli and Galileo, and Canova's monument to Alfieri. Not one of the tombs was perfect — the statues on Michelangelo's supported by metal bars, Galileo looking more like an astrologer in a popular almanac than the great astronomer, and the figure of grieving Italy on Alfieri's too fat. Nonetheless, they had finer monuments than any of France's great men, which pained him.

But what would really engrave Santa Croce in his heart were two chapels the guide insisted he see. Too often in museums he reproaches himself for his coldness, has to squeeze a little excitement from his soul. His admiration is reasoned, not felt. But today in the Niccolini Chapel he was close to rapture. The painted ceiling was beyond his short-sighted eyes, but those sibyls! Especially the one on the right who reminded him of Minette. The same sweet-faced Germanic type, and the combination of grace and grandeur with which he falls immediately in love. For a few minutes he was back in Brunswick. He could have stood there all day admiring her, though he was exhausted from the sleepless night, his feet squeezed and swollen in new boots.

But he'd have missed the real revelation if the guide hadn't dragged him to another chapel. Altarpieces are poorly lit, but this one was delineated with such precision that he needn't strain to see it. The subject was the release of the dead from Limbo. The risen Christ was a triumphant male nude (minimally draped for decency). But what drew his eye was the exquisite female nude alongside, in the classic pose of Venus surprised, one hand shielding a perfect breast, the other hiding the pudenda, transparent drapery drawing attention to the delicate navel. How was such glorious nudity permitted in a church?

'That's Eve,' the guide explained, 'with Judith below her,' but he wasn't listening. What did it matter who they were? The second woman, auburn-haired, bare-breasted, sublimely stern, seemed to return his gaze. A third reached down to help another still struggling up from the darkness of death. That brought tears to his eyes. He'd have wept like a child if he'd been alone.

For two hours he'd been in a state of heightened emotion. But inevitably it couldn't be sustained. Nothing moved him at the Uffizi — except a head of Brutus by Michelangelo. But it only captured his strength, not the gentle soul, the inner combat that Shakespeare portrayed. Everything else left him cold. If it weren't for the emotion he'd felt this morning, he'd believe himself unresponsive to art. When you feel nothing in front of a universally acknowledged masterpiece you can't help but think that the fault's in you. But today he'd started to see why. There's something bland about Italian art. All those perfect faces are empty, any sign of passion or conflict eliminated. *That's* why he stands unmoved in front of them. And it's the same with sculpture. The great Winckelmann was wrong: the Greeks didn't copy nature. They sought the ideal. He must make a note of that in the morning.

And yet in front of the *Limbo* he *had* been moved. Was he merely stirred by beautiful bodies? He must go back tomorrow for another look. Burying his face in the pillow, he tries to call up the picture in his mind. But he can only recover the general configuration — pale shapes that waver like candle flames in a draft, almost extinguished then flaring up again. Two slowly crystallise into lifelike forms — the one leaning down, her beautiful breasts exposed, to help the one below whose face is hidden. He watches her climb upwards; she's almost there, she's about to re-enter the light of day, but with sudden terror, rooted to the spot, he knows what the light will reveal.

Opening his eyes on darkness, struggling to stay awake, he sees it for a delusion — the promise that the dead will rise again intact, his mother still in the bloom of life just as he remembers her, leaning over his bed to kiss him goodnight. They'd told him he'd see her again in heaven, the usual pious lie, but even if it were true he could never recover what he'd lost, never fling himself into her waiting arms, because he wouldn't be seven years old any more, but full-grown, an old man, perhaps; she wouldn't know him. It was a lie, and the painting too, a sublime lie like all art. He must remember to write that down in the morning.

Milan, Thursday 26 September

I was as nervous on reaching the opera house as a girl entering society for the first time, and indeed the evening proved that I am still an innocent in the ways of the world. I should have preferred to hear my first opera without the distraction of society, and I am certain that I made a very gauche impression on Mme Picard and her friends. What foolishness to be intimidated at my age by individuals with whom my parents would not have associated.

It is after midnight now and I am too tired to record my impressions of the evening which are in any case far too complicated to render fully.

She takes off her silk dress and hangs it in the armoire with a feeling quite unlike the anticipation with which she'd put it on earlier, when her appearance had for once given her satisfaction, though it had lasted only as far as the theatre where the sight of the fashionable throng made her want to flee. With his usual thoughtfulness, Larocque had arranged for a fiacre to pick her up and he was waiting for her at the entrance. They'd joined Mme Picard, imposing in a striped silk turban, and her husband, a stout, red-faced man who offered her his arm as they mounted the stairway to the boxes. 'It's your first visit to La Scala, I believe, Mademoiselle? There's something for every taste — one may gamble in the foyer, conduct business in the pit, or entertain friends in one's box. The first two rows of boxes are for respectable society, but God knows what goes on behind the curtains in the upper rows.'

The Picard box was in the second row; once there, she faced her hostess's interrogation.

'So you have been here nearly three weeks already?' Mme Picard exclaimed. 'I'm vexed with you,' she called out to Larocque, who was talking to her husband. 'Why did you not bring Mademoiselle de Vernet to us before?'

'I have spent most of that time with my Italian friend,' she said quickly.

'You have Italian acquaintances?' Clearly this was rare, to judge by Mme Picard's surprise.

'My friend is the widow of a French officer. She is taking me to visit her family in the country next week and then we shall go to Varese and Lake Maggiore.'

'Varese? The cream of Milanese society spends the summer there. Does your friend have a villa?'

She'd mentioned Maddalena only to escape being taken under Mme Picard's wing, but now she'd created a false impression. Before she could correct it, other guests arrived — a plump, friendly older lady and a striking dark-haired woman in a richly coloured cashmere shawl. The musicians were tuning; it was time to take their seats. She had the place of honour beside her hostess at the front of the box, with a sweeping view of the crowded auditorium. In the neighbouring box, a regal Milanese beauty leant out, gracefully acknowledging the salutations of her many admirers among the gentlemen in the pit.

The musicians ceased tuning and the overture began. It was the first time she'd heard any music beyond the church organ and Marie-Cécile's pianoforte, and she was captivated as much by the spectacle as the sound — the candle glow on brass and polished wood, the intentness of the players, arms moving in unison, cheeks expanding and contracting round instruments unknown to her. The singers entered, first an elderly couple engaged in some dispute, then a pretty girl and an officer, who sang a duet once the old couple left. Two new suitors arrived and sang in turn and the pretty girl greeted each with a lively aria that seemed to disconcert them. A comic exchange between the rivals followed, with much crude byplay that the audience relished, and the first act was over.

Even if her Italian had been adequate, she would have had difficulty following the plot, for the audience had not ceased talking except for certain solos or duets, announced by the prompter ringing a hand bell. She asked her neighbour in the cashmere shawl if the Milanese were always as discourteous.

'They only listen to the best bits — they're here most evenings, you understand, and the performance is just an agreeable background to conversation. It's your first visit to La Scala?'

'My first opera, to tell the truth.'

'What a pity it's this second-rate farce. One's first should be Mozart. But naturally the Milanese are prejudiced against anything Austrian.'

'Mme Delavigne is a great admirer of Austrian music,' said one of the officers who'd come up from the pit to pay his respects.

'And she plays it divinely,' said the young lieutenant with him, nervously fingering his small moustache as if to hasten its growth.

It was clear that Mme Delavigne, though no longer in her first youth, could still captivate. Her dark curly hair, worn short, and something unconventional in her manner hinted at an independence of mind that was both attractive and intimidating. The simplicity, even shabbiness, of her dress suggested that all her resources had been used to acquire the magnificent shawl, but she wore it with enviably unselfconscious grace.

Leaving Mme Delavigne to the officers, she listened to the general conversation. It was more amusing than the talk at Marie-Cécile's dinners, but shallow; there could be no meaningful exchange when all the participants were so desirous of being witty. How did Larocque fit in this group, she wondered, glancing at the back of the box where an argument seemed to be under way. She couldn't catch the subject, but his frown, his quick rejoinder, seemed to express dissent, and the way in which he threw up his hands in apparent disgust to the amusement of the others suggested it was a habitual position.

The orchestra struck up again, the curtains unveiled a new decor, and dancers in Grecian dress appeared. A ballerina leapt and twirled with a display of leg that kept Monsieur Picard's lorgnette trained intently on the stage. In the neighbouring box the parade of men hadn't ceased and the laughter had grown more raucous. Mme Picard glared at its beautiful hostess. 'She entertains the entire Viceregal Guard every night.'

In the second interval, Larocque joined the ladies and Mme Delavigne enlisted him in her disparagement of Italian opera.

'I told Mademoiselle de Vernet that she must not judge opera by this second-rate piece. We need a director with the courage to challenge the audience as Mayr is doing in Bergamo.'

'You really think they'd listen to anything not Italian?' he asked.

'If Mayr could get the Bergamo audience to attend to Haydn's *Creation*, why not? Remember their response to the crescendo of "Let there be light"? Three reprises!'

'Yes, that was one of those moments one doesn't forget,' he said. 'Even an irreligious man feels a shiver down his spine.'

Again, she could only listen silently. Before they regained their seats for the second act, she caught a small exchange between Larocque and Mme Delavigne — nothing more than a sideways glance in her own direction, an almost imperceptible lift of Mme Delavigne's fine eyebrows, followed by a question she couldn't hear but sensed had to do with herself. His response elicited a further question from Mme Delavigne, whose face, lifted to his, seemed for a second to betray something more than curiosity.

The action onstage (even the suitors' comic trio which won the audience's full attention) could not distract her from her new perception of Larocque. He was clearly at home in this circle where she felt ill at ease. How naïve she'd been to imagine him living only for his daughter. Obviously, a man his age, even a widower, must need society.

The second act came to an end. The young lovers had triumphed, though their happiness would be short-lived since the handsome officer was summoned to his regiment. But there was still another ballet to come, though it was after eleven. Ices were served, and new visitors arrived, with gossip about a lady who was rumoured to be convalescing in a secluded villa on Lake Como.

'One of those inconvenient maladies that cause a swelling of the stomach,' said a woman in yellow satin.

'Fortunately the cure, once it arrives, is immediate,' said another, to general laughter. She'd been shocked to realise they were discussing the viceroy's sister.

It is not a group she could ever find congenial, she thinks, putting away her evening slippers, the soles already scuffed by their first outing. Tomorrow she will have to call on Mme Picard to thank her for her hospitality. But it's as well she's leaving with the Rossi family on Saturday. On her return she must try to avoid further invitations.

Florence, Friday 27 September

It's impossible to visit a place that's caused so much ink to flow without adding his own observations to the visitors' book of the centuries, but in his determination to avoid the hackneyed, he's often too cold and critical. The sentences he'd composed in his head last night were strong accurate descriptions of what he'd felt, but set down on the page with the cold detachment of morning they didn't capture his sensations. Today he's resolved to record his impressions while they're fresh.

A morning of museums and churches, starting at the natural history museum, where the anatomical exhibits impressed him, particularly the room devoted to childbirth, which was superior even to the one in Vienna.

I recall with pleasure the visit I made to the Emperor Joseph's academy with Lady A., he writes. Conveniently, that initial could as easily denote Adèle, Angéline, or Angela as Alexandrine, though the mention of Vienna is a giveaway. His mind drifts, caught up in the memory. She'd been particularly fascinated by the obstetric models. When the demonstrator manipulated them, she could actually *see* what before she could only feel. It was natural for a woman, even one who'd given birth several times, to be interested in the revelation of all that's hidden in her body, but it had made him shudder at all the pains and mishaps to which nature had doomed the female. His poor young mother, so pretty, so full of life, dead of a botched delivery at thirty-three. The same age as Angela, in her prime. It didn't bear thinking of.

He writes several paragraphs on the other natural history displays. Afterwards, he'd visited churches, richly decorated but lacking in effect. A damn nuisance of a Mass prevented him viewing the Masaccio frescos, like yesterday in Santa Croce when he couldn't see Ligozzi's *Martyrdom of Saint Lawrence*. Though he might as well have skipped it for all the pleasure it gave him today.

I must give vent to my feelings on painting. All these great painters lack expressiveness. The figures they depict engage in extraordinary activities with calm blank faces. Even the beheadings of John the Baptist are tame.

So many of them — Domenichino, Albani, even Titian — seem incapable of rendering passion or complex emotion. And yet they must have had feelings themselves, they lived in a country with a rich language of gesture — why weren't their paintings more expressive? If visitors find them 'divine', it's only because they've read it in their guidebooks (or been told so by some windbag smelling of stale sweat, like today's cicerone).

I'm not saying that these judgements are true for you who read me, but they are for me, M.H.B., born in 1783, and knocked about by eleven years of experience.

He's flouting received opinion, and his readers may feel he lacks discernment. But it's time someone questioned that unthinking adulation of the old masters, someone capable of examining what he really feels in front of a work of art and brave enough to state it honestly.

The valet is hovering. Time for the afternoon round. He rushes to get down everything else he wants to say, however illegibly. His thoughts flow so much faster than his pen that he loses them if he writes carefully. Ideally, he'd dictate them, but you can only be frank if you write for yourself, and even then caution is warranted. There's no knowing what use might be made of his journal if it fell into the wrong hands.

Later, there's time to write a little more while he waits for dinner. He'd returned to Santa Croce but the sibyl wasn't quite as perfect as he remembered, though the *Limbo* still enchanted him — at least until some common fellow came up and started to explain it. *I told him to get himself fucked, and walked away disdainfully.*

Perhaps it was just as well: the painting couldn't have had the same effect in his fault-finding mood today. But has he been too severe, he asks himself, rereading his earlier comments. What proof does he have that his taste is better than the standard authorities? Absolutely none.

There may be no more than a handful of individuals in Europe who think as he does and he'd love to meet them. As for the rest, who stick to the conventional line about the arts, he feels nothing but scorn for them, which would probably be mutual, so it's as well they're unacquainted.

Of course, his judgement may change, because he's starting to see that things he thought ridiculous and unnatural have a purpose — the red highlights in Rubens, for instance, designed to help the short-sighted like himself. (He really needs glasses for anything that's not at eye level, but that would be the final catastrophe for a face like his. Hello glasses, goodbye girls, as the saying goes.)

Nonetheless, there are paintings he'll never enjoy, like that *Martyrdom of Saint Lawrence*. The lack of expression was ludicrous: the saint on the grid over the hot coals, his back starting to roast but nothing on his face to show it, and the other figures crammed so close that the Roman magistrate would literally suffocate in the smoke.

But here's the waiter with his dinner. Finally, a piece of meat from a beast that hasn't died of old age, and fried potatoes just as he likes them instead of the eternal macaroni. Schneider's inn lives up to its reputation.

Restored, he picks at a bunch of grapes. The walk at the end of the afternoon had done him good. The beautiful view of the Arno from the terrace of the Boboli Gardens brought back memories of the Danube and his excursion to Leopoldsberg with Lady A. two years ago — a rare moment of intimacy though he'd been too shy to make the most of it. They'd gone in a group (her husband too busy with the emperor to join them), but she'd singled him out as her escort. Was it because the family connection made it more fitting that he (rather than a mere acquaintance) should lift her down from her horse, or did she want to be held in his arms? Whatever the case, he'd been too timid and too concerned for her safety to take advantage of the privilege. She was in a strangely reckless mood, exhilarated by the gallop, insistent on climbing to the roof terrace of one of the little pavilions, though it meant clambering up a ladder through a trapdoor and crawling across the tiles.

It gave them an extraordinary view — Vienna in the distance and below them the Danube's many channels snaking round islands and sandbars. Remembering it now as he waits for coffee, he sketches a river flowing in a deep serpentine curve round a hill. Something curious strikes him: boats on opposite sides of the hill would appear to be travelling in different directions — one north, the other south — though ultimately both are borne on the same current towards the sea.

This river explains to me how two souls of the same nature but with different levels of intelligence can clash. For example, Mme . . . He scratches out the name he's written till it's illegible, and in memory of the ride to Leopoldsberg writes, *Mme Lb. and I are not dissimilar in sensibility, but lacking my scepticism she believes our directions are opposed.* He draws an arrow on the river pointing north and labels it L, then adds a southward one labelled B for himself. *So I am nothing to her. With a little insight we'd recognise that we're destined to understand each other.*

He's scarcely thought about her in the last few weeks, but now he wonders what will happen when he sees her again. Will his love for her revive, or has Angela taken her place? His little boat has travelled farther downstream on the river of life, and all these new experiences have changed him.

Studying his sketch, he sees a further application. Just as a river's course is altered by some obstacle in the terrain through which it flows, so too the natural inclination of a mind may be redirected by the discovery of some new truth. His sensibility hasn't altered but his thinking has. What he wanted from art twelve years ago would sicken him now. But enough of this — it's time to call on cousin Adèle.

POSTSCRIPT It's midnight but he must write to relieve his feelings. Adèle had given him a chilly welcome that confirmed his view of the Parisian heart. No wonder he prefers Italians! Even her cook had shown him more of the simple human interest that you'd expect from a normal person on meeting unexpectedly after four years. Of course, his visit was ill-timed — Adèle was in bed, recovering from her recent delivery (the infant in its cradle beside her, mercifully asleep). An awkward situation and he'd talked too much. It was a shock to see the slim young girl of his memories metamorphosed into this softer, heavier creature (with a nicely rounded bosom, he couldn't help noticing). At least she had the grace to invite him for lunch tomorrow.

But the meeting revived bad memories. How unhappy she'd made him — or rather, how unhappy he'd made himself because of her. Such a child he was back then, and in the intimidating world of Paris she'd been like a younger sister until their camaraderie became something more. For him at least. A kiss was a kiss, and she'd given him a lock of her hair. Of course, it could never have led to marriage. With her dowry of twenty thousand francs, she and her mother had their sights set higher. Adèle had simply been flirting, practising her first moves in the adult world. Those tender moments which counted so much for him had clearly meant nothing to her. Like the night they'd watched the fireworks at the Café Frascati and she'd leant on his shoulder. One of the three happiest moments in his life, he'd felt at the time. What a fool he was. He should have refused her invitation to lunch.

MILAN, FRIDAY 27 SEPTEMBER

It is four weeks today since I left Nogent. Maddalena reported this morning that her brother saw me at La Scala last night and said that I looked charming. I must admit that it reassured me, though I do not take his compliments seriously. This afternoon I called on Mme Picard to thank her.

The Picard apartment was in a former palazzo now occupied by some branch of the new administration. A dusty shabbiness of offices and clerks had infiltrated the lower level, but the upper floor retained its former elegance, and the salon in which Mme Picard received her friends could accommodate a crowd. At one end stood a pianoforte and a harp with a circle of chairs; at the other, sofas enclosed a more intimate space. The books on a low table included *Corinne*, which provided a convenient topic since she was the first visitor.

'How do you find Mme de Staël's portrait of Italy?'

'Pure romance! An Italy of the imagination without the dirt, ignorance and thievery. And the heroine is a creature of fantasy: a woman who conducts herself with all the *liberty* for which her author is reputed.'

'So the freedom that Mme de Staël attributes to Italian women is exaggerated, you think?'

'Oh, no doubt a half-foreigner such as Corinne may travel in the company of a Scottish lord without fearing ostracism. The extravagant behaviour of wealthy foreigners has always been tolerated here for mercenary reasons. But an Italian woman would be excluded from good society were she to permit herself such freedom.'

The arrival of other visitors interrupted them. Then Monsieur Picard came in with news of the army's autumn manoeuvres, which brought an anxious look to the face of a quiet self-conscious young woman sitting beside her mother.

'Nothing can happen before spring,' the mother said quickly. 'It's impossible to do anything in the Russian winter. And there's still every possibility that war will be averted.'

'A young wife must not regret her husband's chance of promotion even if it deprives her of his attentions,' said Picard, giving the girl a roguish look. 'But there's no cause for alarm. The Russians haven't forgotten the lesson we taught them at Austerlitz. The emperor has only to make a sufficient show of force, and the tsar will capitulate.'

Conversation focused on military affairs for a while. It made her feel her distance from the preoccupations that governed these women's lives. News she might hear with a gravity detached from any personal involvement was of the highest significance to them, for it could spell imminent separation. For that reason, perhaps, conversation soon turned to lighter topics.

She'd half hoped that Larocque would be among the gentlemen callers, but as she turned into Contrada Passerella on her way home, she saw him walking towards her.

'What a happy chance,' he exclaimed. 'I have just left a note to wish you a good journey. Would you have time to take coffee?'

They made their way, not to the fashionable café on the Corsia dei Servi (for which she was grateful) but to a small place where the few customers were engrossed in their newspapers.

'There was talk of war with Russia at Mme Picard's. Do you think it inevitable?' she asked.

He frowned. 'I hope that it will not come to that. It would be absolute folly to engage in a new war in the east while we are still fighting in Spain. But the Russians are seeking a confrontation. It's not just that they're breaking the embargo against English goods by reopening their ports to neutral ships — they've now imposed tariffs on French imports. That's a provocation that the emperor will not ignore. It's no secret that he's building up troops in Poland. We've been ordered to acquire waggons for the supply train that will accompany the Italian army north.'

'If war is declared, will you have to go with them?'

'I hope not. A good part of our forces will remain here. The emperor cannot leave Italy unguarded.'

'But I thought his marriage precluded any further threat from Austria?'

'The threat is internal.' He glanced around and lowered his voice. There'd been peasant uprisings fomented by priests angered by the arrest of the pope. And there were armed groups in the hills, officially passed off as bandits but probably young men evading conscription.

'I saw nothing alarming on my journey here,' she said nervously. 'And Milan seems calm.'

'We have fifteen thousand French soldiers garrisoned here to keep it so. But this is a gloomy subject. Tell me how you found the opera. I trust that it didn't shock you too much. We who live here have become inured to the indecency of Milanese humour — we forget its impact on a newcomer.'

'It was a little coarse at moments, but the performance was very lively.' She did not want him to think her a prude.

'Did you have much conversation with Mme Delavigne? I think that you'd like her — she shares your interest in the arts.'

'She is certainly very knowledgeable about music. I don't believe I met her husband. Is he not a music lover?'

'I'm afraid he spent his evening at the gaming tables below. Gambling is a particular vice among the officers here. His wife has endured a great deal. She's a very talented musician — I hope that you'll have a chance to hear her play one evening.'

'That would be a pleasure,' she said, though she was reminded unpleasantly of Marie-Cécile and the heavy pounding of the pianoforte behind the closed door of the salon on days when Marie-Cécile withdrew into a sullen hostility of which she'd felt her own unwanted presence to be the principal cause. 'I have had few opportunities to hear music.'

'Then I hope that you will have many more. We are promised concerts at the new institute this autumn. There you will hear music as it should be heard, without interruption. La Scala, as you saw, is a place for social intercourse at the expense of music. I only go because otherwise I'd be as solitary as a bear.'

'Those of us who are by nature solitary always feel obliged to apologise for our preference, but is it really a defect?'

'In my case, yes. I'm a surly character except with the few who know how to tame me.'

She'd laughed, while wondering if Mme Delavigne was among the privileged few, but they continued talking so easily that she felt he'd exaggerated his lack of sociability.

Late that night, having packed a bag for the journey, she writes a last few words in her journal before locking it in her trunk to await her return.

I feel a little anxious at leaving this room which has come to feel a haven. It will be harder still to leave it when I set off for Rome. But I am in no hurry to depart. There is still so much to see at the Brera and elsewhere, and the promise of concerts this winter tempts me to prolong my stay. In any case, I have retained my room till the end of October. I need not make a decision yet.

En route to Rome, Saturday 28 September

On the move again, through a grey-green monotone of olive groves. The courier, accustomed to nights on the road, soon falls asleep. He tries to do likewise, but his thoughts keep returning to Adèle. Marriage and motherhood haven't softened her sharp tongue, and her complacent awareness that she's married a man on the rise is sickening. Alexandre, she announced, would be named Baron Petiet in the next official bulletin, and his youngest brother had just been appointed first page to the emperor. Of course it helped to have had a father high up in the administration, instead of a sheep breeder like his own! He tries to console himself with the thought that he's at the centre of things in Paris. But Italy is where he longs to be, and it's too late now: all the best appointments have gone. Florence is wasted on Alexandre. The man's a nullity. What maddens him most is knowing that the position might have been his. Alexandre is only a year older but has several years' advance on him, having dutifully followed the path through the École polytechnique and army that he'd abandoned, and served in enough junior positions to be eligible for this post. And then of course he's married advantageously, though Adèle's dowry is nothing compared to the 500,000 francs that Chancenie brought Martial Daru.

At least Adèle kept a good French cook. A small boy was brought in by his nurse to be displayed — another Napoleon like Mme Daru's. How many thousands of them were now waving toy swords or staring at strangers with precocious arrogance? This one at least was soon dismissed to the nursery. Adèle is less indulgent than Mme Daru, whose children are always with her.

But two in three years! There also, he might have been in Alexandre's place, a paterfamilias at twenty-eight. He isn't sorry to have been spared that burden, however much he envies Alexandre in other respects. Marriage is unlikely to figure in his own immediate future. Attempts to arrange a match for him came to nothing and it was just as well. The girl was nice but dull, the product of a conventional upbringing, her dowry the only thing that could recommend her. In any case, he didn't meet the mother's ambitions. The catch is that while the right marriage would assist his rise to a prefecture or intendancy, without some such position to impress the parents he hasn't a hope of finding a wealthy bride. An intendant needs a private income, especially in the new territories where you must entertain lavishly to woo the local elite. Without it, you're likely to get stuck for life in some provincial hole, which will probably be his own fate.

Stop it, he tells himself. He's falling back into the obsessive thoughts about his future that Italy had banished.

It's hard to resist the pull of ambition, though he's always known it for a sad passion that oppresses those in its grip. Men like Jacqueminot at the office — perpetually discontent, his dull face only coming to life when he reads them some memorandum he's written to contradict Count Daru. And Daru himself not the happiest of men, raging at his underlings because he's terrified of the emperor's rage. Louis Joinville is another — what an enviable life he might have led if he'd been content to stay in Milan as a commissary. A mistress like Angela would be worth the sacrifice of a career. What a woman! A body that any sculptor would want as a model, finer than all the statues he saw in

Florence. Not that a sculptor could do her justice. How could marble capture the mobility of that face in which the constant animation of thought and emotion reveals a soul?

He must find a way to return at whatever cost, and rent a room next time (since it's out of the question she risk her reputation by coming to his inn), somewhere secluded where they can meet soul to soul in those tender moments after desire is sated.

But as though the vehicle has hit a bad pothole, the recollection of Widmann jars his fantasy. How can he compete with a rival who'll continue to see her daily? Will Turcotti's surveillance keep Widmann at bay? Or will Widmann outwit Turcotti as he himself did? It's like the plot of a comic opera — in which he may not be the hero.

Still, Widmann hasn't prevailed so far, while he reached his goal in a mere three weeks. And he'll keep himself in her thoughts this winter with amusing letters from Paris. It was his wit that charmed her, and wit can be exercised from afar.

He starts composing the letter he'll write her from Rome, but the phrases run together like a blurred imprint on blotting paper till sleep finally obliterates them.

La Colombera, Saturday 28 September

A day of new impressions that I hasten to record before the oil in my tiny lamp burns out.

Thankfully she's alone, in the room that would have been occupied by Maddalena's eldest brother and his wife, whose imminent confinement has kept them at home. Somehow or other (little ones with parents, girl cousins together, boys and young men in the hayloft), an extra sixteen individuals have been absorbed into the Locatelli household, including a complete stranger like herself welcomed as Maddalena's friend into this family reunion.

We left at dawn and met the rest of the family at the city gate; after distributing children among the four vehicles our caravan set off. Mid-morning we turned north up the valley of the Olona. Glimpses of the river and its watermills among the trees. The Indian corn has long been harvested, but clover fields still scent the air with late bloom. Women were turning the last crop of hay. The Alps on the horizon throughout the journey.

Her pleasure in the countryside had been slightly troubled, however.

'Don't mention our plans to anyone, will you?' Maddalena said — in French, though Pierino was too busy teasing his cousin Marco to attend to their conversation. 'I haven't told my mother that we're going to Lake Maggiore — she thinks we're just making a pilgrimage to the Sacro Monte.'

'I should not like to deceive your mother.'

'Don't worry, you will not be obliged to lie: since she knows nothing, she will ask no questions. And when we return I'll simply tell her that we decided to go as far as the lake since we were already halfway there.'

She felt uneasy, but Maddalena's chin had the same stubborn tilt as her son's when he was determined to get his way.

They reached the farm mid-afternoon. Like others she'd seen from the road, it was a two-storeyed brick building composed of four wings enclosing an inner courtyard that they entered through an archway, scattering ducks and chickens. Two wings sheltered carts and implements; the other two housed animals and people. An outside staircase gave access to a covered balcony running the length of one wing, which was picturesquely strung with the drying cobs of next year's seedcorn. Signora Rossi's eldest brother and his family lived there with the grandparents and ran the farm.

Their arrival brought the women from the porch where they were shelling beans. Inside the large central room, where the evening soup was simmering in a cauldron over the hearth, the grandparents awaited them — an old man, bowed and stiffened by years of labour, and his alert snowy-haired wife, who greeted the Milanese contingent of great-grandchildren with her blessing.

After the heat and dust of the road the adults were grateful to sit in the cool dim interior, but the children were eager to roam.

'Come and see the puppies, Signorina,' Pierino begged.

'Let the signorina rest!' his mother commanded. But she was glad of the excuse to escape a conversation in country dialect of which she understood very little. The puppies were lazing in a patch of sun beside the stables, but one whose unmatched ears gave him a roguish look came gambolling towards them. Pierino seized the small squirming body. 'He's the boldest.'

'He'll be a good ratter,' said a cousin who was stabling their mules. 'We call him Lupetto.'

They played with the puppies awhile, then went to see the pig, a massive creature oblivious to his imminent fate who refused to stir in spite of the boys' ungentle prodding. By the time they were called for supper, she'd seen the cows being milked and watched with the same horrified fascination as Pierino while a fat hen was isolated from her fellows, carried squawking and flapping to the block and beheaded with a single efficient blow for the Sunday pot.

She found herself thinking of Larocque. When he'd spoken of his desire to farm she'd imagined it through the filter of Roman pastoral verse. But now she'd seen and smelt what the poets left out — the chicken droppings and the manure heap, the flies in the privy, all the inescapable squalor of breeding and slaughter. Yet it had its undeniable pleasures. Looking down over the fields to the green line of willows along the river and up over the roofs and bell tower of the village to the vineyards on the opposite slope, she could see why he might choose such a life.

'We must find you some country clothes,' Maddalena exclaimed at the sight of her dusty petticoat when they returned.

The men of the family came in from their labour and we gathered for the evening meal (vegetable soup and a wedge of polenta). It was an entirely new experience for me (only child and all my grandparents dead before my birth) to see four generations round the same table. Kneeling for the rosary afterwards, I could hear the animals shifting on the other side of the wall that divides the room from the stable.

I am clearly an object of curiosity to these country folk, perhaps the first French person they have seen other than a soldier. I smile a lot to compensate for my inability to speak their dialect. It reminds me of Mrs Godwin's account of her stay with a Swedish family. This opportunity to participate in the everyday life of an Italian household is not granted to the majority of travellers, who meet only innkeepers and servants.

With a final quiver the lamp flame dies, forcing her to undress in the dark. The room has a dusty nose-tickling smell of whatever is stored in the bales against the wall, but she cannot open the shutters for fresh air since the window gives onto the communal balcony. The mattress crackles as she stretches out (straw or corn husk, pray heaven no lice), but the coarse sheets smell of sun and fresh air, and she's dabbed herself all over with lavender oil to repel the inevitable fleas. Despite her fatigue she's not sleepy yet. Words run through her mind — scraps of dialect that she's trying to retain and a mass of unrecorded detail jostling for outlet like the carts at the city gate this morning. She would like to describe it all for Larocque, but where would she post a letter here? In Varese perhaps, but it would make her friends curious. She must save her impressions until they meet again.

SUNDAY, FEAST OF SAINT MICHAEL THE ARCHANGEL *Entering the village church this morning, I compared the people with their counterparts in Nogent. Here, too, the old are bent and twisted by a lifetime's labour, but there are more handsome faces and a greater animation, unlike the brutish endurance that often marks faces in the north. The cause, I suspect, is not some innate temperamental difference between north and south, but the better living offered by this fertile land. Even here though, the poorest look ill-nourished, and some bear signs of a skin ailment that is said to be common among those who consume only polenta. The vehemence of the sermon surprised me, though I did not learn its import till later, for the priest addressed the people in their dialect.*

He was an imposing figure, stern as the archangel with the sword whose feast they were celebrating. Though she caught little beyond the invocation of San Michele and the words *Satan* and *Antichrist*, she was fascinated by his performance. His right hand rose heavenwards with every reference to the archangel, then descended, palm and fingers outspread as if to push down some rebellious element, only to rise again with the index finger shaken in admonition, while the left hand, extended outwards, was flung wide in question or exclamation. Finally he raised both arms heavenwards, approaching the crescendo. She glanced sideways at Maddalena who rolled her eyes expressively. Signora Rossi further down the row looked as if she'd been struck by lightning.

As they walked back to the farm with the other women, she could hear an argument among the men. 'The sermon has stirred them up,' Maddalena whispered. 'I'll tell you later.'

After lending a hand with the morning chores, they escaped for a walk with Giovanni. Pierino had gone off with his cousins, revelling in the freedom of the fields.

'He's a cunning rascal, that priest.' Giovanni pulled a tall weed from the side of the path, nervously stripping its leaves as they walked. 'He said nothing directly but everyone knew what he meant.'

'Did you understand anything?' Maddalena asked her.

'Only a word or two.'

'It was all religion on the surface,' Giovanni said. 'How San Michele threw Satan out of Heaven, the usual story. But then he warned that Satan and the forces of the Antichrist are active here on Earth, engaged in a great struggle at this very moment with our holy mother the Church. You get his meaning?'

She did, all too well. 'The emperor should never have arrested the pope.'

'And then he said that many who think themselves good Christians are allied with the forces of darkness.'

'It frightened Mamma,' said Maddalena. 'She prays every day for God to punish the emperor. But now this priest as good as says that trading with the French is aiding Satan. Father says it's nonsense, of course.'

'I hope your mother does not place me among the forces of evil,' she said, uneasy at being identified as a citizen of a state to which in reality her allegiance was anything but simple.

'You're going to make the pilgrimage to the Sacro Monte — that puts you on the side of the angels,' Giovanni assured her. But she felt just as uncomfortable to be credited with a piety she didn't possess.

Fortunately, the sermon was soon forgotten in the pleasures of the feast day. The polenta was more appetising with a sauce of freshly gathered mushrooms, though as she ate her share of boiled fowl she had to suppress an image of blood dripping from the severed head.

Other family members had come up from the village to join them and conversation turned to births and marriages. 'And you, Giovanni,' a cousin asked. 'Why aren't you betrothed yet?'

'I haven't found a woman willing to take me.' The mock despondency on his handsome face made everyone laugh.

'Who'd want a rascal like you!' his brother asked

'He's still young,' Signora Rossi protested.

'He's twenty-eight — if he waits too long all the pretty girls will be taken,' the cousin said.

'Why do you married folk want to see the rest of us in chains like yourselves?' he protested. 'There's more to life than settling down. I want to see the world before I die.'

'God preserve you!' Signora Rossi crossed herself.

Even before Maddalena's translation, she'd grasped the import of the exchange. The cousins in their patched and faded work clothes were constantly joking at Giovanni's expense, mimicking the way he tossed his long hair off his forehead, teasing him for his lady's hands. She was interested in the contrast between town and country cousins, but it would be indelicate to write about these people while she's their guest. She sticks to generalities.

I had conceived of my journey to Italy as a passage back in time, to antiquity and the Renaissance, yet if I were to publish my impressions I believe that the present condition of the country might interest the public as much as — if not more than — the landscapes and monuments that have been so often described.

But I was naïve not to have foreseen the awkwardness that a traveller from France must feel visiting Italy at this juncture. Preoccupied with my own misfortunes, I have paid too little attention to the great changes taking place here and elsewhere, which now, whether I like it or not, I am forced to consider. My friends shelter me from any hostility I might incur, but I cannot help wondering what it will be like when I set off alone.

Rome, Monday 30 September

When the Angelus bell woke him at first light, he was unsure for a moment where he was. He'd taken a room at an inn, unwilling to mar his first evening with social obligations, and hurried to see Saint Peter's before nightfall. Impressive, though less than he'd expected. He was more struck by the people, the proud independence of ancient Rome still visible in those faces — the powerful nose, the jutting chin, the challenge in the eyes. They wouldn't accept a new government as easily as the practical Milanese, who knew where their interests lay. He was eager to hear Martial's report of the situation.

Bathed and breakfasted, he called for a fiacre and set off for the Quirinal. His cousin was certainly well lodged, he thought, as they halted in front of the palace. At the portal (where the imperial eagle had replaced the papal insignia), he presented his card to the officer on duty and was escorted to the intendant's quarters. He was curious to see his cousin in this new role, but apprehensive. He'd once felt more affection for this man than any other he knew. Martial had been his mentor, his model of how to conduct himself with women, and a true friend, interceding on his behalf with his elder brother when he was in disgrace. But the dignity of Martial's new position might come between them.

He needn't have worried. His cousin embraced him warmly. 'Henri, old man, how are you? We guessed you were on your way — there's post from Milan for you.'

His heart beat faster but he put the letter in his pocket to savour later.

'Come and see Chancenie, then I'll show you around,' Martial said.

She was at her desk attending to correspondence, and their boisterous arrival startled her. Her pale rather earnest face assumed a welcoming smile, and as usual he wondered if she disliked him. 'You'll stay with us, of course,' she said.

'I'm at an inn — I didn't want to disturb you. But I'll gladly accept your hospitality on my return from Naples,' he said quickly, so they wouldn't take offence.

'Naples?' Martial shook his head. 'The roads are much too dangerous at present. The Florence courier was attacked two nights ago.'

'Yes, I heard about it last night. I had a narrow escape — it was the courier with whom I'd have travelled if the seat hadn't been taken. Nasty trick those scoundrels played!' The postilion had spotted a body on the road but, suspecting a trap, didn't stop, though he had to rein in the horses to avoid it. Before they could gather speed again, several men by the roadside had grabbed the reins. The courier and passenger were forced face down on the road, the passenger robbed of two hundred louis. The 'corpse' was, of course, one of the band.

'Wait until the authorities have organised a convoy,' Martial advised.

'But I have to be back in Paris four weeks from now. I can't miss Naples.'

Martial's caution surprised him. Was this the man with whom he'd ridden across the defeated German states five years ago? There were still flashes of the old irreverent wit as they toured the palace, but responsibility had sobered him; his chubby boyish face showed incipient jowls, his temples were greying.

The building was in urgent need of renovation before the emperor's visit in the spring. Its ceilings were cracked by recent earthquakes, its grand salons partitioned into apartments. An odour of fusty celibacy clung to the old-fashioned furnishings and the art was manifestly unsuitable, as Martial pointed out: 'The emperor won't want Moses or Elijah scowling at him.' He'd commissioned the best painters in Rome to replace them with Caesar and Alexander. The renovation was a godsend for artists. Before the war, they could make a living off the English; every milord wanted his portrait painted and a Venus to take home. But there were few travellers now, and even the market for sacred art had diminished since the monastic closures.

They reached a spacious salon with windows on three sides. This was to be the emperor's office.

'You don't need anything on the walls with a view like this!' he exclaimed.

The whole of Rome lay below them. Domes, cupolas, bell towers rose above the rooftops in a harmonious blend of terracotta, white and grey among the green of vineyards and gardens, against a horizon of blue hills. Martial identified the landmarks, his stocky figure acquiring new dignity as he surveyed twenty-five centuries of history on which he too would leave his imprint.

'You're a fortunate man!'

'It's not the ideal posting you imagine. Fever is rampant here — I had to send Chancenie and the children away for the hottest months. It's a primitive place in many ways, a city of contradictions — magnificent architecture and human excrement under every portico!'

Yes, he'd noticed the stench, but up here on the hill you could escape it. And Rome was still extraordinary. If only he'd been chosen as Martial's assistant! It reminded him that he hadn't seen his lucky colleague yet.

'How's Nanteuil?'

'Gone back to Paris.' Martial frowned. 'I advised him to wait for authorisation, but he claimed to have urgent reasons for returning. My brother won't be pleased.'

It gave him a moment's disquiet, given his own irregular departure. But if Nanteuil asked to be relieved of his duties, there might still be a chance for himself. Except that he wasn't there to solicit it — and others were! He must get Martial on his side.

At lunch with Chancenie and the children, whose babble dominated conversation, he was reminded of his first meal in Milan. 'Remember, Martial? You took me to the Casa Bovara and ordered *cotolette alla milanese*. I've just renewed my acquaintance with someone from those days . . . You must recall Mme Pietragrua?'

'The name seems familiar, but we had so many friends in Milan.' Martial's tone warned him not to pursue the subject in Chancenie's presence, and it turned bitter when he added, 'We never doubted our welcome there.'

'Tell me,' he asked, once they were alone again, 'has Rome not received you as warmly as the *Moniteur* proclaims?'

Martial's face lost its jovial air. 'You want the truth? We gave a ball to celebrate the birth of the king of Rome, invited everyone who counts. Three hundred polite regrets! Only a few accepted, like the Duchess Lante. Superb woman! You'll meet her tonight — we have a reception Monday evenings.'

He'd hoped that Martial would ask after Mme Pietragrua and give him an opening for a discreet boast, but once started on the subject of Roman resistance Martial couldn't be stopped. Nobody had foreseen the difficulty of establishing secular government, he said. It wasn't enough to exile clergy who refused the oath of loyalty; they still exercised invisible influence. 'The faithful fear damnation if they so much as sip our champagne!' Then there were the papal functionaries who'd lost their jobs, not to speak of the monks and nuns from the abolished orders, and the poor who'd depended on their charity. 'We've pulled down the old system too fast. Some of my colleagues are more fanatical than priests in their reforming zeal.'

Outside the window a perfect afternoon faded as he listened to Martial's complaints. Back at his inn to change, he opened his letter. It was disappointingly brief. Angela was melancholy. Was it all a dream, she asked.

He'd rather have spent his evening wandering the streets, but he couldn't skip the reception. It was a mixed group, French and Roman, with a sprinkling of architects and artists to leaven the dough of officialdom. He avoided contact with the latter — the fewer people in authority who knew about his journey the better. But he couldn't escape being presented to General Miollis, the acting governor. Fortunately, Miollis was more interested in a dark-eyed Roman beauty who hung on his every word. She turned out to be the Duchess Lante. Martial introduced him as a passionate admirer of Italian music.

'Then you must come to our Thursday concert, Monsieur.' Her French had a delicious Italian lilt. 'We're just a few friends who sing together for pleasure, you understand, but if there is something you would like to hear we will add it to our programme.'

'You are most gracious, Madame. You would bring back the happiest moments of my life with anything from *Il Matrimonio Segreto*.' He wanted to amuse her with the story of his first opera, but another lady joined them, addressing her in Italian as though he weren't there.

'Do you have any news, *cara*?'

'General Miollis has obtained a postponement. Filippo may remain at home until his health improves.'

So that was why she'd been charming Miollis. 'Has the Duchess's son been conscripted?' he asked Martial later, as they admired the moonlit city from the emperor's future office.

'No, His Majesty has decreed that the sons of the Roman nobility are to be educated in France.' Martial hesitated. 'I fear that he has not been fully informed of the resistance here. We cannot afford to jeopardise our relations with the elite. The legitimacy of our government depends on their support. The official justification is that we must form capable men among the younger generation. At present they're educated by priests — more stress on piety than science and mathematics. You can imagine!'

He could indeed, remembering how his tutor, Abbé Raillane, had taught him Ptolemy's long outdated astronomy simply because the Church approved it.

'It's a long way to send a child of eight! Who can blame a mother for resisting? But Miollis can't postpone the boy's departure indefinitely. The duchess will have to exercise her charms at the highest level when the emperor comes. That's if war with Russia doesn't postpone his visit — frankly I almost hope it will, given all we still have to do here.'

Martial fell silent, gazing out across the sleeping city. On the skyline, the dome of Saint Peter's, eternal and invincible, rivalled the full moon in majesty.

La Colombera, Monday 30 September

We rose at dawn to begin harvesting the grapes before the heat of day. Maddalena lent me a skirt and blouse of the kind the peasants wear. The loose blouse is comfortable in the heat, but the skirt is shorter than I am accustomed to which made me self-conscious, though I soon discovered its convenience in the fields. Signora Locatelli found a pair of sabots that fitted me more or less.

The farm produces wine only for the family's consumption, but all hands are needed to bring in the grapes. The men pick from the vines trained up the trees, while the women gather those that border every field.

She worked alongside Maddalena and Teresa, enjoying the novelty of the experience. At first she listened to their talk, hoping that by sheer exposure she would eventually understand Milanese, but her thoughts soon wandered. Giovanni came by at regular intervals and they emptied their baskets into the hod on his back. He too had shed his town clothes and with them the stiff bearing that a cravat and high collar imposed. But even in his open-necked shirt he would not be taken for a countryman; the city sharpness in his face betrayed him even more than his smooth, uncalloused hands, she thought, watching him when they ate their breakfast of cold polenta on the edge of the field.

Evidently he had similar thoughts about her own transformation. 'Country dress becomes you, signorina. You're like the mistress who changes clothes with her maid in the opera. But no one would mistake you for anything but what you are.'

And what was that, she wondered uneasily. What did Giovanni perceive behind the mask of Marie Vernet?

It was time to return to work. Halfway up the field, the other women relieved themselves behind a mulberry hedge, but she was too embarrassed to follow them until her need became urgent. Whatever hardships she'd endured in exile, she'd always clung to certain privacies, but here among these countryfolk she had no choice but to adopt their natural attitude to bodily functions. When nature called, the mistress was no different from the maid.

'Watch out for wasps!' Maddalena called as she resumed picking. The sun was hot now and there were still hours to go. She pulled her straw hat forward and adjusted her kerchief to protect her shoulders against sunburn. The work itself wasn't tiring but she was unaccustomed to being on her feet all day and they ached in the ill-fitting wooden clogs. She would have been more comfortable in her own kid boots, but she couldn't single herself out from the others.

The sounds of flute and fiddle met them on their return to the house. Two itinerant musicians had arrived to encourage the treaders, who were already immersed to mid-calf in a thick pulp from which a purplish liquid oozed. Their legs rose and fell in a kind of primitive dance to the tune of a blind fiddler, whose milky eyes turned upwards as if seeking inspiration in some invisible world. The boy who'd brought him played the flute, or sang in a high shrill untutored voice that was strangely affecting.

Soaping off the day's sweat with the other women in the wash house, she felt no more than a healthy fatigue, but by the time supper was done and they were kneeling on the hard brick floor for the rosary, she longed for bed. The repeated sequence of prayers, led by a cousin in a sing-song voice, seemed endless. Across the circle, Maddalena's younger sister Catarina — sleeping infant on her shoulder — had the air of a young Madonna, in contrast to the careworn face of Signora Locatelli, who bent humbly forward, hands locked in supplication. Maddalena's eyes were closed but her hands were firmly controlling Pierino, who knelt in front of her making faces at his cousin. At the far end of the circle, Signora Rossi, sensing an alien gaze, opened her eyes in a suspicious glare that made her hastily lower her own, though not before she'd seen that Giovanni, kneeling behind his mother, was as distracted as herself. Their eyes met for an instant, guilty in her case, conspiratorial in his.

Neither the journey nor my encounters in Milan have enlarged my experience as much as my participation in this field labour that is the lot of most of humanity. In England I earned money with the work of my hands, but embroidery is lady's work, and it was Jeannette who scrubbed the floor and carried up coal and water. I no longer believe that it is the will of Providence that some are born to labour for others. But I cannot see how the world can change.

Towards the end of the day I stopped to admire the view. Around me, the purple and crimson foliage of the vines displayed the opulence of late summer while on the opposite slopes of the valley the woods are already sprinkled with russet and amber. On the field edge, bright patches of gold emblazon the mulberry trees, as though signalling the lucrative power of the silkworms they nourish. At least the peasants enjoy the ever-changing spectacle of nature, whatever else they lack. But despite the beauty of the scene, I felt rather melancholy. Though I am interested in these good people, I could never feel at home among them and I longed for a congenial mind with whom to share my thoughts.

Rome, Tuesday 1 October

Martial had promised a tour of the excavations, but he had business at the Vatican first. 'You might as well visit the Loggia while you wait.'

It was a long, painted gallery open on one side to the courtyard below with a view across the city to distant hills. Popes and cardinals had walked here, taking the air, pausing to admire the painted birds and animals among the exuberant festoons. Such a combination of elegance and naïveté in decoration was new to him. Overhead, in a scene from the Creation, God looked like a simple Tuscan shepherd surrounded by a flock of exotic animals.

'Enchanting, isn't it?' Martial was already back. 'But damp is affecting the paint. If something isn't done soon, it will be damaged beyond repair.' All the Vatican's treasures were at risk because the roof leaked. The popes had neglected it, like everything else in the city. The new Commission for the Embellishment of Rome, of which he was one of the three directors, had its hands full.

On their way to the Roman Forum, they stopped briefly at Trajan's Column. Darkened by the centuries, its reliefs were rendered unapproachable by the heap of decaying rubbish around the base.

'Romans dump their waste wherever convenient,' Martial said. 'They've done it for centuries. But we shall give the column the setting it deserves. All this will go . . .' With a wave of his arm, he swept away several houses and a convent. 'No problem with the convent — the order's dissolved — and we'll compensate the householders. The site has never been excavated. Just think what might lie twelve feet down!'

The emperor was hoping for some buried masterpiece to grace the museum in Paris. So far, however, they'd unearthed nothing but fragments; all the ruins had been pillaged in earlier centuries. An anxious frown played over Martial's face.

They drove on, down narrow streets that suddenly debouched onto an open grassy area. 'The "cow pasture", Romans call it,' Martial said. 'But we've banned grazing now.'

He stared about him, astounded. Though he'd seen prints of the forum, nothing prepared you for this graveyard of antiquity. In front of him stood a triumphal arch, with saplings sprouting among the weeds along its top. But for every such survivor still standing, a dozen mounds and hollows showed where the rest lay buried.

All this was about to change. They headed towards a work site where the ground beneath three massive archways of an ancient basilica was being cleared The space had been used by an adjoining monastery to pen its livestock. 'It's shocking what the papal authorities allowed,' Martial said. 'There was a fish market under the portico of the Pantheon!'

A cloud of dust hung over the site, where some fifty labourers were at work, among them women and children. 'Is male labour so scarce?' he asked, watching a barefoot woman with a basket of debris balanced on her head. There was an infant in the shawl tied to her bosom.

'We don't turn away anyone able-bodied — it's a form of poor relief, you understand. Better a spade in hand than a begging bowl. And eventually the whole forum will be a park for the common people of Rome.'

No doubt the excavation of the forum was an achievement for which the new French government would be honoured by future generations, but personally he was glad to have seen it in its present condition. The weed-covered ruins, the columns buried like Dante's sinners up to their necks, made tangible the passage of time. Cleaned and preserved, they'd risk becoming lifeless exhibits in a museum.

Nonetheless, he envied Martial as they approached the Coliseum. Here was a project into which he could throw himself wholeheartedly (unlike the reprimanding of a concierge who'd neglected to place dust covers on the furniture during the emperor's absence). Its immensity stunned him. No women labouring here, but convicts in leg irons. The upper galleries and the entire northern section were now almost completely cleared and next would be the arena itself. But the expense of moving such huge loads of debris was eating up his budget, Martial complained. Those in Paris had no idea what a Herculean task it was. And the prefect wanted to put flower beds around the outside! The Coliseum was not a rose garden.

The afternoon was drawing to a close. His cousins, thankfully, had a dinner engagement, so the evening was his. He said he'd make his own way back. 'Don't stay too long,' Martial warned. 'There's a guard on the site, but it isn't safe after dark.'

He settled himself on a piece of fallen masonry. His notebook was in his pocket but he left it there, wanting to absorb the spirit of the place. The convicts were laying down their tools; in the silence that followed their departure, he heard a multitude of chirps above his head where small birds flitted in and out of the upper arcades.

As twilight fell, a single bird began its song. The notes echoed across the empty arena, taken up and answered by another farther away. For the first time he felt truly moved. One had to be alone to experience a place like this. A memory came to him of a blackbird singing from a rooftop that had filled him with hope one spring evening under the reign of Abbé Raillane, the poignancy of childhood longing intensified by the reminder emanating from these ancient ruins of the impermanence of things, of the long generations of dead turned to dust and ashes. It brought tears to his eyes, and yet he felt intensely happy that his soul was capable of such emotion still.

Darkness was falling as he left and the glow of a lantern lit a street sign: Via Alessandrina. He hadn't thought of her for a while. How much softer her name sounded in Italian, unlike the crisp formality of Alexandrine. Walking back to his inn among the evening strollers, his eyes lingered on one feminine face after another, in quest of something that none seemed to offer. It wasn't a girl he wanted tonight, but another soul.

Back in his room, he pulls out a sheet of letter paper. *Today I visited the Coliseum where the song of a bird on the highest arcade moved me to a degree that all the splendour of Saint Peter's could not achieve. The sight of the Via Alessandrina as I left prompted me to send you my respectful homage from the city of the Caesars.*

It's impossible to write freely to a woman whose husband reads all her post. He tears it up and starts a letter to Angela. But the impulse belongs elsewhere; he abandons it.

La Colombera, Tuesday 1 October

I knew nothing hitherto about the production of the staple crops on which we all depend, and even less about the conditions that govern the lives of the producers. Today I tried to ask 'men's questions' like Mrs Godwin.

They were eating the noonday polenta in the farthest field, sitting on the ground. 'Does the farm belong to your grandparents?' she asked Giovanni. The Locatelli family seemed the kind of energetic, enterprising people who might have managed to acquire land. Vigorous and long-lived too, unlike her own family which seemed destined to vanish even without the Revolution.

'No, the count owns it all — the land, the house, the tools. They give him half of everything they produce as rent.'

So nothing had changed here, yet. 'Does the count deal fairly with his tenants?'

'Better than most landlords, my uncle says. But he's very demanding — he's interested in new methods of cultivation and all his tenants have to follow his directions. Some of them grumble, but my uncle is willing to try new ways, and so is Tommaso. He's the eldest — the tall one over there. He's getting married next month to escape conscription. Fathers of dependent children are last on the list.'

'Tommaso will have to work fast,' Maddalena said to general laughter. 'Unless he's already made a start with Rosina!'

Such remarks made her feel conscious of being an outsider and not just because she was a little shocked. The talk of conscription was another reminder of the emperor's power, even if it was exercised under the auspices of the new Italian state. He could pluck young men from this peaceful valley and march them hundreds of leagues to engage in battle with other young men, probably simple peasants like themselves.

Was that why there'd been so few of them at Mass? Larocque had told her they were taking to the hills to escape conscription. Turning to a safer topic, she asked about the farm's most profitable crops.

'Wheat at present,' Giovanni said. 'It seems you've had a second year of bad grain harvests up north, so our farmers may get a better price. But I doubt that my uncle will confess it to the priest! Then there's the silk, though it no longer pays as well. It used to be exported to the German states and England. But now it all goes to Lyon, and their manufacturers set the price.'

She thought of Payot; kind though he was, he would strike a hard bargain.

It was time to return to work and Giovanni held out his hands to help her up, pulling her towards him as she rose, in the same flirtatious manner with which he treated his cousins. 'I know nothing about the production of silk,' she said, to cover her embarrassment. 'Except that silkworms live in mulberry trees.'

'They have to be reared indoors.' Maddalena was shocked by her ignorance. 'So the cocoons will be perfect — outdoors they'd get damaged by rain or birds. I'll show you where when we go back.'

It was long past the season, but they went up to the room on the second floor, directly above the heat of the hearth, where the silkworms were reared on wide shelves that now held only the empty reels.

'What happens to them afterwards?'

'Oh, they drown when the cocoons are put in the hot water. They're fed to the chickens.'

It made her feel squeamish. 'How is the silk extracted?'

'It's not easy. You have to find the end of the filament and start pulling, very gently, so as not to break it. Then you thread it onto the reel and begin winding. It's women's work — men's fingers don't have the dexterity. And it has to be done fast before the cocoons spoil.'

She thought of the dress she'd worn to the opera and wondered how many cocoons it had taken to produce it and how many hours of labour.

Tonight at supper I regarded Signora Locatelli and her daughters with new respect. Painstaking though it is, my embroidery is but the end of a laborious process of which I had hitherto no conception. There is a parallel between the silkworm and the workers whose skill extracts its luxurious thread, for just as the worms will never become moths, these women will never wear the product of their own hands, which all goes to beautify the rich. Admittedly, there is little occasion in the workers' lives for fine apparel, and such a delicate material would only draw attention to complexions coarsened by long hours in the sun and hands roughened by labour. But it seems unjust nonetheless.

My previous indifference to such matters shames me. I scorned the talk of trade at Armand's dinner table, but the well-being of the Locatelli family and their like depends on it. Uncomfortable as it is at moments, my sojourn among these country folk has opened my eyes to the importance of this essential part of society without which the rest could not survive.

Rome, Wednesday 2 October

I've seen Raphael's Loggia, he wrote to Pauline before going out, *and conclude that one should sell one's shirt to see it if one hasn't, or to see it again if one has.*

The day that followed confirmed his feeling that Rome was worth any sacrifice. In the morning, Martial took him to Canova's studio.

'A great man with the simple manners of an artisan,' Martial said. 'But obstinate! The emperor wants to make him director of the imperial museums in Rome. But Canova refuses the oath of allegiance. He'll work with us, but on his own terms: no salary, no oath. You know the penalties for refusing . . . Certain colleagues would arrest him immediately. But you can't coerce a great man: you have to win his loyalty.'

The visit to the studio overturned all his notions of the artist. On arrival, they were conducted to the inner sanctum and greeted by a stooped figure in a dusty coat putting the finishing touches to a Muse, his hair protected by a paper hat that would have made a lesser man ridiculous. Only the eyes — dark, piercing, deep-set beneath a jutting brow — suggested genius. He'd imagined a muscular Michelangelo alone with a block of marble, not this scarecrow. But Canova's health was impaired by years of labour. He now required a platoon of assistants to transform his original clay model into plaster and marble creations.

There was a certain pathos in the contrast between the ageing artist and the noble forms and flawless nudity of his creation. Humour too. At moments, as he showed them round the workshop, Canova sounded like a major-domo introducing eminent guests: 'The Empress Marie-Louise. The Grand Duchess of Tuscany. The emperor's mother . . . His Majesty keeps me busy,' he said, an ironic gleam in his eye. 'Not only have I the honour of portraying his family, but I must fill the pedestals he's emptied in our museums. He's taken the Medici Venus to Paris, but Florence shall have my *Venus Italica* to replace her!' He indicated a surprised nude clutching a drapery modestly to her front, leaving her rear provocatively exposed.

'The world will have gained another masterpiece, Monsieur,' Martial said smoothly.

Dare he admit that she was more to his taste than the Medici, he wondered, eyeing the taut buttocks. Was it art if it made your cock stir?

As if a morning with the greatest modern sculptor didn't suffice, it was followed by the Duchess Lante's musical evening, which proved far more than the salon entertainment he'd expected. The Palazzo Lante had its own private theatre where the duchess's talented friends performed an entire oratorio, Zingarelli's *The Destruction of Jerusalem*, concluding with some lighter pieces, including those he'd requested.

He applauded fervently along with the Italians present, but his compatriots seemed unaccountably restrained. Was Zingarelli's subject — the conquest of a small nation by a mighty empire — a little too near the bone? Or were they shocked to see a duchess perform? The two basses (each a duke or prince, no doubt) who sang the duo from *Il Matrimonio Segreto* had thrown themselves into their roles with all the buffoonery of practised comedians: a departure from the dignity of rank that would be inconceivable in Paris.

The duchess was mobbed by admirers. Finally his turn came. 'You have the voice of an angel, Madame.'

'You are too kind, Monsieur. I am just an amateur.' She was flushed from the performance, her eyes luminous.

Another Frenchman hovered impatiently. He'd noticed him earlier, a self-important talker. Small mean mouth, and something stealthy about the eyes, fixing you with an almost accusing look then sliding away. Let him wait his turn.

'It seemed to me, Madame, if I'm not mistaken, that certain passages in the *Jerusalem* might allude to recent events?'

'It's a purely religious work, Monsieur.'

She wouldn't be drawn. He changed his tack and complimented her on her singing style. 'Our French singers embellish every piece with superfluous ornament. One must come to Italy to learn the art of the natural. It's something of which we French have not the smallest understanding.'

'You are unjust to your compatriots, Monsieur,' she protested. 'I find them true connoisseurs. Monsieur de Norvins,' she turned to the eavesdropper, 'hasn't missed a single one of our concerts.' He sensed she was warning him. Could the fellow be her lover? He bowed coldly.

'Aren't you surprised,' Chancenie asked Martial, once they were safely in the carriage, 'that the duchess would dare perform a work by Zingarelli?'

So his intuition was correct. 'Is the subject too sensitive in present circumstances?'

'Zingarelli is in disgrace, didn't you know?' Martial said. 'He refused to conduct the "Te Deum" at the Sistine to celebrate the birth of the king of Rome. Norvins had him arrested!'

'Norvins?'

'Yes, the director-general of police. Then an order came to send him under guard to Paris. Can you imagine the scandal? Italy's greatest modern composer under arrest! So the prefect invited him to travel to Paris by whatever means he chose and Zingarelli gave his word of honour to do so. From what I hear, the emperor's anger has dissipated. They'll find some way to smooth it over.'

No wonder the duchess wouldn't be drawn with the director of police standing by. And he'd blundered in like an ignorant fool! What an act of defiance to perform the work at such a moment! She'd had seven lovers, Martial said. He would like to be the eighth!

La Colombera, Wednesday 2 October

Maddalena seemed agitated this morning and when I discovered the cause I shared her dismay.

'It will ruin our plans,' Maddalena burst out as soon as they were alone.

Giovanni put a warning finger to his lips. He'd left the men and fallen back to join them as they walked out to the fields. 'Don't oppose her, or she'll suspect something. It's a whim — she may change her mind.'

'Mamma wants to accompany us to the Sacro Monte,' Maddalena whispered. 'The priest has frightened her.'

'Will your father come too?' Then at least Signora Rossi would be in her own vehicle, not squeezed in beside them.

'Father isn't interested in a pilgrimage. He says the Virgin can hear her prayers just as well at home.'

'News from Pulcheria could change her mind,' Giovanni said.

'But then she'd make us go home for the baptism.' Maddalena seemed defeated.

She had shared Maddalena's resentment, suspecting that it was less piety that motivated Signora Rossi's sudden decision than the urge to curtail any sign of independence in her daughter. The day seemed longer, heavy with their disappointment.

When they returned to the farmhouse the music from the grape treading seemed faster and more urgent than on previous nights, but it made her sad: she would never be part of the dance to which it called all listeners. There was an immense golden harvest moon low in the sky and she longed to walk down to the river by herself, away from the shrill cries of the children and the incomprehensible jabber of competing voices around her.

Watching Signora Rossi at supper with Caterina's baby on her lap while his mother ate, she felt guilty for her earlier suspicions. How many infants the signora must have held and comforted over a lifetime. Perhaps her wish to pray at the Virgin's shrine arose from maternal anxieties that didn't cease when the children were grown. But there was no escaping the fact that her presence would take all the pleasure out of their excursion to Lake Maggiore, even if she agreed to it, which seemed unlikely. Maddalena and Giovanni might act behind her back, but they seemed incapable of standing up to her.

The respect owed to parents is even more piously observed here than in France. It is without question a primary social virtue, for otherwise what would happen to those who have given us life, and who deserve in old age the same care they bestowed upon us in youth. Yet it can lead to domestic tyranny when parents continue to rule the lives of their grown children, a tyranny all the harder to resist because religion and the law endorse it. No one can deny that parents would sacrifice themselves for their young, but do they not sometimes demand a similar sacrifice?

The lamp is nearly burnt out. She undresses quickly and gets into bed. The old temptation makes itself felt. Her hand slips under her nightgown and her mind enters the anarchic world of desire where anything is permitted. She's not alone there but she gives no name to the one she meets, though he's a familiar of her imagination. Perhaps he waits for her somewhere in the world. She imagines him lonely too.

On the Road, Thursday 3 October

Twilight is falling over grassland baked golden by summer; the only sign of life is an occasional herd of black cattle, watched by a solitary peasant leaning on a staff. Against the sunset sky, the broken line of a Roman aqueduct — sublime witness to the decay of empire.

His final hours had been taken up by social calls. The duchess, General Miollis . . . but not Norvins. If he'd given offence, it was too late to repair it; he wouldn't grovel to a man like that. A pity so much of his time had to be spent with his cousin. Success hadn't made Martial arrogant, but it had made him dull — obsessed with incompetent workers and obstructive colleagues, and the constant directives from Paris that took no account of conditions on the ground. And Chancenie, self-effacing like the good accompanist that she was, simply provided the continuo for his solo. When he remembered some of the women his cousin had had, he wondered if Martial wasn't bored with such devotion, though there was something rather touching about Chancenie's modest, slightly wistful smile.

The growing dusk makes him nervous. In daylight you have some hope of spotting a threat before it hits you over the head, but at night you're defenceless. Martial and Chancenie had begged him not to take the risk. And shouldn't he be hurrying back to Paris to meet his new chief, Martial asked. But nothing would persuade him to give up Naples. There's probably no safer time to travel than after an attack, when the authorities are especially vigilant. As for Paris, Faure must by now have received his letter and requested an extension of his leave. The matter is in hand. But he's anxious nonetheless. And the courier, who evidently didn't want a passenger, had tried to leave without him and isn't talking. Resigned to silence, he huddles in his corner. Darkness descends like a blindfold.

He wakes with a start; he must have nodded off. They're slowing, the postilion gives a warning blast on the horn. But it's only a post house. As they pull up, he catches sight of the moon, low in the sky and full, as reassuring as a nightwatchman's lantern in a dark alley, till it occurs to him that moonlight favours bandits as much as honest travellers.

He gets out to relieve himself while fresh horses are harnessed. Returning from the privy, he passes two rough-looking men in the yard, a short one with a wide-brimmed felt hat that leaves his face in shadow and another, badly scarred by smallpox, who gives him an appraising glance. He climbs back into the carriage in a state of anxiety that guarantees a sleepless night.

La Colombera, Thursday 3 October

Yesterday's source of anxiety has vanished and we celebrated the end of the harvest with carefree hearts.

A bad attack of indigestion overnight had decided Signora Rossi to return to Milan and her favourite apothecary, though Maddalena was still apprehensive, since her mother was quite capable of changing her mind should anything make her suspect their plans.

By late morning the picking was done and the final loads emptied into the vat. Giovanni swung a bare leg over the edge and plunged into the reeking vinous mass of broken fruit, linking arms with his cousins. The fiddler struck up a tune and the onlookers began to sing. Through song after song the young men kept going, their legs rising and falling in time to the music till at last it wound to a halt and released them. They climbed out, staggering a little, Giovanni like a young Bacchus in his purple-stained breeches. An older man slopped water over their legs. With a wink at the others, he tipped an entire bucket over Giovanni, soaking him from head to foot.

Then came the festive meal. Signora Locatelli and her daughters carried dish after dish to the table — thick bean soup and a salmi of wild pigeon to enliven the polenta, and all the abundance of late summer in the colourful platters of vegetables. Ripe figs in a basket of their own aromatic leaves, with fresh cream cheese to accompany them, were fit for the gods. Faces reddened and shone with every dish that passed. Between courses, they took it in turns to sing, ballads or worksongs picked up by the fiddler from his corner. Even the old grandfather sang a solo in his quavering voice.

Eventually the women started to clear away and the men drifted outside. A minute later, Giovanni put his head round the door. 'Come and see the comet.'

'Blessed Virgin save us!' Signora Locatelli exclaimed. 'Don't expose yourself to its rays!' But the younger folk ignored the warning. The night was cool and the sky clear. The comet had changed since she'd first seen it. Its tail, now branched in two, spread out across the sky growing fainter towards the end, like the straggling remnant of some great cavalcade of which the brilliant head still outshone the brightest star. The watchers murmured solemnly among themselves.

I gathered that the priest had made much of the comet's appearance at this time, and everyone seemed more fervent than usual when we knelt for the rosary. Even if they wish to see the Emperor overthrown, they know that the poor suffer too when the great fall.

I had brought some embroidered handkerchiefs with me as gifts to the women in the family, which I distributed before bedtime. When I thanked Signora Locatelli for her hospitality, she said, 'But you earned your board, Signorina. You are a good worker.' Her words touched me more than any praise I have ever received.

ON THE ROAD TO NAPLES, FRIDAY 4 OCTOBER

Mola di Gaeta. He steps out, squinting in the blaze of light from the sea. A swarm of urchins surrounds him, clamouring for alms. The courier swats them away like flies.

Seventeen hours on the road, and about the same still to go. He's dazed from lack of sleep. Fear kept him awake, apart from a couple of hours' sleep at a filthy inn. But then came the Pontine Marshes, notorious for their fever-ridden vapours that could kill a man in three days. Luckily, he had the recommended prophylactic — the picturesquely named 'four robbers' vinegar'. He'd drenched his handkerchief, kept it over his face the whole way, though the pungent odour of garlic and camphor had nearly knocked him out.

First glimpse of the Mediterranean at Terracina. Palm trees. The women brown, their bosoms flattened by the ugly bodice of the local costume. Towns and people dirtier the farther south you went. Inland again; the wild terrain renewed his fears, though the authorities were taking strong measures against banditry, hanging convicted robbers at the scene of their crime and leaving them to rot as a warning to others.

But here on this balmy coast, fear evaporates. He's never seen anything like it — the glittering sea, the distant islands, and southwards, faint as though an artist had pencilled them on the horizon, the twin peaks of Vesuvius.

A table is set for them a few steps from the shore where fishermen are mending their nets. Bread, olives, wine arrive, then plates of fried fish. He calls for a second helping. This time he's paying for his own meals.

Off again, through country even more fertile than his beloved Lombardy. Orange groves, orchards, trees draped in reddening vines, the scent of aromatic plants in the warm air, and mountains on the horizon to add the note of grandeur that lifts the view beyond mere sensual appeal. The country of Cimarosa and Pergolesi. If his little Angel were here, he'd have her sing for him. How charming she is in the guise of a shepherdess or peasant girl with her luxuriant black curls tumbling over her shoulders. Hers is the type of beauty that answers the promise of this landscape.

But any woman would be a better companion here than one of his male friends. If men had soul they hid it in the company of other men, but women weren't ashamed to reveal it and they felt freer in the country. Mme Daru was another woman at Bècheville, wandering round the garden in her straw hat with her skirts pinned up and a new plant in hand, revelling in the physical freedom that polite society denied her. How charming she'd been that day in Leopoldsberg, rosy-cheeked from the gallop through the frosty air. And he, poor fool, too timid to say the things that perhaps she was hoping to hear. It took him two years to declare his love. With Angela it was only two days.

How sweet it would be to have her beside him now. If she were here, they'd watch the sun set over the water every evening, and then at dawn after a night of love see it rise behind Vesuvius.

What a dream! Reality is the crowd of men around her, the misery of watching her smile and flirt. To hide her love for him, she claimed, but did she tell others the same tale? He's had her, though: even if it never happens again, he's possessed a woman whom all men desire. She'd found something in him that singled him out from the others.

The day is waning; the distant hills turn violet then indigo, the clouds above them rose and gold. When they stop for supper he'll make a note or two. Not that he's much of a hand at description, and anyway if most readers are like himself they'll skip it. Once you've read one traveller's rhapsody you've read them all. Sublime prospect, smiling fields, perfumed breezes, the land where the lemon tree blooms. It's all been written a thousand times.

His head is nodding irresistibly. Huddled in his corner he drops off to sleep.

Varese, the Albergo Reale, Friday 4 October

Peasants in the woods beating chestnut boughs to bring down the nuts. Mushroom gatherers. Church in Castiglione, primitive statues. Bizzozero, sublime view of Alps.

Sitting on the edge of the bed in her nightgown, back discreetly turned while Maddalena undresses, she pencils a few details into her Italian exercise book. She can't risk Maddalena reading her journal over her shoulder and she won't be alone again for the week, since they're sharing a room to save money. Pierino is in his uncle's room, though it took some persuasion.

'Can't I stay with you, Mamma?' He leaned against her, nervously playing with her shawl.

'No, *tesoro*. Signorina Marie is going to share my bed. I'll come to kiss you goodnight as soon as you're undressed.'

It was high time Pierino left his mother's bed, she thought, though she felt sorry for the boy and a little uncomfortable herself with the arrangement. She hasn't shared a bed since she and Jeannette slept top to toe in London. But she's grateful to economise, and the sheets (which she'd quickly inspected while Maddalena was saying goodnight to the child) are clean.

'Are you writing a letter?' Maddalena is in her nightgown, her face aureoled in curl rags.

'Just a few notes on what we saw today. But I'm done now. You can put out the lamp.' It's still early, but Maddalena will be rising at dawn to make her confession and take communion before the pilgrimage.

Her own mind is too busy for sleep. She lies in the dark (not even a glimmer from the shutters, since Maddalena fears the night air) trying to fix the day's events in memory before they fade.

As they'd headed north, the valley narrowed to a wooded gorge where the river foamed between huge boulders. At midday they stopped for refreshment in a village beneath a ruined castle whose grandeur suggested a more prosperous past. Two stone giants flanked the porch of the ancient church — Saint Anthony the Hermit and Saint Christopher, carved in the primitive style of an age when perhaps such men had dwelt there seeking the solitude of the woods.

Maddalena took Pierino inside to light a candle in front of the Virgin. She'd been less talkative than usual all morning, a little frown between her brows. They were by themselves in the carriage, Pierino riding with Giovanni.

'It will be five years this month since my poor husband's death. I pray every day for his release from purgatory. Pierino too. They say God listens to the prayers of children because they're pure of heart.'

'Then God has surely pardoned your husband. He must be in heaven already.' Kindness dictated her response, though purgatory now seemed as mythical to her as the ancient underworld.

But Maddalena's frown didn't lessen. 'Pierre was a good man, but he wasn't religious. I doubt that he would have made his confession before the battle. To die without absolution of one's sins . . .'

'But he died doing his duty,' she said, then remembered the priest's insinuations. Pierre Garreau had fought on the side of the devil. That must be the source of Maddalena's worry. 'May we not hope that God will forgive us our sins just as Jesus forgave his executioners?'

Maddalena looked only half convinced. 'If you make the pilgrimage to the Sacro Monte, you gain a plenary indulgence,' she said, her own solution now emerging. 'All the punishment for your sins remitted. I'm making the pilgrimage for Pierre. I want to feel sure he's entered heaven. That he's happy, that he has no need of us. Pierino asks me the strangest questions. "Can my *babbo* see us?" he asked the other day. What would you have told him?'

Poor child, she thought — trying to make sense of an absence, or haunted in his small misdeeds by the thought that his father was watching from beyond the grave.

'I would tell him that the dead cannot see the living. But they do not forget us.' Let the child believe in his father's continuing love. Maddalena's own anxiety, she sensed, lay behind the question. She felt her way towards an answer. 'I asked a priest that question once, after my mother died, and he told me that the dead are freed from earthly attachments. Their love is purified of any desire for possession.'

'You explain things so well, Marie!'

She was briefly pleased with herself. But what if Pierre Garreau was watching from the shadows, reaching out with impotent longing for an embrace he could no longer feel, like the ghosts Ulysses met in the underworld desperate for news of the living? And her parents too, as in those dreams in which she and her father are taking ship for France and her mother is left behind on the quay. Was she a hypocrite, giving answers she only half believed? But her intention was sincere. Maddalena needed to be released from her obligation to a dead man.

The conversation had freed them to enjoy the long climb through the woods to Varese. In the steepest part they walked to relieve the horses, a necessity for which she was grateful. On foot, she had time to notice the arum berries among the silver-spotted lungwort, and tiny ferns in the hollow of mossy rocks. Near the top, the road turned a bend and suddenly the huge panorama of alpine peaks rose before them like a vision conjured up by an enchanter. If her childhood drawing lessons had continued, she might have been capable of sketching it. But perhaps on her return she can buy a print or engraving. Larocque will surely know where to find one.

Beside her, Maddalena turns and burrows deeper into sleep. But she's still wide awake. How many strange rooms has she slept in since she set off five weeks ago? Ten at least, counting this one (and her room in Milan which now feels like home). From each some fragment remains. A great shadow darkening the moon. The sound of rushing water in the silence of night. Musicians beneath her balcony. And brief flashes of the many strangers with whom she shared a table — the young man with the fancy watch chain and his two Italian companions; Payot and his friendly wife; the dour Genevan pastor; and all those others who'd briefly travelled the same road. Memory can still resurrect them, but soon they'll vanish into oblivion, unless her pen grants them a reprieve. Her writing too will vanish eventually, tossed onto the scrap heap of the century, crumbling into dust. And yet she values the preservation of these ephemera; they are lodged the more securely in memory for having been inscribed. Tomorrow at all costs she must find some private moment to write.

Naples, Saturday 5 October

He arrived at three in the morning and slept till eleven. The sunlight on his balcony was blinding, but there above the rooftops, as the innkeeper promised, was Vesuvius.

After breakfast, he sent a note to his old friend Lambert, then plunged into the city. The din was overwhelming. On every corner, the shrill cries of lemonade sellers vied with the warning bellow of coachmen and barrow boys; housewives screeched from balconies as they lowered baskets to tradesmen below, and through it all, like the drone of insects, came the beggars' sing-song whine — the whole in a version of Italian unlike any he'd heard before. Everywhere, barefoot *lazzaroni* squatted on their heels, awaiting the chance to earn a coin.

Pigs rooted through refuse heaps. A fruit vendor slept on his heap of watermelons.

Back at the inn, he took a nap. By the time he'd spruced himself up, Lambert was waiting below, his suntanned face dark as an Italian's but his slim frame, in the uniform of a deputy inspector in the army administration, no heavier.

'You haven't changed in the least, Léon!'

'But you've prospered, my friend, since we last met!' Lambert's gaze, admiring and ironic, made him feel overdressed.

'You've done pretty well yourself,' he said, congratulating Lambert on his promotion. It made him guiltily conscious of his own good fortune. But Naples was a splendid place to end up, though the poor fellow had endured three years in Calabria first.

Mme Lambert awaited them, a vivacious, self-assured brunette with heavy sensual features and slightly protuberant eyes. Over dinner they reminisced about Marseilles. Lambert hadn't forgotten Mélanie.

'I hope she found a more discriminating audience in Paris?'

'She's in Saint Petersburg now — with a company that's opened a French theatre there.' Poor Mélanie. He'd been sorry to see her reduced to that second-rate troupe. But Russian audiences would be easier to please. And perhaps she'd find a wealthy protector. There'd never been a lack of candidates for the role.

Later, on his balcony, listening to the plink of a mandolin below, he feels a brief nostalgia for those first months with Mélanie. He was twenty-two and at last, after years of sighing after unattainable women, he had a mistress, blonde, beautiful, and with all the allure of the theatre. He'd helped her learn her lines, reassured her when reviews were bad, suppressed his doubts about her talent, telling himself that her acting was simply too subtle for a provincial audience. How love makes you deceive yourself! But what's worse (as memory reminds him, now that he's lowered his guard), he'd deceived his family, told them he was the father of her child (the seven-year-old girl he'd seen just once, with her foster parents in the country). What had possessed him to tell such a lie? He'd been so sick of their attempts to talk him out of living with Mélanie that he had to find something to justify it, and there was a certain pleasure in writing 'my daughter'. It made him feel a man. But one lie had led to another, and each one bobs up in his consciousness now like some repulsive scrap of detritus on the surface of a river. Telling them she was called Henriette after his mother. Using the money his grandfather sent for the child to pay his debts. They must have seen through it eventually. No one has mentioned her since. Pitied him probably — a naïve youth deceived into assuming paternity by a woman of easy virtue. Better to let them think that than admit the deception was his.

He lies more than he should. Every child lies, of course — the tyranny of parents and teachers makes it inevitable. But a man shouldn't need to, except out of kindness. There are various forms of dishonesty he still succumbs to: a tendency to exaggerate his success, the little deceptions of courtship. Harmless enough. But then there are the lies told from expediency or fear. Regrettable if for no other reason than that they could be exposed. Like the deception he's practised over this journey. Martial is bound to mention his visit in letters home, so his whereabouts will be revealed. And it's pointless telling himself that he's no longer under Count Daru's orders, because his cousin's good opinion is even more important now that he's the emperor's right-hand man. All that distinguishes the unknown Henri Beyle from a hundred other aspirants is a recommendation from the Secretary of State. This journey could cost him dearly.

He tosses a coin to the mandolin player and steps back into the room, leaving the curtains open so that dawn will wake him. Even if he loses everything, it will be worth it to have seen the sun rise over Vesuvius.

Santa Maria del Monte, Saturday 5 October

To the Sacro Monte. Beautiful views as we climbed the Via Sacra to the Virgin's shrine.

She stops, frustrated. Maddalena is moving restlessly round the room, folding garments, shaking out the creases in the dress she plans to wear tomorrow, obviously wanting to talk. Her own thoughts tonight are complex, demanding time and concentration for their full expression. An account of the Sacro Monte would take pages; she must confine herself to a few headings and hope they'll jog her memory later.

History of Blessed Caterina di Pallanza. The old nun. Closure of convent. Unexpected arrival of Captain Trezzano.

Unexpected by herself, anyway. But Maddalena must have known all along, hence her despair when her mother thought of accompanying them. The captain would have made the day's journey for nothing if Signora Rossi had been there. It had tired him, his limp more evident as he entered the dining room at the inn to their exclamations of genuine or feigned surprise.

'You're not displeased, Marie, that Trezzano has joined us?' Maddalena is sitting up in bed, her face framed in curl rags, the anxious little frown back between her eyebrows.

'Of course not. I like him very much.' Resigned to conversation, she puts her notebook away and gets into bed.

'He wanted to surprise us. He'll be company for Giovanni.'

Maddalena is being evasive. But then so is she, for in truth she'd felt a little duped when the captain arrived. Was this why her friend had been so eager to have her company on the journey? Giovanni and the child are surely sufficient as chaperones, but the presence of another woman makes Trezzano's reason for being with them less obvious. Whether this was Maddalena's motive or not, she feels implicated in the deception of Signora Rossi, but she cannot let it trouble her.

Today's pilgrimage seems to have marked a turning point in Maddalena's widowhood, the fulfilment of some ultimate duty. Her fervour was sincere. She'd refused breakfast, in order to make the pilgrimage fasting. Even Giovanni had been serious for once as they passed through the entrance to the sacred way.

Fifteen halts punctuated the winding route up the mountainside — not the simple wayside shrines she'd expected but small chapels resembling the pavilions in a nobleman's garden, each one distinctive, as though the architect had scoured a design book for elegant variations. The first represented the Virgin's girlhood home and they peered through a window into the room where the Angel Gabriel was making his announcement. There was a real bed and even a washstand. The two holy figures were life-sized statues.

'Look at the Virgin's slippers under the bed, Mamma!' Pierino was fascinated.

She studied the scene as Maddalena led them in the rosary, wondering why it left her cold. She might have ignored the sentimentality of the portrayal, but something in the combining of the real and the artificial troubled her. With a picture, you never forgot that it was painted canvas, whereas these life-sized figures surrounded by actual objects aimed to create the illusion of real presences. They were as counterfeit as opera scenery but they aimed to compel belief. That was what made her uneasy. Watching Pierino absorbed in the details of each scene, she saw their power.

The effect became more disturbing once they reached the chapels of Christ's sufferings. There was something almost shameful in looking at the naked victim, seeing the pain on his face and the pleasure of inflicting it on the faces of his tormentors. Had there been such looks on the faces below the scaffold as the late king died? She closed her eyes against them.

When she opened them again, she saw that one of the pilgrims ahead was making the climb to the Crucifixion on his knees, dragging himself over the stones until he collapsed and had to be supported under his arms by his companions. She glanced quickly at Maddalena, fearing she might be inspired to follow suit, but her friend's face expressed only horrified pity.

They held back to let the penitent complete his personal 'calvary'. Maddalena's head was bowed in silent prayer but Giovanni and the child moved towards the view. They were high enough now to glimpse the distant rooftops of Varese and the shining expanse of a lake beyond. In the green calm of the trees below the parapet, a flock of small brown birds flitted from branch to branch with gentle chirps. It was a relief from the drama on the hillside.

There were five more chapels still, but finally they reached the summit and recited the final prayers in front of an ancient wooden statue of the Virgin — carved by Saint Luke the Apostle, the sacristan assured them. He recounted the history of Blessed Caterina, who'd led the life of a hermit on the mountain, living in a cave with her two companions before the convent was built.

'She recited a thousand "Ave Marias" every Saturday.'

'A thousand!' Maddalena was awestruck.

And we've barely managed 150, she thought. The ability to withstand tedium seemed a necessary part of sanctity as the Church conceived it. She'd noticed the former convent as they climbed the hill, fortress-like with its tiny windows, immuring its denizens in chosen silence. Centuries of a way of life now deemed worthless. Since the suppression of the order, the convent had become an inn. A few aged nuns who had no family to return to had been allowed to stay.

They encountered one, bent double by age and infirmity, as they left the church. Maddalena pressed a coin into her hand.

'Please, sister, will you pray for the soul of my late husband, Pierre Garreau — the boy's father.' She drew Pierino forward to present him.

No words but a solemn nod of acquiescence. For an instant the old face, pale as ivory and scarcely wrinkled, was lifted towards them with a kind of wonder, then she made the sign of the cross on Pierino's forehead and shuffled on.

The last obligations of piety fulfilled, they could admire the view from the belvedere. A man with a telescope, leaning idly against the parapet, sprang to attention and offered his services. To the north above the wooded hills rose the Alps. Southwards lay the immense sunlit plain of Lombardy, dotted with towns and villages, among which, with the telescope's aid, they could just pick out the silhouette of the Duomo in Milan.

But now they were ravenous. 'There's nothing like prayer to give you an appetite, eh Signorina?' Giovanni said. The meeting with the old nun seemed to have completed the exorcism of Maddalena's ghosts; her mood was as effervescent as the wine they drank with lunch.

But, of course, she thinks, still mildly resentful, Maddalena was anticipating Trezzano's arrival. Acquitted of her obligation to the dead, she could welcome him without guilt. Still, the captain was a pleasant addition to their group. He was an intelligent man, more reflective than Giovanni; it was possible to have a conversation with him that didn't always end in a joke. Over dinner, they told him about the sculpted scenes in the chapels, which Maddalena so much regretted he had missed that she was ready to make the pilgrimage again, though Trezzano showed no inclination to do so.

'And what did you think of them, Signorina?' he asked.

'They are beautifully done. All the details — the Virgin's slippers, Saint Veronica's veil . . .' She hesitated, not wanting to spoil Maddalena's pleasure, yet feeling a need to be honest. 'But a little theatrical, I thought, a little too close to entertainment.'

'But it makes you feel you were there!' Maddalena exclaimed. 'The Crucifixion brought tears to my eyes!'

'It moved me too.' She didn't wish to seem cold. 'But as a play in the theatre might do. Not as a spiritual experience.'

'I don't see the difference.' Maddalena frowned.

But Trezzano seemed interested. 'I believe your reactions demonstrate the differences in national character. It's generally agreed that people in the south are more emotional — or more ready to show emotion — than the inhabitants of colder climates. So our religion demands more dramatic expression. But northerners being more reserved, their religion is more inward. That's why Protestantism developed in the north.'

'You may be right,' she said. 'In England the churches are bare, no statues, no holy images —'

'You've been to England, Signorina?' Giovanni caught the implication before she had time to cover her slip.

'When I was a child.' She couldn't lie, though the curiosity on their faces made her regret it. Trezzano asked if her family had emigrated during the Revolution.

'We fled the violence as many did. My father found employment in London as a teacher.' She tried to make it sound as though it had been his normal occupation.

'So you've been to England, Signorina, and our Lena to Germany, and Fedele to Spain. I've never been anywhere!' Giovanni sounded envious. Exile wasn't a pleasure tour, she wanted to say, but she'd revealed too much already.

'The Revolution in France has affected us all,' Trezzano observed. 'It has changed the world and we have not yet seen its full import.'

He and Giovanni exchanged a significant look. They believed in it still, she saw, and Larocque too in spite of his disillusion. She felt very lonely.

Naples, Sunday 6 October

He woke in the grey light of dawn and stepped out on the balcony. The air was salty and pure, blowing in from the sea. On the horizon the twin peaks stood out black against the pale gold sky and, as he watched, the rim of the sun appeared between the cones. A sublime moment, worth all the risks and discomforts of the journey.

At midday he met his friends and this time Louis Barral was there. They embraced warmly. Barral was his oldest friend, born on the same street (though in a grander residence than his own family's dark old house farther down). They hadn't met till school brought them together. He remembered sitting in a mathematics class admiring Barral's stylish blue jacket. Barral was shabby now, a bad sign, though his long narrow melancholic face hadn't lost its air of distinction, a covert inspection revealed as the four of them set off towards the sea.

It was a year since the night Barral confessed to him that he'd just gambled and lost what remained of his wealth. Surely now, he'd thought, his poor friend would come to his senses. But today he saw at once (the evasiveness in his eyes, the haggard look) that nothing had changed. They were several days into the month; Barral would have collected his allowance, redeemed his belongings from the pawnshop and paid his rent, then returned to the gaming tables. He'd run through the fortune inherited from his mother and all he had to live on now was the small monthly allowance from his father, the *ci-devant* Marquis de Montferrat. Enough to survive on in Naples, but not in Paris. The ex-marquis wasn't stingy, but what could you do with a son like that, short of locking him up? Barral is the best-hearted of men, but away from the tables everything bores him.

They'd reached the waterfront. 'My God, what a view!' he exclaimed. For once the guidebooks hadn't exaggerated. Nothing could be finer than the sweeping curve of the bay, the white sails on the blue expanse, the islands. 'So that's Capri? I hadn't realised it was so close. To think the English held it!'

'All the islands are garrisoned now,' Lambert said. 'But we'll never be safe from the English till we drive them out of Sicily. They boast of their freedom, but they don't want to extend it to others. They've already made one attempt to restore the Bourbons to the throne of Naples. If we let them win, they'll restore all the old monarchies and set back the advance of progress a century. What makes them think they have the right to rule the Mediterranean?'

'There was an English corvette in the bay this summer.' Mme Lambert's rather bulbous eyes widened theatrically. 'Just anchored there, out of reach of our cannon, you could see the officers on deck with their spyglasses!'

'That was just a provocation,' Lambert interrupted. 'But two years ago they landed troops on the island of Ischia — over there, behind the headland. They had two hundred and fifty warships waiting to attack Naples. And all we had was two! It was an uncomfortable few days, believe me! We thought they'd bombard us like they did Copenhagen, set the city alight. Fortunately, the news that the emperor had just defeated the Austrians and would march down here to defend us scared them off. They'd be a bigger threat if their army wasn't fully occupied in Spain. They don't have the troops to support an invasion here. All they can do is stir up discontent in Calabria. I saw enough of that when I first arrived, I can tell you!'

He put his hand on Lambert's shoulder to calm him. 'I'd like to taste some Neapolitan ice cream before the English fleet returns.'

Afterwards, they headed to the parade ground where the king was to review the troops. 'He's as good a spectacle as Vesuvius,' Lambert said. 'Enough gold braid to blind you.'

'And his breeches so tight it must take two valets to get him in and out of them.' Mme Lambert's eyes bulged expressively.

'A man who's turned the course of battle as often as Joachim Murat can permit himself a little flamboyance,' he said. There was something almost operatic in the rise of this innkeeper's son, educated for the priesthood till the day he followed a cavalry regiment down the street and exchanged his cassock for the uniform of a *chasseur*. And now here he was, the most gallant and reckless of the emperor's generals, replacing a Bourbon on the throne of Naples. King Joachim. Of course, he owed his elevation to his wife. Caroline Bonaparte was said to be as intelligent and able as her brother. 'Will the queen be present?' he asked.

'She's just left for Paris. Something's going on, some struggle between the emperor and the king.' Lambert was trying to appear in the know. Murat, he claimed, wanted to owe his power to his own popularity, not to his imperial brother-in-law, so he was favouring Neapolitans in every way he could.

'There's a rumour that he's in disgrace.' Barral emerged from his lethargy. 'That his wife will govern in his stead.'

'It's what she's been waiting for,' Mme Lambert sneered. 'She made a spectacle of herself when the English threatened us — riding round town in a military uniform to rally the people!'

'Her abilities have earned the admiration of many discerning men,' he said curtly. 'If Elisa Bonaparte can govern Tuscany, why shouldn't her sister rule Naples?'

Mme Lambert was starting to irritate him. He looked at his watch. The gardens of Chiaia were pretty but he was bored. Another hour passed without the king's appearance. Finally the troops were dismissed, red-faced and sweating.

As they were returning to the Lamberts' apartment for dinner, they found the neighbourhood celebrating the feast of the local Madonna with an enthusiasm more pagan than Christian, and when they set out again for the opera, past the illuminated shrine, urchins tossed firecrackers at their feet, to the great vexation of Mme Lambert, who feared for her dress.

He'd looked forward to some music and the grand new opera house impressed him. But it wasn't La Scala. Neapolitan men were better looking than the women, who favoured combinations of colour as loud as their voices, and the production — Fioravanti's latest — had lots of comic play with local dialect that pleased the audience, but nothing to stir the soul. 'It's hard to believe this place produced Pergolesi,' he remarked to Barral.

'Music's in decline here, like everything else,' Barral said gloomily.

How often in Paris they'd walked home together discussing a performance. But tonight his friend had nothing to say, and his own animation felt forced. He'd have liked to exchange some news of their scattered classmates, but Lambert had dominated conversation. It was unwise to mix friends from different epochs of your life, he decided. And Mme Lambert was a bore. How could Lambert, whom he had always thought more discerning, have ended up with this vulgar woman?

She isn't coming on tomorrow's excursion; perhaps without her they'll regain their old ease.

Laveno, the Albergo del Posto, Sunday 6 October

Never have I seen a more enchanting view than the one we enjoy here — the lake and its islands, the little white towns and villas along its hilly shores, and above it all the majestic snow peaks, very clear in this beautiful autumn weather.

She can write more freely this evening since she has the room to herself while Maddalena is with Pierino. The child has been clinging jealously to his mother all day, no more deceived than herself by the fiction that the captain is there to keep Giovanni company.

They'd left Varese this morning after despatching a message to Signora Rossi to announce their delayed return. Maddalena wore her new hat. The substitution of a fashionable bonnet for the widow's black veil could not have conveyed a clearer message, and Trezzano kept turning in his saddle to glance back at her as the two men rode ahead of the carriage.

'How long have you known the captain?' she asked.

'About six months. But Giovanni has known him longer. They met in some club that Giovanni is not supposed to talk about.'

It was what she'd suspected. The possibility that they might belong to a political group explained their unlikely friendship, the younger man so frivolous, the older informed and serious. Sometimes she had the feeling that all men belonged to a secret society — not one of the many such associations rumoured to exist, but a club in which they held membership simply by virtue of being male. Armand and his acquaintances were irritatingly prone to mysterious allusions and knowing looks. Trezzano, though, had an earnest sincerity in his manner that inspired trust.

'The captain is a very thoughtful man,' she told Maddalena.

'Yes, Giovanni admires him greatly. He needs a friend to steady him — or a sensible woman, if he can find one who'll accept him!'

The journey took them through thickly wooded hills where occasionally the roof of a villa appeared among the trees. How she would love to dwell in such verdant seclusion, to open the shutters every morning to this sweet air uncontaminated by the city's stink. She imagined the garden she'd create; it would not be elaborate but simply a perfecting of what was already there — a sunny glade with a rill of clear water running down from the woods where birds and animals would come to drink. She'd plant wild flowers dug from the woods and meadows, and train wild roses and honeysuckle to form a fragrant bower above a rustic seat. Near the house, she'd have a vegetable patch, and a strawberry bed. She could manage without a servant, she was sure. But could a single woman live safely in isolation? All her dreams came up against that obstacle.

Late in the morning they reached Laveno, a prosperous little harbour curved around a bay of Lake Maggiore. There was only one inn, but it was clean, with a landlord solicitous of their comfort, and the view was beyond compare. As they walked along the shore after lunch, she had an opportunity to become better acquainted with Trezzano. Maddalena had given in to Pierino's insistence that she join his exploration at the water's edge, and Giovanni had wandered off to talk to the boatmen.

'I am curious to hear what you think of the English, Signorina,' Trezzano said. 'You have lived among them, while I know them only as our adversaries in Spain.'

'But I had no close English acquaintance, so I know them from the outside only. And my impressions are often contradictory.' On the one hand, there was the civility of the respectable classes and the solemn hush of the English Sunday. But was the raucous behaviour outside the alehouses not equally characteristic? She tried within the limits of her Italian to convey something of this. 'Perhaps every nation is composed of contradictory elements, and one should not speak of a national character.'

'There's certainly a contradiction in the present attitude of the English that I find surprising,' he said. 'For a long time enlightened thinkers everywhere have considered the English system of government a model — the limitation of the monarch's power by Parliament, the two chambers, and so forth. But in the present wars they have allied themselves with the absolute monarchies. It's said that they funded Austria's last offensive against us.'

He talked about it a little, proud to have fought with the army that had driven the Austrian archduke's forces out of Italy.

'I would have expected that you, as an Italian, would be grateful to the English,' she said. 'They lead the opposition to a man who seems determined to add all the small states of Europe to his empire.'

'It may surprise you, but many of us see the benefits of his conquests. Ten years ago, Italy was nothing more than a collection of small backward states, each with its ruler, its dialect, its particular institutions and customs. But under the unifying effect of French rule we shall become one people. It's a paradox, I know, but I believe that it is the French who will make Italians of us, rather than Lombards and Tuscans and Venetians as we are at present.'

'But how can you be Italians under the domination of a foreign empire?'

'That's a question for the future. The task of our generation is to surmount our divisions.'

'But have the French not added to those divisions? There are those like yourself who welcome French rule, but are there not many others who oppose it?'

'The opposition comes mainly from the Church, and from the peasants. But once the people recognise the benefits of enlightened government they will cease to resist it. Meanwhile, those who co-operate with the French, in government, in the army, are helping to shape a new Italy and gaining the experience to govern it when the moment comes. It will take time, but I truly believe that this new century will see the creation of a united and independent Italy.'

Not without more bloodshed, she'd thought. Trezzano might regret it, but as a soldier, he'd accept the necessity of violent struggle, and was no doubt prepared to shed his own blood for the cause. It found an eloquent defender in him, she could not deny, looking at his lean, intelligent, serious face in which there was no hint of doubt, or the disillusion that marked Larocque. It was easy to see why Giovanni admired him, but the conviction that shone in Trezzano's eyes was not less to be distrusted because of its utter sincerity.

He reminded her of Armand, and the way Armand had justified his service of the Revolutionary. 'I was a soldier,' he said. 'It was my duty to defend France against foreign invaders, even those who promised to restore the monarchy.' For men like Armand and Trezzano, it was the future that mattered, and they could set aside their reservations about the current government. With Larocque, she thought, it was different; he'd once believed wholeheartedly in the new republic, but now he served its successor only because he had no other means of supporting himself and his daughter.

Trezzano had given her a view of Italy that Mrs Godwin would certainly have recorded. Personally, she found its individual conflicts — the profound opposition between Signora Rossi and her aspirant son-in-law — as interesting as the larger questions. But the dinner table was calling them, and over a dish of rice with mushrooms (a welcome change from polenta), followed by fried lake perch, their conversation was light-hearted.

Just before sunset, as the church bell tolled the angelus, they'd walked to the end of the promontory that enclosed the bay. As the sun descended, a blaze of gold fell on the water like a path to the farther shore, till a sudden breeze sent a shiver of ripples across the surface, splintering the gold in a million fragments. Great flocks of birds wheeled over the lake on their way to roost. The peaks turned rose, then silver as the light waned. It was inexpressibly beautiful, yet she was sad. She'd enjoyed the journey today, despite the difference in sensibility between herself and her companions, but at moments like these she longed for a fellow spirit.

Giovanni offered her his arm as they made their way back along the path among the trees. The others were ahead, Maddalena leaning against Trezzano's shoulder, Pierino tugging at her hand on the other side as counterweight. Giovanni was silent for once, but the warm pressure of his arm against hers in the dark made her keep up a nervous flow of conversation until they reached the inn.

Naples, Monday 7 October

'Is this really the Grotto of Posillipo?' Where was the romantic cavern he'd imagined?

'Everything here has some fanciful name.' Lambert raised his voice to compete with the echo of hoof beats against the vault. 'It's always been a tunnel. The Romans cut through the headland to shorten the route to their villas.'

'And we imagine we're innovating! But you should see the Gondo tunnels in the Simplon. The emperor will give Italy a network of highways such as it hasn't known since the Romans. And with roads comes progress.'

'There speaks the optimism of Paris! Don't underrate Italian resistance.'

'It will cease once our reforms take root.'

'Don't bet on it. Look what's happening in Spain, and here in Calabria. The rebels have the advantage of their wild terrain, the peasants' support, the sanction of the Church. They call themselves defenders of the faith, but they're no better than savages. If you knew what they did to prisoners, or to local officials who've supported us! The worst is that it forces us to take brutal reprisals, then they hate us all the more.'

Lambert had the look of a man who'd seen things best not talked about. It was a relief to emerge into the sunlight above the calm blue water of a bay. They headed down to the shore and after some haggling with a guide embarked for the opposite headland.

Cape Miseno, and Baia, named for the comrades whom Aeneas, and before him Ulysses, had buried there: they were entering the realm of poetry. Along the shore and below them in the translucent water, they glimpsed the ruins of elegant villas, tumbled long since by earthquakes or swallowed by the sea. Who hadn't owned a villa here, if one believed the guide? Augustus. Caligula. Nero. Caesar — and his future assassin, Brutus! That surprised him. But was it any more inconsistent for a virtuous republican to possess a villa than for a supporter of the Revolution to own a château, like Barral's father?

Disembarking on the barren shore, he felt an agreeable shiver at setting foot on such fated ground. They picnicked among the ruins, then continued to Nero's baths (so-called), which proved to be a thermal spring reached by a tunnel no wider than a man. Their guide put four eggs in a pail for some demonstration, then lit a pine torch, and in they went. The tunnel was hot as a furnace and he gave up halfway. When the others re-emerged sweating, the guide's pail was filled with boiling spring water in which the eggs had cooked on the way out. They shelled and ate the eggs while sitting on the rocks in the afternoon sun.

The boat took them back to their carriage. He'd had enough by then, but there was still the Solfatara crater, a rocky hollow that spewed out sulphurous vapours and jets of boiling mud that might have inspired one of Dante's descriptions of Hell. Even the ground on which they stood was hot.

'They say that so long as Solfatara is active, Vesuvius won't have a major eruption,' their driver said. 'But we place our trust in San Gennaro and the Blessed Virgin.'

No wonder these people were superstitious, living under a volcano. But even with that threat hanging over you, what a place! The bay was shimmering in the radiant light as they re-entered Naples.

'Weren't you surprised that Brutus owned a villa?' he asked the others over dinner. 'A man who'd sacrifice himself to save the republic! *The noblest Roman of them all*, Shakespeare calls him. What a play! I'd sell my shirt to see it performed!'

'The times aren't favourable to plays that glorify republican conspiracies,' Lambert said drily. 'Especially since our own Caesar has had his share of would-be assassins.'

'None of our dramatists can touch Shakespeare,' he said, ignoring the interruption. 'His genius is that at the height of the drama he introduces some ordinary human detail and that's what gives his plays their truth, truth of a kind our tragedies will never possess while they stick to the old conventions. It's time for a revolution in the theatre.'

Their faces had the rigidity of feigned interest, Barral clearly waiting for the moment when he could decently excuse himself and head for the dice, Lambert barely suppressing his yawns. He gave up.

Back at the inn he strips off his sweaty clothes and stands naked as a statue in the cool air from the balcony, the first time he's felt comfortable since morning. The Romans knew how to dress for this climate. Impressions of the day come back to him. Their picnic in the Temple of Apollo, the look on Lambert's face when he talked about Calabria, Barral fumbling in his pockets for something to tip the boatmen and coming up empty-handed. He should have written a detailed account, but he's too tired. The heat is enervating. How had the Romans found the energy to extend their empire to the boundaries of the known world?

Laveno, Monday 7 October

Today we took a boat across the lake to the Borromean Islands, of which all travellers speak so enthusiastically. It took an hour and a half to reach

Isola Bella with two rowers, and I must confess to a certain anxiety when we embarked.

It is not the only thing she might confess to, but the rest is inadmissible.

'How deep is the lake?' Maddalena asked as they pulled out of the harbour.

'As deep in the middle, Signora, as the spire of the Duomo of Milan is high,' said the boatman.

The thought of the abyss beneath them terrified her. The boat seemed dangerously low in the water with the five of them aboard, squeezed together on the narrow seat encircling the stern. Giovanni rested his arm along the rail behind her; its proximity was reassuring, though she didn't lean back (as Maddalena was doing against Trezzano's). At one point, as he turned to look at the receding shore, his knee had touched her thigh, so lightly she would have thought the contact accidental were it not repeated a minute later. She was not unfamiliar with such moves on the part of Armand's dinner guests. Self-respect as much as decency required an adjustment in her own position that discouraged further advances. But in the natural intimacy of their little group and the excitement of the excursion she could pretend not to notice, lulled into acquiescence by the rhythm of the oars and the soft morning air.

They were heading for Isola Bella. From a distance it seemed a mirage — a faerie island floating on the lake as lightly as a water lily. But its substantiality was all too apparent once they drew close enough to see the palace and the pyramidal garden rising above. The island was misnamed, she thought, as they reached the landing stage; there was nothing beautiful about this opulent piling-up of stone, which vied ineffectually with the grandeur of the mountains.

Giovanni sprang ashore and offered her his hand. She gathered up her skirts and stepped nervously over the side.

The family being absent, they could visit the palace. She had never entered a residence of such grandeur before. Armand's house, like Mme d'Aumont's (which she could still not think of as her own), was no more than a substantial bourgeois dwelling, and her childhood home, though ancient and dignified, had not been ostentatious. She felt a strange emotion as they followed the custodian through a series of ornate salons. Not envy — what would she do with all these rooms and the servants necessary to tend them? — but bitterness that some could still take such wealth for granted. She stared resentfully at the Borromeo portraits as the custodian recited his history of their illustrious line. His stories about the visit of Napoleon and Joséphine, some fourteen years previously, were more entertaining.

'Thirty guests they'd told us, then twice that number arrived. We were hard put to satisfy sixty appetites, I can tell you! We ran out of sugar for the ladies' lemonade.'

'And General Bonaparte, what was he like then?' Trezzano wanted more than domestic anecdotes.

'Very serious, Signor, always thinking. They say he carved the word *battle* with his sword on a tree, but I couldn't swear to that. What I can tell you, because I saw it with my own eyes' — the lowered voice promised something scandalous — 'is that the lace cover on his bed was torn. But not because of any amorous battle — no, his spurs had torn it! The general was too drunk to take off his boots when he went to bed.'

How utterly trivial, she thought, compared with the immense human destruction Bonaparte had wreaked since, but it still loomed large in the custodian's mind. Such reverence for his master's possessions would be almost contemptible were it not to be pitied.

Outside, they were handed over to a gardener, who led them up ten stacked terraces bristling with urns, obelisks, statues and topiary, to the amphitheatre at the top dominated by the sculpture of a rearing unicorn mounted by Eros — no vision of enchantment, to her critical eye, but the ultimate excess in the whole extravagant creation.

The view, however, was truly ravishing and she drank it in. Above them towered the Simplon peaks against a brilliant azure sky; down below, on the narrow strip of land between the steep wooded slopes and the lake, whitewashed villages basked in the morning sun.

'That must be the Paris diligence!' Trezzano pointed out a speeding vehicle on the road along the shore.

Only five weeks ago she'd been seated in the cabriolet behind the galloping horses. She had the odd sensation of seeing herself through a telescope — but a different self . . . Could a single month have made such a change?

'A fine life — to be the driver of a diligence. Or a mail courier.' Giovanni sounded genuinely envious. 'But even the humblest *vetturino* knows more of the world than us. Perhaps I shall set myself up with a carriage and mules. Then I could take Signorina Marie to Rome.'

'What an idea!' Maddalena exclaimed. 'You've never been farther than Lodi. You'd get lost in the mountains. Poor Marie!'

'You imagine it on a day like today,' Trezzano said. 'It wouldn't be pleasant in the rain.'

'They think I'm joking,' Giovanni told her as they returned to the boat. 'But I'm serious. I've had enough of being my father's messenger boy. With father and Roberto in charge I'll never amount to anything. I must find some business of my own. Or enlist.'

The last words were spoken so quickly that she had no time to respond before they re-embarked. When they reached the Isola Madre — another Borromeo residence, where roses were still in bloom despite the advance of autumn — she waited until the others were ahead with a gardener before she spoke. 'I hope that you are not seriously thinking of enlisting. It would cause great pain to your mother.'

'The army is one of the few paths open to a man with no particular talent. I don't have an aptitude for figures or writing reports; I couldn't work in an office. But the army offers a future. If my parents had let me go when I was called I might be a captain by now.'

'Or buried in Spain.' He needed to face facts.

'A man, if he's a man, is willing to take the risk.'

'He also risks causing great pain to his family and friends.'

'You are very kind to interest yourself in my fate, Signorina.' He said something to the gardener, who cut a rose for her. The gallant gesture made her uncomfortable and to cover her embarrassment she questioned the gardener about his plants.

There was no lack of exotic species to arouse her curiosity on the sheltered terraces and around the house. But beyond, even more beautiful to her eyes, the island's native vegetation had been left untouched — a dark grove of ancient evergreens through which a path wound among huge mossy boulders down to the water's edge. It reminded her of the garden in Desio; she wondered if Larocque had been here.

They lunched in a little town on the mainland. It was warm enough to eat outside. As they sipped their wine with the view spread before them, there seemed little wanting to the perfection of the day, yet she was melancholy. Trezzano and Maddalena were so absorbed in each other that it was almost embarrassing. She and Giovanni kept the conversation going and entertained the child.

Back in Laveno, they took their sunset stroll after dinner, Trezzano and Maddalena alone together at the water's edge, Giovanni distracting Pierino with a game of ducks and drakes. When he offered her his arm on the path back she held herself stiffly and he made no move to draw closer. Perversely, she was disappointed. The soul's imperatives weren't always in accord with the body's desires.

To escape her mood, she makes herself write as full a description of the day as Mrs Godwin would have given.

The islands have been likened to the isles of the blest in Greek mythology, but I saw nothing to merit the comparison. Such artifice, when all around lie the beautiful works of Nature, such extravagance to please the tastes of a few when the multitude lacks basic necessities, simply demonstrates the decadence of a class whose self-indulgence led to the Revolution and brought suffering upon many who had not deserved it.

Are you not merely jealous, her conscience asked, because you yourself might have possessed such a garden — which, had the world not changed, you would have enjoyed without a thought for those outside its gates? Is it the deprivation of the poor that you lament, or your own because the Revolution has disinherited you?

It's an uncomfortable thought in which she has to recognise some truth, and it's not the only troubling discovery she's made. She'd judged herself immune to merely sensual temptation, and it shames her to discover her weakness. She can only hope Giovanni didn't notice the effect he'd had on her. It means nothing to him, she's sure: in the absence of younger, prettier objects he exercises his charm on any woman at hand.

Or has she imagined the whole thing? Were those slight contacts that aroused her nothing more than the accident of their proximity on the boat? It's humiliating. What could be more foolish than an old maid imagining herself the object of desire.

She feigns sleep when Maddalena returns from her prolonged goodnight to Pierino, though she's still wide awake, her body as well as her mind restless from the day's emotions. Desire, illusory or not, seeks satisfaction. But with Maddalena beside her, she can't resort to the usual relief, only to a fantasy that is perhaps a more dangerous indulgence.

Naples, Tuesday 8 October

They left early to reach their destination before the midday heat and drove down the coast along a road lined with wealthy villas amid luxuriant vegetation. An idyllic landscape, but always in the volcano's shadow. One little town had been destroyed and rebuilt nine times in its long history. They passed through another renamed Gioacchinopoli in honour of the new king, who'd established manufacturing there.

'I'm glad to see that Joachim is trying to abolish indigence.'

'He won't succeed with the *lazzaroni*,' Lambert said. 'Why would they slave in a factory twelve hours a day when they can earn as much by their wits in an hour? As long as they have a bowl of macaroni they're content to sleep under a bench without a thought for the morrow.'

'They should be forced to work,' his wife exclaimed. 'I'm sick of the beggars, the outstretched hand wherever you go!'

He'd had the same reaction himself, but he was annoyed to find himself in agreement with Mme Lambert. It made him feel contrary. 'We're bringing all the advantages of modern civilisation to Italy. Let's hope that in so doing, we don't destroy everything that makes it happier than France.'

Before she could answer, the driver pulled up on a stretch of arid wasteland. On the other side of a fence lay an enormous pit where only a grid of low walls indicated there had ever been a city. So this was Pompeii. Just another excavation. Here, as in Rome, the debris was carried away by women, their bare feet grey with dust.

A guide led them down a ramp, past labourers freeing a row of columns, and they walked up and down the streets. In a roofless house, the guide dipped a sponge in a pail of water and moistened a wall, briefly reviving painted birds and plants that faded quickly in the dry air. In another, they saw a series of tiny rooms, mere cubicles with graffiti that indicated their purpose. He wanted to ask if any of the girls and their customers had perished in the act, but the question seemed heartless.

Back in the nearest town they found an inn. The appearance of four foreign signori caused a great shaking-out of table linen and recitation of menus.

'No soup, no macaroni!' Lambert was brisk. 'Just fish if you can guarantee it's fresh. What's the price of your best wine?'

'You have to be firm with these people, or they rob you.' Mme Lambert didn't trouble to lower her voice.

He stood at the window looking out. Two bare-legged men in broad-brimmed hats conversed with eloquent gestures. A woman with a basket paused at the stall of a cheese merchant who was suckling her baby under the shade of its awning. Next to them, a scribe had set up his table and was writing to the dictation of a young peasant.

The entire life of this people took place on the street. They lived in the exterior in every sense of the word — he couldn't imagine them possessing an inner life. The introspection of the northern character had no place in a land of eternal sunshine. Perhaps that explained his boredom in the midst of all this beauty.

On the way back, Lambert had the driver stop in a village beneath which lay another Roman town. A man with a pine torch led them down through a trapdoor into a Roman theatre. A comic actor's mask — had it fallen from his face as he tried to flee? — had left its impression in the hardened flow of ash. It stared up at them in the flickering torchlight, a mocking reminder of the vanity of human aspiration.

You too, stranger, will one day bare your teeth in the final rictus. It was the one memorable thing in a disappointing day.

Laveno, Tuesday 8 October

A long journey today, first across the lake and then by mule cart to see the statue of San Carlo Borromeo that stands on a hill above the shore, visible from afar.

Another sacred mountain with a pilgrims' way, but today Maddalena showed no pious inclinations. The statue was their goal, and as they rounded the final bend it appeared with the brazen suddenness of a god, sunlight flashing from its copper robes, a huge hand outstretched in blessing.

'They say it's the eighth wonder of the world.'

Maddalena was easily impressed. For her own part, she thought it a hideous imposition on the landscape.

'Look what big ears he has!' Giovanni said to Pierino. 'It must be from listening to all those confessions. They got bigger with every sin he heard.'

'You can climb up a ladder inside the statue, right to the head, if you have the courage,' Trezzano said. 'There'd be a magnificent view from the top.'

'And you'd find out if a cardinal has a' — Giovanni used a dialect word she didn't know, though she guessed its import from Pierino's giggle — 'under his robes.'

'What are you teaching the child! Don't let *la nonna* hear you say that,' Maddalena told Pierino.

It wasn't the only shocking thing he was likely to tell his grandmother. A small boy couldn't guard his tongue like an adult, and the captain's presence on their journey would not long remain a secret. But, one way or another, Signora Rossi couldn't be kept in ignorance much longer, she thought, as they walked back to the boat, the child between Trezzano and his mother, swinging from their hands. Even Signora Rossi's heart might soften at the sight.

'Lena must remarry,' Giovanni said, as though reading her thoughts. 'She's too young to be shut away with my parents for the rest of her life. But she'll have to fight for her happiness.'

'How could your parents object to Captain Trezzano once they know him?'

'My mother won't forgive her if she marries another man in the service of the French.'

'But will he stay in the army? Is his lameness not an impediment?'

'Only to active service. But his role with recruits is just as important. He's a man who inspires others.'

She could well believe it, remembering Trezzano's dream of a future Italy. Training young men, even reluctant conscripts, Trezzano would give them a new consciousness of themselves as Italians; he was creating the future army of an independent Italy. More than likely he was the inspiration behind Giovanni's talk of enlisting. But if Giovanni enlisted, Trezzano would have stolen two children from Signora Rossi. It was difficult to see how the signora would ever become reconciled to the marriage.

After dinner they took their usual sunset walk. She could not refuse Giovanni's arm, though she tried to maintain her distance.

'I hope that you don't think me a fool, Signorina — I like to joke, but I'm more serious than everyone thinks.'

'I know.' She was uncomfortable, not sure where he was leading.

'When I talk to you I feel capable of becoming another man.'

'Not a soldier, I hope?' she interrupted nervously.

'No, no. I'm thinking of becoming a courier. What better life for a man of no talent who wants to see the world?'

'Why are you so certain that you have no talent?'

But he'd reverted to his joking manner and there was no further serious talk between them, only the playful gallantry that put an end to the tentative frankness they'd achieved earlier.

It's not something she can record, except obliquely. Maddalena may return at any moment and she would not feel comfortable writing certain things in her presence. But self-censorship makes for a boring narrative; she adds a postscript.

A certain acquaintance of mine disguises his aspirations by playing the clown, but it is not the whole man. Yet who does not play a role in company? Perhaps we all resemble the islands on the lake, of which only the uppermost fraction is visible while the rest is submerged.

Naples, Wednesday 9 October

I wanted to use the other notebook to write about Naples, but I couldn't find it. I haven't noticed anything else missing except a penknife. Nothing to get upset about. There were only a few words in the lost notebook about the Valais and Rome, the D-ss L, and the veil of boredom thrown over Rome by the tedious house of Pacé.

It's a good thing, though, that he'd disguised Martial under the usual sobriquet, because it could be embarrassing if the missing notebook fell into the wrong hands. He must have left it in the post vehicle or at an inn. He'll make enquiries on the way back. There can't have been anything too indiscreet in its pages, but it's a loss for his description of the Simplon road, which he can barely remember now. His recollections of Rome are still clear, but it would be an effort to set them down again. Better to record his impressions of Naples while they're fresh.

He manages three paragraphs on the journey and arrival before the urge to write starts flagging. Here he is, in one of the most beautiful places on Earth, and he's unhappy. The problem is that he's seeing it in the wrong company. This enchanting landscape deserves better.

During the journey I observed that I think tenderly of five women and that a rendezvous with any one of them would give me pleasure. These five women are: Mme P., Mme Palfy, Mélanie, Livia B., and Ang.

I believe I am in love with the first. At least, since Bologna, I would rather have been with her than wherever I was at the time.

It must be love when his pulse quickens at the mere thought of her, and seven or eight times a day he finds himself lost in a tender reverie from which he emerges reluctantly. He's dying to get back to Milan.

He'd expected so much from his journey south, but lack of the right company and all the many irritations of an uncivilised society have spoilt it. In fact, he'd be glad to get back to Paris if it weren't for Angela. If only he had entrée here to a circle like hers or Mme Lamberti's, Naples would be more interesting, and of course if he'd heard music by some of the great Neapolitan composers — the divine Pergolesi, or his beloved Cimarosa — that would have changed everything.

But he must stop complaining and bring his diary up to date. He forces himself to write a perfunctory account of each day since his arrival, then puts away his notebook with relief. In a few hours they'll be leaving for Vesuvius. Lambert assures him you have to see the volcano by night. Perhaps this will be the experience that redeems Naples.

Laveno, Wednesday 9 October

This afternoon I went fishing with Giovanni and Pierino on the lake, an experience as new to me as to the child. Maddalena was tired and preferred to watch us from the shore.

Trezzano, too, refused, saying he had letters to write. 'But you'll come with us, Signorina, won't you?' Giovanni gave her a significant look.

'With pleasure.' The moment had come to cease playing chaperone. When they were far enough from shore to glance back discreetly, she saw that Trezzano had joined Maddalena.

Once the lines were cast, they were silent so as not to frighten the fish. Seated in the stern out of the others' way, she watched their intent faces. Pierino's features were still undefined, but now and then one caught a hint of what they'd be when his round cheeks gave way to a masculine leanness and his snub nose lengthened to the Grecian line that gave Giovanni's profile its distinction — unless he took after his father, of whose features his own might be the sole record. But the eyes were definitely from the Rossi side. Giovanni had the same black pupils.

As though conscious of being watched, Giovanni turned and met her eyes. She smiled, nodding towards the child who was utterly absorbed in watching his line. Giovanni put his hand on the little boy's bent head, caressing it affectionately. A shock of longing ran through her. Not since childhood had anyone caressed her, and at that instant she would have sacrificed independence, even honour, for it. But she knew herself too well to imagine finding happiness with a man who was neither her social nor her intellectual equal, though that recognition did not banish longing.

An exclamation broke the silence and moments later a fish was writhing in the net. Pierino watched its death throes, fascinated and repelled. Some ten minutes later his own line jerked and with Giovanni's help he pulled in a sizeable perch.

'Who's going to eat this fine fish, Signorino?' the boatman asked.

'Me. But I'll share it with Mamma.'

'Won't you give Signorina Marie and our friend Trezzano a taste?' Giovanni asked.

'No, just me and Mamma.'

They exchanged wry glances over his head, both conscious of what might be taking place on shore, though on their return it was unclear what had happened, Maddalena less animated than usual and the captain silent and preoccupied. The child had dominated talk at dinner.

Poor little fellow, she thinks now. But perhaps it will be easier for him to let go of his mother now that he is moving into the world of men.

The fishing trip was an initiation: a first experience of slaughter, a first sight of death. Men have to learn a hardness of heart that a woman need never acquire, a lack of pity for which we sometimes unfairly reproach them, forgetting that it relieves us of the necessity of painful tasks. But even so, it is one thing to gut a fish and another to bayonet a fellow man. I cannot imagine any man of my acquaintance capable of such an act, yet I know —

The door creaks open and Maddalena tiptoes in.

'You're still writing, Marie! I thought you would be in bed.'

Sensing Maddalena's embarrassment, she ventures to be direct. 'Please forgive me if I'm being indiscreet, but it is impossible not to be aware that Captain Trezzano is in love with you — has he spoken to you yet?'

'Oh, Marie, I've been longing to tell you! But I was afraid you might disapprove.'

'On the contrary, my dear! I wish you both all the happiness you deserve.'

But the situation, she learns, is not so simple. Trezzano has asked Maddalena to be his wife, but she won't marry him unless he resigns his commission. 'I've lost one husband to war, I could not bear to go through such anguish again! But it's hard for Fedele, he's a soldier to the core. I'm asking him to abandon his calling. Do you think me selfish?'

'Not at all. A married man has responsibilities that are not easily compatible with a soldier's life. But your brother told me that the captain is no longer fit for active service, in any case. Could you accept that he continue training recruits?'

'If I could trust that he would never be sent into the field. But who can be certain that there won't be another war in which every officer, fit or not, will be needed?'

'He will be more acceptable to your mother if he is no longer in the army.'

'Oh, she'll disapprove no matter what he does! We have a battle ahead!'

'She must accept your marriage eventually, even if you have to wait awhile —'

'I'm not willing to wait. I've been alone for five years.'

And I, for how long now? she thinks silently, trying not to envy Maddalena.

Naples, Thursday 10 October

At one in the morning we set off for Vesuvius.

I was surprised at not seeing hell boiling in the crater. Description to be added when I have more time.

The view from the hermit's house is probably the most beautiful in the world. There's a visitor's book in which we found a platitude signed by Préameneu, the Councillor of State. Not a single sensible remark, which is astonishing. The names of Mme de Staël and Schlegel.

Now *there's* a way to see the world in comfort! Attach yourself to the household of a wealthy woman as tutor and literary adviser. August Schlegel might even get to England if Mme de Staël annoys the emperor enough. The malicious said it was he who'd written her book on Germany—as if a woman wasn't capable of it, especially that one.

Nonetheless, he'd been surprised to see that she really had made the ascent — or as far as the hermitage anyway. But Mme Lambert was proof a woman could do it, though she had to be carried in a litter by two peasants since no side saddle was available and she couldn't decently straddle a donkey in a dress.

They'd ridden by moonlight up the lower slopes to the famous hermitage where a tall figure bearing a pine torch met them. His monkish robes and gaunt sun-blackened features gave him the air of a desert saint, but he was more innkeeper than holy man, offering them an omelette and slices of sausage. They rested, then set off on foot to ascend the cone.

It was a hellish climb over a shifting surface of cinders and small rocks that made you slip back two steps for every three you took. He was soon out of breath and had to pause. Lambert had already reached the summit. Barral had gallantly turned back to help Mme Lambert, who'd given up halfway. One of the guides unrolled a length of canvas which he passed around her waist and attached to a rope round himself. Thus harnessed, she was hauled up the slope like a bale of merchandise.

It was still dark when they reached the main crater. He'd expected the lurid glow of fire, but there was only smoke and a stink of sulphur. The guides' pine torches provided the lone flames. Had Mme de Staël really seen molten lava? More likely, she'd stolen her description from a writer who had.

What redeemed the experience was the view. As dawn broke, earth and water emerged from darkness, reborn with the rising sun as fresh as the first morning of Creation. As they staggered back down the cinder slope, a vast panorama spread before them. On the plain below, the scars of ancient lava flows were easily visible, but so too was the land's prodigious fertility as the sun's first rays illuminated fields and vineyards. Beyond lay the sea, dotted with the sails of fishing boats and in the extreme clarity of the air, Naples itself and the offshore islands stood out distinctly. Could there be any sight on Earth more beautiful?

Their awe was tempered by hilarity at the sight of each other's grimy faces. 'You resemble a chimney sweep, my love,' Mme Lambert told her husband, wiping the smuts from his face with her handkerchief. She shook the dust from her petticoats, revealing a shapely calf. He was grateful he'd worn old boots. His gloves were blackened beyond redemption by the final ascent where he'd advanced on all fours across the cinders.

Back at the hermitage they sampled a bottle of the famous wine produced on the slopes. It was revoltingly sweet instead of the good thirst-quenching muscat he'd anticipated.

'Aren't you going to sign the visitors' book, Henri?' Lambert asked.

He hesitated, torn between a comic pseudonym and the desire to inscribe his obscure name in the same volume as the famous, to be recognised in its turn by some later traveller when he'd made his mark in life. How agreeable it would have been to sign 'Baron Henri de Beyle, Prefect', or better still a simple 'Henri Beyle' that any theatregoer would know.

He took the pen Lambert held out to him, and beneath his friend's elegant signature he scrawled: 'HB, who came, saw, and ruined a pair of gloves'.

Back in Naples, he reserved his seat with the Rome courier for the following night. He's seen all he came to see.

Laveno, Thursday 10 October

Our last day here and a final excursion across the lake to Intra. From afar, it is just another picturesque lakeside town, but its position between two fast-flowing mountain torrents has made it a centre of cloth manufacture. Captain Trezzano wished to visit a cotton mill owned by a Swiss manufacturer who has introduced the new English spinning machines. The mill occupies a former Franciscan monastery. Maddalena and I were deterred by the hot humid atmosphere and the noise of the machines, but the captain spent some time observing their operation. The new spinning mule, he told us, had increased the production of cotton thread tenfold.

'Where does the mill obtain raw cotton now?' she'd asked. The shortages produced by the blockade had been a frequent subject of conversation at Armand's table.

'From Egypt at present. But the new government of Naples is promoting its cultivation there. Soon Italy will produce all we need. And even the restrictions on trade that hurt others benefit us indirectly. Now that Swiss cotton manufacturers can no longer export their wares, Muller has opened his mill here — as an Italian manufacturer he can market his goods in Italy, and he brings us his machines and his expertise! Ultimately, we shall be the gainers.'

She was impressed by Trezzano's grasp of such matters. If he turned his energy and intelligence to a similar enterprise, he would serve the new Italy he dreamt of as much as by training its future soldiers. The army had always been the noblest of careers, but even her cousin was not ashamed to have interests in manufacture now. The world was changing.

She could write more tonight since she's alone, but she's not in the mood. It isn't easy to be an extra on the margin of someone else's happiness. She'd done her share all day, along with Giovanni, in distracting the child, but it was an effort at supper to keep up a lively flow of conversation when Maddalena and Trezzano were silent, their desire to be alone together evident in every glance. She has no wish to listen to her friend's confidences tonight. She will feign sleep.

A tug on the bedcovers, as Maddalena slips into bed in the dark, pulls her out of a dream. She has no idea what time it is, but the lamp has burnt down and the grey light of dawn is visible round the edge of the shutters. Out of consideration for Maddalena, she gives no sign that she's awake. Clearly, the sooner their marriage takes place the better. She'd thought Trezzano a more honourable man. But who is she to judge them?

Naples, Friday 11 October

His last day in Naples and he'd watched hopefully as the sun rose behind the twin summits of Vesuvius. There's talk of an imminent eruption, though there'd been no sign of activity yesterday, other than the fumes that stung their eyes. He'd cut out his visit to Livia for a chance to witness it. But there's not even a wisp of smoke from the summit.

He writes a few lines, though it's an effort. A week in this soft climate and his wits are dulled. His account of Naples can be rounded out later by the book he's bought, which will supply the facts, along with the comments Lambert has pencilled in at his request. Sarcastic for the most part, he sees, leafing through. Not surprising in this backward place. He's tried to refrain from any talk that might feed Lambert's envy, but he's uncomfortably aware of his own good fortune and a little guilty. Lambert had once asked if he'd put in a word for him with the all-powerful cousin and he'd refused. It was bad enough to have his father and grandfather bombarding Daru with pleas on his own behalf. He hadn't dared irritate his cousin by requesting help for friends.

It will be good to be on his own again. He'd looked forward to seeing his two old friends, but neither measured up to his memories. Had he overestimated them? Or was Naples to blame and its enervating way of life — all pleasure, all surface, stimulating the senses but not the mind? The intellect flourishes best in a cool climate.

Still, there are worse places to be stuck, he thinks, as they take a last walk around the bay in the limpid afternoon light. 'I shall envy you here under the palm trees of Chiaia when I'm dodging the potholes in Paris,' he tells Lambert.

The sunset sky is aflame as he settles in beside the courier, a small compensation for the missed eruption.

Milan, Friday 11 October

Here I am at last back at my table writing without danger of interruption. But I cannot help wondering what is happening across the street. It seems inevitable that Pierino will make some allusion to Captain Trezzano and Maddalena will have to face her mother's questions. I advised her to remain calm however much her mother provokes her, for it is the best way to show that she is fit to decide her own future. Women have always been considered too emotional to govern themselves and we must prove that we are as rational as men if we are to claim the right to independence. But to counsel calmness to an Italian is like telling a dog not to bark.

Happy though I am to regain my solitude, it was with sorrow that I left the beautiful lake country where I had had a poignant glimpse of what life might be, intensified by an experience on the journey home.

They'd paused frequently to permit Trezzano to dismount and stretch his leg. On one of their halts in a wood where the others looked for mushrooms, she'd lingered behind them on the path. Doves cooed above her head, a squirrel watched her with its bright brown eye as it stripped a chestnut. She stood very still not to alarm it. A sudden little gust of air showered her with a rain of yellow leaves, and at the same instant, somewhere below in the valley, a cock crowed. Sound and colour fused, filling her with a wave of happiness. Whether through some effect of the light or simply her intense concentration, she felt she was seeing with absolute clarity, as if through an optical instrument that magnified the smallest detail. Each of the scattered leaves at her feet stood out distinctly, an individual differentiated from the others by some slight variation of the gold overtaking the green — some still perfect, others papery, curling. The bark of the tree beside her was encrusted with a thick green layer of moss. She laid her hand on it and felt a cool spongy resilience pressing back against her palm almost as a cat or dog might respond to a caress.

Pierino came running down the path in search of her. The squirrel leapt for safety, the doves flapped away. The moment was broken. But she'd possessed it, or rather been possessed, lifted out of mundane awareness into a vision of things as they were, a world of multiple existences in which hers was merely one, of no more significance than that of the doves and the squirrel, or the trees even, live presences around her, their smallest twigs like delicate antennae reaching out towards the light.

It was not a state that could be prolonged, or not in company, though all the way back she felt its transformation. But the first sight of the city walls, even with the grand spectacle of the Duomo rising above them in the rosy aura of sunset, filled her with a melancholy reinforced by the odours assailing her nose as they passed through the city gate. There was comfort, nonetheless, in recognising familiar streets where the lamplighters were starting their rounds, and as they turned onto the Contrada Passerella she felt she was coming home.

To her surprise there was a letter from Armand and a note from Larocque, who'd evidently remembered when she was returning and looked forward to hearing about her journey. She wrote a quick reply for Perpetua to take in the morning, saying she would appreciate his help in finding a print of Lake Maggiore whenever he had time.

Armand was writing because he had news of his own. He was delighted to inform her that his wife was awaiting a happy event in the spring. 'If you are back from Italy by then, my dear cousin, we would be delighted if you would consent to be godmother to the new member of the family.' She was momentarily touched, though she quickly discerned the motive. A childless spinster, with property to bequeath, was a desirable godparent.

The letter ended with a postscript: 'I am pleased to hear that Larocque has been of service. I always found him trustworthy despite his brusque manner, because he still showed the respect due to our family, which in those days was all too rare. I would not otherwise have recommended him to you.'

The judgement angered her, not so much for what it said as for all it omitted: Had Armand perceived nothing of Larocque's intelligence and cultivation? But Larocque would not easily reveal himself, and an officer of Armand's rank would see no reason to become acquainted with a subordinate. Armand has learnt to show a democratic amiability in the circles he now frequents, but he would never promote an inferior to the rank of friend. He finds whatever human affection he needs at home; all other relationships are cultivated for their usefulness or tolerated for their necessity.

She is being unfair, she admits, putting the letter away and starting to get ready for bed. As a member of the former nobility in a fanatically republican army, always vulnerable to accusations of royalist sympathies and even imprisonment as the nephew of an émigré, Armand must have learnt to make himself acceptable to all, while trusting none — a situation that would not favour the development of friendship.

She had learnt the same distrust — the wariness of a sheltered child cast abruptly into a strange new world, all her capacity for social intercourse shrivelling like the buds of a hothouse plant exposed too soon to the chill of the outside world — a distrust reinforced by her return to a radically changed society in which she could never tell what hidden animosity might lie behind the faces around her.

Stretching out in bed she is grateful for the luxury of unshared space after the week with Maddalena. Not that she had found it distasteful. There'd been something comfortable about their nightly exchanges, the kind of intimate talk she might have had with her long-dead sister if they'd grown up together. With Maddalena, of course, the confiding had all been on one side, though Maddalena was not incurious and had indeed embarrassed her today on the journey back by asking if she'd never thought of marrying. Giovanni, she said, thought perhaps she'd vowed fidelity to a man who died in one of the recent wars. It was flattering that he saw her as a woman who'd known love, though she'd quickly corrected such a romantic notion. Marriage had been out of the question while her father needed her. And she was too accustomed to her independence now, she'd added. The last thing she needed was Lena matchmaking on her behalf.

SATURDAY *A crisis has broken out in the Rossi household, though I did not learn this till my return from a pleasant afternoon with Monsieur Larocque, who had the kindness to accompany me to a bookseller's.*

She'd breakfasted early, expecting a message from Maddalena since they were planning to go to the baths together. Her laundry despatched, she unlocked her trunk to shake out the creases from her winter wardrobe. Its sombre grey and indigo oppressed her now she was no longer in mourning. If she were to spend the winter in Milan she might permit herself the luxury of a new dress. Otherwise, she must conserve her resources for the journey.

No word had come from Maddalena so she headed out alone to the Alamanni baths for the luxury of a soak after her travels. On her return she found a message from Larocque to say he was unoccupied this afternoon and would be pleased to help her find a print.

He was wearing a new coat, she noticed when he arrived, or perhaps merely a warmer one for the change in the weather. The dark-brown broadcloth and black cravat suited him better than his uniform. On their way to the shop she asked after his daughter.

'We are reading the fable of "The Fox and the Crow". We take roles — she insists on playing Master Fox so I am Master Crow.' He hunched his shoulders and put his head on one side with such perfect mimicry that she was charmed.

'What a happy method of education!'

'She learns best when she's entertained. But what can you teach a child in an hour or two a week?'

'Have you thought of initiating her to botany?' she asked, tentatively, because some educators held that botany, with its discovery of sexual propagation in plants, was unsuitable for girls. The suggestion did not appear to shock him so she continued, 'It was my favourite pastime at her age. There's the pleasure of collecting plants for a herbarium. And she can draw and colour her favourites, which teaches observation. At the same time you are giving her some notions of scientific classification and even a little Latin —'

'An excellent idea. But I shall have to educate myself on the subject first. Perhaps the print shop will have a book for beginners.'

They crossed its threshold into an odour of leather binding that resurrected memories of her father's library. She made her enquiry in Italian with a new confidence that clearly surprised Larocque.

The merchant nodded. 'We have views of the lakes, Signorina, but we have also just received this new book on the Simplon route. It's fully illustrated.' He set a large volume on the counter and left them to examine it while he fetched the prints. She turned the pages, and Geneva, Saint-Maurice, Brigue, Domodossola passed before her eyes. Everything was there, from the most dramatic points on the new road to the beauties of Lake Maggiore. It would be a perfect record of her journey. But the price made her hesitate.

'Will you permit me to offer it to you as a gift?' Larocque asked quickly. 'It would be a small return for all your father's generosity.'

'You are too kind — I cannot let you indulge in such extravagance. I may get it, but I should like to see the prints first.'

While she examined them, Larocque asked the man if he had any books on botany suitable for a child, and he brought out a copy of Rousseau's *Elementary Letters on Botany*.

'But that's the very book my governess used!' She felt a thrill of pleasure at seeing the familiar plates.

'Then I must get it,' Larocque said.

As it was being wrapped, she made her own decision: 'I will take the book on the Simplon road.' It was worth the sacrifice of a new dress.

There was a small café on the corner, too unfashionable to attract anyone they knew, she saw with relief. They settled at a table and he asked about her trip. She said little about her friends, whose personal affairs could not interest him, but told him about the farm and her participation in the grape harvest.

'It's the best moment of the year on a farm,' he said. 'I'm glad you enjoyed yourself.'

He must think she'd been playing at rustic life like the late martyred queen and her ladies in their shepherdess attire. But of course, he was right. She knew nothing of the back-breaking toil of weeding or hay raking in the midsummer heat. Feeling a little humbled, she said no more about the farm but asked if he knew Lake Maggiore. Since he too had been there, she unwrapped her new book so they might view certain scenes together. The pictures had a satisfying exactitude, but something indefinable was missing. The colour was monotone, lacking the richness and variety of nature, and the reduction in size to the pages of a book could not capture the immensity of lake and mountains.

'The old painters knew better how to render space, did they not? I am impatient to visit the Brera again.'

'I'm at your disposition whenever you wish.' He smiled at her enthusiasm.

They agreed to meet on Monday.

Maddalena had left a note in her absence. The Rossi household was in turmoil. Pierino had immediately recounted their adventures, in which, naturally, Trezzano figured. A furious scene ensued and no one had slept. 'Fedele has spoken to my father this morning,' Maddalena wrote. 'Father has made no difficulties, but Mamma has said unforgivable things. She accuses me of bringing shame on the family by displaying myself with my lover. I beg you to avoid her for the next few days. I'm embarrassed to say that she's angry with you too.'

No doubt Signora Rossi considers me a bad influence. It is an unpleasant situation, but any resentment that I might have felt at being embroiled without my consent in Maddalena's affairs is banished by my conviction that she deserves to be happy. Whatever deception there has been was necessitated by Signora Rossi's unjustifiable opposition to her daughter's remarriage.

Rome, Sunday 13 October

He reached Rome as the sun's first rays illuminated the countryside. The return journey was uneventful, but his enquiries about his lost notebook at every halt were unavailing. Unfortunately there was no seat with the courier for another two days, so he couldn't escape Chancenie's hospitality. His plans were continually frustrated in this backward country. Did he dare take the extra time for Ancona without knowing if his extension had been granted? But he'd announced his arrival to Livia; it would only add a day or two.

His cheerful mood was jolted when Martial asked what he'd said to the police chief at Mme Lante's concert.

'Nothing directly. He was eavesdropping on my conversation with the duchess. Why?'

'He asked me if you had authorisation for your journey. As an auditor you need it.'

'But I'm travelling as a private citizen.'

'I told him that you had a leave of absence. But be prepared for a reprimand. I fear he may mention you in his reports. You should have paid him a courtesy call.'

For the rest of the day his heart raced whenever he thought of it. He tried to calm himself. Thanks to Mme Lante's caution he'd said nothing outrageous in Norvins' hearing. Surely the man wasn't petty enough to denounce him for failing to call. It was a mistake to have had any contact with official circles; he should have travelled incognito.

In any case, it was too late to remedy it now. Martial at least would send a positive report to his brother. And Chancenie's opinion was important too. The women in the family corresponded; he liked the thought that news of him might reach Mme Daru. He went to romp with the children — always a sure way to a mother's heart. Young Jerome, like Mme Daru's Napoleon, liked playing horse and rider. Crawling round the nursery with a child on his back gave him a perfect view of the nursemaid's ankles.

He was anticipating a family evening, but he'd underestimated Martial's hospitable nature. Colleagues, both French and Roman, dropped in after dinner for music and conversation. Martial introduced him to a middle-aged man with an ironic smile hovering at the corners of his mouth.

'Monsieur Landi is Italy's foremost modern painter. He's advising me on art for His Majesty's suite, and contributing a work of his own — Pericles watching the building of the Parthenon accompanied by artists and poets.'

'An ambitious subject, Monsieur!' he said politely, adding as Martial greeted another guest, 'And a *flattering* theme' — to show he wasn't a fool. The painter merely smiled but asked how long he was staying in Rome. 'Only a day, unfortunately — what do you advise me to see in that brief time?'

'Ah, but you've already seen the best Rome has to offer — in Paris.' It was said politely, but he felt the reproach.

'With all the riches that Rome still contains, it will never lose its pre-eminence,' he replied in his official manner, adding in his natural tone, 'I hardly know where to begin.'

'If you've time for nothing else, visit the Raphael rooms at the Vatican.'

'You place Raphael above Michelangelo?' He found a scrap of paper to write on and asked the painter to rank the greatest Italian artists.

Landi listed a dozen names. 'But Raphael, Correggio, Annibale Carracci are the greatest.'

'Carracci? But his paintings are so black! I saw some in Bologna.'

'They've darkened with time. He used cheap materials because he was poor. But he rescued art from the mediocrity into which it had sunk.' The Carracci family were revolutionary in their way, the painter explained; after the great flowering of the Renaissance there'd been a decline into artifice till the Carracci led a return to the natural.

Did this explain his lack of response to Italian art? That *Martyrdom of Saint Lawrence* in Santa Croce, for example. He'd been wasting his time on the practitioners of a dead tradition. It's the same in literature — all those hidebound imitators of the classics, repeating the stale figures of an outmoded rhetoric when a new language was needed, suited to the rapid tempo of modern life. Literature too needed a revolution. His mind filled with parallels.

When the guests left, he complimented Chancenie on the evening's success. The importance of these gatherings was obvious

— champagne, music, urbane conversation would slowly erase the memory of General Radet and his troops breaking down the palace doors in the night and rushing the pope away in a closed carriage. He congratulated himself on his own part in spreading goodwill. And the painter had offered to show him some of the city's lesser-known treasures in the morning. He'd made a friend there, he thought with satisfaction.

Milan, Sunday 13 October

No word from Maddalena. Anxious to avoid Signora Rossi, I attended Mass at San Babila instead of the parish church. After lunch I walked in the public gardens, then wrote to Armand.

She'd intended no more than a note of congratulation on his news, but she couldn't resist describing her journey. Her vague allusion to travelling companions will make him curious, but she judged it best to be unspecific. He would question the wisdom of involving herself with individuals who are not her equals, and Marie-Cécile would be scandalised to hear that she'd worn peasant dress and worked in the fields. An agreeable sensation of defiance fills her at the thought.

But it's galling nonetheless that her limited resources and the fact that she's travelling alone (which must certainly raise eyebrows if not actually close doors to her) make it difficult to enter the circles to which her birth should admit her. Armand's letters are all addressed to minor officials, well placed to offer practical assistance but not to provide entrée into the best local society. Does he lack connections with more important men, or was he embarrassed that she was travelling unaccompanied? In any case, she cannot regret that it's led her to make Larocque's acquaintance. She adds a postscript.

Monsieur Larocque's gratitude to my father has led him to offer me invaluable assistance since my arrival. His intelligence, his cultivation, his goodness of heart fully justify my father's faith in his capacity to profit from education. My father would have been happy to learn that his protégé has not forgotten him. The true monument of a benevolent man is found in the lives of those whom he has assisted, and is more substantial than the most grandiose tomb.

The final remark is one in which Armand can deservedly recognise himself, even if she had not intended it for him.

MONDAY *The fifth anniversary of the battle of Jena. Maddalena came with Pierino after attending Mass for the repose of her husband's soul. I could not help thinking of the thousands of Prussian families who must also mark the anniversary. Surely there will not be war with Russia. Has the Emperor not put enough families in mourning! This afternoon I went to the Brera with Monsieur Larocque.*

He'd started reading Rousseau's botanical letters and was grateful for her suggestion. 'It's exactly what she needs. I've discovered that a child — this one, anyway — learns best through activity, not parroting texts as I did at her age. Of course, it's not the season now for identifying plants, but in the spring we shall be prepared when we go to the woods.'

She would be gone by then, she thought with a pang.

'By the way, I received a message from Mme Picard,' he said, as they turned into the Brera. 'She requested your address so that she may invite you to a musical evening. I did not like to give it without your permission —'

'But of course you may.' She was grateful nonetheless that he hadn't offered to bring the invitation himself. The less that lady knew of their friendship the better.

The old cicerone greeted them but left them to themselves. As usual, there were no visitors or copyists in the Bellini room.

'Here's another landscape for you,' Larocque said. 'If you can ignore these holy persons who so inconsiderately block the view.'

It had become a joke between them. The main obstruction here, apart from the seven saints attending the Virgin, was two plump cherubs suspending a scarlet drapery. She eyed them with distaste. 'Why did artists portray angels as naked infants when we are taught that they are spiritual beings superior to mankind?'

'Do these fit your idea of angels better?' He pointed upwards at a large canvas of three archangels casting Satan into Hell — glorious figures whose scarlet and ochre garments shone in the rising sun. There was some incongruity still: even Michael with his upraised sword had a feminine grace that made it hard to believe him a warrior. The naked figure of Satan was unquestionably male, however, and his face bore a marked resemblance to the emperor that would have pleased the village priest, though the fifteenth-century painter could not have foreseen it. She told Larocque about the sermon. He was not surprised.

'It's well known that the priests are preaching rebellion. But it's impossible to arrest them all. In any case, their influence will diminish as the people reap the benefits of our presence. There are enlightened priests who see the necessity of social change, but for every good one, like our old *curé* in Vernet, who tries to educate his flock, there are a dozen who keep them ignorant the better to tyrannise them.'

There were many such figures on the walls around them — stern theologians and confessors, inquisitors with burning eyes. But their power was waning. She could almost pity them, falsely secure in their gilded frames, unaware that their churches had been despoiled, their monasteries closed, their authority challenged.

She moved to an altarpiece in which the Virgin was almost eclipsed by four gloomy ecclesiastics. 'That one with the corners of his mouth turned down looks particularly glum. He must have eaten a sour apple, as my nurse used to say.'

'He reminds me of a priest at the college, a brute who took pleasure in whipping any boy who failed his interrogation. Enough of these evil old men! It's too beautiful a day to be inside.'

She would gladly have spent another hour at the gallery, but she accepted his change of mood. It was indeed a perfect afternoon to drive around the ramparts. The wave upon wave of green beyond was now splashed with gold and amber, and in the crisp autumnal air the entire Alpine chain was visible on the horizon. For an even better view, Larocque said, they should climb to the roof of the Duomo one afternoon. There was a gallery round the spire from which you could see half of Lombardy. It was especially beautiful towards sunset.

When they reached the Porta Romana she was reminded of the decision she must take and asked if he'd ever been to Rome.

'Unfortunately, I've not had the opportunity. May I ask if you still intend to travel south before winter sets in?'

'I find Milan so agreeable that I may wait until spring.'

'All your friends will be very happy if you decide to prolong your stay.' The words were merely what the moment called for, but the warmth in his eyes was genuine and she was touched.

'It will be hard to leave. I cannot hope to meet with as much kindness in Rome as I have found here.'

'Will you return to France afterwards?'

'Nothing calls me back. I have no ties there, apart from my cousin and his wife. I set off with the idea of settling in Rome . . .'

'That might be unwise. From what I hear, the Roman summer is dangerous because of the endemic fever. Of course, there's fever here too in the rice-growing districts, anywhere there's stagnant water, but it's much worse in the south. Fever has depopulated the countryside round Rome. I advise you to be prudent.'

'Thank you for the warning. I may have to reconsider my plans. But in the meantime I should like to see more of Lombardy in this beautiful autumn weather.'

'The poplars on the canal must be turning colour now. We should see them before the leaves fall.'

They parted with an agreement to drive out there the following day.

After dinner, Maddalena came to beg her company. As she pinned on the veil she'd bought in Milan, it struck her that she was moving between two contiguous but separate worlds. She was Signorina Marie in one, but still Mademoiselle de Vernet in the other, an odd disjunction, though the two worlds were not impermeable, as she discovered when she joined her friends. Allowing the lovers to make up for three days of separation, she and Giovanni hung back.

'You've been hiding something from us, Signorina,' he said playfully. 'Who is the gentleman who came for you in a carriage on Saturday and again today?'

'I am hiding nothing.' The question was impertinent and her tone showed it. 'Monsieur Larocque is an acquaintance of my cousin. He had the goodness to take me to a bookseller on Saturday and to the Brera gallery today.'

'Forgive me, Signorina. I did not mean to offend you. This gentleman works at the army commissariat, doesn't he? My father has done business with him.'

'I'm not offended.' He was merely teasing her as he did his sisters and cousins. But it was disagreeable to be reminded of Larocque's mundane employment, and even more disagreeable that she found it so. Were her prejudices so ingrained? She turned the conversation away from herself. 'Do you know if the captain has offered his resignation?'

'Yes, but it's not to take effect immediately. He wishes to find alternative employment first. He's a prudent man, our friend.'

He himself was the opposite, she thought, everything he did impulsive — the way he'd take off at a canter on his horse, or speak without considering his words. There was a recklessness about him that could lead to some foolishness he might regret. Maddalena had it too, though Trezzano steadied her.

There are prudent characters who can delay happiness in order to place it on a secure basis, and reckless beings who seize their happiness in both hands when they believe they have found it. The prudent are undoubtedly wiser, yet I envy the reckless their passion. But I too have been rash in setting off with only the dream of Rome to guide me, and what Monsieur Larocque told me today about the Roman climate has forced me to recognise my foolhardiness. Still, if I reach Rome by late November I could safely stay there until May. Then Florence perhaps, or somewhere cool in the mountains for the summer. But the thought of becoming a perpetual wanderer frightens me.

TUESDAY *Signora Rossi still refuses to meet Captain Trezzano and Maddalena is in a state of nervous exasperation. But Pierino had a surprise for me this morning. Signor Rossi has brought back one of the puppies from the farm — Lupetto, the children's favourite — to deal with the rats in the courtyard. It has happily diverted the child's attention from the tension surrounding his mother's remarriage.*

My excursion this afternoon with Monsieur Larocque aroused thoughts of the past that seemed to find an echo in tonight's music. Mme Delavigne plays like an angel.

Their return to the canal had been perfectly timed. The poplars were at the height of their beauty, their green transmuted to gold by the alchemy of the season, shimmering like candle flames in the canal's dark mirror. But it brought back memories of the carriage rides with her mother and their homesickness that first autumn of exile. They'd consoled themselves with the hope that they would soon return. Yet here she was, all these years later, still an exile, uprooted from her place in the world, a stranger passing through.

'You have a wistful air. Does this bring back too many memories?' Larocque seemed to divine her thoughts.

'Beauty itself sometimes makes one sad, irrespective of its associations, don't you find?'

'Because it's ephemeral. It reminds us of mortality. Especially at this time of year. *Sunt lacrimae rerum —*'

'*Et mentem mortalia tangunt,*' she completed the quotation. There are tears in things, reminders of mortality that touch the mind. She took some consolation in knowing that the ancients had known such emotions too.

A boat had just passed through the lock and was gliding towards them pulled by a horse. It was a picturesque sight and she remarked that it might figure in the background of a painting. 'But the poplars alone would almost suffice for a subject, don't you think?'

'In the eyes of a few, perhaps. But for the general taste a landscape must have figures, from myth or poetry if not scripture. At the very least some picturesque peasants.'

She evaded the mild irony in his tone and asked him if Bellini or Previtali, who so obviously loved the countryside, had never painted it for its own sake without a religious subject.

'Not to my knowledge. At least, there's nothing of the sort in the Brera.' But the collection had been brought together from churches and monasteries, so naturally its subject matter was religious. 'In fact I believe I've only ever seen one landscape without figures — a small piece by a Flemish painter at least a century later. It's in the collection at the Ambrosian library. We could go there next week, if you like.'

They were to see each other in the evening at Mme Picard's. When Larocque came in, she was seated beside her hostess, and he came over to greet them, giving no indication that he'd parted from her an hour or two earlier. She was grateful for his tact.

Two officers opened the evening with comic duets, followed by a lady singer whose pleasant voice was marred by a coquettish manner. The main offering was a pianoforte performance by Mme Delavigne that began with two bagatelles familiar from Marie-Cécile's after-dinner entertainment. But Mme Delavigne was not a stiff performer like Marie-Cécile. Indeed, as she embarked on her next piece, it seemed as though she were improvising, her hands hovering above the keyboard while she waited for inspiration, the first notes falling from her fingers in a soft ripple of sound that awaited a theme.

When it came — three slow resonant notes, repeated in a haunting sequence — it seemed to embody all the longing for things irrevocably lost that she'd felt by the canal. Her eyes sought Larocque, but his were on the musician. Would he hear what she heard in those sounds? Did they evoke the same emotions for all listeners? She was too musically ignorant to judge. And for him they might carry other associations, not least with Mme Delavigne herself, a romantic figure in her simple white dress, her dark curly head bent over the keys.

The pensive opening gave way to a more cheerful movement that in turn was ousted by something furious and dramatic. Though she felt its passion, she could make no sense of the violent onslaught of sound, which tested all the performer's considerable skill and met with cries of admiration when it concluded. A fierce irrational envy shot through her, not because of the applause, but because Mme Delavigne possessed this means of expressing what words could only clumsily convey. She felt dull in comparison, the writing over which she laboured flat and passionless.

At that moment, though, Larocque made his way across the room, ostensibly to greet a friend, stopping as he passed, to say in an undertone that could not reach Mme Picard's ears, 'That first movement reminded me of our conversation. *Lacrimae rerum.*'

Something *had* passed between them. She felt a surge of gratitude. He addressed no further remark to her, as though obeying some tacit agreement to shield their friendship from gossip. When the evening ended, she gratefully accepted the offer of the plump lady, Mme Bouchot, to convey her home, and was taken to her door in a babble of conversation.

Her candle is almost burnt down, but she must finish capturing her thoughts of the day before she sleeps.

In the past few years I have lived in a poverty of the senses that desolates me now that I recognise it. The beautiful and the sublime existed only in books; they were intellectual experiences that came to me through words and only engaged my imagination. But while rejoicing in this tardy discovery of art and music I could weep for the years passed in ignorance. How much lost time I must make up for!

WEDNESDAY *As we passed Pontarelli's, Maddalena admired a reticule in the window and the idea came to me to make her one to match her new hat — a small gift before my departure. I went back later to check the design and purchase some dark green velvet and embroidery silks before calling on Mme Picard.*

To her disappointment, Mme Delavigne was not among the visitors.

'Gabrielle's days are busy,' said Mme Bouchot in answer to her enquiry. 'She has many pupils. And she continues to study herself, with a professor at the conservatory. He is probably in love with her like all the men.'

The quiet young woman was not there either. She was, her mother confided, in an interesting condition and needed to rest. 'Our little Sophie! Already!' exclaimed Mme Bouchot. The news gave the possibility of war with Russia new poignancy.

At the end of the afternoon the gentlemen arrived. Larocque was not among them. She knew he'd be stock-taking for the next two days. What a waste of his intelligence, she'd thought. It surprised her that he'd freed himself two afternoons running, but probably he worked late to compensate for any liberty he allowed himself during the day.

'I hope we shall have the pleasure of seeing you tomorrow evening,' her hostess said in parting. This would be the rhythm of her weeks if she stayed in Milan, she thought, returning home. A musical evening, an afternoon call, the opera on Thursdays, her daily walks with Maddalena. Far livelier than Nogent. But not enough to keep her from Rome, were it not for the Brera and her country excursions with Larocque.

Ancona, Thursday 17 October

In bed at last (not Livia's, though he'd probably be welcomed there), he tries to fix the last three days in memory for later recording.

Still worried about his missing notebook and the awful possibility that it could end up in the hands of the director of police, he'd judged it safer not to write another word in Rome, not even to describe his tour with Landi. His final hours were spent among the tombs at Saint Peter's — a fitting end to his visit. The whole city is a cemetery, crammed with relics of a grander past.

It was a relief to be heading north again — till he heard that he was travelling with the courier who'd been attacked two weeks earlier. Despite telling himself that misfortune wasn't likely to strike the same man twice, he slept uneasily through the night, waking to a shrill female voice at the carriage door: 'The best grapes in Italy! Taste them, Signor!' At every halt there's a hand held out and a scowl if you don't put a coin in it. Whatever this creature muttered in her dialect when he refused was neither a compliment to his ancestors nor a blessing on his journey. Travel, he'd written to Pauline, would show him a cross-section of Italian life, but it's a cross-section of the lowest class of society, and the Italian lower class is the most exasperating in the world. Indisputably, civilisation has reached a higher level in France. If it weren't for the passionate sensibility that makes Italians excel in the arts, their country would be intolerable.

In Foligno, he had to find a courier going east, and had a moment's hesitation. If he continued north he could reach Milan in four days. But Livia was expecting him; it wouldn't be fair to disappoint her. Their brief acquaintance was like something in a novel in its unlikeliness, though it must be one of many in this new empire, which was bringing together individuals who would never have met in the past. In this instance, you had a Polish soldier, inspired by Bonaparte's sympathy for his oppressed country, who joins the emperor's legions, fights in the Italian wars, marries a pretty Italian who accompanies him on the next campaign, and they end up in occupied Brunswick, where an assistant war commissioner by the name of Henri Beyle plays cards with the charming young wife, then (after the unfortunate Pole gets himself killed in some skirmish) escorts the grieving widow on the first stage of her journey home. No, he couldn't give up this detour. It wasn't often that life offered you a second chance.

By good luck he'd met a Milanese businessman returning home via Ancona who suggested they travel together sharing expenses, and whose cheerful company had made the journey tolerable. The roads in the former papal states were appalling and frequently obliged them to get out and walk. At the highest point in the Apennines, the route funnelled them between sheer rock walls into a village whose inhabitants seemed to have no other means of existence than beggary. A troop of ragged women and children mobbed them, undeterred by the postilion's whip.

Milan, he realises, had given him a false impression of Italy eleven years ago. What he'd seen then was a region that had prospered under the enlightened rule of Austria. Most of Italy was still in the Dark Ages. But now, thanks to the emperor, all these small, ill-governed states were being lifted out of their backwardness and brought into the modern world.

Casati, his fellow-traveller, agreed with him that Milan was the most civilised town in Italy. 'And I don't say that because I'm Milanese, but because I've seen all the others!' Just talking about it made him long to be back there. Nothing on the journey, not even the Bay of Naples, could compete with the joy of seeing Angela again. As they travelled through the second night he rehearsed the tender things he'd tell her once they were alone together.

He woke to his first glimpse of the Adriatic as they entered Ancona — a little town of tall brick houses and narrow streets, hemmed in between its harbour and two steep hills. He had himself shaved at a barber's, then asked his way to Livia's house. A maid with an ingratiating manner admitted him, and a moment later Livia appeared, as pretty as he remembered and no longer wearing the mourning in which he'd last seen her, but white muslin that showed her figure to advantage. Her father pressed him to stay with them in that hospitable Italian manner that brooks no refusal, and he accepted.

After breakfast, Livia took him down to the waterfront — a barren, rocky, treeless shore with none of the luxuriant beauty of the Bay of Naples. But the natural harbour created by a curved headland had given it importance from early times, and there was a well-preserved Roman arch celebrating the exploits of some emperor and a papal arch rebaptised the Gate of France. It was a naval base now, with frigates patrolling the Adriatic against the threat of the English navy, and the anchorage was being enlarged by the extension of the ancient Roman breakwater.

'A pile of money it's costing,' Livia's father grumbled over the midday meal. 'But it will be good for us in the long run once the war ends and business returns to normal.' The port was suffering from the ban on trade with England, though there was a lot of smuggling, he admitted slyly. A shrewd fellow, with a frank unpretentious manner and a good heart, but he was living openly with the maid, which made Livia unhappy.

After lunch they'd climbed up to the citadel. Its guns threatened any English vessel that tried to enter the harbour, but the blue expanse of the Adriatic, sparkling in the afternoon sun, was disappointingly peaceful.

'Now you've seen all there is to see,' Livia said. 'It's a boring place. I'd love to live in a big city, even outside Italy . . . '

'But you must have some amusements here?'

'Amusements!' She shrugged. 'I walk twice a day — you've seen both walks — I go to the theatre with my cousin. I take singing lessons, though I don't know why since there's no one to notice whether I've improved. Your arrival is the first new thing that's happened in a year.'

'I bet you have lots of admirers,' he said gallantly. 'You're still as pretty as ever. I'm surprised you haven't remarried, with all these officers in town.'

'I made that mistake once but I won't repeat it. To love a man and then lose him like that . . . '

But weren't there other men, he asked. None that interested her, she'd said. Naturally, she wouldn't settle for some dull merchant after her dashing Polish colonel. But the man had been dead three years now — a long time for a woman to be without love, especially one with Livia's temperament.

After dinner they went to the theatre. Livia had dressed with care. Her figure wasn't unlike Angela's, and with the deep brim of her bonnet hiding her face, he'd had the illusion for a delicious moment that he was back in Milan. But conversation in the cousin's box was dreadfully provincial. He'd had difficulty stifling his yawns.

When they said goodnight Livia had lifted her face to his for the kiss he felt obliged to give. He could have her, he's sure, but her kisses don't arouse him like Angela's. In any case, he's only here for a couple of days, till Casati has completed his business. Five days from now he should be in Milan!

Milan, Thursday 17 October

Maddalena came early with the good news that Signora Pulcheria has been safely delivered of another boy, which must surely distract Signora Rossi from her anger.

I spent the afternoon drawing a design of wild roses for Lucia's sash. Pink will please her, I hope. I went out afterwards to purchase the materials.

Tonight good Mme Bouchot took me in her carriage to the opera. A conversation with Mme Delavigne made me feel (contrary to my first impression) that I should like to know her better.

There was something disarmingly natural and uncalculated about the pianist's appearance — the unadorned white muslin, the dark curly hair that almost certainly required no curl rags — yet the effect was seductive. Her features were imperfect but that was part of her charm; the tiny mole above her upper lip (like the speck a mother would brush away with the tip of a forefinger) seemed less a flaw than an embellishment that drew attention to the sensitive shape of the mouth.

At their first meeting, Mme Delavigne's musical sophistication had intimidated her, but now she welcomed the opportunity to offer compliments. 'You must spend hours every day at the pianoforte.'

'Not as many as I would like. I give lessons, which takes up much of my time.'

'But you transmit your love of music to the young . . .'

'To a few. For most it's drudgery that their mothers impose. I would not teach if I did not need the money. You will have heard, no doubt — in this circle there are no secrets — that my husband is a gambler?'

Such frankness surprised her. Pity was not the appropriate response. She chose her words carefully. 'When circumstances, whatever they may be — and I have known hardship myself — oblige us to earn our living, we demonstrate that women are capable of independence, which society is not yet ready to admit. You set us an example.'

'You too. Travelling alone is certainly a mark of independence.' The little beauty spot was like a punctuation mark to the smile. 'It takes courage to brave the roads.'

'It takes more courage, I find, to face society's disapproval. The risk of losing one's reputation is greater than the dangers of the journey.'

'Oh, reputation! If one wants to be happy one must learn to ignore public opinion.'

She could not feel as defiant herself. 'The threat of being excluded from polite society frightens me, as it does most women, though exclusion might have the advantage of liberating one from social obligations. Solitude is precious.'

'But complete solitude would be painful. One puts up with society in the hope of encountering those few individuals whose conversation is interesting.' It was said with a smile and the exchange ended there as the young lieutenant joined them.

In the neighbouring box a continuous parade of guardsmen paid homage to its beautiful hostess, though as soon as the second act started all left but one.

'The current favourite,' Mme Picard observed. 'As a colonel, he has privileges to which the lower ranks cannot aspire.' Like a hawk hovering above a meadow, she was alert to any movement in the vast auditorium. Giovanni's discreet bow from the pit did not pass unobserved.

'Who is that handsome young man who just saluted you, Mademoiselle de Vernet?'

'The brother of my friend. Signor Giovanni Rossi.'

'Ah, he's Milanese. I thought perhaps he was one of the new contingent of officers.'

Giovanni's looks were evidently not enough to overcome the disadvantage of being Milanese. She wondered if her hostess knew any Italians beyond servants and tradesmen.

Larocque didn't arrive till the end of the first ballet, still in uniform. 'I had work to finish,' he said in answer to Mme Picard's playful reproach. He stayed beside them a moment, before ceding the place to another man. When next she looked his way, he was involved in some discussion of which she only caught snatches. Sensing her gaze, he turned and gave her a smile, so open and intimate that she prayed no one else had observed it. Perhaps Mme Delavigne was right, and one could worry too much about one's reputation, but her fear of public judgement was of too long date to be easily brushed aside. She was careful not to look his way for the rest of the evening.

Ancona, Friday 18 October

They climbed up to the promontory to visit the Duomo, which had served for centuries as a landmark for seafarers. The stiff breeze off the water flattened Livia's dress against her body, revealing a shapely bottom. He put his arm around her waist and squinted at the horizon, hoping for an English warship in full sail, but there were only small craft hugging the safety of the coast. Livia leaned against his shoulder, warm and yielding. He slid his hand downwards.

'*Impertinente!*' she said, but didn't resist. There was no one to see what his hand was up to, so he made full use of the opportunity till she slipped from his grasp, laughing.

'Let's go inside. You must see the Virgin of the Miracle.'

'What miracle?' he asked, pulling her back to him.

It had happened the day the French first arrived. All the women in town were in the Duomo beseeching the Virgin's protection when suddenly the Madonna opened her eyes and smiled. The priests said it was a sign that the French would be defeated.

'Perhaps she just wanted a look at them,' he said. 'What woman isn't aroused by men in uniform? Virginal eyelids must have fluttered all over Italy!'

'Blasphemer!' She put her hand over his mouth.

'You're not telling me you believe it?'

She wasn't sure; she was only twelve at the time, kneeling there with the others, and when someone cried out that the Virgin's eyes had opened she'd fixed her own eyes on the painting and she thought she saw it too. The smile certainly.

An optical illusion, he said. Caused by the flicker of candlelight or a slight change in the angle at which the painting was hung, which could be manipulated. 'Besides, she didn't have much success, your Virgin — we're still here, fourteen years later!'

'Maybe she averted the worst that was to happen.' General Bonaparte had asked to see the painting, and he took off the pearl necklace attached to it, and said he'd give it as dowry to an orphaned girl. 'Can you imagine! No girl would take the Virgin's necklace and risk damnation! And then he turned deathly pale and put the necklace back and told them to cover the painting. He'd seen it too. The Virgin had looked at him. He was afraid!'

'Nonsense! The emperor is an intelligent man. All he'd seen was that it was foolish to offend a population he hoped to win over.'

'Why are you always so sure you're right?' she burst out.

They went back down the hill in silence. He'd thought her too intelligent for such nonsense, but it was ingrained in the Italian character. Everywhere you went in this country there was some miracle-working statue or relic. Could you ever civilise such a people?

'So, Signor Beyle, did the Virgin smile at you?' Livia's father asked, as they sat down to dinner. The smirk on his face brought a scowl to his daughter's.

'I didn't dare enter the church. I was afraid she'd give the evil eye to a Frenchman, as Signora Livia is doing.' He gave Livia's knee a little nudge under the table.

Her father launched into an attack on the priests. The so-called miracle was a fraud perpetrated by a clergy that feared the loss of its wealth and power. It was a bad time for them — church treasures seized, monasteries closed, the gates of the ghetto torn down and four Jewish merchants on the city council. The faithful were scandalised.

'Your emperor is in too much of a hurry. You can't force new ways on people, you've got to bring them round gradually. And now there are these damned restrictions on trade! We've lost our principal market: before the wars we sold wine, silk, straw hats and naval supplies to the English and bought their cotton goods in return. Now we're told to grow our own cotton. But the farmers aren't going to uproot their olive trees for a crop they've never tried. And all these new trade regulations favour France!'

It made him uneasy. Here was a man with liberal ideas, supporting the new government but frustrated by its policies — and better informed than himself, so he couldn't argue. It was like the conversations with Lechi in the diligence. Fortunately, none of this diminished the good man's hospitality, even to a visiting Frenchman (whose leg was now entwined with Livia's under the tablecloth), and with another glass of grappa they drank a toast to a prosperous future.

Milan, Friday 18 October

After calling on Mme Picard this afternoon, I went up onto the roof of the Duomo with Monsieur Larocque. He had warned me that there were 150 steps, but the view of Monte Rosa on the horizon was worth the effort. We could have gone higher still, to the gallery that encircles the spire, from whence one can see the entire plain of Lombardy, but I suffered an attack of vertigo.

It keeps coming back — not the fear but the dangerous impulse to give way to it, to surrender to the weakness in her limbs, to the almost voluptuous sensation that she's going to faint. To write is to indulge it, but the temptation is too great.

I climbed the spiral staircase without difficulty, only a little breathless when we reached the top. Fortunately the attendant was busy with a party of Germans who wished to go higher, so we had the roof terrace to ourselves. Hundreds of statues surrounded us, mounted on slender pinnacles lining the roof and buttresses. I dared not imagine how they had been placed in position. The very thought made me dizzy. Some pinnacles were still enclosed in scaffolding on which stonemasons were at work. I could not bring myself to watch but turned my eyes to the inner walls. Everywhere that a niche or pedestal can be fitted stands some figure bearing the symbol of martyrdom or sainthood.

Circling the roof, they tried to identify the figures: Saint Apollonia to cure a toothache, Saint Roch to protect against plague, Saint Raymond for women in childbed — 'though he doesn't seem to have the ear of God,' Larocque remarked with quiet bitterness.

She thought of his wife, and Mrs Godwin, of her own mother's mother dying ten days after an apparently safe delivery. The loss of life among childbearing women, though individual and uncounted, was surely no less tragic than the carnage of a battlefield. Nature was cruel, and its Creator vengeful to curse all women for Eve's sin. Even as a child, she'd felt the injustice. No wonder the faithful had always turned to human intermediaries.

'There seems to be a saint for every need or fear.'

'And now they've even found a Saint Napoleone. A miracle — given that the Church hadn't noticed his existence before.'

'You think it a deliberate invention?'

'There was a Saint Neopolus, apparently, and Neopolus to Napoleone is but a step. A tribute to the emperor who reinstated religion. The Revolution made life difficult for the Church, which will do anything to regain its power.'

They'd arrived in their exploration at the west end. 'Come and see the view of the piazza,' he said. 'It's amusing to watch the crowd from this height.'

She peered through an opening in the parapet. Down below, small figures with exaggerated shadows moved across the empty space like automatons. Something inside her contracted in fear. Until that moment she hadn't registered how high they were. Reason assured her she was safe, but her body refused to believe it. Her forehead turned ice cold.

'I'm going to faint,' she managed to say. Through the wave of dizziness that was turning everything black, she felt him draw her away from the edge. She tried to pull herself together, apologising for her weakness.

'No, it's I who must apologise,' he said. 'I should have realised that you might suffer from vertigo. Sit down here on the step till it passes.'

It's coming back as she sits before her notebook and this time, eyes closed, she doesn't resist — free-falling, out of reason's control, reliving the sensation of his arm around her shoulders, and her desire to be enfolded in its embrace.

She pushes back her chair, incapable of writing more, and goes to the window, staying well back from the balcony. There are voices below — Perpetua on the doorstep, gossiping with another maid. A masculine voice breaks in, and the girls respond, their voices loud and shrill.

Is she too as giddy as any servant girl in the proximity of a male?

But what happened today wasn't just a physical response, though it was that too and it sweeps over her again with a deep shudder of pleasure as she recalls it. She's come to feel a unique affinity with this man despite everything that separates them. Over the past few weeks their exchange of confidences, their discovery of shared tastes has brought them to a rare and intimate understanding. That it should have created an attachment is only natural.

Nonetheless, it's as inadmissible as her passing attraction to Giovanni. Family honour, filial respect prohibit it. What would her parents have said, what would Armand say, if he knew? They would have warned her that she was setting herself up for misery in befriending a man who was not her social equal and now she's reaped the consequences. What could be more painful than to feel desire for a man with whom she cannot possibly envisage the union that would sanction it?

Besides, what makes her think her feelings are reciprocated?

But this is a dangerous temptation, as she recalls looks, words that have seemed to hint at something more than friendship on his part. Each recollection induces a shiver of happiness that she can't help prolonging. If she had leant back against his arm this afternoon, rested her head on his shoulder, what might have happened?

And if he too . . . if the attachment was mutual? She would have a companion with whom to follow all those paths she could never explore alone. They might see Rome together! They would bring Lucia to live with them, she would undertake the child's education . . .

An image of Mme Picard intrudes. Could she endure being patronised by that woman for the rest of her days?

The thought brings her back to reality. To be the wife of an adjunct commissary, a position that he himself despises though he's trapped in it, to lose her name and all that it represents — it's simply unthinkable. She must leave Milan. There's no other recourse. She cannot live with a daily struggle to suppress feelings that are unlikely to vanish now she's recognised them for what they are.

How blind she's been! If she'd left for Rome a month ago, she'd have felt at most a mild regret, but now she could weep with the sense of loss that overwhelms her. And Rome has lost its appeal — what will she do there alone? She is losing not only a friendship of a kind she may never encounter again, but the very motive of her journey.

The window closed now against the night, she returns to her journal in the hope of reasoning herself back into equanimity. But it's impossible to set down her feelings in black and white, not just because she cannot bear the thought that anyone else should ever read them, but because the sensations that rise in her at the very thought of expressing them are dangerous. The blank page must serve as her sole reminder.

Ancona, Saturday 19 October

I am writing these lines in Livia's room at her table, facing the sea which closes my horizon beyond all the chimneys of Ancona.

Livia is busy this afternoon, so he has time to describe the town. A sketch map first, to show its position between citadel and cathedral and the layout of the harbour with its two grand arches.

In Livia's absence he can write about her too, though he tries to put it in English for discretion's sake. *I have find her much below my ideas, but for the figure and for the witt.* The problem is that she's bored in this small town and it makes her lethargic and irritable. This morning she'd have skipped her singing lesson if he hadn't teased her into going. It did her good to sing for him. He makes a note of her voice range to send her some sheet music by Mozart from Paris.

You could win the heart of a bored woman, he notes, by tactfully leading her into more activity until she came to see you as a source of pleasure. Not that he wants to win Livia's heart, but it's an insight worth recording. Boredom is the bane of women's lives. It leads to inertia, which redoubles the boredom, unless like Mme Palfy they escape it through frenetic activity. Even Angela, a woman who's the life and soul of every group, complains of boredom — the same callers every afternoon and again at the opera every night, the same routines year in year out. Part of the problem is their education — if a smattering of languages, geography and carefully censored literature deserves that name. It doesn't develop their minds, in fact the reverse: it aims at a docile acceptance of tradition that stifles independent thought. And women lack that invaluable resource against boredom — work. In his own case, it had taken him some time to realise that he needed work to be happy — not the drudgery of his early days, but some task that makes demands on his intelligence.

That's what he's been missing for the past month, he realises, though it hadn't dawned on him till yesterday when he picked up one of the books he acquired in Rome and read for a while. And, of course, he's lacked stimulating conversation. All his friends in Italy are less intelligent than he thought them. *It seems that I have advanced a few leagues further along the river 'of knowing'*, he adds, with a little English flourish.

'Are you writing the history of your life?' Livia's step is so light he hadn't heard her return. He closes his notebook quickly.

He could have her within another day or two, he's sure, but he doesn't really desire her. They've both been trying to recapture something that stirred them three years ago. But the moment has passed, it can't be revived. It's time to be on his way. This morning he called on Casati, who's ready to leave tomorrow morning. By Wednesday he'll be in Milan.

He writes some observations on yesterday's reading, copying out a passage that particularly struck him. If he had a secretary he could dictate another five or six pages of useful notes, but handwriting is tiresome. He makes one last note before he stops, about three Italian writers whose works he must read on his return to Paris. The very thought is stimulating.

Milan, Saturday 19 October

Being indisposed, I spent the day in my room alone except for a visit from Maddalena.

Punctual as clockwork, her monthly flow had started. She worked on her travel notes all morning to keep her mind from obsessive thoughts, but after lunch, in the languor induced by a dose of paregoric, she could no longer keep them at bay.

She tried to examine her feelings rationally. How could she be sure that the emotion that swept her yesterday was love? It could have been nothing more than a response to his kindness, which she has hungered for in her lonely self-sufficiency. She longed to see him, to test her feelings in the reality of his presence.

When Perpetua tapped at the door, her heart leapt in anticipation of a message, but it was only to announce Maddalena. For a moment she was tempted to confide in her friend, but it was impossible to admit to the conflict in her heart, which Maddalena wouldn't comprehend. In any case, Maddalena had news of her own. She'd persuaded Trezzano to attend Sunday Mass at the parish church and meet them on the way out. Her father would greet him cordially, and in such a public space her mother could hardly refuse to acknowledge him.

'But something's up with Giovanni,' she said. 'We've scarcely seen him for two days and when he comes in he doesn't say a word.'

Here was her chance to drop a warning hint. 'Could he be looking for employment? You remember he told us that he envied the life of a courier or a diligence driver.'

'He wasn't serious.'

'He's more discontented than you realise. You should talk to your father, tell him that Giovanni needs more responsibility, or perhaps help in establishing his own business.' It was the best she could do without betraying his confidences.

'If he showed any sign of settling down, getting married, father would treat him as a man. But he's such a boy still. A sensible woman might settle him,' she added thoughtfully. 'And he's affectionate. He might make a good husband.'

Alone again after dinner, she struggles to prevent her thoughts going where good sense forbids. It's time she planned her journey. She must leave at the latest before mid-November, when rain swells the rivers and make many roads impassable. Only a little over three weeks from now. The thought of all the dangers and discomforts, of fending for herself again in a strange city, is daunting. Remembering the book that had given her courage before, she reaches for *Corinne* and opens it at random, hoping for a sign. But the page she lights on only echoes her fears:

> Travelling, whatever may be said of it, is one of the saddest pleasures of life. When you find yourself comfortable in some foreign city it begins to feel, in some degree, like your own country; but to traverse unknown realms, to hear a language spoken which you hardly comprehend, to see human countenances which have no connection either with your past recollections or future prospects, is solitude and isolation.

Looking for something less discouraging, she picks up Mrs Godwin's travels and lets it fall open where it will:

> Sitting then in a little boat on the ocean, amidst strangers, with sorrow and care pressing hard upon me, — buffeting me about from clime to clime, — I felt
>   'Like the lone shrub at random cast
>   That sighs and trembles at each blast!'

Her mentors are not encouraging tonight. The young man from the diligence was wrong: far from spinning illusions, travellers' tales are full of the physical and mental hardships the traveller faces.

Still, Mrs Godwin's words are less desperate than they seem, for though they describe a perilous voyage along the Norwegian coast on a rainy night, the writer found safe haven on an island. It's an episode she'd forgotten — the little house on the shore, the kindly old hostess, the clean bed that was almost too soft. She reads to the end with pleasure.

She at least won't face the open sea. And there will be beacons of civilisation like Florence along the route, however primitive the inns between. But she need not decide anything yet. Her room is paid till the end of the month. Monday, perhaps, if she receives one of Larocque's unexpected messages (her heart turns over at the thought), she'll see her way more clearly.

On the road, Sunday 20 October

A stiff breeze off the water brought an invigorating tang of salt into the carriage. They were following the coast, speeding north on a superb new road. It was a relief to leave Ancona. By the end Livia made no effort to hide her sadness, but he didn't let it affect him. He couldn't be her saviour.

Casati is a genial companion, natural and unaffected like all Milanese. Helpful too, teaching him how to avoid being cheated by couriers and innkeepers.

Outside Pesaro they stopped to visit the gardens of Count Mosca, opened to the public in a grand gesture inspired by the visit of General Bonaparte fifteen years ago. Terraces, cascades, and best of all an outdoor theatre — clipped cypress hedges framing a stage that seemed expressly designed for the moonlit garden scene in *The Marriage of Figaro*.

Was this Mosca a genuine adherent of the Revolution like Lechi and his brothers, he wondered, as they headed on. Or a man who saw the wisdom of accommodating himself to new realities? It would be interesting to study such a character — a man of superior intelligence, astute enough to turn circumstances to his own ends, and prescient where others were too blind to recognise the inevitable course of the future.

'Does Count Mosca support the new government?'

'Yes indeed. For the last few years, he's been director of police.'

His heart contracted. He'd managed to suppress any thought of Norvins for the last few days, but now it would nag him all evening. Fortunately, Casati distracted him with an amusing story about a recent scandal. He was about to respond with one of his own when the postilion's horn blared a warning.

'What the devil!' Casati exclaims. The driver pulls up so sharply that they're pitched forward, then tipped sideways as the carriage overturns. Bandits, he thinks. We're done for.

A minute later, a rough but not unfriendly voice asks if they're all right. Arms reach in to extricate them from their undignified position. The postilion is abusing a goatherd, whose flock, all jangling bells and anxious bleats, is huddled along the roadside. Half a dozen sturdy peasants soon have the carriage righted. The horses, by some miracle, aren't injured. The postilion shouts a final curse at the goatherd, and they're on their way again.

Milan, Sunday 20 October

Still indisposed, I did not attend Mass. No news from Maddalena. I have spent the day in total solitude, sewing.

She hasn't attempted anything as complicated as these palm leaves on the reticule for a long time, and her eyes ache from the strain of accurately placing her stitches on the dark green velvet. But it's time she started work on Lucia's sash. Whether she leaves or stays, it will be a way to thank Larocque for all his kindness over the past two months.

Only six weeks, in fact, she reminds herself, since that first encounter in his office, and their meetings fewer than she'd thought. The intimacy of their conversations makes it seem as if they've been acquainted much longer. Six weeks' acquaintance is very little on which to judge the permanence of an attachment. Of course, many marriages are based on far less — a few meetings, always chaperoned, enough to establish mutual acceptability before the contract is signed. But how can she think of marriage when she knows in her heart it's impossible? You are dishonouring our family, Armand would say: it's an insult to your father's memory. It hurts to imagine his dismissal of Larocque. In this at least she trusts her own judgement. Larocque's intelligence and education are equal to her own, indeed superior; he's a man of integrity, a tender father, a thoughtful friend. She esteems him more than any man she's ever known.

Why would she nonetheless be embarrassed to announce her marriage? Is it just lingering prejudice? Nobility with all its claims and entitlements was abolished twenty years ago by the Revolution. It is merit, not birth, that determines a man's position now — she has no quarrel with that principle. But birth hasn't ceased to count: many former nobles hold office in the new imperial state and their titles still possess a lustre that the new ones lack. In her heart of hearts it matters that she (and any children she might bear) would lose all claims to nobility by marrying a commoner. And to marry into a family that has profited from the confiscation of her father's land! Could love overcome such objections?

More and more her departure seems a necessity. It would be folly to abandon her dream of seeing Rome for this uncertain promise of happiness. Again, she turns to her bookshelf for support, pulling out Chateaubriand's *Letter on the Roman Countryside* and skimming its pages till a passage seizes her attention:

> I look back at my past life; I feel the weight of the present, and I try to penetrate my future. Where shall I be . . . what will I be twenty years from now? Whenever one looks inward, one finds an invincible obstacle to every vague plan one forms, an uncertainty caused by a certainty: that obstacle, that certainty is death . . .
>
> Have you lost a friend? In vain do you think of a thousand things to tell him: miserable, isolated, wandering the earth, with no one to tell your sorrows or pleasures, you call out to your friend but he will come no more to relieve your ills or share your joys . . . Now you must walk alone.

She closes the book in anguish, seeing herself, not twenty years from now but in two months: alone in Rome, having lost a friend, not to death but to foolish prejudice and a cowardly conformity to the world's judgement.

If it were possible at this moment she would throw on her cloak and go to him. But it's night, she doesn't even know where he lives. Thank heaven there's no possibility of a foolish gesture that could only embarrass them both. In the solitude of her room, though, she can imagine what she likes and she gives herself up to it. She undresses, her skin contracting against the chill of her nightgown, extinguishes the lamp, and draws the bed curtains, slipping into a darkness where the demands of honour and propriety hold no sway, and fantasies of impossible happiness can briefly reign.

Parma, Monday 21 October

The road they travelled today followed the ancient Via Emilia; straight as a hurled javelin, it sped across the plain to the horizon. What single-minded characters those Romans were.

They're spending the night in Parma, capital of a duchy whose Bourbon ruler had the tact to die leaving only a child heir, thereby allowing his realm to be annexed as a French department. The ducal palace houses the French prefect now, another of those fortunate young men whose rapid rise has fed his own ambition — auditor on the Council of State at twenty-two, a post in Germany, prefect of a department by twenty-four, and now this enviable position in Italy, though it must require a Machiavellian cunning to govern a state with Parma's history.

But what a place to study the Italian character — and no more than a day's ride from Milan! He'd do anything for a post in one of these fascinating old cities. Everything hangs on the success of his visit to Grenoble. He's held his present appointment for over a year and promotion would come much sooner if he had money behind him. It's expected that every high official have the personal income to uphold his position with dignity. If only he can make his father see this. Does the old man still not trust him, or is he simply too tight-fisted?

His grandfather says it isn't avarice but lack of funds. And Pauline's husband warned him that his father has heavy debts. He hadn't taken it seriously but now that he adds it up — the grand new house on Place Grenette, all the extra parcels of grazing land for the sheep — it's clear that his father must be borrowing to finance his acquisitions, and probably at 5 percent for land that may never justify the expense. Of course, the demand for fine merino wool must be high — his father is surely too prudent to speculate without the certainty of future gain. But in the meantime he has a son who lacks the means to advance in his career.

Still, there's no point brooding about the future now. This time tomorrow night he'll be in Angela's box at La Scala!

Milan, Monday 21 October

Maddalena told me that, as she hoped, on leaving church under the eye of many neighbours, her mother could not refuse to meet Captain Trezzano.

Signor Rossi invited the captain to call. Now he may court Maddalena officially, which will permit the announcement of their betrothal.
Monsieur Larocque invited me to the Ambrosiana this afternoon.

Much as she longed to see him, the invitation threw her into a state of anxiety. As they headed to the gallery, she reverted to an awkwardness that would have made her despair had she not counted on finding their usual connection in front of the paintings.

In this gallery too, Larocque seemed to be well known, and they were allowed to proceed without a cicerone. They made their way through a room where the blank spaces on the walls bore silent witness to the absent masterpieces now in Paris, and entered another that they had to themselves. Here, for once, landscapes predominated, though some still had a sacred pretext, if only the presence of a hermit or penitent saint. But what unnaturally dramatic landscapes they were — mountainous, for the most part, and lit by moonlight or the lurid glow of lightning. She paused before one in which a torrent overarched by a frail bridge tumbled through a chasm overhung by craggy cliffs to which a ruined tower clung precariously. It seemed as though in the absence of a sacred event the painter felt compelled to create an alternative drama in nature.

'Perhaps I am contradictory,' she said, hesitant in case these were his particular favourites, 'but a patch of meadow between the heads of two saints gave me greater pleasure. Here, the landscape is everything, which should satisfy me, but . . .' She stopped, unable to articulate her feeling.

'But it's melodrama!' he offered. 'And you are not deceived by its artifice. Come and see something simpler.' He took her over to a group of six small works. The first — a snowbound scene with peasants carrying firewood home — had the kind of simple truth she'd admired in Bellini, but it was spoilt by a heavenly cloud of cherubs.

'Sentimental piety,' he said. 'Inserted at a patron's request, probably. It spoils a picture one would otherwise admire. But here's the one I wanted to show you . . .'

Trees overhanging a stream. No saint or hermit in sight, not even a solitary herdsman. Only the birds — ducks going their placid way, a pheasant on a fallen tree trunk, a songbird on a branch. It was summer, to judge by the water iris, yet there was an autumnal tinge to the foliage that gave the scene an elegiac quality. Here at last was landscape without drama or story, painted for its own sake. She started to relax, sensing they'd found the subject that would restore their ease with each other. They were alone still, though she could hear a cicerone's voice in the adjoining room.

'Nothing could be truer to nature than those tree roots, that patch of muddy ground,' she said.

'There's still a certain artifice,' he demurred. 'The way these branches frame the scene: that's a painter's device — or a gardener's. Nature is more random. But I thought it might please you. It's no masterpiece but it reminds me of a spot I loved in my youth.' It was the sanctuary he'd sought in his holidays from school, a stream overhung by trees, where he could revel in solitude after the forced cohabitation of the dormitory. 'I used to take a notebook into which I'd copied poems I liked — I had no books of my own as yet.'

She had a sudden perception of his loneliness — cut off from his family by his education, but never a part of that other world to which it had seemed to promise entry.

'Which poems?'

'Latin mainly. Horace's odes about his farm . . .' He broke off, a look of intense annoyance hardening his face. The voices in the next room were louder, coming their way. To her horror she recognised a familiar tone: it was Mme Picard accompanied by another lady and a cicerone. There was no avoiding the encounter. She felt her cheeks flush to an incriminating hue.

But Mme Picard's eyes were not on her. 'So, Larocque, you are not at work this afternoon?' she said archly. 'What have you been showing Mademoiselle de Vernet?'

He'd turned his back on the woodland scene. 'We were discussing the evolution of landscape painting. What do you think of those?' He pointed (a little unkindly, she thought) to the paintings they'd dismissed.

Mme Picard was not caught out. 'You will say they lack the genius of the quattrocento. But you cannot deny their mastery. This one, for example, it's sublime! The fleeing travellers, the ray of moonlight piercing the clouds —'

'It's not the moon, Signora, but the light of heaven.' The cicerone reasserted himself. 'The scene represents the conversion of Saint Paul.' He was launched on his exposition and she could see no way to escape without being discourteous. She dared not look at Larocque.

When the tour was over, they had no option but to leave with their companions since the gallery was closing. Outside on the street, it was raining heavily. Mme Picard's carriage drew up to meet her and she insisted on sharing it. 'We can deposit you at your lodging, Mademoiselle, it's directly on our way.'

'You are too kind, Madame.' Flustered, she didn't know how to refuse.

'I'll walk, thank you,' Larocque said curtly. 'I'm going in the opposite direction.'

He could no more resist than she could. He was too discreet to claim for himself the right to take her home, which would have been tantamount to declaring a relation that might embarrass her. No gentleman would do that. It was a woman's prerogative in such situations to indicate what she wished and instead of exercising it she'd submitted to Mme Picard. But how could she have done otherwise?

She regained her room in a state of agitation. To the conflict in her own heart and the uncertainty of his must now be added the indignity of gossip. Their presence alone in the gallery, without even a cicerone, would not pass uncommented. Of course, it was hardly Mme Picard's fault that she'd chanced upon them, and her offer of a place in her carriage was merely polite. But it could not have happened at a worse moment.

After dinner she took a volume of Horace from the shelf, turning the pages till she found the lines she sought: *Hoc erat in votis: modus agri non ita magnus . . .* (Yes, this is what Larocque would ask for: a piece of land, not large, with a garden, and close to the house a spring that never dries up, and a patch of woodland as well.)

Enough land to be self-sufficient, he'd said, the day they went to Desio, and leisure to read the Roman poets in the heat of the day. It would be enough for her too. A rustic retreat, far from the judgement of society. They need not depend on the generosity of his former father-in-law — she would sell the house in Nogent. He could plant the trees he'd admired at Desio . . .

No, she must not permit herself to dream. She is still as uncertain of his feelings as before, and going back over their conversation she finds nothing to enlighten her. They'd been interrupted just as they were beginning to feel at ease. She must write to him tomorrow and suggest they resume the conversation so that he not think her indifferent to the memories he was confiding.

On the road, Tuesday 22 October

'Lodi,' the postilion announced.

Only five leagues to Milan. But he couldn't go through Lodi without seeing the famous bridge. They walked down to the river and there it was — perched on its timber supports, just wide enough for seven or eight soldiers marching abreast.

'It takes true courage to face cannon fire under those conditions,' Casati observed.

Or a kind of madness that overrides the instinct of self-preservation. Moving forward, stepping over the bodies of comrades who've been mown down, until you were directly in the line of fire. But if you were among the lucky ones who made it across and up the slope to the Austrians, you were a hero. So the grenadiers had marched forward, shouting, '*Vive la république!*' The irony of that would have angered him once. But their deaths weren't pointless, even if that republic is now an empire. It's only fifteen years since that battle. Who would have predicted then that a virtually unknown twenty-seven-year-old would rise to be emperor? Or that Europe would be altered forever?

It had given him a desire to see action again. If the rumours of war proved correct, it would be fascinating to accompany the army to Russia in the spring. But for now his heart urged him back to Milan. It was too late to catch Angela alone, so he must find some discreet way to convey his feelings. As he spotted the walls of Milan in the distance it came to him: Nothing in the whole of Italy, not even the Coliseum, had given him as much joy as the sight of the Porta Romana tonight.

Nine o'clock So much for phrase-making! He tears off his cravat and slumps into a chair. Nothing turned out as he'd hoped. He'd hurried to La Scala, but her box was empty. He ran to her parents' shop, where he was greeted by Mme Borroni. At Santa Maria del Monte? And where was that? Near Varese. When did she expect them back? Not before next Monday.

But by then, unless his extension's been granted, he'll be halfway to Paris. It's incomprehensible. She knew he'd be back this week. Have her husband and Turcotti carried her off? Is she offended that he didn't return sooner?

But he mustn't despair. A letter from Faure in the morning could change everything. If his leave is extended, an excursion to Varese would round off his tour of Italy. If there's no news from Paris, though, he'll have to take desperate measures.

Milan, Tuesday 22 October

She's sitting, pen in hand, in front of a blank sheet of notepaper, paralysed with indecision. She'd planned to write to Larocque this evening suggesting they return to the Ambrosian. But after what's just happened it's no longer as simple.

There was no musical evening tonight since Monsieur Picard and many of the officers were celebrating some important anniversary — or so Mme Bouchot had let slip, in a tone of wifely indulgence at men's mysterious doings. Larocque had been on his way there, perhaps, which would account for his haste just now.

After all the evenings when she might have run into him with her friends, it was odd that it should happen tonight when there were fewer strollers about because of the change of season. The nights were still mild, but after sunset a heavy mist drifted in from the meadows — a phenomenon peculiar to Milan, she'd been told. It created a strange kind of intimacy, separating each little group of strollers like conspirators, an impression reinforced tonight by Giovanni's behaviour. He'd waited till the lovers were ahead, out of earshot, before telling her his news. But first he'd made her promise secrecy.

'I shan't tell anyone else till Lena is married. I don't want to put any obstacle in her way. You know my mother! But I've made my decision: I'm enlisting in the cavalry.'

'Is that wise now with all the talk of war with Russia?' How far had he engaged himself, she wondered, and could he still be deterred?

'It's the best possible moment.' He'd been speaking to a recruiting officer. A new campaign offered a chance of rapid promotion, besides the adventure of traversing all those unknown lands. Clearly, he already saw himself galloping across the steppes.

'But what quarrel does Italy have with Russia?' she asked, to bring him down to earth. 'Why would you risk your life for the interests of the French Empire?'

'The interests of Italy cannot at present be separated from those of France.' He sounded like a schoolboy repeating a lesson. 'In any case, it may not come to war — the Russians are too busy fighting the Turks. And if it does, they just need a little reminder of Austerlitz.'

It was what they all said, except Larocque, who pointed out that the Russians had learnt from Austerlitz and that they were winning their war with the Turks. Should she tell Giovanni that, or would it only strengthen his resolve?

They'd been so intent in conversation that they were hardly aware of their surroundings. As they reached the end of the Corsia dei Servi, a man turning out of a side street almost bumped into them. It was Larocque, and the surprise and pleasure of seeing him brought a blush to her cheeks that deepened to scarlet as she sensed both men's eyes upon her. Maddalena and Trezzano turned back to join them and she made the introductions with what composure she could muster. For a moment she hoped Larocque would join them, but after a brief exchange he'd wished them good evening and gone on his way.

'I'm not the only one with a secret, I think, Signorina,' Giovanni murmured. Maddalena, too, had given her a searching glance.

'I have no secrets,' she lied, though in a sense it was true, since her feelings were now plain for all to see. And Larocque must have seen them too, for how else could he interpret her blush than the natural shyness of a woman in the presence of the man she loves. Even now, sitting alone in the candlelight, she wants to cover her face at the recollection. But painful though it is to have had her innermost feelings laid bare, it brings relief. She must dismiss all her qualms and reservations. There is no going back now: her future is in his hands. A frisson, not unlike the vertigo that overcame her on the Duomo roof, traverses her from core to extremities, whether joy or fear she scarcely knows, a surrender so dizzying that she is faint with it, and yet she has never felt such trust, such readiness to risk everything.

A knock at the door brings her back to reality — Perpetua with the bedtime jug of hot water. Abandoning the unwritten letter, she undresses and fills the basin on the washstand. But as she raises soapy hands to her face, the familiar stranger who looks back with wary eyes from the mirror seems to caution her. She still knows nothing of his heart; she can only wait now for a sign from him.

Four

Autumn Fog

> The admission of women to complete equality would be the surest mark of civilisation; it would double the intellectual capacity of the human race and its potential for happiness.
>
> — Stendhal, *Rome, Naples and Florence* (1826)

Milan, Wednesday 23 October

A letter from Faure at last! He scanned it rapidly. No objections raised to extending his leave, decision pending.

If there were no objections, why no decision? What was going on? If Daru were still his chief it would be simply yes or no (most probably the latter), but with the new man in charge he didn't know where he stood. He'd been counting on this extra month and now he was in trouble. To reach Paris by November 1 with a halt in Grenoble he should take the Turin mail courier tonight. But if he left without seeing Angela one last time, she'd think she meant nothing to him. He *had* to hold her in his arms again, just to know it wasn't a dream.

Varese, her mother said. He could make a detour if he took the Simplon route. But that would cut out Grenoble. It's five years since he saw his grandfather and this might be the last time. Checking the letter again, he saw it was dated twelve days ago. Confirmation must surely be on its way since there were no objections. It would be stupid to leave for Paris tonight, when tomorrow could bring good news. It was a gamble, but he'd risk it.

The fine rain darkening the cobbles outside the post office didn't dampen his resolve, nor the length of the journey. Six hours to Varese, the *vetturino* informed him — just as well he had a new book to hand. He'd always meant to read Ossian and what better time than now: he could almost fancy himself in Scotland in this autumnal landscape with wraiths of mist drifting through the pine woods like the ghosts of ancient warriors. He felt exalted by his decision. He was putting his career in jeopardy for Angela, but it lifted him above the calculations of Paris — the hypocrisy, the compliments, the tedious evenings in knee breeches and silk stockings playing cards with boring old women who could put in a word for him with someone influential. Ambition had shrivelled his soul to the point where he feared he'd lost it. But on this lonely road in the gathering twilight, he felt heroic.

The outskirts of Varese. Only a few miles separated them now.

'Impossible, Signor,' the driver said. 'It's another league to the Sacro Monte and there's no moon tonight.'

The innkeeper shook his head. On horseback, alone? The track up the mountain to the village was dangerous in the dark.

Resigning himself to a night at the inn, he ordered a horse to be ready at dawn.

Milan, Wednesday 23 October

Another misty day. The end of the month is approaching, and Signora Colomba asked if I wished to keep my room in November. I have promised to let her know shortly, though I feel no closer to a decision.

This morning I had difficulty eluding Maddalena's curiosity, aroused by our encounter last night. Fortunately we are now accompanied on our walk by Lupetto, whose antics interrupt conversation. On our way back we visited Signora Pulcheria to admire the new baby, which provided another distraction. I worked on Lucia's sash all afternoon, having no wish to go out.

The truth is that she'd stayed in expecting a message from Larocque, but nothing had come. She tries not to read anything into his silence. After all, her blush may have taken him by surprise and he might be asking himself what it meant, afraid to misinterpret it, and needing time to examine his own feelings. Which, she forces herself to acknowledge, may be no more than friendship. His attentiveness, she feels sure, stems from something deeper, but is it intuition or her own desire that makes her think so?

In the midst of it all, she hadn't forgotten Giovanni's news. He wasn't with them tonight, so when Maddalena went into a shop, she seized the chance to sound Trezzano. She felt guilty disregarding Giovanni's request for secrecy, but she was sure Trezzano wasn't unaware of his friend's intentions.

'Do you think that Signor Giovanni is seriously planning to enlist? It would grieve his mother dreadfully. His sisters too.'

It was a covert appeal to Trezzano's self-interest, but he wouldn't be drawn, and she could only hope that he might be moved to act by the loving trust on Maddalena's face as she took his arm when she rejoined them. He was giving up his own career for her sake. Would he not see the necessity of saving Giovanni from a step that might prove fatal?

It is possible that military service may allow Signor Giovanni to develop capacities for which his present existence offers no outlet. But there must be other spheres in which he might prove himself. We live in terrible times indeed when the pursuit of war offers the best or the only employment for ambitious young men.

Shall I find it strange (years from now rereading this journal) that I interested myself in his fate? If so, let me remind myself of the impotent anger I feel (and am surely not alone in feeling) that the Revolution's attempt to eradicate the absolute power of the monarchy has only produced a dictator in whose wars the youth of France and indeed of Europe are being sacrificed. If I can but save one young man from his grasp, I shall have done what little a woman can do to resist.

Varese, Thursday 24 October

Today I had Ossianic weather and adventures.
  For the first hour or two, anyway — until he reached Angela's lodgings and entered the realm of comic opera.
  He pauses to choose his words since he intends to show her this, when next he's permitted to see her. If he can only make her grasp the state of mind he was in, surely she'll forgive his lack of forethought.
  This morning at sunrise he'd set off on horseback to ride the last three miles to Santa Maria del Monte. As the road climbed, he looked down on a dense white mist through which only the tops of the lower hills emerged, like islands in a sea of clouds. As the sun burnt through the mist, the lakes came into view, but he was too impatient to stop and admire them. He didn't slow down till the steep path up to the village forced him to dismount — at which point whom should he meet but Pietragrua on his way down! Fortunately, he had his alibi prepared (rendezvous with his German friend, Strombeck) and their brief exchange was affable enough.
  He reached the village, enquired for her lodging, knocked with his heart in his mouth, and there she was. He moved to embrace her in the French fashion.
  'Please remember it's not the custom in Italy,' she said sharply. Her hair was loose, her feet in slippers. He should have known better than to arrive so early. No woman liked to be caught unawares.
  'You must forgive the impatience of a man who hasn't seen you for a month.'
  'How did you get here?'
  'On horseback.'
  'My God, you must have met my husband on his way down!'
  He had to admit it.
  'What were you thinking of! Didn't you get my letter?'
  It must have reached Rome after he left.
  Well, he'd better be aware that her slut of a maid (who was being courted by Turcotti) had told tales about their meeting at the

Alamanni baths. His unannounced appearance here would confirm her husband's suspicions.

It was impossible to say any of the tender things he'd prepared on the road from Rome. And worst of all, she accused him of planning in advance to add her to his list of conquests. All because he foolishly let her read Faure's letter and a slightly ambiguous sentence gave her the wrong impression. He'll have her reread it. She'll see that it only proves his ten years of enduring love.

She relented enough to offer him breakfast, after which they went for a walk. That too was doomed. Every hill for miles around was densely wooded, but on this damned holy mountain there wasn't a single tree — nowhere to find a moment of privacy. It was even worse at her lodging with the boy Antonio wandering in and out and the husband liable to appear at any time. He begged her to return to Milan. He was too insistent, but he couldn't help himself. A lover is never very lovable when he's pressing his claims.

And now she's banished him for two days to avert her husband's suspicions, told him to visit Lake Maggiore. He's trying not to worry about Paris, counting on the hopeful words 'no objections raised'.

Milan, Thursday 24 October

Maddalena has started a novena in preparation for the Feast of All Souls and on our way to the baths we stopped at the Church of the Holy Sepulchre. (It is just behind the Ambrosian gallery and I felt a pang as we passed the entrance.) After we took our baths I let Maddalena arrange my hair in the new style. I have capitulated to fashion, but I have to admit it becomes me.

This afternoon I went to the Brera, having taken the precaution of informing Perpetua of my destination just in case anyone should ask for me.

The old cicerone greeted her warmly. 'We have not seen you for some time, Signora. The signor is not with you today?'

'I have come by myself to make some notes,' she told him so that he would not offer to accompany her.

She had indeed brought a notebook and pencil, for she'd resolved to be methodical today and examine all the paintings in the Sala Bellini to which they'd paid no attention. But circling its walls she felt that Larocque (and her own instinct) had already led her to the best. What remained for the most part left her cold.

There was — surprisingly, given its huge dimensions — a Bellini they'd not looked at, but it was the work of his elder brother and of a very different character: a crowded scene in a city square. Ostensibly, it depicted Saint Mark preaching in Alexandria, but the group of veiled women in the foreground were the real subject, she felt — more conspicuous than the saint on his pulpit, more exotic than the camel and giraffe in the background, more emblematic of the Mohammedan world than the turbaned men and the minarets. It would give her something to talk about when she saw Larocque in the evening under Mme Picard's sharp eye, a moment that she longed for and dreaded.

She was more self-conscious than usual on entering La Scala, though Mme Bouchot complimented her on her coiffure. A new production had opened — Paisiello's *Barber of Seville*. 'And about time too,' said Mme Picard. 'I've had enough of those deluded suitors.'

It was another tale of young lovers outwitting an elderly guardian, with many comic scenes and a charming mandolin serenade that received three encores. But her mind was elsewhere. She wasn't surprised when Larocque did not appear before the overture. He was probably detained by work. But there was still no sign of him in the second interval.

'Where is Larocque tonight?' Mme Picard enquired, as though she must know.

'He's not the only one absent.' Mme Delavigne rescued her. 'Where is our beautiful neighbour?' The box next door was silent, its curtains closed.

'Even that impossible woman would have stopped talking for the serenade,' said Mme Bouchot. 'What an enchanting piece!'

'You forget the sequel,' Mme Picard said scornfully. 'In three years' time Almaviva will have tired of his Rosina and started seducing her maids.'

'Let us enjoy our illusions at least for an hour!' her friend protested.

'Lieutenant Richard wants to sing it at one of our evenings,' Mme Delavigne told them. 'But none of our gentlemen play the mandolin, so he will have to make do with my accompaniment.'

'Will you be playing for us next week?' she asked. 'I should so much like to hear the opening of that sonata again.'

'The adagio? I'll be happy to play it for you whenever you wish — come and see me Saturday afternoon if you are free. I have no pupils then.'

She was pleasantly surprised by the invitation, though it could not take her mind off Larocque's absence. Mme Picard asked several habitués where he was, but no one knew.

Alone in her room at midnight, she wonders if he'd stayed away to escape Mme Picard's predictable raillery about their encounter at the Ambrosian. His silence since that moment is heavy with implications that she can't decipher. If only she'd written immediately to suggest they resume their interrupted conversation; it would have been only polite to do so then. But even now, if she words it carefully, it is not too late. She will try in the morning when her mind is clear.

The room is chill as she undresses. Italy is not the land of endless summer it has seemed for the past few weeks.

Isola Bella, Friday 25 October, nine o'clock

Perhaps it's in the nature of a soul that's capable of great things not to be very pleasing at the moment of action when it's mustering all its strength. Anyone who reads this will scoff at the adjective 'great' applied to my actions yesterday.

But truly, riding though the mist, he'd felt capable of any sacrifice for love. Greatness doesn't always lie in the act itself, but in the mind that refuses to be defeated by circumstances. Like Ulysses trapped in the Cyclops' cave: it took true greatness to escape a situation that would have been nothing to a stonemason with a jack. Still, he won't risk Angela's mockery by letting her read this. Besides, once she had the notebook in her hands, there'd be nothing to stop her leafing back and finding something incriminating. Livia, for instance. He's in enough trouble already.

On his guard now, he rereads the eight-page letter he's written to beg her forgiveness for his behaviour yesterday. It's frank — too frank, perhaps? What if she showed it to Widmann or Turcotti, just as she'd let him look at theirs yesterday? (Only a single sentence in Turcotti's: What hadn't he been allowed to see?) But he'll judge more clearly in the morning. Tonight, listening to a thunderstorm rage outside, snug beside a blazing fire in his comfortable lodging on Isola Bella, he wants to record the day.

He'd left Varese on horseback early. A three-hour ride through country that offered everything his heart could desire. In Laveno he'd hired a boat, which took him through rain to the Isola Bella. He visited the palace and the garden, constructed in 1670 — the same period as Versailles and just as incapable of touching the heart. But the weather had cleared by the time he reached the topmost terrace, and both shores of the lake were visible with a glimpse of the Alps through drifting cloud — a view as grand as the Bay of Naples, but much more affecting. Was it because Angela was there, on one of those hills he could just make out in the mist? Or because his sensibility, shaped by the mountains of his childhood, could never be as deeply moved by the sea, even Homer's Mediterranean? Whatever the cause, he couldn't imagine a finer landscape. And only six hours from his beloved Milan, which he'd prefer to Rome or Naples even if it wasn't Angela's home.

With relief, he feels his love return. Yesterday all he'd felt was a desperate need for proof that she loved him, which had made him push his claims too insistently. Tomorrow he'll show more discretion.

Milan, Friday 25 October

She has opened her notebook but she cannot bring herself to confide her thoughts to the waiting page, though the day's events lie as heavily on her mind as Friday's penitential salt cod on her digestion.

She'd risen early to write to Larocque — a brief note, regretting the interruption of their conversation at the Ambrosian and hoping that when his responsibilities permitted they might resume it. Such a note was entirely proper, she told herself, with no hint of feelings that could embarrass either of them. She asked Perpetua to deliver it to Larocque himself, and waited impatiently for her return. Yes, the girl said, she'd given it into the hands of a gentleman but not the French gentleman because he'd gone away.

'Gone out?'

'No, gone away.' Perpetua was certain.

'And did the other gentleman say for how long?' The girl shook her head.

He hadn't mentioned any imminent journey, but there was no reason why he should inform her of his comings and goings. Still, she regretted even more that she hadn't written at once.

She was working on Lucia's sash, but it could not distract her. There seemed something definitive in Perpetua's 'gone away', though perhaps that was just the girl's manner. Still, there was an obvious explanation:

the army's suppliers must be scattered around the countryside and he would deal with them wherever they were. But thinking back to their accidental encounter three evenings ago, another possibility struck her. He had been stiff, distant, almost abrupt — making his escape the instant it was polite to do so. Was he avoiding her, aware now of feelings that he could not reciprocate? The thought was crushing.

Her afternoon call on Mme Picard had lowered her spirits further.

'Ah, Mademoiselle de Vernet, we were just speaking of you,' said Mme Picard when she entered. 'Mme Martin asked if you were related to Colonel de Vernet.'

A plain little woman smiled at her nervously from the edge of the circle.

'You know my cousin, Madame?' She tried to sound as if it gave her pleasure, though the immediate fear crossed her mind that any gossip might travel back to Nogent.

'My husband served under his command until Marengo. I never had the honour of meeting the colonel myself, but my husband had a great respect for him.'

'I will mention your husband's name to my cousin when I write,' she said, relieved there was no lasting connection. 'He will be pleased to have news of a former comrade.'

Mme Martin looked gratified and asked if she found Milan to her liking.

'It's a most agreeable city. I had not anticipated that there would be so much to see.'

'Indeed. One could spend every afternoon looking at pictures,' Mme Picard said archly.

The remark, anodyne on the surface, confirmed her suspicion that her hostess had told the others about finding her at the Ambrosian with Larocque, but in her embarrassment she could think of nothing to say.

What she should have done, she recognises now too late, was to look her hostess boldly in the eye and engage her in discussion of the pictures they'd seen together, refusing to let herself be embarrassed. Fortunately the arrival of Monsieur Picard had distracted their attention, though among his news a casual remark that Larocque had gone to Bergamo had filled her with an anxious desire to hear more that she dared not satisfy.

The odour of fish through the kitchen door as Perpetua let her in had done nothing to lift her mood. Nor had her walk after dinner

— Giovanni had not joined them, so she made an awkward third with the lovers, unsure whether they'd included her out of kindness or whether Milanese convention still demanded a chaperone even now they were officially betrothed.

If she and Larocque had been accompanied by a friend on their excursions, any gossip (for there would always be some) would have been attenuated. But they could never have spoken so freely about the past in the presence of an outsider. Even their discussions in the Brera would have been more reserved. Friendship cannot develop without intimate conversation. She has nothing to reproach herself with. It's time she ceased worrying what others thought.

But it takes courage to brave the judgement of society. Reminded of a passage she'd marked in Mrs Godwin's travels, she takes the book from the shelf and leafs through until she finds it:

> All the world is a stage, thought I; and few are there who do not play the part they have learned by rote; and those who do not, seem marks set up to be pelted at by fortune; or rather as sign-posts, which point out the road to others, whilst forced to stand still themselves amidst the mud and dust.

The image is painfully apt. Mrs Godwin's book had indeed pointed out a road to her, but that poor lady's life was a sad example of the consequences of defying public opinion. She sees her again, not as she likes to imagine her — rowing across a Norwegian bay to bathe in a secluded cove — but as she'd last seen her: trapped in the public gaze, her body swollen by the pregnancy that had forced her to marry Mr Godwin and thereby reveal to the world that she had not been married to the father of her little girl, a sin for which respectable society would not forgive her. What strength it must have taken to face public opprobrium, what private pain lay behind the mask of indifference!

But even in an unblemished life one must guard one's reputation. It isn't sufficient to be virtuous: one must have every appearance of virtue. The mildest gossip is dangerous. Insinuations will stick, and like the burrs that adhere to petticoats on a country walk, they aren't easily removed.

She puts Mrs Godwin's travels back on the shelf, and tries to dismiss her anxieties. If she leaves for Rome, she will have been no more than the conversational titbit of an afternoon, soon forgotten as the gossips move on to other fare. And if she stays . . . But she must not permit herself to envisage that possibility until she knows Larocque's heart. Selfishly, she has been thinking only of her own good name when he too has to live with their insinuations. A man's reputation cannot be as fatally damaged as a woman's, but gossip would embarrass him if only for her sake, and for the respect he bears her family. Could it be that he has gone away for a while to confound Mme Picard's suspicions? There is no way of knowing, but the thought comforts her.

Santa Maria del Monte, Saturday 26 October

This journal is written for Henri, if he's still alive in 1821. I don't want to give him occasion to laugh at the Henri who's living now. The Henri of 1821 will have become cold and more full of hatred.

It's coldness he fears more than anything — the ageing of the soul that withers the capacity for passion. Another ten years in Paris, watching fools compete for preferment, and his fire will be quenched. But on this splendid autumn day, the sky clear, the summits gleaming with freshly fallen snow, he'd felt capable of anything. It was perfect weather for the boat trip back across the lake and the three-hour ride to Santa Maria. He stopped for refreshment at the inn below the village, chatting with the landlord and a customer to broadcast his alibi of a rendezvous with a German friend. By then, it was pouring with rain again, so he had to resign himself to being carried up to the village in a *portantine* — a canvas seat on poles with an umbrella over the top. Not the most dignified of conveyances.

This inn is at the far end of the village, but the innkeeper insisted on lodging him in this annex in the centre, just a few steps from Angela's accommodation. Convenient but dangerous. All the more so because it was dark and the innkeeper escorted him with three torchbearers who conducted him, brilliantly lit, up a narrow alley past the door of the Pietragrua lodging, which just happened to be open!

He'd bent over double and hunched his shoulders, but fortunately no one had been looking out except Angela, who arrived at his door a moment later (accompanied by her son) and passed him a note instructing him to come at midnight. He'd have to leave before seven in the morning, as her husband's suspicions were aroused. The only problem, she'd whispered, was that two nuns were lodged in the antechamber through which he'd have to pass.

Nuns! Has Pietragrua placed them there to guard her virtue? It's more and more like a comic opera — the lover creeping past the jealous husband's door, the amorous wife with the billet-doux, the sleeping nuns. She said she'd do everything possible so he could come to her. Does she plan to drug their supper?

Still three and a half hours till midnight. The wait is making him nervous. Not just the obvious risks, but their effect on his performance. He hadn't been impressive in that first rushed encounter a month ago; tonight he'd hoped to do better.

In romance the obstacles are worthy of the hero, whereas he must contend with a husband and nuns! The latter liable to shriek and swoon, the former . . . Where is Pietragrua anyway? He must be on duty at a Customs post, or patrolling the road from Switzerland for smugglers. What else could take him out on a night like this? The storm that's rattling the windows could bring him home, though. And don't nuns get up in the night to pray?

But Monday she'll be back in Milan. He can only hope that the letter granting his leave will be there too. Because even if he were to set off tomorrow morning and cut out the stop in Grenoble, he hasn't a hope now of reaching Paris by the end of the month. Does she have any conception of what he's risked for her?

He picks up Ossian, stretches his legs towards the fireplace, and tries to relax.

A persistent tapping slowly penetrates his consciousness. Good God, he must have fallen asleep! Cautiously, he opens the door a crack and peers out. The boy Antonio hands him a note and darts off. Tearing it open, he already guesses the contents. 'No hope left.'

Perhaps it's just as well. After all those hours on horseback today, he's ready to drop. In future, he must take an afternoon nap as a precaution against oversleeping in a perilous situation, or not being up to full enjoyment of his happiness. But those nuns — were they real, or just an excuse? No, she couldn't invent something so preposterous, they must be real. And a place of pilgrimage like this must still harbour them since the convent's closure. As Martial said, some of those poor creatures have nowhere else to go. You can't just put them out on the street.

Pitiful or not, they've wrecked his chance of a night with Angela. And she's ordered him to leave first thing tomorrow before her husband gets back. But she'll be in Milan by Monday evening. Even if there's a letter demanding his return to Paris, he won't leave Milan without taking her in his arms one last time.

Milan, Saturday 26 October

Only five days till the end of the month. Feeling I should not make Signora Colomba wait for my decision, I have retained my room till mid-November, which is the point by which I can no longer postpone my departure for Rome without facing the risk of roads and bridges washed out by rain.

This afternoon I visited Mme Delavigne. I begin to feel at ease with her, but I could not broach the subject that was the secret purpose of my visit.

The Delavigne apartment was above a draper's on a populous but respectable street. She caught the faint sounds of a piano behind the door as she knocked.

'Am I disturbing you? Would you rather I came back another day?'

'No, no! I'm delighted to see you.'

Apart from the piano, the room was sparsely furnished — a few shabby chairs, a table piled with books and sheet music, and a chessboard set out at one end.

'My last game with Olivier.' Mme Delavigne followed her glance. 'I haven't the heart to put it away. He's my youngest — he's just joined his brothers at school.' The three boys were at one of the new schools in France. It was the best education to be had, and she'd resigned herself to parting with them because it promised a secure future. All three had scholarships as an officer's sons. 'They have that advantage at least from their father.'

'You must miss them.'

'I'd be lost without them if I didn't have my piano.'

She asked what Mme Delavigne had been playing when she arrived.

'A sonata I shall play on Tuesday at Mme Picard's if I have mastered it. But I promised to play the adagio — would you like to hear it now?'

'It would give me great pleasure, if you are not tired?'

The first notes rippled into the room like the gentle current of a stream. Then above them, as if a walker were slowly pacing its bank, rose three lingering, resonant chords that seemed to contain all the sadness of lost things. Repeated in a different key, they became a dialogue (or so she heard it), a higher voice asking 'Must it be?' and a deeper one answering 'It must be.' Unceasing, beneath the voices, the stream flowed on, relentless as time.

She felt it more intensely now that she wasn't perched self-consciously on a hard little chair in Mme Picard's salon. Unobserved, she could abandon herself to the music, feeling again all the sadness of irretrievable loss that she'd felt by the canal. She was there again, he was there beside her; but the poplars must be bare by now, their leaves borne away by the current.

The adagio gave way to a bright little tune, falsely consoling. Then, abruptly, the mood changed. It was jarring, a sudden wild rush of notes like the hooves of a galloping horse, whipped on by a frantic rider. A more lyrical phrase, like the memory of happiness, kept surfacing, briefly audible behind the thudding hooves, but always obliterated by their onward drive.

It was coming to an end, reaching a standstill, as if horse and rider were exhausted. But no, they were gathering their forces again for a final impassioned charge. One last echo of the melancholy question from the opening, then a dramatic finale as though horse and rider had leapt off the cliff that had always been their destined goal.

Mme Delavigne's hands fell to her sides. 'Forgive me! You asked for the adagio and I have made you listen to the whole sonata. I can never resist the final movement. It has such energy, such passion!'

'But it seems to end in catastrophe . . .'

'Is that what you hear? For me it's the antidote to the resignation of the first movement.'

'I have no musical knowledge. I can only say what it makes me feel.'

'But I too speak of my feelings, not the rules of composition. This composer overturns them, in any case. Listen to this: Does it not make you desire something more passionate, less constrained than the life we lead?' She lifted her hands, played a passage again, ferociously this time, hammering the keys. 'It's like a storm in the mountains — listen!'

Her fingers mimicked the drumming of rain on a roof, the sudden crash of thunder. The stream had become a torrent, sweeping rocks and trees in its path. The musician herself seemed a force of nature at that moment. It was easy to see why she drew men. Had Larocque felt that attraction? The first time she'd seen them together at the opera, she'd sensed the familiarity of long acquaintance. But was it something more? It was naïve to imagine that he would not overcome whatever moral scruples he possessed to win the love of this exceptional woman, who by all accounts had a husband who didn't deserve her. The possibility of a love affair, so inconceivable in a small town like Nogent, was greater in a city like Milan. The animated social life, the presence of an army and so many single men, the climate even — breeding more ardent temperaments and constantly arousing the senses — all contributed to laxer attitudes. Maddalena and Trezzano on their last night in Laveno . . . But no, she must not let herself suppose more than she knew. In any case, she would not condemn them now as she might have before. And she would not relinquish the chance of friendship with a woman like Mme Delavigne even if her life was not blameless, though she hoped there'd been no affair of the heart with Larocque.

But for her own part she could not contravene the standards of her upbringing, nor could she overcome her fear of public opinion. For even if morality was less severe in this pleasure-loving city, gossip still thrived so long as curiosity and malice were part of human nature.

On that score at least, she was somewhat reassured on leaving by Mme Delavigne's invitation to return. If her new friend had heard any talk about her, it clearly made no difference. But the possibility continued to trouble her; her inner conflict was painful enough without the humiliation of public commentary.

SUNDAY *I attended the baptism of the new Rossi grandchild. Afterwards, a succession of relatives, neighbours and business associates came to offer congratulations, including Captain Trezzano's family, since the celebration was also an occasion to make public Maddalena's betrothal, to which Signora Rossi has grudgingly consented. I was relieved to be in the signora's good graces again, but I am ashamed to admit how much I still fear her disapproval. The desire to placate is a sign of a weak mind.*

After dinner, she accompanied her friends to the promenade on the Duomo square. Night was falling, and the sight of the statues along the roofline against the darkening sky made her ache with longing. She could barely maintain a pretence of interest in Giovanni's banter.

'You're quiet tonight, Signorina. Sad, I think?'

'Just a little tired. Has the captain had any success in finding employment? I do not like to ask him.'

'Nothing so far, or nothing he will accept. Lena is wrong to ask him to leave the army. He'll be unhappy and she'll regret it.'

'But does a married man have the right to risk his life when others depend on him?'

'Why did Lena encourage him if she was not prepared to marry a soldier?'

'One cannot always control one's heart.'

'In any case, he's in no danger here in Lombardy training recruits.'

But it was only two years ago, she thought silently, that the Austrians had attempted to recover their Italian domains. Who was to say that they wouldn't invade again? And a patriot like Trezzano who'd fought them valiantly on that previous attempt would certainly take arms again. The emperor's marriage to the Austrian Marie-Louise made another invasion unlikely, but circumstances could change. History was full of broken alliances. Maddalena was right: her happiness would never be secure unless Trezzano left the army. And why shouldn't she try to keep him safe? Were the claims of the family not more primordial than those of the nation?

As they circled the piazza, she noticed fewer uniforms among the men. Autumn manoeuvres had taken them away. It struck her that the danger she feared for Trezzano and Giovanni applied equally to Larocque — in the event of war the supply corps would accompany the army. Even now, on his trip to Bergamo, he might be preparing for a campaign. He had mentioned some time ago that he was purchasing mules and supply waggons for the march north. She'd been puzzling over his absence as if it concerned her only, forgetting its larger implications.

But perhaps it was her own morbid nature that made her think of war.

I have a tendency to fear the worst. No doubt this pessimism results from my experience, but it may be no less ill-founded than the optimism that governs individuals like Signor Giovanni. Surely the Russians will know better than to provoke the Emperor to an invasion of the kind that Prussia and Austria so disastrously incurred. And the Emperor himself, recognising that Moscow lies many weeks' if not months' farther march than Berlin or Vienna, must see the imprudence of undertaking such a protracted campaign. Thinking of all those I know whose lives might be forever altered by his decision, I can only hope so.

Milan, Monday 28 October

God, what happiness! He reads the letter again to make sure he hasn't misunderstood. But no, Faure's news is definite: a whole month's leave. Quickly, he calculates how much of it he can spend with Angela. If he takes the courier to Turin, then the diligence via the Mont-Cenis pass, it's roughly three days to Grenoble. A day there to see his father and grandfather, two days with Pauline and her husband on the way to Lyon, then three or four days to reach Paris — and he needn't leave till November 20, or even the 22nd if he takes the courier from Lyon instead of the diligence. That gives him three whole weeks in Milan!

Practicalities first: he'll need a room for his assignations with Angela. He makes enquiries and finds one above a wig maker's on a side street off the Piazza del Duomo, close to her parents' shop. He gives a false name, naturally. If only Angela were here to share his joy! But she'll be back tonight. He might even see her at the opera.

Another month of freedom! If he'd been prudent, he'd be halfway to Paris by now, but he gambled on freedom and won. He strides up the Corsia dei Servi like a god in winged sandals, released from the weight of mortal obligations. No fashionable beauties at this hour, but other eyes meet his as he passes, with that split second of mutual evaluation that puts a spark in the day. He crosses Piazza San Babila onto the Corso Orientale and past the imposing gateway of the seminary, where a young man in the garb of a future priest stares at him. One of those beautiful youths that Italy produces, with a natural grace the cassock can't hide and eyes that will spellbind every woman in the congregation when he preaches. Vowed to celibacy, what a waste! Thank heaven *he* isn't a eunuch, however unblessed with looks.

Walking on, past a succession of elegant new residences, then across the canal, he reaches Casa Bovara (the window of his former room a poignant reminder of his adolescent self), then follows the avenue of trees alongside Villa Bonaparte, where the viceroy resides, and into the public gardens, full of nursemaids with their charges at this time of day.

A puppy runs across his path tugging a small boy behind him, scattering a pile of newly raked leaves in their exuberance. He too could kick up his heels with joy at his freedom. But he'll need something to occupy his time when he's not with Angela. He'll look for that history of painting his Roman friend recommended. Even if it doesn't expand his taste it will develop his critical judgement.

But he's already too critical — that's his problem, he thinks, climbing the ramparts. It's a curse, this critical nature: it chills his response to art and makes him too conscious of other people's flaws, whether they're friends or lovers. Without it he'd be the happiest of men. And his love of the arts is partly to blame. If he hadn't formed his idea of life from literature he wouldn't so often be disappointed by reality. Art is responsible too — what face, what body, lives up to the perfection of Raphael or Canova? And music most of all, lifting you so high above the everyday that you can't fail to be dissatisfied when you descend. He might have been happier if he'd never discovered the arts. Yet they themselves are one of the greatest sources of happiness; he couldn't live without them.

The Alps are hidden by cloud today, but the ocean of foliage beyond the ramparts is view enough. He's always loved trees. The limes at Furonières, the beech woods above Les Échelles. To enter their shade on a summer's day was like a dip in a mountain stream. He'd had his first intimations of beauty at Les Échelles, the summer after his mother's death, sent to stay with uncle Romain and his pretty young wife and her family of smiling sisters who all seemed to find him lovable and clever. Nobody scolded him, even when he threw stones at the young men who came to court the girls. He was in heaven. But then it was back to Aunt Séraphie and the Latin tutor and the gloomy house on Rue des Vieux-Jésuites where his mother's room was permanently locked. If it hadn't been for his good old grandfather, he'd have been the loneliest child on earth.

Old people tell the young that childhood is the happiest time in one's life. He'd have despaired if he'd believed them. Fortunately he'd seen through such platitudes at an early age.

But in one respect at least he was fortunate to have had an unhappy childhood. It gave him the strength of character to rebel. Without it, he'd still be in Grenoble, leading the same narrow existence as his father. But he'd made his escape and then he'd had the luck to see Italy at seventeen, and not just any Italian town but this one in all the euphoria of liberation.

Memory has brought him along the ramparts to the Porta Nuova. He'll walk back that way, complete the magic circle of his first days in Milan. Down past the Customs post where the driver of a hay waggon is protesting as guards poke and prod his load. Back across the canal onto Corso Porta Nuova and there ahead of him is the very spot where, riding into the city in June 1800 — a day that will forever stand out in his memory — he ran into Martial. There began those glorious months that gave him a glimpse of what life could be, until Count Daru got him his commission and sent him off to the army to be knocked into shape. Striding down Corso Porta Nuova now, eleven years later, he measures the change in himself with satisfaction.

Back at the inn, he composes a letter to Angela. The challenge is to voice his frustration without complaining, which would only irritate her. But a lover who's been dreaming of a reunion for a month has the right to call himself unhappy when everything conspires to frustrate it. It takes a while to find the right tone, but he's satisfied with the result — expressed with delicacy, but in a resolute style that could have figured in a novel by Duclos. He leaves it with Signora Borroni, who promises to give it to her daughter as soon as she returns.

Later, in the faint hope that Angela might be back, he goes to La Scala. But her box is empty. In the pit he runs into Widmann and announces the prolongation of his leave with all the joy he's feeling, though he feels some slight compunction on seeing the dismay that Widmann can't hide.

The Disappointed Suitors has ended after a successful run, and it's Paisiello's *Barber of Seville* now — pleasant melodies without depth. He only stays for the first act. He needs an early night, to be in good form tomorrow. In his note to Angela, he's promised to wait for her all morning in the rented room.

Milan, Monday 28 October

I believe I saw the young man from the diligence in the public gardens this morning. He was too lost in a dream to notice me and almost tripped over Lupetto. Can he have been in Milan all this time?

It is hard to believe that only two months have passed since that supper conversation. If I were asked to define happiness now I might give a very different answer.

Indeed, it strikes her painfully that her answer would be identical to the one he'd given. To read love in the eyes of the one I love. But how much more elusive that happiness is than the one she'd wished for then. Now it depends on a man who seems to have disappeared into thin air. It's almost a week since she last saw Larocque in that brief encounter with her friends and she's had no word. But none of this can be confessed to her journal, though it weighs on her like the mist that shrouds the city most days now.

She'd embroidered all morning and by two o'clock her eyes needed a rest. She was making good progress, alternating the two pieces, but they had to be completed before she left for Rome. *If* she left for Rome. All her plans, indeed her entire future, were in a state of suspension until Larocque's return. To distract herself she'd decided to take a long walk to some point of interest. Leafing through the guidebook Larocque had given her on that first day, she'd chosen the church of Sant'Eustorgio because the martyred inquisitor was buried there in a tomb said to be a masterpiece of quattrocento sculpture. Her route would take her past a surviving Roman colonnade (and it was near Larocque's office).

As she entered the church a rattle of keys announced the custodian. 'The visit must be made with a guide, Signorina!'

'I only wish to see the martyr's tomb.'

'Ah, the Signorina suffers from headaches?'

'Occasionally.' She was puzzled.

'Many ladies come to seek a cure from the reliquary which contains the saint's head. A piece of cloth that has touched it will protect from headache for a year.'

Naturally, a martyr with a cleaver in his skull would be sympathetic to headache sufferers! She wished Larocque were with her to share a smile.

The tour of the church, which the custodian insisted on giving (perhaps afraid that his tip would be reduced otherwise), might itself induce a headache, she thought, enduring his sing-song recitation. But the martyr's tomb was worth the visit. The sarcophagus, naïvely sculpted with scenes from his life, was raised on pillars, supported by graceful feminine figures representing the virtues — Charity with babes at her breast, Hope gazing heavenwards, Faith holding a Bible.

'And this one?' She was puzzled by the triple-faced head.

'Prudence, Signorina. Guided by the past, anticipating the future, vigilant in the present.'

Perhaps it was the grotesquerie of the three-faced head, but there was something repellent about the virtue, she thought. It was cautious, calculating, small-minded, lacking generosity and fire. Prudence would have kept her in Nogent, growing more reclusive every year like a grey house spider in its corner. But she'd committed the grand imprudence of setting out to see the world. And however the world might judge her friendship with a man beneath her own class, it was an imprudence she was proud of. Even if it were to end unhappily, it would be an unhappiness that had come from opening herself to new experience, not the melancholy of an unlived life.

Declining the opportunity of touching the martyr's reliquary with her veil, she left. But the defiant mood that buoyed her up on the long walk home did not survive the disappointment of learning that no message had been left in her absence.

Milan, Tuesday 29 October

I was going to begin by copying the letter I wrote to Angelina, but that would be even more boring than writing it.

His eloquence hadn't met with success.

'You wouldn't write like that if you were really unhappy.' She shook the rain off her cloak and sat down without embracing him. 'It's nothing but literature!'

'I swear to heaven it's what I was feeling!'

An example of different schools, different ways of seeing nature, he writes, his head full of the history of Italian painting he'd bought last night, which he'd started to read while waiting for her. What seems natural to one is artifice to another. He thought his letter a model of sensitivity; she found it detestable. Their first chance to be alone, and they were off to a bad start. And when he announced his good news her reaction was disappointing.

'But you can't stay in Milan! My husband is suspicious. He found out about your second visit from the porter who carried you up to the village.'

'Does he have spies everywhere?'

'It was sheer chance — the porter mentioned a foreigner.'

'Our love is cursed!'

'I know. If one of my friends told me such a tale of misadventure, I'd tell him it was a novel, I'd make fun of it.'

The situation seemed more tragic than funny to him. 'You don't really want me to leave?'

'You're putting me in an awkward situation — Turcotti comes back tonight.'

'Surely he can't follow you everywhere?'

'Of course not, but I mustn't let him suspect anything.'

It was clear there was something between her and Turcotti; not love he was sure, or not on her side, but some question of mutual interests. Turcotti struck him as a shrewd manipulator. As for Pietragrua, he didn't believe the man had enough feeling to be truly jealous. He was simply concerned for appearances.

'In any case, we're going to Novara on Saturday till the fifteenth,' she added.

Two whole weeks, out of the three that yesterday stretched ahead so promisingly. He was crushed. 'But I requested my extension with the sole desire of spending it with you!'

'Don't look so sad!' she said, abruptly tender. 'Come here.'

He tried to hold back, but after a month without a woman the inevitable happened. He did his best to compensate with finger and tongue, but time was running out. Any minute now the Angelus would ring. Sure enough, just as he felt ready for a second round, the bells began their clamour. 'My God, midday already!' she exclaimed. 'I must run.'

She was right to be alarmed. He saw for himself, later in the afternoon, how her husband reproached her (and in front of him too) for her absence and for sending Antonio home with the umbrella. Worst of all, the rascally wig maker from whom he's renting the room had followed her. So now there's the possibility of blackmail on top of everything else. It's an opera buffa, without the transforming grace of music.

But late tonight, at her parents' shop, while her mother was busy with the assistants, they enjoyed half an hour in paradise. She looked truly in love and all the more beautiful for it. With others around, they could only banter, but playful tenderness is the mode in which he's most himself, and he could see in her eyes and in the flush on her cheeks the effect that naturalness in a great soul has on a heart of the same nature. She said she'd write their story while she was away; she spoke of leaving everything and going back to Paris with him.

That alarmed him. It would be a disaster if she meant it. He couldn't afford to support her, and it would scandalise all the people on whom he counts to advance his career. And how would she feel as a kept woman in Paris, without the social position she has here? But she's not serious. She's bored, that's her problem. Her superiority to all other women guarantees that any man who comes under her spell will always be at her feet. It flatters her, but the predictability makes her yawn.

He records that thought as proof of his lucidity, so the Henri of 1821 won't mock him. But that cold-eyed future self has made him censor his emotion. Rereading his account, he's struck by its flatness. Four pages of dull sentences. Still, he's not Leonardo trying to produce a masterpiece every time. And on top of the long letter he'd just written Pauline, it's hardly surprising he's worn out his eloquence and this wretched chicken quill.

Time for bed if he's to be on form tomorrow. She's promised to come at ten. He's missed a lot of sleep in the past month. Too much coffee and all those nights on the road. He's even lost weight. But he's in excellent shape. If only she were here with him now he'd get up to a very respectable number . . .

Milan, Tuesday 29 October

This morning's walk was interrupted by a downpour that forced us to take shelter in a café. The weather is colder and I took my winter cloak from my trunk before going to the Brera.

'The signor is still away, Signora?' the old cicerone asked as she entered.

She nodded, not knowing what to say, touched by the old man's friendly interest but embarrassed at the misapprehension he might entertain.

Inevitably, she was drawn back to Bellini's Pietà as though it would summon Larocque's presence. But once in the side room where it hung, she felt she should give some time to paintings they had not examined. To her surprise one was a Raphael and she wondered why Larocque had never called her attention to it. Did he not admire the great master of the Renaissance?

The painting depicted the betrothal of the Virgin to Saint Joseph and the foreground was occupied by the Virgin's attendants on one side and Joseph's defeated rivals on the other, with a bearded priest in the centre joining the hands of the future spouses. In the middle ground, small groups of figures were conversing in front of an elegant temple that dominated the scene. But beyond, and all the more inviting because half concealed, lay a misty landscape of meadows and low wooded hills, against a pale sky.

Standing back to take in the scene as a whole, she saw its mastery. Yet she could not quite feel the admiration it deserved. The colours were rich and subtle, the attitudes graceful, everything (except the faces of the rejected suitors) breathed harmony and order. But there was something too studied in the placing of the groups of figures that irked her. And the feminine figures all seemed struck from one mould — the same doe eyes and rosebud mouth, the same demure and docile gaze.

'What an achievement, eh Signora?' It was the old cicerone who'd followed her. 'And he was only twenty-one when he painted it. So young to create such a masterpiece!' And so sure of himself, she thought silently — inscribing his own name in large letters above the temple door as though he were the divinity worshipped there.

The old man pointed out how the artist's use of perspective directed the eyes to the temple that symbolised the presence of the Eternal. Then, tactfully, he left her to her own contemplation. She'd learnt something from him, she had to admit, letting her eye be drawn through the temple door to the vanishing point in the open doorway beyond, which framed a blue infinity of sky. But it gave her a strangely empty feeling, as did the blind windows of the great dome above, which seemed only to enclose a void. Was it inherent in the painting itself, or a consequence of her own loss of faith? She withdrew her gaze from infinity and fastened it on the hills to the side where the artist had painted the delicate silhouettes of trees against the sky. Here was the only salvation she recognised.

She wished she could hear what Larocque thought of it. Perhaps he'd be at Mme Picard's tonight, though the possibility of his return filled her with as much anxiety as hope. To meet him in public under the knowing gaze of Mme Picard for the first time since that awkward encounter with her friends would be torture. It was almost with relief that she looked round the familiar faces in the salon and saw only his lacking.

A lady harp player opened the entertainment, then two officers sang comic duets. Her thoughts wandered until Mme Delavigne announced a sonata. It was not her sonata, but she recognised the composer's style. Again that dialogue between two voices (or so she heard it), though this piece lacked the poignancy of the other. If certain combinations of sound veered towards melancholy, it was kept at bay. When the sonata ended with calls for an encore, Mme Delavigne announced the adagio from sonata fourteen — 'for a friend'. As the first notes rippled into the hushed room, she raised her fan to her face so that no one could see her emotion.

Between art and music the day was richer in experience than I could ever have dreamt in Nogent. Only one thing was lacking. Attachment is a hazard of travel that I had not foreseen. The wise traveller would stay no longer in a place than its sights required and would avoid making any acquaintance.

Milan, Wednesday 30 October

At two of o'clock the fair Antonio gives me the following letter, he writes in English, then copies the letter into his notebook in its full extravagant Italian:

'*A single line to remember myself to you whom I love more than my life, and to tell you that the most fatal circumstances kept me tied up until eleven o'clock; I went immediately to the meeting place but you had already left!*' She must have mistaken the time; he was there reading till half past eleven. '*Tomorrow at ten I hope to be more fortunate and to be able to tell you how much I love you and how much I'm suffering for you!*'

She's adorably imprudent: her letter is too incriminating to keep. What a risk to send it with her son, who could so easily be suborned by his father! And such artlessness! No wonder she disliked his polished letter. Of course, most Frenchmen would find her language exaggerated, but an Italian heart can't be judged by the standards of Paris.

A postscript tells him to meet her at the Caffè Sanquirico this evening at six.

He rises from his chair and burns her letter.

A quick calculation of his remaining funds reassures him that with the money he changed yesterday he has enough for another month. He doesn't want to think how much he's spent of the three thousand francs he set out with two months ago. Even in Italy, travel isn't cheap. If he's going to come back in the spring he'll have to raise the money somehow.

It's still too early for his afternoon call. Come late, she told him yesterday, and don't stay long. He'll drop in at the Brera for half an hour first which will give him something to talk about. Art is the perfect alibi for his extended stay in Milan, given his professional connection with the emperor's museum. And his reading of the history of Italian painting last night will make him sound more authoritative. He's now read the preface and several chapters on the Florentine School of painting. It's as dry as you'd expect from an elderly Jesuit scholar, but useful for anyone who wishes to understand the development of the art.

Now *there's* a way to make some money, he thinks, as he knots a fresh cravat: translate it! With all the Italian art in Paris now, a history of Italian painting would surely sell. There's nothing like it in French yet. He could dictate a translation. The words would flow easily if he didn't need to write legibly.

How long would it take? He picks up the book and improvises aloud a translation of the first two pages. Four minutes by his watch. Next to no time, even allowing for hesitation and second thoughts. At two minutes a page, that's thirty pages an hour. If he dictated for two hours every morning, he could complete it in thirty or forty days. Find a publisher, and he'd be set. It's a brilliant idea.

It still seems inspired at bedtime. He's purchased the remaining volumes of the *History* and been back to the Brera, where he saw a Giotto and a Mantegna that interested him because of this new project. All evening he's been floating on air, buoyed up by the happiness of seeing Angela at the café. Young Antonio was with them but he'd drifted away to watch the billiard players, so they were able to talk freely.

'Must you stay away so long?' he asked. 'What shall I do in Milan till you get back?'

'Go to Genoa or Venice. You can be there in twenty-four hours. You can't claim you've seen all of Italy till you've been to Venice.'

'It would spoil Venice to see it when my heart is elsewhere. I'd like to see it with you!'

'What's the time?' she asked. 'I must go in a minute.'

Always the time! But at least she'd granted him this stolen half-hour. In some ways these were the sweetest moments, when he could gaze at her with no aim other than to memorise every feature to carry back to Paris — the lower lip that always looked swollen by kisses and that way she had of looking down, head on one side, a half smile flitting across her face. This evening, in her white veil, she resembled a Madonna. But when she raised her eyes and looked into his, it was another matter: she was Circe the enchantress, and he was hers for life. He'll work like a man possessed this winter to earn the money to come back.

Milan, Wednesday 30 October

A bright morning. We left Pierino and the puppy with his cousins since Maddalena wished to look at apartments. She hopes to be married and in her own home by the new year, though the captain has still not settled his future. But his promise to resign his commission appears to satisfy her.

Inspecting apartments (and briefly imagining each as her own possible home), she couldn't help envying Maddalena, who — whatever difficulties lay ahead — was moving towards a chosen future. Two months ago she too had had a goal, which she's lost sight of in the last few weeks. It's time she faced up to the reality of Larocque's silence and made enquiries about travelling to Rome.

She began at the diligence office, but her call there only confirmed that there was no service to cities farther south. The clerk, a fatherly man, advised hiring a *chaise de poste* and driver with fresh horses at every halt so as to spend the nights in the larger towns and avoid the posting inns on the road.

'But that would be very expensive. Is there no cheaper way?'

'The *vetturini* offer a cheaper service but they're too rough for a lady, and very slow. An open vehicle is tolerable for a short distance in good weather, but not in November. Try the mail courier, Signorina.'

On the street outside the post office, a handful of *vetturini* awaited customers. One of them, a coarse-looking fellow in a dirty coat, made an elaborate bow as she passed and his companions sniggered. It was inconceivable that she could entrust herself to such a man.

The postmaster was brusque. When did she want to leave? She didn't know yet. 'Come back when you've decided. At least three days in advance. The places are taken fast. But I warn you, some couriers refuse women passengers — they don't want the responsibility of protecting them. You'll be travelling with your maid, of course?' he added.

She nodded, though it hadn't occurred to her. But of course she couldn't possibly spend nights alone on the road with a courier. Yet another expense, and necessarily long-term, for if she engaged a maid here she couldn't cast her off in Rome. The one solution, if only she knew how to set about it, was to find respectable private travellers willing to take a passenger in their carriage or share the expenses of travelling in a hired vehicle.

But the whole problem might vanish with Larocque's return. For there was no companion with whom she would sooner enjoy the happiness of seeing Rome; she would gladly postpone the journey until such time as he could travel with her. That dream buoys her up as she walks back. But there is still no message waiting when Perpetua admits her.

Milan, Thursday 31 October

It's a mad idea, this scheme he's conceived, but the pile of new books at his elbow is a pledge to carry it through. (Three volumes of Lanzi's *History*, eleven volumes of Vasari's *Lives of the Artists*, Bossi on *The Last Supper* — a hundred francs' worth. Fully justified if it earns him enough to return to Italy.) His first thought had been simply to add some footnotes to Lanzi — personal touches to enliven its antiquarian style. But then it came to him: Why not write his own book? Crib the facts from the *History* but give them the colour, the life, the anecdotes they lack. The thought had him so excited that he'd started drafting an announcement for the newspapers. 'A work in two volumes to appear in Paris at the end of 1812. Fruit of three years' travel and research. The author has made use of the Abbé Luigi Lanzi's *History*.'

Of course, it's presumptuous when he still has everything to learn. But that will give his writing the freshness of discovery, and between this stack of books and all the Italian masterpieces now in Paris, he'll soon know enough. And his own honest reactions will be livelier than the old Jesuit's scholarly account.

Elated with his project, he'd welcomed Angela with a gratifyingly sustained performance, followed by a second as rapidly as he could wish. She came three or four times. Or at least she seemed to. Women often pretend, little Angel says. With her, there's never any doubt, but with Angela there isn't yet the complete frankness between them that comes with time.

Afterwards, he went to the Brera with new excitement now that he had a purpose. He began with the scene of Hagar's dismissal that Angela so admired. Without her distracting presence he could give it his full attention.

The face was alive: it seemed to change before his eyes, revealing everything a discarded mistress might feel — disbelief, pain, humiliation, a last glimmer of hope as she pleads with Abraham. There was an emotional depth here that few painters approached.

This wasn't some stock figure from the repertoire, but a real woman, red-eyed with weeping. And no seductive Magdalene, just a maid, pleasing enough to catch the master's eye but not young, and the hand clutching the handkerchief had clearly worked hard. Guercino had taken the plight of a servant and her bastard child and made it a subject for tragedy.

But admirable though it was, the canvas alongside solicited his attention. One can't help but be drawn to a beautiful woman, and this one in her yellow robe had such a graceful attitude, half turned towards the man addressing her. *The Samaritan Woman at the Well.* Annibale Carracci. No wonder his Roman friend placed him in the first rank. His eyes moved back and forth between the two pictures. The lovely Samaritan was eloquent in her hesitation, her profile luminous against the dark background, but there was no complexity to her. Unquestionably, *Hagar* was truest to nature, and that must be his touchstone.

Wanting to look at some of the early painters mentioned in the *History*, he continued to the room where he'd seen the Mantegna yesterday. Beside it hung a gilded altarpiece of the type he usually ignored. But there was something interestingly peculiar about this one. The Virgin, richly dressed and crowned, had the sullenly resentful air of one of those unfortunate princesses married against her will to seal an alliance (like poor young Marie-Louise, swept off to the imperial bedroom within minutes of her arrival so the emperor could start begetting an heir). And the Holy Child, clutching a live bird in one tight little fist, had a stubborn look that said, 'Let nobody take this toy away from me.' On each side stood a pair of saints — Saint Peter with the suspicious glare of a maniac, holding a set of giant keys, and a monk rolling his eyes in the throes of ecstasy or a very bad stomach ache. Opposite them, another monk — with a cleaver in his head and a sword plunged deep in his chest — stood beside a fashionable youth whose short tunic and scarlet hose showed off his legs to advantage.

And they called this genre a *sacra conversazione* — not much conversation among this unlikely group! It was almost caricatural. But the artist was undeniably skilled. The fruit and flowers round the base were painted in such perfect *trompe l'oeil* that you could almost reach out and pluck one. The name Crivelli was new to him.

Something told him he was being observed. A woman in a doorway across the room who vanished as soon as he turned. He almost followed her. Art is a respectable pretext to engage in conversation with a stranger, as he'd discovered in Bologna. Perhaps that's what they hope for, the women who come alone.

He must bring Angela to see the Crivelli. It's a perfect target for his wit.

Milan, Thursday 31 October

Late this morning I put the final stitches to Maddalena's reticule. It will be a wedding gift if I stay, a farewell gift if I leave.

After lunch I returned to the Brera. The old cicerone was conducting a group but I did not join them though no doubt I might have profited from his explanations. I wanted to see the Raphael again to understand why, despite its beauty of colour and form, it had not moved me.

Recalling the cicerone's instructions, she positioned herself in the spot from which the artist intended it to be viewed. Again, her gaze was drawn to the oblong of light framed by the temple doorway. But this time, she moved closer, right up to the frame where, examining the surface of paint and varnish, she escaped the artist's direction. To her surprise, the oblong wasn't entirely filled by the sky — across the bottom was a faint blue line of distant hills. So it was not infinity that the painting invited her to contemplate but the horizon, though so distant that it seemed an image of futurity, of all the centuries to come.

But that too made her feel empty. She'd set off two months ago towards the horizon, and indeed she'd reached it and crossed into another world, but her ultimate destination seemed as far away as ever. The temple itself with its blind windows, perhaps a replica of some ancient Roman model, seemed a warning that she would not find what she sought in Rome.

In despair, she decided to leave. But as she was about to re-enter the main Bellini room, she spotted another visitor and paused. It was a man with his back to her but something familiar in his stance and the Parisian cut of his coat told her it was her fellow-traveller from the diligence. He turned and she stepped quickly out of sight but she'd seen enough to confirm his identity. Once she was sure he'd left, she couldn't resist going to see what had caught his attention.

It was a strange painting of the Madonna and Child with attendant saints, one of several heavily ornamented works by an artist whom

Larocque had dismissed. It was hard to see what the young man had found to admire in it, apart from the exquisitely lifelike foliage and fruit. But why had the artist painted a large fissure in the marble dais beneath the Virgin's throne? To show off his skill at creating illusion, or to suggest a crack in the foundation of Christian belief?

She longed to discuss it with Larocque, and the Raphael too, indeed everything she'd seen this afternoon had raised so many questions in her mind that she felt his absence acutely. It was over a week now since he'd left, so he might very well be at the opera tonight, though she told herself not to hope. Nonetheless, like a creeping plant that sends out runners in every direction and roots wherever it finds even the smallest space, her mind seized every possibility, so that when he had not appeared by the second interval the disappointment was crushing. Her only comfort was to be spared the malicious observation of Mme Picard, whose barbs were directed at the hostess of the neighbouring box and her many admirers.

Among them, to her surprise, was the young man from the diligence, looking very pleased with himself. He seemed to be everywhere all of a sudden.

She talked for a few moments with Mme Delavigne, who invited her to visit again. It made her feel less lonely to have found one fellow spirit among the group, though it could not compensate for Larocque's absence. The officers were talking gravely among themselves about the latest news from Spain. Two weeks ago Larocque had been part of that group; their eyes had met in an intimate exchange that she had surely not imagined. It was the day after their walk along the canal but before their climb to the Duomo roof.

As though her thoughts had conjured up the man himself, she heard a new arrival tell Mme Picard that he was back: 'I ran into him at the stables — he'd just got in from Bergamo. I'd have brought him with me, but he said he was in no fit state to meet ladies.'

There was no time to hear more as they took their seats for the second act.

I was grateful that in the Picard box the convention of silence during the performance still prevails so that, whatever my social obligations during the intervals, at least while the singers were onstage I could let my thoughts wander where they wished.

Autumn Fog

Milan, Friday 1 November

All Saints Day, and every church bell in the city ringing. Fewer of them now since the closure of the monasteries, and less festivity. Eleven years ago, every feast day brought candlelight processions through the streets in clouds of incense. They were banned now as a threat to public order. An ill-judged move, he thought. Desirable though it might be that Italy escape the thrall of religion, the people loved a spectacle. It was unwise to forbid their pleasures. His main concern, of course, was how far the holy day would interfere with his own. Fortunately, whatever rites Angela conformed to didn't preclude their meeting, and as the bells pealed their salute to the saints in paradise she was halfway to heaven herself.

At a loose end afterwards with the Brera closed, he'd thought of trying a church or two for their frescos. But in the grey November weather there was insufficient light and the dim glow of an altar lamp illuminated nothing. Towards the end of the afternoon he paid his respects in Via Meravigli. Light-headed with the knowledge of his possession, he was afraid even to look at Angela lest his eyes betray him. The magnetism between them was so strong that he was sure the others must sense it. Turcotti was too clever to betray any suspicion, but Widmann seemed moody, leaving the conversation to pick out a tune on the piano. It was one of the popular romances that Mme Daru liked to sing, and it gave him a momentary pang as he remembered how much he'd read into the words back in June. Irrationally, since she'd rejected his love, he felt almost guilty that he'd forgotten her so quickly with Angela.

No chance of a rendezvous tonight because every citizen of Milan is attending the All Souls vigil. He can hear the muffled dirges as he wanders the empty streets, but in his jubilation he's impervious to their gloomy message. He knows it's dangerous: he'll suffer all the more when he leaves for Paris. But better to have experienced it and suffered than to be as phlegmatic as an Englishman.

Milan, Friday 1 November

The Feast of All Saints. My call on Mme Picard was brief, since I was invited to dine with the Rossi family before the vigil of All Souls. A curious, indeed rather primitive, feature of the occasion is the little cakes known as 'dead men's bones' that we ate at the end of the meal to fortify us for the long church ritual ahead. Unfortunately they did not sweeten all tempers.

'At least they've left this feast where it belongs,' Signora Rossi complained. No one responded, but she wouldn't allow the subject to drop. 'It's an insult to the blessed memory of the saints to forbid the observance of their holy days.'

'Would you have us go back to the way things were before?' her husband asked. 'A day off for every saint in the calendar even if we're in the middle of a job!'

'And the Blessed Virgin? You don't care that they've stolen her feast for their San Napoleone? They give freedom of religion to heretics and Jews and take it away from good Christians!'

'Can't we enjoy our soup without a sermon?' Signor Rossi held out his bowl. 'Give me some more and let us eat it in peace!'

It was an awkward moment. She wanted to apologise to Signora Rossi for Saint Napoleon if nothing else, but whatever compunction she felt was wiped out by a further outburst as they set off for the vigil. Maddalena had faithfully observed the preparatory novena, praying the past nine days for her late husband, in case her pilgrimage to the Sacro Monte hadn't sufficed to release him from purgatory. Trezzano, who'd been invited for the meal, was accompanying them to church, and as they stepped out into the street, Maddalena took his arm.

'Show a little decency on this night of all,' Signora Rossi hissed. 'Do you think God listens to the prayers of a widow who's found herself a lover?'

'Mamma!' Teresa exclaimed. Maddalena grabbed Pierino's hand and set off at a run, leaving them all behind. Trezzano hesitated an instant then followed.

Unaccustomed to such outbursts, she was trembling as she followed with the rest of the family, but the scent of incense and the solemn hush of the vigil calmed her. The church was in complete darkness except for the red glow of the sanctuary lamp on the main altar, but slowly, as the priest and his assistants processed from chapel to chapel, lighting candles on every black-draped altar and in front of every statue, it re-emerged from the shadows. Even without the recollection of her own dead, the ritual would have moved her — all the tiny candle flames springing up in the darkness, frail but persistent like the memories of lost ones in each heart.

'*Mater Misericordiae*,' the priest intoned. 'Mary, Mother of Mercy, intercede for the souls in purgatory. Pray for us also who are still in danger of eternal damnation.'

'*Ora pro nobis.*' Shrill and fervent, Signora Rossi's voice rose above the others. How were mother and daughter going to face each other afterwards? She felt for Maddalena, who had veiled her face so the effect of Signora Rossi's words was not visible.

'Woe unto us miserable beings, who have deserved the punishment of Hell,' the priest declaimed. 'May God grant us time to atone for our sins before we die.'

When the church emptied, Signora Rossi remained behind in ostentatious prayer. Outside, Maddalena whispered urgently to Teresa, who sighed and nodded.

'We're going to stay at Teresa's tonight, Marie. I cannot sleep under the same roof as Mamma. Come, Pierino.'

'These women! What can you do with them?' Signor Rossi clapped Trezzano on the back. 'Don't worry, young man — it will all blow over by tomorrow.'

Giovanni offered her his arm but since she had only to cross the road to reach home, she declined it, and he headed down to the café alone.

Through all this, she'd not forgotten that Larocque was back. Returning from her walk this morning she'd hoped, unreasonably, to find a message, and tonight the same unreasonable hope was disappointed again. But he'd scarcely been back a day; tomorrow, surely, she would hear from him, if only the reply to her own note that courtesy dictated.

She scarcely knew what she hoped for except to see him. Ten days had passed since their accidental meeting and her uncertainty had grown. It would only be if she could see him again, alone, that she might judge how things stood between them.

MILAN, SATURDAY 2 NOVEMBER

Without a doubt the most beautiful woman I've had, and perhaps that I've ever seen, is A. as she looked this evening in the glow of lamplight from the shops as we walked through the streets.

Seeing her in public through the eyes of strangers, and as he now knew her from the privacies of the bed, he felt like a mortal loved by a goddess, perceiving her divinity even as he penetrated her human form. She's not unaware of her effect. Some of her friends, she said (quite naturally, without vanity), have told her she's frightening. It's true.

Her eyes were shining, her face half lit had a soft harmony and yet at the same time there was something terrifying in its supernatural beauty. She seemed like some superior being who had taken on the disguise of beauty but whose penetrating eyes could read to the depths of your soul. That face would have made a sublime sibyl.

Yet he's possessed her. And she appears to love him. And to be satisfied by his lovemaking.

They'd met at six near the Sanquirico, their usual rendezvous. He escorted her to her sister-in-law's and waited for her in a café. Afterwards, they had coffee in the deserted back room of a shop, then finally, after half an hour's walk, they parted on Piazza Mercanti. All this in the company of young Antonio. No chance for a last embrace, only his lips briefly grazing her hand, their eyes locked an instant.

He's evaded the awful finality of it till this moment, but now the exaltation that's buoyed him up for the last few days collapses. If he returns to Paris — as he must — it may be six months before they meet again, or longer. He feels close to tears, like an abandoned child. But she'll be back by the fifteenth, they'll have a few last days together before he leaves. He clings to that.

Reading over what he's written, it strikes him that this is where his 'Tour', if he publishes it, should conclude. He adds a footnote in English: *The last part of a tour throught* — then, uncertain of English spelling, switches back to French — *Italy presented in all humility to Monsieur H de B aged 39 years, who will be alive perhaps in 1821, by his very humble and more cheerful servant, the HB of 1811.*

Where will he be in 1821, on the verge of middle age? Prefect in a town close enough to Paris that he can get to the theatre once or twice a month if he's lucky. Or better, perhaps, secretary to a minister, so his evenings at least will be interesting however tedious his days. Will his play be finished by then, or will he still be squeezing out scraps of dialogue in the intervals of work? With his hair receding and his girth expanding and his disposition soured by daily exposure to the petty vanities of Paris, just another eunuch among the sycophants at the court of the great sultan who has taken all power unto himself.

A dismal thought. He heads to the Caffè del Duomo for the consolation of a sorbet. There's a full moon high above the city and the great cathedral has never seemed lovelier. The white marble has the beauty of Gothic without its gloom, a typical Italian transmutation of a northern style into something lighter, more frivolous, yet with its own special melancholy which resembles that of love. A good observation: he scribbles it on a scrap of paper for future reference.

The café is busy as usual even though it's the Day of the Dead, and his spirits are restored by the lively crowd. The Milanese are a congenial people. He likes their sagacity, their good nature and their blunt laconic humour, so akin to his own. He's even grown accustomed to their nasal dialect. True, its contractions cut off the vowel endings that make classic Italian the most melodious language in the world, but though it sounds abrupt to most foreign ears, it doesn't to his. He feels more at home here than anywhere else in the world. If he could only find enough to live on, he'd come back for good, rent a room off the Corsia dei Servi, write the books he has in him, see his Angela whenever she permitted. What else matters in life but happiness? Each individual pursues it in his own way, but most are deluded as to its source. It doesn't lie in the fleeting satisfactions of worldly success. This year has taught him that, if nothing else, though he's only fully grasped it in the last few weeks. Perhaps he needed to be several hundred leagues from Paris to see it.

Milan, Saturday 2 November, Feast of All Souls

This day on which everyone goes to the cemetery I can only pass in silent recollection. I received a brief note from Monsieur Larocque.

It lay on the table in front of her in all its terse formality. He thanked her for writing and hoped she was well. He too regretted the interruption of their conversation. Unfortunately he was very occupied at present but he hoped to pay his respects to her at Mme Picard's on Tuesday.

To see him, for the first time in two weeks, at Mme Picard's, would be almost worse than not to see him at all. She was sure now that he was avoiding her. Of course it had been dictated to his clerk, but still she felt a distance that had not been there before. It was only when she threaded her needle with pink silk to embroider another rose on Lucia's sash that she found an explanation. How could she have forgotten that he and the child would be visiting his wife's grave today! It was selfish of her to have hoped for anything this day of all days. She must not jump to conclusions.

She worked on Lucia's sash till it was time to visit Mme Delavigne. A loud male voice rang out as the maid opened the door: Lieutenant Richard was rehearsing his serenade.

'Do not stop on my account, I beg you. I should like to listen, if it does not disturb you.'

He smoothed his moustache and went through it again, hand on his heart, gazing soulfully at Mme Delavigne across the piano until she sent him away.

'He's really more suited to Figaro, poor man,' Mme Delavigne remarked after he left. 'But he fancies himself in the role of Almaviva so I humour him.' She began putting away her music, and added, 'I hear Larocque is back.'

'Do you know where he's been?' She tried to sound indifferent.

'On one of his tours of inspection, I imagine — his pretext when he's had enough of society. He's a moody man.'

'You know him well?'

'We used to confide in each other at a time when we were both unhappy. And sometimes he'd bring his little girl into town. He thinks the world of her. It's probably the reason why he hasn't remarried. He certainly hasn't lacked the opportunity. We'd go to the marionettes with my Olivier — my poor boy. I had a letter from him today and I'm worried. We agreed on a code to use in our letters — the notes of a musical phrase — because the boys' letters home are read by the master so they can't write openly, and he used the code for 'unhappy'.

'Poor child! Can you reply freely?'

'Their letters are opened. I must be careful not to betray him. All I can do is ask his brothers to look after him. It breaks my heart to send them so far away. But it's in their best interest — or at least I hope so.'

Sympathy made her encourage Mme Delavigne to confide her worries, and for the remainder of the visit no natural opportunity presented itself to learn more about Larocque. She did not like the feeling the conversation had aroused, which she was forced to acknowledge as jealousy. She'd imagined herself his only confidante and now it appeared he had another. But there was something selfish in wishing that she'd been the first in his life; true affection should make her rejoice that he'd had a friend in his loneliness. What was love if it did not put the well-being of the beloved first? Yet despite her self-reproach, she could not help feeling reassured that Mme Delavigne had spoken of these events as past.

Autumn Fog

Milan, Sunday 3 November

A morning so dark that he needs candles to read by, and after an hour he rubs his eyes and pushes the book aside. History can't hold him today. Milan is desolate without Angela, his freedom meaningless. But there's no point sitting here brooding. He rouses himself to take a walk, but just as he enters the Duomo square, the downpour that's been threatening since breakfast sends the pedlars and street musicians scurrying for shelter. A priest with a huge umbrella, his soutane hitched above thin black-stockinged ankles, runs clumsily through the puddles towards the Duomo, shaking himself in the portal like a wet dog before entering. On impulse he follows. He hasn't been inside in years. There's bound to be something of interest.

Mass is over, but an officious sacristan bars his way. 'The church is closed, Monsieur.' He stands his ground, asserting his right to look even if he can't go further. In the echoing central nave, workmen are attaching swathes of red damask to the pillars and suspending huge paintings between them. A handsome young priest directs operations, even hoisting his cassock and climbing a ladder himself. Sad to see a young fellow fussing over draperies like a woman, when he might be wearing the uniform of the Italian army. He asks the sacristan what's happening.

'Tomorrow is San Carlo's Day, Monsieur. We're decorating in his honour.'

A sentence shapes itself; he scribbles it on the back of a bill he finds in his pocket: 'The sainted cardinal is Milan's chief deity after the Virgin, though the pious also pray to God, just in case.' Just the kind of quip his 'Tour' needs. Apart from a page or two at the beginning, he's written nothing about Milan that doesn't revolve around Angela. He should use his remaining leave to fill out his portrait of the city, as it was when he first saw it and now, after a decade of change.

Outside, it's still raining too heavily to make a dash for the café. He stands in the doorway, surveying the deserted square.

Of course, if he publishes his 'Tour', he'll have to cut all personal references, not just to Angela and her circle, but to everyone he's met in the last two months. A pity — it's those encounters and conversations that make it more than another tedious compendium of monuments and masterpieces. Take out the people and what's left? He could give them false names as he already has in his journal, but they'd recognise themselves. He can't risk giving offence or exposing Angela. And in any case it would be highly imprudent to reveal where he's spent the last two months. He'll have to use a pseudonym himself. A foreign name would be the most effective disguise — German, since they're the only other foreigners in Italy now that the war keeps the English away. And after his two years among the Germans in Brunswick he knows them well enough to fabricate a plausible character. A northerner coming under the spell of the south — a man like his good friend Strombeck, or the art historian Winckelmann, who found his life's purpose in Rome.

The rain shimmers like blown gauze across the deserted piazza, reminding him of the wet November day five years ago when he'd travelled from Berlin to Brunswick with Martial. The main road was blocked by French troops since Magdeburg had only just capitulated, so they'd had to make a long detour north through a succession of dreary towns, of which the only one he recalls is Winckelmann's birthplace. No wonder he'd fled to Italy, they'd agreed. 'All this Lutheran gloom!' Martial exclaimed, grimacing at the ugly red-brick church whose disproportionately high towers dominated the little town. But what was it called? The name escapes him.

The rain is tapering off at last; he turns up his collar and crosses the empty piazza to the café. Taking the last free table, he considers the question of a pen name. On the one hand, it permits everything — irreverent thoughts, scandalous admissions, unpalatable truths. On the other hand, publishing pseudonymously won't bring fame to Henri Beyle. But a 'Tour' isn't likely to achieve that anyway. It's simply a first step towards the more substantial book he'll write one day. Till then, it's wise to use a pen name.

But if by some happy chance his first writings gain the respect of the few who matter, why not adopt the pseudonym as his true name? Shed the identity of Henri Beyle, fat boy of the École centrale, failed dragoon, adjunct commissary, official drudge. His pen name, free of whatever embarrassment has attached itself to the name of Beyle, will become his true identity.

Of course, he must choose it carefully. He can't publish a book under one of the comic aliases he uses with Pauline. It should be unique or very uncommon, with a more distinguished sound than Beyle, which to a Parisian ear sounds like the bleating of his father's merinos. German for the disguise, but something that sounds good in French, not some alien explosion of consonants like Pfitsch or Knistedt. A German cultivated enough to write in French, a cosmopolitan with enough experience of the world to view it with irony, but a poetic sensibility and a northerner's enthusiasm for the south.

To be honest, he's personally as often infuriated by the south — its dirt, its backwardness, its beggars. That's why he prefers Milan to Rome or Naples, or even Florence. Governed by the Austrians for so long, yet profoundly Italian still, Milan combines the best of north and south. It's a city where one could live without irritation or gloom.

A wave of affection fills him as he looks around the café at the Milanese crowd — the young officers flirting with their girls, the bluff good-natured merchants discussing the affairs of the day, the government officials not too puffed-up with self-importance to relax among friends. He'll portray this world in his 'Tour' — its blend of superstition and practical realism, its earthy humour, its devotion to pleasure, and the unique charm of its women, that pensive yet sensual Lombard beauty with which Leonardo and his followers endowed Virgins and courtesans alike. Italian women are the most womanly in the world, and those of Lombardy above all. He'll dedicate his 'Tour' to the loveliest, his 'Lady Simonetta', for she's the true source of this new power he feels in himself.

MONDAY All the bells in the city are pealing for San Carlo's feast. On his way to the Caffè Nuovo, he runs into Widmann — he, too, at a loose end with Angela away. It's a dangerous pleasure to talk about her. He does his best to hide his secret, but he can't keep it out of his voice, though he's careful to refer to her as Signora Pietragrua, not 'la Gina' as the others say.

Widmann asks when he's leaving.

'Not for another two weeks. There's a lot I haven't seen yet at the Brera and elsewhere.'

'Don't delay too long. There's snow in the passes already.'

'Oh, I've braved snow before — in the crossing of the Saint Bernard,' he says casually.

No doubt the poor fellow will be happy to see him go, though he's as courteous as ever. Apart from Lechi (who's left for his villa), he hasn't made any friends in Milan, though there are two or three men in Angela's circle whose company he might have enjoyed. But love is an unsocial state; it isolates you from others. What man doesn't forgo the opportunity to spend time with friends if there's even the smallest chance of being with the woman he loves?

The mention of snow was a jolt, but he can't let the weather deprive him of his last five days with Angela. Meanwhile, he must make the best possible use of time till she returns. Now that the holy days are past, the Brera will reopen. He'll go tomorrow, spend the afternoon there. He needs some good pages on art for his 'Tour', and apart from Florence he's kept few notes on what he's seen. With his poor memory, everything fades unless he writes immediately.

What was the name of Winckelmann's birthplace? It's been on the tip of his tongue all day. Steindal? Stendal? It has a good ring to it and it's not unpronounceable. He scribbles it on the back of the menu, as the waiter arrives with his sorbet.

Milan, Monday 4 November

I wrote nothing yesterday. Without news from Maddalena, I talked to no one but Perpetua. Needing to rest my eyes after hours of sewing, I went out when the rain ceased, but the sunlight piercing the clouds gleamed on every wet surface, and I could scarcely bear the brilliance. The Corsia dei Servi was crowded and the cheerful atmosphere so much out of harmony with my mood that I fled to the sanctuary of my room.

It was a malaise that she'd first experienced in London as a girl thrown from a sheltered home into the public gaze of the street. Today, as then, she'd hugged the walls for safety like an animal — a dangerous state of mind that she must not succumb to now that she may soon be on the road again.

But Mrs Godwin too had suffered from the stares of the curious in Norway. A woman could never move through the world with the ease of a man. She almost envied the Egyptian women painted by the elder Bellini, shrouded from head to toe. Yet even veiled they were conspicuous; invisible, they nonetheless magnetised the eye — a paradoxical state.

Still, the veil — its Milanese version at least — had lessened her discomfort in public, made it easier to explore the city alone. But will she enjoy the same freedom of movement in the south? Her dream of an independent life in Rome may prove illusory, the stuff of novels, just as the young man in the diligence warned.

Today is San Carlo's feast and like all Milan I ate chick pea soup in honour of the great cardinal, who apparently favoured it. Perpetua believes it has healing properties. I wish that it could cure melancholy.

Maddalena is home so we took our usual walk this morning. Mother and daughter are not reconciled, but a truce has been reached. Maddalena has no choice but to remain under her parents' roof until her marriage. Unfortunately, there is no possibility of advancing the date since weddings are not performed during the penitential season of Advent which, under the Milanese rite, begins two weeks from now.

'Does Pierino know that he will have a new papa?' The child was ahead of them patiently waiting while Lupetto lifted his leg against a stationary carriage.

'Children are so funny — I told him that we are soon going to live with Fedele and he said he wanted to stay with Lupetto! I had to promise that Lupetto could come too.'

They were walking along the inner canal, keeping pace with a loaded barge. The sight reminded her of Larocque. She'd heard nothing more from him, but of course this succession of holy days explained it. He must be spending them with his daughter. That's why he'd said in his note that he would see her at Mme Picard's. It lifted her spirits to have found an explanation.

Milan, Tuesday 5 November

Another rainy morning. He went to the Brera to see works by Leonardo's followers. A guard directed him to the farthest room, which was empty except for a woman in a grey cloak and Milanese veil, examining a picture on the far wall. He glanced at a painting or two, then looked her way. She hadn't moved. What had caught her attention? He made his way stealthily around the room and using the emperor as his cover took a quick glance sideways. A pale, fine-boned face, almost translucent skin — not Milanese, he was sure, in spite of the veil. Her eyes were closed — bizarre. But he'd seen that profile before . . . It was the woman in grey from the diligence!

The temptation to approach her was irresistible. If she snubbed him, he'd gracefully withdraw. He cleared his throat to alert her to his presence and caught a split second of welcome in her blue eyes before recognition dawned. 'Forgive me for disturbing your reverie, Mademoiselle, but I believe we've met before. We ate supper together at a village inn in Burgundy two months ago, if I'm not mistaken?'

'There were three of you,' she nodded. 'You were talking about happiness.'

How much else did she remember, he wondered uneasily. But this was his chance to wipe out any bad impression. 'I know it's inexcusable to intrude on you like this, but it's so improbable that our paths should cross again that I could not resist addressing you. Will you permit me to introduce myself?' He gave her his card.

She took it but did not offer her own name. He was tempted to ask if she often looked at paintings with her eyes closed, but he didn't want her to know he'd been watching. 'You like the painters of the fifteenth century?'

'Some.'

It was clearly not going to be easy, but he persisted.

'Personally, there's little that interests me in the early period apart from Raphael. But I'd sell my shirt to see the Raphael rooms in the Vatican again.'

'You've been to Rome?'

Now he'd caught her interest. 'I made two visits on the way to Naples and back.'

'How did you find it?'

'In a shocking state of decay. But the new government is taking things in hand. My cousin is the Intendant of Crown Possessions there, so I heard everything from the source.'

He told her of the changes underway and the obstacles to progress, described his meetings with Canova and the duchess's musical performance. She had, unlike many women, the capacity to listen intently, and it led him to talk too much. He tried to compensate: 'But I haven't asked what brought you to Italy?'

'Books — as you may remember. You mocked my faith in travellers' accounts.'

Her smile belied the slightly accusing tone, but he was abashed. 'I only meant to caution, not to mock you. But I'm often too trenchant in the heat of discussion, my friends tell me. I hope you'll forgive me?'

'I have to admit that you were right in one respect at least. I intended to continue to Rome, and the books that inspired me gave me the illusion that a woman could travel alone. But everyone tells me that it's too dangerous.'

'It's true, unfortunately. Much of Italy is barely civilised. I had a narrow escape myself. The courier with whom I might have travelled was attacked outside Rome.' He told the story. The fear in her eyes made him pity her. 'You must find some travelling companions. Official if possible — someone who will travel with an armed guard. Go and see the consul, he'll know who's leaving. You may have to wait a while but there's sure to be someone suitable.'

'I had not thought of asking the consul's assistance, but I shall do so at once.'

She looked so grateful he was touched. It made him feel a veteran of the road. 'When you reach Rome I advise you to engage a manservant as guide. It will cost you almost nothing — the servant class are desperate for any pittance — but it will protect you from petty annoyances with cab drivers and beggars.'

The guard interrupted to announce the gallery was closing. As they made their way out, he pointed to the Crivelli by the archway. 'Look at that poor Virgin, what company she's in! A demented pope, a hysterical monk — this one with the cleaver in his head who insists on showing off his wounds for all eternity — and a young fop who's worried that his stockings bag at the knee. No wonder she's pouting!'

She laughed and he felt he'd passed the outer ring of defences.

'It's a very strange painting,' she agreed. 'He's a master of illusion — those plums are so real that a wasp might be deceived. But have you noticed that fissure in the marble? What do you make of it? Could it be a covert expression of doubt?'

'You think he was an early Protestant?' He was annoyed that he hadn't noticed it himself.

'A crack beneath the Virgin's throne must have some significance, don't you think?'

'Signori, if you please!' The guard hurried them out.

They descended the stairs to the courtyard: another moment and she'd be gone. It was only two o'clock and he had a whole afternoon to get through without Angela. Could he invite her to a café? She was wearing sturdy ankle boots, he'd noticed — obviously a walker — and the sky above their heads was clear again. 'Would you like to take a stroll on the ramparts? One needs fresh air, I find, after a museum.'

She hesitated, then to his surprise accepted, and they set off towards the Porta Nuova. He asked about her experience of Milan. Like himself, she'd made Italian friends but they sounded ordinary. His acquaintance with Milanese society was much broader. Angela's friends were men of distinction even if her parents were shopkeepers. But then beauty like hers raised a woman above her class. This one appeared to have sunk. Her speech and deportment left little doubt about her origins, but the unfashionable cloak suggested straitened circumstances.

It turned out that she'd also been to Lake Maggiore and they compared notes with all the pleasure of shared experience.

'If I could find a small house near Laveno,' she said, 'the humblest even, I'd be content to spend the rest of my life there.' The fresh air had put some colour in her pale cheeks.

'I had a similar thought myself. The inn on Isola Bella would be a perfect place to write. It's a little piece of heaven fallen to earth. Nothing in Rome or Naples compares with that view.'

'Rome disappointed you?'

'It's backward and shabby — even the grandest buildings are neglected. An immense graveyard of a once great city. You know the one thing that truly moved me? The birds in the Coliseum at twilight. It brought tears to my eyes. That, and a picture in Florence — Bronzino's *Limbo*. Don't miss it when you're in Santa Croce. I've never seen anything so moving, all the dead rising out of oblivion, unchanged, just as they were in life.'

This was the way to her heart, he saw. Her face was unguarded for the first time since he'd addressed her in the museum. Impulsively, he went on, 'Sometimes I feel I've lost my soul, do you know what I mean? When you're young you feel everything with such intensity and then somewhere after twenty it starts to fade and you think your soul is dead, and then unexpectedly an experience like that brings it back to life.'

'I felt something similar in the woods near Laveno,' she said. 'I was alone, the leaves were falling — it was as if I were seeing everything for the first time. I hadn't felt so alive in years.'

'If only it were possible to live with that intensity all the time,' he said.

'Yes, the life that one would like to lead seems always out of reach.'

They climbed the ramparts and paused to admire the view. The Alps were barely visible — a silver foam-crest on a sea of grey cloud.

'Do you know what form it would take, your ideal life?' he asked. 'For my part, I'm still uncertain.'

'Last year I would have asked only to live somewhere beautiful in the depths of the country. With a well-stocked library. But since my arrival here I would now place art and music among my requirements.'

'I love the country too, but I couldn't be happy without the theatre and the opera. A good library, of course. I'm lost without books. What did you bring with you for the road?'

'Books by the two women travellers who inspired me — to maintain my courage. And Monsieur de Chateaubriand's *Letter on the Roman Countryside* —'

'Chateaubriand . . .' He restrained himself.

'And Dante to read in Florence, and Machiavelli —'

'Machiavelli! That's an unusual choice for a woman.'

'But essential for Italian history, don't you think?' She sounded apologetic. 'And then for Rome, everything that I could fit in my box. History, of course, Livy and Tacitus —'

'I thought of bringing Livy myself,' he said, not to be outdone. But she wasn't trying to impress him: it was the enthusiasm of a passionate reader. 'You enjoy Roman history?'

'My father gave me a taste for it. But I've also brought the poets. It's my dream to reread *The Aeneid* in Rome.'

'Which translation do you have?'

'I read it in Latin.' Again that apologetic note.

'You have the Latin to read Virgil? That's rare for a woman.'

'My father had no sons to educate so he passed on his learning to me.'

'I learnt nothing from mine. It's not that he lacked the time or education to teach me, but we were always at daggers drawn.'

'How sad!' She looked at him with shocked sympathy. 'My father was demanding and I feared not meeting his expectations, but he was an excellent teacher. He would repeat certain lines so expressively that even before I understood them they sounded beautiful.'

'You were lucky! My first Latin tutor simply made me memorise rules. The next had me and my two companions in misery parse the *Georgics* — can you imagine! We were ten years old, barely understood a word! But I'd found a French translation — we hid it in a cupboard in the privy so as to consult it unbeknown to him on the pretext of relieving ourselves.' Had he gone too far? No, she was smiling. 'Of course we were found out and punished. It wasn't till I was sent to school that I read Latin with pleasure. But then I discovered a talent for mathematics. I saw it could be my escape.'

'What did you want to escape?'

'Home — I had a miserable childhood after my mother's death, always in trouble for one thing or another, not allowed to play with other children or swim in the river like other boys. It wasn't till I was seventeen and came to Italy that I discovered happiness.'

'It was the reverse for me. An only child, indulgent parents, brought up with every advantage — my childhood couldn't have been happier. But it all changed when I was eleven.'

'The Revolution?' he guessed. 'You emigrated?'

'We spent ten years in England.'

'England — what luck! It's my dream, once the war ends, to see Shakespeare in an English theatre. Did you have the opportunity to see any of his plays?'

'The theatre was beyond our means,' she said sharply, and he thought he'd lost her. Abruptly, she changed the subject and asked what books he'd brought for the journey.

'Only a couple. In fact, I've scarcely opened them, being with friends in Rome and Naples. But I've bought books here on Italian art. In fact, it's given me a project. My travels have made me feel my ignorance and it occurred to me that by translating a history of Italian painting I could instruct myself and assist other travellers.' He wasn't ready to disclose his new plan yet.

'What an excellent idea! I should have liked to read a history of art before visiting a gallery. But the friend who took me to the Brera said that one should begin by following one's inclinations.'

'Your friend is right.' (Male or female, he wondered; something in her voice told him it was a man.) 'It's important to discover what one really feels and not what good taste dictates. But a simple chronology of artists and schools, like the one I'm translating, can be useful. It doesn't tell you what to think, like a cicerone. I detest them. It's always better to look at art alone.'

'But it can be good to share impressions with a thoughtful companion . . .'

Definitely a man, he decided, seeing her blush. But they were approaching the Porta Orientale, and he was afraid she'd want to turn back. It was only mid-afternoon and he was enjoying himself. 'We can leave the ramparts here and return through the public gardens if you wish. Or can I persuade you to continue a little farther?'

To his surprise she agreed. She was a good walker, not needing his arm like Mme Daru, nor constantly distracted by others like Angela.

'What I'd like to understand,' she took up the discussion again, 'which perhaps your history will tell me, is what brought about the change in the quattrocento. Before that, judging by what I've seen — which isn't much, I know — artists represented saints like statues on an altar, as in that picture we just saw together. But then they began to paint them as human beings in a natural setting. What was happening — in the church or in artistic circles — to bring about that change? That's what I would like to learn from a history of art.'

'It was probably no more than a change in taste,' he temporised, feeling at a loss. Nothing he'd read answered this kind of question.

'Just as the generation that followed the Renaissance masters emphasized style or "manner", until Guercino and the Carracci led a return to the natural.' He felt on safe ground repeating his Roman friend.

'But even if it was simply a change in taste,' she persisted, 'that still leaves the question as to what caused it. Besides, I find so much truth in certain painters of the quattrocento that I see their work as an advance in . . . how should I put it? . . . the depiction of reality. Why would the next generation abandon that?'

'Because the public — or at any rate the patrons who pay the artist — prefer the ideal to the real. You yourself, if I dare say so — you've brought Chateaubriand because his eloquence fits your idea of Rome. But when he writes of moonlit ruins he doesn't tell you that you'll have to pick your way delicately among the stones with a handkerchief to your nose because the Roman populace answers the call of nature wherever convenient. We talk about truth in art but do we really want it? Great art always tends towards the ideal.'

'I do not think that art need descend to the sordid to be truthful,' she said a little stiffly. 'Though you may be right that I have succumbed to the spell of Monsieur de Chateaubriand's style.' She was silent a moment. 'And I *am* inconsistent. When I first looked at paintings the landscapes that pleased me most were idealised. But I soon saw that they were purely imaginary. And now I find that I am most moved by those artists who seem to have copied directly from nature. There's truth in their most ordinary detail — haystacks, stubble fields, the muddy bank of a stream —'

'But who wants to look at a patch of mud?' he interrupted.

'Because the artist is showing the world as it is — the mud, the nettles, the . . . horse droppings on the path, as well as the blue sky above and the beauty of the trees. It's the real world, not a romantic fantasy.' She was another woman, he thought, when she spoke passionately like this. 'And the artist who paints the mud,' she went on, 'will also portray people as they are, not just ideal beauty.'

'You approve Guercino's *Hagar* then! Have you not seen it? It may be the Brera's greatest possession.' He began to describe it, but the sky was darkening — rain threatened.

'I think we should turn back,' she said.

They left the ramparts, feeling a first raindrop or two, their conversation less animated, and as they approached the centre she reverted to her former stiffness. When they reached the street where she lived she came to a definitive halt on the corner. 'We part company here, Monsieur. I am happy that chance brought us together again. This has been a truly interesting conversation. And I am most grateful for your advice to seek the consul's help.'

'Don't give up your goal, Mademoiselle, however difficult it seems.' She nodded, but she was already detaching herself. He made one last attempt to retrieve the lost connection: 'When you hear the birds in the Coliseum, have a thought for me at my desk in Paris.'

He walked back to his usual restaurant and ate his solitary dinner, wishing he'd suggested another meeting. It was the most stimulating talk he'd had in months. And he'd managed — quite gracefully, he felt, and not untruthfully — to dispel any suspicions she might have had about him that night at the inn. He'll go back to the Brera tomorrow, on the chance of finding her. He'd like to show her the Guercino.

Milan, Tuesday 5 November

To the Brera, where I wanted to try an experiment. Unfortunately I had only just begun when I was interrupted by the young man from the diligence. I should no doubt have rebuffed him, but the coincidence of this meeting was too strange to ignore and our conversation proved most interesting.

She'd been standing in front of the Madonna of the meadow, wondering if it were possible to memorise a painting as one could a poem. She stared intently at the Virgin's blue cloak, echoed by the paler blue of hills and sky, then closed her eyes. For a few seconds she could see it still in the darkness of her head, then it faded and she was left only with the impression of where it lay in the frame. She repeated the experiment, concentrating all her effort on the colour and this time it remained a little longer on her inner eye. She tried other elements. Eyes closed, she could summon an image of the shepherd and the plank bridge; with every try it grew clearer. If she persisted, she might be able to store the whole in her memory and carry it always with her. But that would take an immense amount of time. If only there were some easier means. Engravings were a poor substitute even if she could afford them. What was a painting without colour? Colour wasn't a superfluous ornament but an integral part of the effect. That blue in its subtle gradations penetrated the soul. She closed her eyes again.

'Forgive me for disturbing your reverie . . .'

For a joyful instant she thought it was Larocque, but the voice, though French, wasn't his. A plump face, framed by curly black sideburns, brown eyes twinkling with amusement — the young man from the diligence.

She glanced quickly at the card he proffered. Auditor in the Council of State. A man of some standing, though his intrusion was unconventional to say the least. But she too was struck by the unlikeliness of their meeting, and curiosity overcame caution. He'd been to Rome, he said. She wanted to hear more.

He had plenty to tell, though she suspected he was largely echoing the important cousin. *We*, he kept saying — we shall free them from the tyranny of priests, from the stagnation of papal rule, from their appalling backwardness. He reminded her of the visiting experts at Armand's table — engineers, agronomists, administrators, all formed from the same mould, forward-looking, energetic, impatient, convinced of the superiority of their government and the benefits it was bringing to every country under its sway. Behind this particular example of the type rose the incarnation of their hopes, the statue of the naked emperor (whose virility his young acolyte was fortunately concealing). But this man, she sensed, was not a wholehearted believer. He admired Romans for their resistance, reporting incidents that showed their independent spirit.

She looked again at the card he'd given her — Henri de Beyle. So he was of good family. And yet, poor man, he had the physique of a tradesman despite his fashionable clothes. But you forgot it listening to him talk. His eyes sparkled with the pleasure of discussion.

She'd almost refused his invitation to walk for fear of encountering Mme Picard, but it would at least confuse that lady's previous suspicions. And in the unlikely event of their running into Larocque it would amuse him, she thought, to meet one of the philosophical gentlemen from the diligence. And he'd correct some of the young man's mistaken ideas about Italians. It wasn't enough to know those who'd adopted French ways; you needed to meet people like the Rossi family or their cousins. It was the weakness of all those attached to the new government. They underestimated the resistance of Signora Rossi and her like.

It wasn't till they were walking on the ramparts that she'd seen there was more to him. Behind the blunt pugnacious manner that she'd found so offensive at their first meeting lay a sensitivity she wouldn't have guessed. Everything else — the dandified appearance, the constant effort to be amusing — was a facade. She wanted to tell him that any woman with a heart would prefer the man who'd shed tears in the Coliseum to the witty raconteur.

We experienced a moment of fellow feeling. When he talked about the painting of Limbo, his voice faltered. He too has known bereavement, and at such an early age. I wanted to tell him about the adagio — the way it captures the feeling of loss — but perhaps such a rare moment of intimacy between strangers could not be prolonged. I am astonished that it was possible to speak so easily with a man to whom I had taken a firm dislike in our previous encounter. It should teach me to guard against my tendency to jump to false conclusions.

There had been one awkward moment, though it put that first meeting in a new light.

'You have seen so much in such a short time!' she'd said. 'Have you kept a full account? I remember you writing in your notebook on the halts.'

He'd begun with the best intentions, he said, but it was hard. 'There's so much to record, and my hand can never keep up with my thoughts. What reaches the page is poor compared to my original sensation. I lack the descriptive talent. But you write too, don't you? I saw you that night at the inn when I went to close my door.'

'I was waiting for the chambermaid,' she said, her cheeks flaming. 'And then I got lost in my writing and forgot to close the door.'

'You were deep in concentration — quite admirable, I thought, after a long day. If I'd had as much discipline I'd have the manuscript of a book by now. Do you think of publishing your travels?'

She wrote only for herself, she said, ashamed to have misjudged him and unwilling to admit her ambition.

'But a woman's point of view would be interesting — provided you don't imitate Mme de Staël! Her inflated style takes people in, yet underneath she's just repeating the same commonplaces as everyone else. But you have something original to say about art. Only, you must be natural. It's the only thing that lasts, unlike the grandiloquence of the De Staëls and the Chateaubriands who won't be read a hundred years from now.'

She has been trying to capture as much of their conversation as she can recall, but it's time to close her notebook and get ready for the evening at Mme Picard's. Now that cold weather has arrived she can wear the dark blue winter dress in which she knows she looks her best.

She brushes out her hair and arranges it in the new style Maddalena has devised.

Midnight Larocque arrived late. She was talking to Mme Bouchot and didn't see him until he stood in front of her. Painfully aware of a rising blush, she saw him register the change in her appearance and immediately regretted making it. She had no opportunity for anything but the usual polite enquiries before the ladies took their seats for the music and he joined the other men at the back of the room.

She couldn't see him without turning her head, but he absorbed her thoughts. Even Mme Delavigne's performance couldn't hold her attention. He was changed. There was no longer the intimate acknowledgement of shared experience in his eyes, but a wariness that she hadn't seen since they first met. It was only when she'd asked after his daughter that he smiled. She'd been tempted to tell him about the sash, but she wanted to keep it a surprise.

When the music ended she hoped in vain for some further exchange, but he didn't approach her. On previous occasions she'd appreciated the tact with which he avoided drawing attention to their friendship, but tonight she'd have welcomed any indiscretion as proof that it still existed. At the end of the evening when he came to take his leave, with others around she could only wish him goodnight.

Now she sits pen in hand a long moment, then closes her notebook. What she cannot bring herself to confess is the awakening of desire. Standing light-headed with the reality of his presence, then, after the music, with every quick glance across the room renewing her sense of him as he talked to others, she'd felt the same longing as on the Duomo roof. He could not be called a handsome man — his features were unrefined, every line of his face written by harsh experience — but it was that she liked: his knowledge of life, his gravity, the hesitant smile that seemed both to doubt the possibility of happiness and to promise it.

The parish bell sounds one o'clock. Methodically, she unpins her hair and plaits it for the night, hangs up her dress, folds petticoat and chemise for the laundry. But once the lamp is out and she burrows into the darkness, it's impossible to evade the truth any longer. Her feelings are as strong as ever, but he does not share them: there is no remedy but to leave.

Milan, Wednesday 6 November

I went to see Bossi's Last Supper *at Rafaelli's workshop. I was displeased with it on account of 1st the colour; 2nd the expression.*

Any attempt to copy Leonardo's faded masterpiece was doomed to failure and Bossi had made the colours too bright — effective in the obscurity of a church, but lacking the sombre majesty of Leonardo. As for the faces, they had the blandness he's found in so much Italian art. *Judas is simply a good-hearted man with the misfortune to have red hair. Without any exaggeration the face of M. Ns (in Rome) would make a better Judas.*

That bastard Norvins with his shifty eyes would be the perfect model for a traitor. The thought brings back his anxiety about the director of police. God knows what the man has said about him in his reports to Paris. It may have been unwise to stay away so long, even with an official extension.

And Milan is empty without Angela, her darkened box at La Scala depressing. His meeting with the woman in grey has made him aware of his loneliness. How often has he talked as freely to anyone as he did on the ramparts yesterday? Occasionally in a letter to Pauline, he confides feelings he'd never admit to Faure or Crozet. He'd promised himself to be natural with Angela, but he's not yet sure enough of his place in her heart to take the risk. He's still playing a role. With this woman, though, he'd sensed that he could speak of his emotion in the Coliseum without sounding ridiculous. Was she exceptional — a rare kindred spirit — or was it simply the circumstances: two strangers safely opening their hearts because they'll never meet again?

He went back to the Brera in hopes of finding her, combed all the rooms without success, then lingered near the entrance so as not to miss her if she came. But there was no sign of her. Afterwards he walked up the Corsia dei Servi to the side street where they'd parted. There was a café on the corner. It was still mild enough to sit outside and he ordered coffee and the newspaper to make his presence seem natural if she chanced to walk by.

The ease of their conversation yesterday had surprised him. So often with women he either talked too much in an attempt to impress or he was paralysed by shyness, unable to utter a word. But it's longing that makes him speechless, which didn't enter into the situation here; all he'd wanted was her company to while away the afternoon, though he recognised now that she wasn't unattractive once emotion animated her frozen face. It was a rare thing in his experience to talk to a woman whose education equalled his own. Most women were so constricted by a conventional feminine upbringing that they could only deal in platitudes and trivia. Angela's conversation was interesting precisely because she'd had no education to speak of. Her mind hadn't been deformed and with her natural intelligence she'd picked up ideas from books and from associating with cultivated men.

Of course, education didn't guarantee good conversation, and he'd far rather talk to an ignorant but charming woman than a pedantic man. But the combination of a feminine sensibility and an educated mind was agreeable. How interesting social life would be if there were more women like his companion yesterday. Shy though she was, she hadn't hesitated to engage with him. That was a good question she'd raised about changes in art, to which Lanzi's *History*, so far as he could see, offered no answer. Was it simply a shift in taste, a desire for novelty, or was it a reflection of broader developments in society?

A question of that kind makes him feel out of his depth. Perhaps he should simply stick to translating the book. But once he's back in Paris with the resources of the Imperial Library, he can set about finding an answer. The prospect of his return begins to seem a little less gloomy.

Milan, Wednesday 6 November

I resolved this morning after a sleepless night that whatever difficulties faced me I would not return to Nogent. If the journey to Rome proved impossible for the moment, I would look for some closer destination — Venice perhaps. Somehow I would revive the spirit of adventure that possessed me on my arrival here. But my call on the consul was discouraging.

'It is out of the question that you travel alone, Mademoiselle, even to Venice,' he said, regarding her with alarm. 'The roads are rife with bandits. The mail couriers now have armed escorts in the most dangerous areas, but the authorities cannot prevent everything. What a pity that you did not come to see me earlier. There are few travellers once the days shorten.' He paused as though an idea had struck him. 'There may still be one possibility. If you wish, I could enquire whether this person would accept a passenger.'

She accepted his offer and left, scarcely knowing what she hoped for but grateful nonetheless that yesterday's encounter had at least set her on the right track.

At Mme Picard's in the afternoon there were visitors enough to require no great conversational effort on her own part. Larocque's return was not commented on, for which she was grateful. Making her way home, she half expected to run into him as she had after her first call on Mme Picard almost six weeks ago. But that hope, like the faint possibility that a message might await her, was disappointed. It confirmed her decision. To stay in Milan would be to torture herself with the continual expectation of seeing him. The only cure for this sickness was to leave, the sooner the better. Since it was now too late in the season to reach Rome, she would book a seat on the diligence and return to Geneva. It would be a safe and pleasant place to pass the winter and she was as likely to find fellow-travellers there for the journey to Rome as in Milan. It seemed the only rational solution, though she found no comfort in it.

The pleasures of Milan that seemed limitless on my arrival have paled. To stay here without my guide, my companion in discovery, would be merely to accumulate empty experience — another church, another fresco, another painter. I know that I must leave, but whether I go to Rome or Geneva I see nothing ahead but lonely days in which my notebook will be the sole companion of my thoughts.

THURSDAY *Maddalena was in high spirits this morning. She has set her wedding date for the week after Christmas.*

With Maddalena's marriage imminent, Giovanni's enlistment appeared inevitable. It grieved her to think of the dangers to which his impulsive character would expose him, but there was nothing she could do. Her stay in Milan had coincided with a critical period in his and Maddalena's lives, fostering an intimacy unlikely in normal circumstances. But that would naturally diminish once Maddalena was married, and then she'd have no real friend in Milan except Mme Delavigne, who was occupied with her pupils. With Larocque's now unmistakable withdrawal there was nothing to keep her any longer in the city.

He was not at the opera. Someone told Mme Picard that he'd gone to Brescia. The spectacle onstage could not fill the emptiness in her heart, and the haunting serenade when its moment came seemed tinkly and trivial — a cruel reminder, nonetheless, of all she'd missed in life. She would never know the happiness of hearing a man declare his love, and she was past the age of serenades. The musicians below her window on her first night on Italian soil had expected payment; it was a purely commercial enactment of the romance of Italy.

Lieutenant Richard was standing behind Mme Delavigne, his body unconsciously mimicking the tenor's stance. During the applause, he bent forward to say something in Mme Delavigne's ear, his hand on the back of her chair a finger's breadth from her shoulder. It was obvious that he was in love with her and equally obvious from her scarcely perceptible movement away from him as she leant on the balcony that he was doomed to frustration.

The arts were dangerous, she thought; they created the illusion of a richer emotional life than most individuals could ever attain. Neither the would-be Almaviva (whose hand, she intuited, longed to rest on Mme Delavigne's beautiful nape) nor the tenor who would triumph at the end of the opera could achieve the plenitude of which music held out a deceptive promise. And the serenade (now receiving its third encore) had an underlying melancholy that acknowledged it. It was wiser to content oneself with experiences that did not deceive, like her solitary moment in the woods.

Milan, Friday 8 November

A dense fog had enveloped the city overnight, muffling its normal clamour as for a funeral. He called at the post office hoping for a letter from Angela, but there was only a note from his sister, asking when to expect him. It made him feel guilty. The five days he'd spend with Angela on her return were days he could be spending with Pauline, whom he hadn't seen for five years. But he needed those last few days with Angela. He must leave an indelible impression on her heart.

Outside the post office he hesitated, at a loose end. No point in walking on the ramparts in the fog. He'd read as much as he could absorb for the moment. He could return to the Brera, have another try at finding the woman in grey, but he had the intuition that she'd avoid another meeting.

In any case it was Angela he missed this afternoon. In a sentimental mood, he thought of following the route they'd taken on their last evening together, but the fog was clammy and cold, so he made his way instead to the Caffè Sanquirico where she'd given him the rendezvous. He was settled in the window, idly watching the passers-by, when a woman caught his eye, darting across the little piazza like a wary cat. Her face was concealed by the hood of her cloak, but he was sure it was the woman from the diligence. He dropped a coin on the table for the waiter and hurried out.

For a moment he couldn't see which street she'd taken, then he spotted her, walking so fast he had to run to catch up. 'Mademoiselle!' he called. She didn't stop — was he mistaken? If only he knew her name. 'Mademoiselle!' he called again, more urgently, and this time she heard him and turned.

He saw from her face that she was in distress. 'Forgive me for intruding again. I hoped I could presume to greet you after our conversation the other day. I only wanted to ask if you have been to see the consul.'

'Yes. I've just received a message from him. There's a lady travelling to Rome with an escort —'

'But that's excellent news!' He was delighted with himself for having given her the solution. But to his surprise her eyes filled with tears.

'Something's wrong? Can I be of any assistance?'

'Forgive me, Monsieur. You are very kind . . .' She fumbled for a handkerchief and dabbed her eyes.

'You're sad to leave Milan?' he persisted. He couldn't let her go like that.

She pressed her handkerchief to her face again. 'Yes. It's foolish. For so long I thought only of Rome. Milan was to be just a halt on the way.'

'It's a city to which one becomes attached. I know from my own experience. And if one is also attached to a person, it's even harder to leave.' After weeks of hugging his secret to himself he was tempted to confide in her, but she was staring at him, her eyes brimming with tears.

'How did you guess? I have formed an attachment that might have kept me here . . .' She put her hands to her mouth to hide her trembling lips.

'But something went wrong?' he ventured.

'I thought that he too . . . But suddenly he withdrew, avoided me.' Her face worked painfully.

He wanted to comfort her. 'Perhaps it's just a lover's ploy? To test your feeling . . .'

'He would never do such a thing.' She was indignant. 'He's the most sincere man I know, always honest even when the truth is painful.'

He felt rebuked and responded coldly: 'Then there are two possibilities. Either he doesn't share your feelings and has withdrawn to avoid a difficult situation, in which case, you'll be wise to leave —' She nodded dumbly and he softened his tone. 'Or he does share your feelings, but he's afraid to speak. It takes courage for a man to declare his love, you know. I can tell you from my own experience — the stronger the feelings the more likely one will be paralysed.'

Especially, he thought, with a woman like this one. It wasn't that she was haughty, as he'd first thought, or cold either, though she might appear so to the world. But call it what you will, modesty or reserve, she wouldn't easily reveal herself. She must be in deep distress to be so open with him now. 'May I ask if you have given your friend any indication of your feelings?'

'Not in so many words. But I am sure that he must know . . . My face betrays me, I blush so easily.'

'But, my dear Mademoiselle, a blush could mean anything! A sign of discomfort, an indication that you didn't wish to see him! I'll wager that he's as uncertain about your feelings as you are about his. You have praised his honesty — then you must be honest with him, give him some sign that you wish him to speak, some encouragement. Believe me, a man needs it!'

'But he's gone away!' Her eyes filled again. 'And if I accept this lady's offer of a place in her carriage five days from now, I may not see him before I leave!'

'In that case, you must write to him.' He saw the expression on her face. 'Yes, I understand, propriety holds you back. And the fear of making yourself ridiculous. But you will be far away when he receives it; you will not have the embarrassment of meeting him if your feelings are not reciprocated.' He saw that she might be persuaded. 'What do you have to lose?'

An impatient shout from a coachman told them that they were obstructing an entrance. She flinched at the rough voice, and he offered her his arm. 'Will you permit me to escort you home?'

'Thank you. You are very kind.'

He felt protective and brotherly, a pleasant sensation that lasted only till he realised they would have to walk past the Borroni shop. What if Angela were to hear that he was seen in intimate conversation with another woman? There was no telling how she'd react. But evidently his companion felt a similar discomfort for she disengaged her arm from his as soon as they entered the busy shopping street.

They reached the Duomo, which was utterly transformed by the fog — the statues on the roof no longer saints in glory but prisoners bound to stakes, each one isolated from his fellows. 'It's a vision from Dante!' he exclaimed. 'A multitude of lost souls in the fog of ignorance!'

She made no reply but drew her hood further over her face. His eloquence was wasted. As they walked up the Corsia dei Servi, he sought some final word to leave her with. They'd almost reached her street; she would dismiss him on the corner if he didn't speak now.

'Listen, Mademoiselle,' he said urgently, 'it's presumptuous of me to offer you advice, but we may never meet again. I understand everything that holds you back. But I beg you to reflect. If you leave without telling him what you feel for him, you will have deprived yourself — and your friend — of all the happiness that love can bring, simply because of a ridiculous social convention that says a woman must not speak first. You are courageous, I think, or you would not have come all this way alone. Have courage now — don't let a foolish propriety hold you back in what may be the decisive moment of your life! Love is worth the risk!'

She looked at him uncertainly. 'I will think about it. You have been more than kind, Monsieur, and I thank you with all my heart. But I must go now . . .' And with that she turned and walked away.

He felt slightly foolish as he went off to dinner. What had possessed him to speak of love like a sentimental novelist when he of all men knew its disappointments? He wasn't in the habit of offering advice to strangers. Something had come over him. But he'd experienced a rare fellow feeling with this poor soul, and not just because he knew all too well what it was like to be hopelessly in love, but because for a few moments the other afternoon on the ramparts they'd spoken heart-to-heart.

The unusualness of such a conversation, he thought, sipping his burgundy (always reliable at Veillard's, like the *bifteck* he'd ordered), demonstrated the artificial nature of social relations between men and women. He himself, despite his hatred of falseness, could rarely be natural with a woman. But he regretted it, and when she praised her friend's sincerity just now he'd felt it as a reproach. It wasn't that he was insincere by nature — on the contrary, with his male friends he was often too frank. But with women he was always playing a role. With this one, though, it had been different, and not merely because the possibility of conquest hadn't entered into it, but because he'd been too caught up in the conversation to worry about the impression he was making. If he were ever to marry, he thought, as the waiter brought his beefsteak, that's what he would want in a wife — the promise of a conversation that would continue to engage him even when they were old and grey on either side of the fireplace.

He felt sorry for this woman. With all her intelligence and insight, she was still in thrall to the conventions that restricted her sex. Would she find the courage to reveal her love, or would propriety win? She'd lowered her guard today, but he was a stranger whom she'd never meet again, and he didn't know her name: her secret was as safe with him as in the anonymity of the confessional. And the strange twilight of the fog that muffled voices and turned passers-by into wraiths had created its own protective veil. The whole encounter was dreamlike.

Well, he'd done his best for her. He empties his glass and calls for the bill. It's Friday, still a penitential day even in this pleasure-loving city, so the theatres will be closed; another empty evening stretches ahead. He could catch up with his journal, but his room will be cold and he hasn't felt like writing since Angela left. He heads for the Caffè Nuovo.

Settled in its convivial atmosphere, a coffee with whipped cream before him, he picks up the newspaper. A victory and a defeat in Spain. The Russians have encircled a Turkish army. Enthusiastic crowds greet the emperor in Amsterdam. Creation of a new imperial order, celebrating the union of France and Holland. For services to government. He might be entitled to a decoration for the work he's done on the Holland file. It's all vanity, of course, in this empire of the vanities, but it would improve his chances of a higher appointment. He'll drop a hint to Daru on his return, he decides, spooning the last froth of cream from the rim of his cup.

Milan, Friday 8 November

She is in no state tonight to record the day's events, though her thoughts are so confused that setting them down might help to bring some clarity.

In mid-afternoon as she was working on Lucia's sash, Perpetua had brought up a note. She felt light-headed with expectation when she saw it, but it was only from the consul. What he had to announce, however, had thrown her into turmoil. He had spoken on her behalf to a French lady who was visiting friends in Milan and would shortly be leaving for Rome, where her eldest son occupied a high position in the administration. This lady had space in her carriage and might be willing to consider a passenger. Her son would ensure that she had an armed escort for the entire journey. Naturally, the lady would like to meet her first, tomorrow morning if possible since she planned to leave on November 13.

Five days from now! She couldn't possibly be ready so soon. And if Larocque had not returned from Brescia by then, how could she leave without saying goodbye?

But it was too good an opportunity to refuse. She sent back a reply to the consul before she could change her mind. Five days! She started to list all she would have to do before leaving, but nothing really mattered except to find out when Larocque was expected back. She must go to his office, tell his clerk that she wished to consult him on a matter of business. And if by some lucky chance he'd already returned, she could tell him in person about the consul's message. His reaction to the possibility of her departure would determine her decision.

She'd thrown on her cloak and made her way through the fog to the office only to find it closed. An indifferent concierge told her it would not reopen till Monday. That was a mere two days before her departure. She turned homewards on the verge of tears. She hadn't gone far when a voice called 'Mademoiselle!' and she'd turned with the sudden hope that it was the clerk. But it was only the young man from the diligence, hurrying after her. She couldn't refuse to greet him, though at that moment she'd wanted more than anything to be alone. And his sympathy had made her lose control. From that point on, her one thought was to compose herself and get back to the shelter of her room, but the young man wasn't so easily shed.

When finally she reached the door, Perpetua was on the threshold looking out for her and Signora Colomba hovering behind, because she was late for dinner, which had never happened before, and they feared she was lost in the fog. They had hot soup waiting, and though she could scarcely swallow the first spoonfuls, their solicitude was comforting.

Back in her room, where Perpetua had placed a little brazier of burning coals against the evening chill, she thought over what Beyle had said. He meant well, his kindness seemed genuine, but his advice came from another world. How could he imagine that Larocque's absence might be calculated to test her! Perhaps young men of his kind played such games with women, but Larocque had suffered too much himself to make others suffer. And then to urge her to reveal her feelings, without thought for the embarrassment it would cause a sensitive man if he didn't share them. No doubt the young man frequented the kind of circles in Paris where women behaved with greater licence. Or he'd read too many novels. But life is not a novel, as he would certainly be the first to tell her.

No, she must rouse her courage and go to the appointment at the consul's tomorrow. If she and this lady reach an agreement to travel together, she will write to let Larocque know and leave the sash for Lucia. If he returns in time for her to say goodbye in person, and if his reaction to her departure gives her reason to hope, she will come back to Milan in the spring. But if it's clear that there's no hope, she must say goodbye and thank him for all the things they have enjoyed together, without losing her dignity or causing him embarrassment. She will neither burden him with her feelings nor risk losing his respect.

If he's not back before she leaves, though, how will she ever know what he felt?

Of course, he's bound to write and thank her for Lucia's sash, and she will reply. And perhaps in writing they might regain something of their previous intimacy. But recalling the cold formality of his recent note, she loses even that faint hope.

Her eyes well with tears again but even here in the safety of her room she dare not succumb to them, for if she gives way to the desolation that threatens she will lose the will to continue. She must not give up Rome, for it is the one thing left to her now.

Milan, Saturday 9 November

A chill dark morning, the city still shrouded in fog. He read another fifty pages of the *History*, went back to the café on the corner of the Contrada Passerella and drank too much coffee, without a glimpse of the woman in grey. He would like to have returned to the Brera in her company, though in the state in which he'd left her yesterday that was unlikely.

At a loose end, he decided to walk, and his heart instinctively took him past Angela's apartment, as if it could conjure up her presence. There was a church beyond with frescos by a follower of Leonardo that might be worth a look. But as he neared it he caught the sound of drums. Ahead of him at the crossroads, the first soldiers of a battalion were marching from their barracks to the parade ground beyond the city walls. Curious, he joined the crowd on the great open field where half the Italian army seemed to be marshalled for review.

It was an eerie spectacle in the fog — the farthest ranks barely visible, an army of ghosts that gave him a sudden shiver. But he was well positioned to see the dignitaries as they arrived. There was General Lechi, Monsieur Lechi's handsome brother Teodoro, whom he'd met in Mme Lamberti's box, with that amusing idiot Migliorini in attendance. Then the viceroy arrived, Joséphine's son, controlling his spirited horse with graceful nonchalance, the officers of the Royal Guard behind him, Widmann at their head, and Cosimo Del Fante farther back among the general staff with others he recognised from Angela's box. How a helmet ennobled a profile! He almost envied them, though not for anything in the world would he return to the army. But he'd had enough of the imperial household. It was time he found a position in an important ministry.

The parade over, he walks back along the Contrada dei Meravigli feeling a little flat. Without Angela here exercising her spell, he's like Ulysses on Calypso's island. It's fine to be the lover of a goddess but sooner or later comes the thought that a man's life is about more than love. It's a mistake to see life as a choice between happiness and ambition as he's been doing the past few days. Ambition is the horse you ride to where you want to be. Once there, you can hunt happiness in whatever way you choose.

MILAN, SATURDAY 9 NOVEMBER

I went to meet the Countess de T. in great uncertainty, almost hoping to find some pretext for refusing her offer. I had feared that the mother of such an important man would be condescending, but my apprehensions soon vanished. The way she spoke of the husband she has recently lost (whose title was not bestowed by the Emperor, but ancient and honourable) immediately gained my sympathy. *She too has known hard times during the last twenty years, and 'rolled up her sleeves' to survive, as she put it.* But she appears to have no qualms about her son's acceptance of the new regime and is proud of his position.

They'd talked for some time, then the countess outlined her plans: 'My son is covering all the costs of the journey. You will have nothing to pay except your own expenses at the inns. But I must warn you that I wish to reach Rome as fast as possible: I do not intend to linger on the way, even in Florence. I hope that will not disappoint you?'

Here was her chance to back out gracefully if she wished, but she did not take it. The bargain was struck: the carriage would call for her at sunrise on Wednesday.

'I am delighted to have met you,' the countess said. 'My maid is a good creature but one needs intelligent conversation on the road. We shall find much to talk about, you and I.'

Outside on the street, she'd panicked at the rapidity of the decision. But there was no time for regrets, with all the practical matters to attend to. First, though, she had to tell Lena.

'But it's so sudden, Marie! We thought you'd decided to stay. Giovanni was sure!'

She knew they'd guessed something, but there was no point in confiding now. 'It was always my intention to continue to Rome, as you know, and now this opportunity has arisen, I could not refuse it.' She brought out her gift to avert further questions.

'It's the most beautiful thing I've ever had!' Maddalena exclaimed, stroking the dark green velvet on which the gold palm leaves stood out resplendently. 'I will carry it on my wedding day. But you won't be here!' Maddalena's eyes filled with tears and it was all she could do to control her own as they embraced. Whatever its limits, this friendship had broken down self-imposed barriers. It had taken her into another world and opened her eyes to much she'd previously ignored. She would miss Lena and little Pierino, and all of them.

But now she had every excuse for a letter to Larocque. She'd kept it brief, saying simply that she hoped to thank him in person for all his many kindnesses before leaving. She wrote 'Urgent' on the front and told Perpetua to give it to the concierge if the office was closed. She could finish Lucia's sash by Monday if she simplified the final sprays. Surely he'd be back by then!

I am on the point of realising my dream, but far from feeling anticipation I am plunged in melancholy. Had I met the countess six weeks ago, I should have rejoiced at my good fortune, for I shall have not only a congenial travelling companion but an introduction to the best circles in Rome. Good breeding does not guarantee compatibility of mind and tastes, though, and high-ranking individuals may be pompous and self-important. The friend whom I have found here is irreplaceable. Such affinities are rare. I can only hope to find in the spectacle of Rome itself some consolation for what I have lost.

SUNDAY *I worked all day on Lucia's sash until my visit to the Rossi family. Maddalena had told them that I was leaving but they seemed puzzled. The idea of travelling for its own sake does not enter into their experience.*

'Are you making a pilgrimage?' Teresa asked.

'I have always dreamt of visiting Rome.' She could not say that her Rome was the ancient city, not the capital of Christendom.

'But what is Rome without the Holy Father?' Signora Rossi lamented.

'Do you not know *anyone* there?' Caterina seemed appalled at the thought.

'The lady with whom I shall travel is very pleasant and I shall meet her son. But I shall never find friends as kind as you.'

'So the die is cast, Signorina,' Giovanni said, as they set off for their evening stroll.

'And for you too?'

'For me too. It's time I became more than a messenger boy.'

'I understand the reasons for your decision,' she said carefully, wondering if she could make one last effort to dissuade him. 'You and Lena have become like brother and sister to me, Giovanni. You must forgive me if I feel a sister's anxiety for you. You know the story of Achilles? He was offered a choice between a long, happy, obscure existence, or a brief life with glory. He chose glory and died at Troy. But when Ulysses met him in the underworld, Achilles said he would rather be a landless peasant than a dead hero.'

'But a hero may live to be an emperor like your Bonaparte. One must take the risk, Signorina. Your example has inspired me — if a woman can find the courage to leave home and set off alone to a foreign country because she wants more from life, why should I too not seize this chance to see the world? The dice may fall well. For you too, I hope.'

I felt like Cassandra, foreseeing the future but powerless to prevent it. But perhaps it is only my tendency to take everything tragically. I try to reassure myself with the thought that war may still be averted, but the history of the past decade offers little reason for optimism.

Milan, Monday 11 November

Another damp grey day, but his call at the post office is rewarded: a letter from Angela! He opens it eagerly, but the news stuns him. She isn't returning on the fifteenth as expected. Her husband's business in Novara requires another week. They won't be back till the twenty-second at the earliest.

But he must be gone by then if he's to reach Paris before his leave expires; he daren't postpone it any longer. Retreating to a corner of the post office he reads the rest. 'Truly, our love has been ill-fated,' she writes. The past tense stabs his heart. But hasn't he known all along, deep down, that she would finally elude him? This is just another broken rendezvous. Perhaps she already knew when she left that they wouldn't meet again. She'd granted him those few hours in the rented room safe in the knowledge that they were the last. His hope of five more days was always a delusion. Prudence had triumphed. Or perhaps she'd never really loved him: it was just a diversion from her boredom that she'd mistaken for love.

Blindly he leaves the post office and paces the narrow street alongside — where there are few passers-by — trying to regain control of himself. There have been moments, surely, when she loved him; how else to explain the tears in her eyes when he told her of his boyish adoration, or the tender way she spoke his name? And she'd talked of leaving everything for him, coming to Paris. It was his own failure to leap at the possibility that had made her see the limits of their love. It wasn't indifference but simply the recognition of reality.

He pulls himself together and returns to the post office. There's no point lingering in Milan now. If he leaves with the courier tonight he'll have a longer visit with his grandfather and a day or two more with his sister. And perhaps all things considered, it's just as well. He'll push his father on the financial settlement, then the minute he's back in Paris he'll go to see Daru about a transfer to a ministry.

Unfortunately there's no seat with the Turin courier until tomorrow night, which leaves him at a loose end. Feeling a need to confide in someone, he thinks of the woman in grey. But though he posts himself on the corner of her street for nearly an hour, there's no sign of her. Perhaps by now she's on her way to Rome or, if she took his advice, in the arms of her lover. He takes his sorrows to the Caffè Nuovo and orders a last cup of coffee with whipped cream.

Milan, Monday 11 November

I stayed in all morning in hopes of a message, but nothing came. By two o'clock I could no longer postpone my farewell call on Mme Picard. To my relief Mme Bouchot was there, which eased a difficult encounter. She at least was kind as ever.

'You're leaving us already? And just as we were getting to know you! We shall miss you, my dear.'

'You do not know how lucky you are to be alone and free, Mademoiselle,' said Mme Picard. 'Many would pity you, but I envy you. I too have dreamt of travelling. To see other towns, new faces. There are days when I'm so bored that I'd welcome the diversion of an Austrian attack. But a married woman is stuck where her husband's career fixes him.'

'There are worse places to be stuck than Milan,' Mme Bouchot intervened. 'Remember our winters in garrison in the north!'

It was a relief when she'd acquitted herself of everything politeness required and could take her leave, though the conversation echoed in her mind as she made her way to Mme Delavigne's. There was spite as well as bitterness in the reference to her single state. But Mme Picard had delivered a salutary reminder of what would face her were her desire fulfilled. A married woman took on her husband's social position; his situation in life determined not only where she lived but how she was seen. The stigma of being an old maid might be easier to live with than social descent. But she hated herself for the thought.

Mme Delavigne was also surprised by her news. 'I had hoped you would stay. I'm not the only one who will regret your departure,' she added with a significant look.

'I shall miss you very much — and one or two other friends,' was all she could reply.

'But Rome! How I envy you.'

They'd talked about the experiences that awaited her, then Mme Delavigne asked if she'd like to hear her sonata one last time. She'd hesitated, agonisingly aware that a message from Larocque might be waiting, but she couldn't refuse. The familiar notes of the adagio filled the room. Today more than ever they captured the essence of loss, but now it was the recognition of what might have been. Larocque, she recalled, had seemed as moved by it as herself. Had he remembered his wife as he listened? Perhaps loyalty to that first love made it impossible for him to form another attachment. If it was the explanation for his withdrawal, she understood and respected it, however painful it was for her. He had never gone beyond the bounds of friendship; it was her own desire that had made her imagine something more.

Mme Delavigne glanced at her, then played on. And finally the drama of the third movement made sense, for it was herself now that the galloping hooves would carry away, and the rapidity of the pounding keys seemed inexorable. Everything was happening too fast, but it was too late to change her decision. The music tried to resist the fatal impetus with a repeated softer passage that echoed the adagio, and then came a pause where everything seemed to hang in the balance, a brief suspension of sound that seemed to promise rescue from the relentless onward rush, but there was no stopping it as it hurtled towards the cruel finality of the ultimate notes.

As though sensing her distress, Mme Delavigne rose and embraced her. 'You'll come back to us, won't you? Rome is unhealthy in the summer, they say — you must come back then!'

They parted with a mutual promise to correspond, then she hurried home. But no message awaited her. No one had called, Perpetua assured her. Up in her room, she mastered the impulse to fling herself on the bed and weep. There was still one day and she had Lucia's gift to deliver — an excuse to go to his office in the morning.

It is raining this evening so we cannot take our usual walk. I have packed my trunk except for the few last things to be added tomorrow night, so now I am alone with my thoughts at this table where I have recorded so many new experiences over the past nine weeks. But the melancholy of departure would not be alleviated by expression. It is time to pack this notebook. I shall start a new one in Rome.

Placing it in her book box with the stack she's filled since leaving Nogent, she feels an impulse to reread them all from start to finish. The first brings back many small forgotten details of the journey. But as she reads on, the idea of publishing seems presumptuous. Her descriptions are conventional, her comments trite. The scenes over which she'd laboured are the ones every traveller records. And her earnest comments on social conditions are tiresome. Readers expecting alpine sublimities would resent being made to feel guilty about the labour that puts food on their tables and silk in their wardrobes. She should have slipped such details in unobtrusively, like the humble figures in a landscape, without sermonising. Only her descriptions of paintings possess any originality, but they are almost too painful to read, each one the distillation of a meeting with Larocque.

How foolish to imagine that she could write a book as substantial as Mrs Godwin's. She's always overestimated her own powers, a consequence of being a precocious and isolated child, her puny efforts lauded to the skies by poor Mademoiselle Robert.

What depresses her most is the diarist's voice — bland, careful, suffocatingly proper. What the journal lacks, what *she* lacks, is the courage to express the feelings that decorum prohibits. But Milan has changed her; she's overcome old prejudices, opened herself to friendship. Perhaps in Rome she will finally escape the constraints that bind her. She thinks of the words from Corinne that she'd inscribed on the title page of the first notebook: '*In Rome one can enjoy a life both solitary and lively, freely developing all that Heaven has placed in us.*' Solitary but lively — the linking of those words had always pleased her. It's perhaps the life most suited to her temperament. She's glimpsed one kind of happiness here, but there are others. She pictures herself reading Virgil in the shade of a parasol pine on the Via Appia, or listening to the birds in the Coliseum like her fellow-traveller. She doesn't require much society, but she will surely meet a few congenial souls through the countess. And her hunger for that other happiness will diminish with time.

Tonight, though, it overwhelms her. It was a mistake to reread her journal, for each account of a meeting with Larocque was a painful reminder of what she's losing. How unconscious she'd been that she was falling in love when now it leaps out at her from every page. But is it the only thing she's been blind to? She'd persisted in ascribing Larocque's attentiveness to his desire to repay her father's generosity, but had it not, almost from the start, been something more? He hadn't confined himself to the practical assistance that was all Armand's letter requested. He'd sought to find things that would please her, shown her the things that meant the most to him, confided in her and invited her own confidences in a way that no man had ever done before. And how happy he'd looked when he'd welcomed her back from Laveno — it was obvious that he'd missed her, though perhaps that was simply a result of his loneliness. But wasn't it possible that he too had been on the brink of love? That night at the opera when he'd sensed her eyes upon him and turned to meet them, there'd been such warmth, such intimacy in his own that she'd turned away, afraid that others would see it.

Others, always her stupid fear of others, of Signora Rossi peering from her balcony, of Mme Picard telling her circle that she'd found them alone together at the Ambrosian, of Armand learning from gossip that she was consorting with a man who was her social inferior. Even if she were strong enough to ignore Armand's disapproval, she couldn't deny her own qualms about the social descent such a marriage entailed. But if that reality was inescapable in her own mind, it would surely occur to Larocque too. She recalled his diffidence, his sudden momentary withdrawals when she sensed she'd touched a raw nerve. Would he not be painfully aware of the difference in their position? For impecunious though she might consider herself, she possessed the means to travel, and a house to return to, while he had no home to offer her, and a poorly remunerated position that he despised. And if she had all too easily imagined Armand's indignation at their marriage, Larocque would certainly anticipate it too. He was a proud man; it would sting. He might feel that he was abusing her father's generosity in even considering it. Could that explain his withdrawal?

It is up to her to speak, she sees, with the sudden force of a revelation. Larocque will never declare his feelings without encouragement: her father stands between them. Respect, gratitude, deference will forever prevent him from aspiring to her hand unless she holds it out to him. The strange young man from the diligence was right — now, on the point of departure, when she may never see Larocque again, she has nothing to lose.

Replacing the notebooks in the box, she leaves the padlock open: she may still need her writing materials tomorrow if he hasn't returned.

Milan, Tuesday 12 November

Midnight. His final hour in Milan and here he is once again in the café by the post office, awaiting the courier's summons. Last time he sat here, almost two months ago, about to leave for Bologna, he was happily recording his victory. But he has no urge to write anything tonight. He's hardly written a page since Angela left.

He'd spent the morning writing her a long farewell, not an easy task given her dismissal of his last letter as insincere. Then he called on Signora Borroni, who luckily was alone in the shop. He explained that he couldn't postpone his return to Paris any longer, and asked her to tell her daughter how it grieved him not to be able to say goodbye to her in person. The good woman nodded sympathetically, but he hadn't dared say more in case she was one of Turcotti's spies.

The *servente* himself was nowhere to be seen, but on the Corso Orientale he ran into Widmann coming off duty. Reluctantly, he announced his departure.

'Shall we see you again?' Widmann asked.

'Next summer, I hope.'

'Who knows where we'll be by then,' Widmann replied with a soldier's fatalism. 'At the gates of Moscow perhaps!'

The one other person to whom he would have liked to say goodbye was the woman in grey, if only to know whether she'd taken his advice. But a sudden misgiving crosses his mind. Supposing he'd led her to incur a painful rejection? Urging such a shy, reserved being to reveal her heart might have been a cruel mistake. He can only hope the man had sufficient gallantry to save her pride if he didn't love her.

There's a copy of the latest *Moniteur* at the next table but he doesn't reach for it. It was in its pages the night he left for Bologna that he'd learnt the news of Cadore's appointment and felt a surge of relief at escaping his cousin's jurisdiction. How carefree he'd felt that night with a month of freedom and the rest of Italy ahead. But now it's the muddy streets of Paris that await him and a new chief to grovel to. And possibly an official reprimand for his absence if Norvins has reported his unauthorised journey. Of course, his little Angel will be there to console him, but that's small comfort when his heart yearns for Angela. If only the courier reached Novara at some reasonable hour so that he might have one last glimpse of her, but it's not to be.

Milan, Tuesday 12 November

Tomorrow I leave Milan and I wish that a storm might flood the roads and prevent my departure. But everything is set in motion. I cannot change my mind now.

She'd risen early and made her way to Larocque's office with the package containing Lucia's sash, only to learn that he was still away.

'When do you expect him back?'

'This afternoon, perhaps, Mademoiselle. Or tomorrow. I cannot say for certain.'

She requested pen and paper and wrote hastily, *An unexpected opportunity of travelling to Rome in the private carriage of a lady has arisen. I leave early tomorrow morning. I had hoped to thank you in person for the great kindness you have shown me, and I very much regret not finding you. This small gift for your daughter must serve as an expression of my deep gratitude to her father. I hope one day to have the pleasure of meeting her. Your affectionate friend, Marie-Honorine Vernet.*

She would not say more for the moment since there was still the chance of seeing him. In person, watching his face, she would have a better sense of how far she could go without embarrassing them both. She asked the clerk to give it to Larocque as soon as he returned.

The afternoon went by with no word from him, but just as she was finishing dinner Perpetua announced that the French gentleman would like to speak to her if convenient.

He was waiting in the hall in greatcoat and muddy riding boots and apologised for his appearance. 'I've just returned from Brescia. I found your two letters, and the beautiful gift for Lucia. I cannot thank you enough. I know it will delight her. I hope you will give me an address in Rome so that she may write herself to thank you.'

For an instant everything felt as before, but there was too much to say, and the hallway was not the right place. Could she suggest a walk? As she hesitated, there was a knock on the door and Perpetua admitted Maddalena and Pierino, followed by Giovanni.

'We'll come back later,' Maddalena said quickly. But Larocque turned to leave.

'I must not take up your last hours in Milan. I wish you a safe journey.'

She followed him to the door and stepped outside with him, putting her hand on his sleeve to stop him: 'I had hoped that we would have time to talk before my departure . . .'

A clatter of hooves on the cobbles announced Trezzano's arrival. Defeated, she could only hold out her hand. 'I cannot tell you how much I shall miss you . . .'

He took her hand in his. 'I shall miss you too, very much.'

For a brief moment their eyes met, though her own filled with tears. Then Trezzano greeted them and Larocque turned to go, this time finally.

Her friends were waiting; she must compose her face and accept their invitation to a farewell glass of wine. 'Why are you leaving, Marie?' Giovanni asked in a low voice. 'I think you're making a mistake.'

It is impossible to change my mind now, as I told Giovanni, and in any case nothing has really altered. I have spoken — as much as circumstances allowed — but the response was too uncertain to admit of hope. There is nothing for it but to bid farewell to Milan.

MILAN, WEDNESDAY 13 NOVEMBER

'We're ready, Monsieur,' the courier announces.

They load his portmanteau and an extra bag with all the books he's acquired, and he climbs aboard. The courier follows, the doors are slammed, they're off, the horses' hooves reverberating in the silence as they traverse the darkened streets. Leaning forward in his seat he strains to read the names at the lantern-lit corners. Then suddenly they're on familiar ground — there's the Caffè Sanquirico (and the piazza where he saw the woman in grey hurrying through the fog), and now they're turning up towards the Contrada dei Meravigli, past the church on the corner where he watched for Angela's signal, past the entrance to her apartment, and all too quickly they're through the Customs post at the Porta Vercellina and onto the highway under the pale light of a waning moon.

A low mist blankets the fields, spreading its damp chill over everything — a foretaste of the northern winter that awaits him. But he won't let its gloom infect him. For nothing can take away the new life he feels in himself, thanks to Angela. It's not given to every man to possess such a woman, and in the risks he's taken for her he's felt himself capable of greatness. Like the emperor before him, he's found his destiny in Italy, and he's ready for the battles that await him in Grenoble and Paris. The future is his to grasp.

He turns up the collar of his greatcoat and folds his arms, rehearsing the arguments he'll present to his father.

Autumn Fog

Parma, Wednesday 13 November

Has there ever been a day in my life like this? I am utterly exhausted but I must record it before I rest.

She'd slept little the previous night in the anxiety of departure. The countess's carriage arrived at the agreed hour. Maddalena was there to kiss her goodbye and make the sign of the cross over her for a safe journey.

As she was settling into her seat, Perpetua came running. A messenger had just brought a package. She knew instinctively who it was from, though she couldn't open it till she'd blown a last kiss to Maddalena. Once they'd turned the corner, she unwrapped it. The first three volumes of Vasari's *Lives of the Artists*. She opened the first to see if he'd inscribed it and saw the letter he'd slipped inside.

She turned her head to the window and watched familiar streets recede through a blur of tears. They passed through the Porta Romana and picked up speed. On the horizon a red winter sun was climbing above the mist.

At the breakfast halt in Lodi, too agitated to take more than a cup of chocolate, she waited till the countess was occupied, then took the letter to the window. It was in his own shaky and uneven hand but covered both sides of the page. There was no salutation, as though he hadn't known how to address her:

I find despite my best resolution that I cannot let you depart without confessing the feelings that you have inspired. If I thereby risk offending you I beg you to read no further.

She read on, her hands shaking:

When you arrived so unexpectedly two months ago I thought only of repaying, through whatever assistance I could offer, the debt I owed your father. But the similarity of our tastes, the sympathy that developed as we talked of the past, made possible a friendship to which I would not have dared aspire. I tried to convince myself that it was no more than that, until our chance encounter one evening made me suspect an attachment between you and the brother of your friend. My only recourse, given the strength of my feelings, was to avoid you, much as it cost me to do so.

Everything was beginning to make sense. How could she have been so blind?

But your words and your look tonight as we parted seemed to give me reason to hope. Nonetheless, recognising the difference in social position that separates us, I dare not aspire to anything other than friendship.

I am conscious that in thus exceeding its bounds I may have made its continuation difficult, but my heart tells me to speak. Whatever your response I beg you to believe me always your most devoted friend,

Jean-Philippe Larocque

As she stood at the window, filled with wild, confused thoughts, a mail coach rolled into the yard and the stable hands ran to unharness the horses. It must be the Milan-bound courier. There was no sign of a passenger, she saw with sudden hope. But she could not turn back without seeming crazed; she'd struck a bargain with the countess that she must keep. The courier was entering the inn: he might accept a letter, if she acted fast. Her writing case was in her luggage, but she had a new notebook in her overnight bag. Tearing out a page, she requested pen, ink and sealing wax from the servant. They took a long moment to arrive while she watched the inn yard anxiously. She wrote rapidly, the blunt quill scratching untidily across the page:

My dear friend, I have just read your letter. My heart is full. The Milan courier is about to leave and I seize the opportunity to respond immediately though there is no time to say all I feel. Now that I am embarked I cannot do other than continue to Rome, much as I might wish to turn back.

Fresh horses were being led out. She hurried to finish.

I shall return to Milan in the spring. In the meantime, my absence will give us time to know each other's hearts by corresponding. I promise you that my letters will be frequent and I shall wait for yours with the greatest impatience. The courier is ready — I have only time to assure you of my deepest esteem and affection.

She sealed and addressed the note and gave it to the courier herself with a large tip to ensure its arrival. The countess was looking her way curiously and she was tempted to confide her secret. But she hugged it to herself, and all day long as they sped south across the plain under a grey November sky his words ran through her head, suffusing everything she saw (the bare fields and rain-swollen streams, the leafless trees, the red-tiled villages and farms) with the glow of happiness.

Autumn Fog

Paris, Tuesday 31 December

Imagine a man in a ballroom, he'd written to Pauline — candlelight, perfume, beautiful women, amorous glances. Then that man is obliged to leave. Outside in the dense fog of a rainy night he stumbles into a pothole full of horse manure. *There you have the summary of my return to Paris.*

He was already depressed by the time he got there. Grenoble was miserable. 'This will be our farewell,' his grandfather said, but he hadn't needed to be told, seeing the old man sick and withdrawn. His father was more evasive than ever about money, and the visit to Pauline too rushed. And no little Angel waiting to console him in Paris: she was away for two weeks. But the following day an icy interview with Count Daru, almost worse than if his cousin had roared at him in the usual way.

'It did not occur to you, Beyle, when you took off without the courtesy of informing me, that you might be needed? On September 6th, believing you still in the office, I sent you an urgent message concerning the Holland accounts of which His Majesty had requested a detailed report. I had specifically asked, you may recall, that you remain in the office until Lecoulteux returned from his leave. But evidently you were in too much of a hurry. And all this, I'm told, in pursuit of a singer. I believed you beyond the age of such escapades, Beyle, but evidently I was mistaken.'

Where had that story about the singer originated? Norvins? But there was little point in telling Daru that he was misinformed, because the truth about his relations with Angéline (and Angela) would only reinforce Daru's disapproval. And in any case there was no denying his dereliction of duty. To have been embarrassed by a family member whose career he'd advanced was something Daru wouldn't easily forgive, though out of concern for his own reputation, he'd concealed his protégé's irresponsible behaviour. But the worst part — and Daru had not refrained from rubbing it in — was that he'd missed a chance of being transferred to a position in one of the ministries. No hope of any promotion now. Daru is no longer speaking to him. And he daren't make any appeal to Mme Daru to soften her husband's anger, because she too must be disappointed in him, especially if Daru has told her this ridiculous story about a singer.

Fortunately his new chief, the Duke of Cadore, seems to know nothing of his misdeeds. The man's a nonentity if ever there was one — a member of the old nobility who still wears a wig! He's less demanding than Count Daru but punctilious on everything relating to his own dignity.

He's ending the year in disgrace with the one man who could advance him; he may never rise above second inspector. But he has no regrets. Italy has revived his soul. The aridity of middle age, of which he'd been feeling the first premonition, is postponed by at least ten years. Prior to his return to Italy he'd been deceived by the mirages of ambition, that will-o'-the-wisp that leads unwary travellers astray. But he knows now where the life he wants is to be found. You can live on a shoestring in Milan, and he'll support himself by writing — translations, biographies, the sort of work you can turn out in a few months. But first he must do what he can to pay off his debts and earn the money to win his independence.

For the last three weeks he's been dictating his 'History of Painting in Italy'. It's dedicated to Angela. He thinks of it from the moment he wakes every day, longing to get to the museum and its pictures, and every time he looks at one of Raphael's Madonnas their beauty is a promise of happiness.

Rome, Sunday 2 February 1812

The days are lengthening now and the piping of a small bird in the tree outside her window hints at the approach of spring. It's chilly still, but a fire of pine logs glows in the hearth, filling the room with its resinous scent. Happily, such comfort is not beyond her means, for though the *pensione* had catered to wealthy English travellers before the war, the owners are now grateful for any visitors they receive. It's pleasantly situated among vineyards and gardens on the slopes above the city and she could ask for no greater luxury than the view from her window of the distant domes and bell towers of Rome.

Two months have passed since she arrived and from the start — thanks to the countess, with whom she developed a genuine friendship on the road — she was introduced to the governing circles of what is now the French department of the Tiber. She has even met the cousin of the young man from the diligence, though she did not mention their acquaintance. But she does not feel at home among these people, well-bred and cultivated though they are. If anything, she pities them. Behind the mask of official optimism she senses that they are baffled and frustrated by Rome's resistance to their programme of modernisation and civic improvement.

There is only one individual with whom she can truly be herself, and she's felt it more, not less, as the weeks went by. Post between Milan and Rome is slow, but his letters are so frequent that her daily call at the post office is generally rewarded. He writes in his own hand now, sometimes in pencil from a place she knows.

I am sitting where we sat in the garden at Desio, the Alps very clear on this frosty day. I wish you were by my side.

Today, I walked to my favourite viewpoint on the ridge, she replied. *I looked across the Tiber at the dome of the Pantheon and wished that you could see it too.*

Would you permit me to join you in Rome? came the response, and without hesitation she'd answered in the affirmative. A note announcing his departure with the courier had reached her by return post and, barring the unexpected, he will be here any day now.

She longs to see him, to share her discoveries, to make new ones in his company. Yet she's anxious. Last night, though she'd fallen asleep in the recollection of his arm around her on the Duomo roof, she woke in the small hours fearful that she was making a mistake, sacrificing her name, her social position, her precious independence for what could prove to have been no more than a passing desire of the kind she'd felt for Giovanni, induced by proximity and need. But she had only to reread his letters this morning to know beyond any doubt that he is the true companion of her heart.

The subject of marriage has not been broached in their correspondence, but his question and her response have been implicit in everything they've written. With her official connections here, the formalities for a quiet civil ceremony should be settled quickly and then they may travel together without fear of public censure.

As for the future — where and how they will live, or what she will say to cousin Armand — she refuses to think of it for the moment. The world will encroach on them soon enough. But for these few precious weeks of freedom they will wander wherever desire takes them, perhaps even southwards where spring is more advanced. For though there are great riches of art to explore in Rome, her fellow-traveller was right — it is a melancholy place, distressingly poor and squalid despite the efforts of the new administration. The journey south is dangerous, she's been told. But she will no longer be facing the road alone, and it will be worth the risk to walk among blossoming almond trees, to visit Virgil's tomb and stand on the shore of Homer's Mediterranean together.

Epilogue

1812 and After

By the early months of 1812 the Great Comet had vanished from western Europe's skies, travelling eastward and into the pages of another fiction, where it would be spotted (with some poetic licence as to dates) by Tolstoy's Pierre Bezukhov above the roofs of Moscow on a warm September night as the French army was entering the deserted city.

With them was Henri Beyle. He'd left Paris in July carrying despatches for the emperor and a draft of his history of painting in Italy, which he hoped to revise en route. He caught up with the vast army of French and allied troops (their ranks already decimated by typhus) near Smolensk. With Count Daru he witnessed the Battle of Borodino, the burning of Moscow and the catastrophic retreat through the Russian winter, losing everything but the clothes he was wearing, including his precious manuscript. By the time he recrossed the French frontier, he was considerably thinner and chilled to the core by what he'd seen.

It was the start of a sequence of events that would culminate at Waterloo in 1815. The candle snuffers had triumphed, Beyle would write in his journal; the light of the Revolution was out. He liked to

Epilogue

joke that he had fallen with Napoleon, but the collapse of his career freed him to return to Milan and Angela, though his love did not survive his discovery of her deceptions.

In 1811 he'd addressed his journal to the Henri of 1821, whom he imagined colder and more cynical. But when 1821 arrived he was once again hopelessly in love. Unluckily for him, the object of this new passion belonged to a group of Italian patriots whose arrest by the Austrian police led to his permanent expulsion from his beloved city.

For Milan was in Austrian hands again. The Congress of Vienna that followed Napoleon's final defeat restored the annexed states to their previous rulers. As Metternich, the Austrian foreign minister, notoriously said: 'The word "Italy" is a geographical expression, a description which is useful shorthand, but has none of the political significance the revolutionary ideologues try to put on it.' The dream of a united Italy cherished by Giacomo Lechi (and the fictional Captain Trezzano) went underground for another half century, though Lechi's younger brother, General Teodoro Lechi, would live long enough to see the start of it and bring out the Napoleonic Eagle he had hidden for over thirty years.

But the war with Russia had been devastating for Napoleon's Italian troops. Of the fifty thousand men who marched north with the viceroy, fewer than three thousand returned. Widmann, Beyle's rival for Angela Pietragrua's affection, died of his wounds there, as did another member of her circle, Cosimo Del Fante (whose gallantry is memorialised in his birthplace, Livorno). But the fate of many (such as Giovanni Rossi) would never be known.

As for the army of French administrators in Italy, they returned to France, either to join the rush for positions under the restored Bourbon monarchy or to retire from public life, like Beyle's cousin Martial Daru. Count Pierre Daru, loyal to the emperor until the bitter end, withdrew to his country estate, mourning the loss of his wife, Alexandrine (object of Henri Beyle's unrequited love), who died at thirty-two from the birth of her eighth child.

The Austrians might have allowed a minor French official with family ties in Lombardy to stay, but perhaps Larocque and Marie-Honorine would have chosen to return to that region between the Loire and the Yonne from which circumstances had uprooted them in their youth. Life there would not have been easy at first: occupied by allied armies for three years, burdened with a war indemnity of 700 million francs and mourning the loss of half a million to a million men, France had also to endure food shortages and epidemics following the harvest failure of 1816 — the 'year without a summer' (caused by the worldwide atmospheric pollution released by an Indonesian volcano). But those who'd survived the great upheavals of the Revolution and the empire had the fortitude to endure such crises and can be imagined happy in obscurity, cultivating their garden. When Marie-Honorine looked back at the year of the comet she would spare a grateful thought for the fellow-traveller without whose urging she might not have found the courage to declare her love. She would wonder perhaps what had become of him and watch the booksellers' in vain for a history of Italian painting translated by a Monsieur de Beyle.

Traditionally, novels celebrate the triumph of domesticity, but such was not the case for Henri Beyle, in life or in his fiction. Living on a tiny inheritance from his grandfather (since his father left him only debts), then on the salary of a French consul in Civitavecchia, he self-published his first books under the name Stendhal. It was not until he was forty-seven that he published the novel for which he's best known, *The Red and the Black*, followed eight years later by his great Italian novel *The Charterhouse of Parma*. Its opening vividly portrays the tumultuous years of Napoleon's Italian kingdom, from the ironic perspective of a narrator who witnessed its euphoric start and its ultimate collapse. Perhaps Beyle was recalling the hopes and fears aroused by the comet of 1811 when he drew the mocking portrait of a village priest, the Abbé Blanès, who climbs his bell tower every night to scan the heavens through a cardboard-barrelled telescope for the signs that reveal 'the exact date of the fall of empires and the revolutions that change the face of the world'. But it is also possible that those words contain a subtle hint to his readers of 1839 that even the most repressive regime is not eternal and that the world will change again. Henri Beyle did not live to see the revolutions of the mid-nineteenth century or the achievement of Italian unification, for he died in 1842 of a stroke at the age of fifty-nine.

To the Reader

> Perhaps I ought to apologise to you for my presumption in striking out of the high road of literature into an unbeaten path and attempting to combine the real scenes and adventures of an actual tour with a fictitious story and imaginary characters, for the incidents detailed in these pages are true, the tale alone is invention.
>
> — Charlotte Anne Eaton, *Continental Adventures* (1826)

If the ghost of Henri Beyle has been reading over my shoulder, I owe him an apology for the liberties I have taken with his life and character. I hope he would not feel misrepresented by my fictionalised portrayal of his youthful self, or the role I have made him play in the life of Marie-Honorine de Vernet. Being himself a shameless pillager of other writers' work, he could hardly reproach me for my use of his diary. As Goethe remarked wryly about *Rome, Naples et Florence en 1817* (Beyle's first publication under the name Stendhal): 'He knows well how to appropriate foreign works. He translates passages from my Italian Journey and claims to have heard the anecdote recounted by *a marchesina*.'

Discouraged by his lack of success, Beyle liked to predict that he would not be understood before the year 2000 and then only by 'the Happy Few'. Little did he foresee the horde of biographers and Stendhal specialists, even less the novelists who would reincarnate him in their fictions. A recent essay on Stendhal studies notes that he figures as a character in four French novels (to which can be added W.G. Sebald's *Vertigo* and Jack Robinson's clever metafiction *An Overcoat: Scenes from the Afterlife of H.B.*), and it suggests that 'the novelist would have been far more delighted to learn that twenty-first-century novelists would seek inspiration in his work than to hear that he was going to be a hit in twenty-first-century universities' (Francesco Marini and Maria Scott, 'Stendhal in the 21st Century').

My own portrayal of Beyle is based largely on his diaries and other autobiographical writings in the two-volume 1982 Pléiade edition of the *Oeuvres intimes*, as well as his correspondence. The translations are my own. For full details of the many Stendhal sources I consulted, please go to www. annpearsonauthor.com.

For the most part I avoided biographies, wanting to create the character as I experienced him in his personal writing, though Paul Arbelet's *La Jeunesse de Stendhal* proved vital for its exposure of Beyle's fabrications (particularly his military exploits). Crucially, Monsieur Henri Daru's recent biography of his ancestor Martial Daru revealed from private correspondence between Pierre and Martial Daru the seriousness of their younger cousin's 'truancy' in 1811.

At twenty-eight, Henri Beyle could often be irritating — brash, crude, self-centred, arrogantly convinced of his superiority to others. It wasn't till I read the autobiographical *Vie de Henry Brulard*, an account of his early life written as he approached fifty, that I began to like the self-questioning older man and to sympathise with the lonely child and adolescent. One of the high points of my long immersion in his world was the day I saw part of the original manuscript in the Grenoble library where it is preciously conserved. Waiting my turn in the dimly lit room among a small group of the 'happy few' (like the faithful in Milan's Duomo filing past the saint's preserved corpse), I could well imagine Beyle's caustic comments were he to witness the scene. It moved me, even so, to view this specimen of his notoriously illegible handwriting on a page that included the sketched floor plan of one of his childhood homes, where the librarian pointed out a tiny *H*, labelled below: 'Moi'.

Despite my interest in the future Stendhal, I would never have thought to make him the protagonist of a novel were it not for the intriguing and altogether unexpected mention of the book that he came across in the cabriolet of the Paris–Milan diligence. Like Beyle himself, I wondered who it belonged to. Almost certainly a woman, I felt, but not English, since France and England were at war. This unknown reader piqued my curiosity and one morning I woke with the sentence 'For the first time in my life I am completely alone'. The idea for a novel was born. But rather than simply telling the story of this solitary woman traveller, I decided to narrate her journey in tandem with Beyle's for the contrast of male and female experience. I set out with no clear sense of the destination, only the idea that the protagonists' paths would cross wherever the gaps in Beyle's journal gave me leeway to invent.

Had I known the amount of research involved I might have been daunted. 'The past is a foreign country', as the narrator of L.P. Hartley's *The Go-Between* remarks — quite literally so in the case of my project, where the foreignness of the times is doubled by that of place and language. We can take a package tour there, lured by the promise of romance and adventure, or we can immerse ourselves in a historical moment and culture, returning with a fresh perspective.

The project put me quite literally on the road, specifically Napoleon's road through the Simplon pass. But much of my journeying took place at my desk, reading guidebooks of the period and reports by the many travellers whose published diaries and letters home served as a kind of nineteenth-century TripAdvisor. The Italy these visitors encountered was very different from the Italy of modern tourism, and it charmed and exasperated them in equal measure. But from 1796 to 1814 it was also a country in the throes of social and political change that no visitor, however thirsty for art and classical antiquity, could fail to notice — even one from the twenty-first century. The histories of Napoleonic Italy that I read opened my eyes to its laudable aims and genuine achievements, as well as to the self-interest and blindness of a powerful state imposing reform on a weaker one by force (with the often tragic outcome that we have witnessed in our own times). But whatever criticism may justifiably be levelled at the emperor, he was a moderniser, supporting the sciences, rationalising public administration, introducing educational reforms, undertaking ambitious infrastructure projects. I have tried through the French and Italian voices of my characters to offer a somewhat different view of the Napoleonic era than the one that has tended to prevail in English-language fiction (with its cliché of the indomitable island nation battling the continental tyrant).

The danger for a novelist lies in including so much local colour and historical detail that the manuscript reaches unpublishable proportions. All too many fascinating discoveries (about émigrés in

To the Reader

London or Napoleon's cultural thefts, for instance) did not survive the cuts to the first draft, which was more than double the length of this final published version.

It was Anna South at The Literary Consultancy in London whose evaluation made me see the necessity of major cuts and pushed me to find deeper connections between my two protagonists. I am deeply indebted to Anna for her enthusiasm and encouragement as I worked through two further drafts.

Many good friends offered support along the way. I am especially grateful to those who read and commented on part or all of the manuscript — Evelyn Cobley, Susanna and Kieran Egan, Ronda Larmour, Margot Maclaren, Bonnie Moro, Magda Pavitt, Vera Rosenbluth, Kay Stewart, Sue Tauber, Carol van Rijn, but most of all to my partner, Allan Smith, without whose belief in me the manuscript might have ended up like others in the back of the cupboard.

A special thank you to Bruce Fraser, who sent me to Granville Island Publishing. From the moment I entered Jo Blackmore's office, with its expansive view of boats, water, and mountains, I felt I was in good hands. Cheryl Cohen, my patient copy editor, weeded out a heap of hyphens, 'buts', and worse and imposed consistency on spelling that fluctuated between British and Canadian.

Thanks to Omar Gallegos for his eye-catching design, and to the whole team at Granville Island Publishing — Rebecca Coates, David Litvak, Sam Margolis — my sincere thanks for your vital contributions.

Ann Pearson grew up in Suffolk, England, and did an honours degree in French at the University of London before moving to Vancouver, where she completed a PhD in French literature. Subsequently, she taught French for a number of years before joining the Arts One programme at the University of British Columbia. She is currently working on a second Napoleonic-era novel, set in Cornwall this time.